"Time to soar," she whispered, and punched her arms forward as if diving into the waters of Lake Pleasance.

Bree twisted herself parallel to the ocean, and though her descent slowed, her speed remained, and like a shooting star she entered the great shadow cast by Weshern and began circling the Fount. Laughing, Bree continued spiraling downward, looping the twisting waters, feeling the wet spray across her face, her long hair wildly flapping behind her like a cape. Harder and harder she pushed at the toggle, willing herself faster, feeling more at home in that moment than she ever had staying at Aunt Bethy's.

And then a fisherman flew in her path.

His back was to her, legs and net dangling as he lifted dozens of fish. He was returning to the docks, and with her rapid descent she was on a direct collision course. Panicking, she felt her mind go blank, felt her body lock up. Deep in her stomach she knew it was the worst possible reaction, and as she careened toward the man she forced herself to do the only thing she could think of: she rolled. Shoulder over shoulder she twirled, ending her curved path around the Fount and sending her flying off and away. The roll gained her the few feet necessary to prevent herself from slamming into the fisherman, but her relief lasted all of a split second, for as she tried to right herself, she found herself spinning. Head over feet she rolled, and it seemed every twist of her waist and pull of her shoulders was in vain.

She was falling.

By David Dalglish

Seraphim

Skyborn

Fireborn

Shadowborn

Shadowdance

A Dance of Cloaks

A Dance of Blades

A Dance of Mirrors

A Dance of Shadows

A Dance of Ghosts

A Dance of Chaos

Cloak and Spider (e-only novella)

SKYBORN

SERAPHIM: BOOK ONE

DAVID DALGLISH

orbit

www.orbitbooks.net

Copyright © 2015 by David Dalglish
Excerpt from *Fireborn* copyright © 2015 by David Dalglish
Excerpt from *The City Stained Red* copyright © 2014 by Sam Sykes

Orbit
Hachette Book Group
1290 Avenue of the Americas
New York, NY 10104
www.orbitbooks.net

Printed in the United States of America

RRD-C

First edition: November 2015

10 9 8 7 6 5 4 3 2

Orbit is an imprint of Hachette Book Group.
The Orbit name and logo are trademarks of Little, Brown Book Group Limited.

The Hachette Speakers Bureau provides a wide range of authors for speaking events. To find out more, go to www.hachettespeakersbureau.com or call (866) 376-6591.

The publisher is not responsible for websites (or their content) that are not owned by the publisher.

Library of Congress Cataloging-in-Publication Data

Dalglish, David.
    Skyborn / David Dalglish.—First edition.
        pages ; cm. — (Seraphim ; Book 1)
    ISBN 978-0-316-30268-5 (trade pbk.)—ISBN 978-1-4789-6046-1 (audio book downloadable)—ISBN 978-0-316-30271-5 (ebook)
    I. Title.
    PS3604.A376S57 2015
    813'.6—dc23
                                                        2015023404

To my mom, who's been waiting for me to write something like this for years.

PROLOGUE

Breanna Skyborn sat at the edge of her world, watching the clouds drift beneath her dangling feet.

"Bree?"

Kael's voice sounded obscenely loud in the twilight quiet. She turned to see her twin brother standing at the stone barricade that marked the end of the road.

"Over here," she said.

The barricade reached up to Kael's waist, and after a moment's hesitation, he climbed over, leaving behind smoothly worn cobbles for short grass and soft dirt. Beyond the barricade, there was nothing else. No buildings. No streets. No homes. Just a stretch of unused earth, and then beyond that...the edge. It was for that reason Bree loved it, and her brother hated it.

"We're not allowed to be this close," he said as he approached, each step smaller than the last. "If Aunt Bethy saw..."

"Aunt Bethy won't come within twenty feet of the barricade and you know it."

Wind blew against her, and she pulled her dark hair back

from her face as she smirked at her brother. His pale skin had taken on a golden hue from the fading sunlight, the wind teasing his much shorter hair. The gust made him stop, and she worried he'd decide to leave her there.

"You're not afraid, are you?" she asked.

That was enough to push him on. Kael joined her at the edge of their island. When he sat, he sat cross-legged, and unlike her, he did not let his legs dangle off the side.

"Just for a little while," he said. "We should be home when the battle starts."

Bree turned away, and she peered over the edge of the island. Below, lazily floating along, were dozens of puffy clouds painted orange by the setting sun. Through their gaps she saw the tumultuous Endless Ocean, its movement only hinted at by the faintest of dark lines. Again the wind blew, and she pretended that she rode upon it, flying just like her parents.

"So why are we out here?" Kael asked, interrupting the silence.

"I was hoping to see the stars."

"Is that it? We're just here to waste our time?"

Bree glared at him.

"You've seen the drawings in Teacher Gruden's books. The stars are beautiful. I was hoping that out here, away from the lanterns, maybe I could see one or two before..."

She fell silent. Kael let out a sigh.

"Is that really why you're out here?"

It wasn't, not fully, but she didn't feel comfortable discussing the other reason. Hours ago their mother and father had sat them down beside the fire of their home. They'd each worn the black uniforms of their island of Weshern, swords dangling from their hips, the silver wings attached to their harnesses polished to a shine.

The island of Galen won't back down, so we have no choice, their father had said. *We've agreed to a battle come the midnight fire. This will be the last, I promise. After this, they won't have the heart for another.*

"It is," Bree said, wishing her half lie were more convincing. She looked to their right, where the sun was slipping beneath the horizon. Nightfall wouldn't be long now. Kael shifted uncomfortably, and she saw him glancing behind them, as if convinced they'd be caught despite being in a secluded corner of their small town of Lowville.

"Fine," he said. "I'll stay with you, but if we get in trouble, this was all your idea."

"It usually is," she said, smiling at him.

Kael settled back, sliding a bit farther away from the edge. Together they watched the sun slowly set. In its glow, they caught glimpses of two figures flying through the twilight haze, their mechanical wings shimmering gold as they hovered above a great stretch of green farmland. The men wore red robes along with their wings, easily identifying them as theotechs of Center.

"Why are they here?" Kael asked when he spotted them.

"They're here to oversee the battle," Bree answered. She'd spent countless nights on her father's lap, asking him questions. What was it like to fly? Was he ever scared when they fought? Did he think she might become a member of the Seraphim like they were? Bree knew the two theotechs would bless the battle, ensure everyone followed the agreed-upon rules, and then mark the surrender of the loser. Then would come the vultures, the lowest-ranking members of the theotechs, to reclaim the treasured technology from the fallen.

The mention of the coming battle put Kael on edge, and he fell silent as he looked to the sunset. Bree couldn't blame him for his nervousness. She felt it, too, and that was the reason she couldn't stay home, cooped up, unable to witness the battle or know if her mother and father lived or died. No, she had to be out there. She had to have something to occupy her mind.

They said nothing as the sun neared the end of its descent. As the strength of its rays weakened, she turned her attention to the east, where the sky had faded to a deep shade of purple. The coming darkness unsettled Bree. Since the day she was born, it had come and gone, but it was rare for her to watch it. She much preferred to be at home next to the hearth, listening to her father tell Seraphim stories, or their mother reading Kael ancient tales of knights and angels. Watching the nightly shadow only made her feel . . . imprisoned.

It began where the light was at its absolute weakest, an inky black line on the horizon that grew like a cloud. Slowly it crawled, thick as smoke and wide as the horizon itself. The darkness swept over the sky, hiding its many colors. More and more it covered, an unceasing march matched by the sun's fall. When it reached to the faintly visible moon, it too vanished, the pale crescent tucked away, to be hidden until the following night. Silently the twins watched as the rolling darkness passed high above their heads, blotting out everything, encasing the world in its deep shadow.

Bree turned her attention to the setting sun, which looked as if it fled in fear of the darkness complete.

"It'll be right there," she said, pointing. "In the moment after the sun sets and before the darkness reaches it."

Most of the sky was gone now, and so far away from the lanterns, the two sat in a darkness so complete it was frightening. The shadow clouds continued rolling, blotting out the field of stars that the ancient drawing books made look so beautiful, so majestic and grand. But just as she'd hoped, there was a gap in the time it took the sun to vanish beyond the horizon and for the rolling shadow to reach it, and she watched with growing anticipation. She'd seen only one star before, the North Star, which shone so brightly that not even the sun could always blot it out. But the other stars, the great field...would they appear in the deepening purple?

Kael saw it before she did, and he quickly pointed. In the sliver of violet space the star winked into existence, a little drop of light between the horizon and the shadows crashing down on it like a wave. Bree saw it, and she smiled at the sight.

"Imagine not one but thousands," Bree said as the dark clouds swallowed the star, pitching the entire city into utter darkness so deep she could not see her brother beside her. "A field spanning the entire sky, lighting up the night in their glow..."

Bree felt Kael take her hand, and she squeezed it tight. Neither dared move while so close to the edge and lacking sight. Perfectly still, they waited. It would only be a matter of time.

It started as a faint flicker of red across the eastern horizon. Slowly it grew, spreading, strengthening. Just like the shadows, so too did the fire roll across the sky, setting ablaze the inky clouds that covered the crown of the world. It burned without consuming, only shifting and twisting. It took thirty minutes, but eventually all of the sky raged with midnight fire, bathing the land in red. It'd last until daybreak, when the sun would rise, the fire would die, and the smoky remnants would hover over the morning sky until fading away.

A horn sounded from a watchtower farther within their home island of Weshern. The blast set Bree's heart to hammering.

"They're starting," she whispered.

Both turned to face the field where the two theotechs hovered. The horn sounded thrice more, and come the final call, the forces of Weshern arrived. They sailed above the field in *V* formations, their silver wings shimmering, powered by the light element that granted all Seraphim mastery over the skies. Hundreds of men and women, dressed in black pants and jackets, armed with fire, lightning, ice, and stone that they wielded with the gauntlets of their ancient technology. Despite her fear, Bree felt an intense longing to be up there with them, fighting for the pride and safety of her home. Sadly, it'd be five years before she and her brother turned sixteen and could attempt to join.

"Bree..."

She turned her head, saw her brother staring off into the open sky beyond the edge of their island. Flying in similar *V* formations, gold wings glimmering, red jackets seemingly aflame from the light of the midnight fire, came the Seraphim of Galen. The two armies raced toward each other, and Bree knew they'd meet just above the fallow field, where the theotechs waited.

Bree pushed herself away from the edge of the island and rose to her feet, her brother doing likewise.

"They'll be fine," she said, watching the Weshern Seraphim fly in perfect formation. She wondered which of those black and silver shapes was her mother, and which her father. "You'll see. No one's better than they are."

Kael stood beside her, eyes on the sky, arms locked at his sides. Bree reached for his hand, held it as the armies neared one another.

"It'll be over quick," she whispered. "Father says it always is."

Dark shapes shot in both directions through the space between the armies, large chunks of stone meant to screen attacks as well as protect against retaliation. They crashed into one another, and as the sound reached Bree's ears, the battle suddenly erupted into bewildering chaos. The Seraphim formations danced about one another, lightning flashing amid them in constant barrages. Enormous blasts of fire accompanied them, difficult to see with the sky itself aflame. Blue lances of ice, colored purple from the midnight hue, shot in rapid bursts, cutting down combatants with ease. The sounds of battle were so powerful, so near, Bree could feel them in her bones.

"How?" Kael wondered aloud, and if he weren't so close she wouldn't have heard him over the cacophony. "How can anyone survive through that?"

Boulders of stone slammed into the fallow field beneath, carving out long grooves of earth before coming to a stop. Bree flinched at the impact of each one. How did one survive? She didn't know, but somehow they did, the Seraphim of both islands weaving amid the carnage with movements so fluid and beautiful they mirrored that of dancers. Not all, though. Lightning tore through chests, lances of ice with sharp tips punctured flesh and metal alike, and no armor could protect against the fire that washed over their bodies. Each Seraph who fell wearing a black jacket made Bree silently beg it wasn't one of her parents. She didn't care if that was selfish or not. She just wanted them safe. She wanted them to survive the overwhelming onslaught that left her mind baffled by how to take it all in.

The elements lessened, the initial devastating barrage becoming more precise, more controlled. Bree saw that several combatants were out of elements completely and forced to draw their blades. The battle had gradually spread farther and farther out, taking them beyond the grand field and closer to the edge of town where Bree and Kael stood. Not far above their heads, two Seraphim circled in a dance, one fleeing, one chasing. They both had their twin blades drawn. Bree watched, entranced, eyes wide as the circle tightened and the combatants whisked by each other again and again, slender blades swiping for exposed flesh.

It was the Galen Seraph who made the first mistake. Bree saw him fail to dodge in time, saw the tip of the sword slice across his stomach. The body fell, careening wildly just before making impact with the ground. The sound was a bloodcurdling screech of metal and snapping bone. Bree's attention turned to the larger battle, and she saw that more had been forced to draw their blades. The number of remaining Seraphim was shockingly few, yet they fought on.

"No one's surrendering," Kael said, and she could hear the fear threatening to overtake him completely. "Bree, you said it'd be quick. You said it'd be quick!"

The area of battle was spreading out of control. Galen Seraphim scattered in all directions, loose formations of two to three people. The Weshern Seraphim chased, and despite nearing town, they still released their elements. Bree screamed as a pair streaked above their heads, the thrum of their wings nearly deafening. A boulder failed to connect with the fleeing Seraphim, and it blasted through the side of a home with a thundering blast.

"Let's go!" Bree screamed, grabbing Kael's hand and dashing toward the barricade. More Seraphim were approaching, seemingly the entire Galen forces. They wanted to be over the town, Bree realized. They wanted to make Weshern's people hesitate to fight with so many nearby. As the twins climbed over the stone barricade, the sounds of battle erupting all about them, it was clear their Seraphim would have no such hesitation. Lightning flashed above Bree's head, and she cried out in surprise. She ducked, stumbled, lost her grip on her brother's hand. He stopped, shouted her name, and then the ice lance struck the cobbles ahead of them. It shattered into shards, and Kael dove to the ground as they flew in all directions.

"Kael," Bree said as she scrambled to her feet. "Kael!"

"I'm fine," he said, pushing himself to his hands and knees. When he looked to her, he was bleeding from several cuts across his face and neck. "I'm fine, now hurry!"

The red light of the midnight fire cast its hue across everything, convincing Bree she'd lost herself in a nightmare and awoken in one of the circles of Hell. Kael pulled her along, leading her toward Aunt Bethy's house, where they were supposed to have stayed during the battle, waiting like good children for their parents to return. Hand in hand they ran, the air above filled with screams, echoes of thunder, and the deep hum of the Seraphims' wings.

They turned a corner, saw two Seraphs flying straight at them from farther down the street. Fire burst from the chaser's gauntlet. It bathed over the other, sending her crashing to the ground. Kael dove aside as Bree froze, her legs locked in place from terror. The body came to a halt mere feet away from her, silver wings mangled and broken. Her black jacket bore the blue sword of Weshern on her shoulder, and Bree shuddered at the sight of the woman's horrible burns. High above, the Galen Seraph flew on, seeking new prey.

"Bree!" her brother shouted, pulling her attention away. He'd wedged himself in the tight space between two houses, and she joined him there in hiding.

"We have to get back," Bree insisted. "We can't stay here."

"Yes, we can," Kael said, hunkering deeper into the alley. "I'm not going out there, Bree. I'm not."

Bree glanced back out of the narrow alley. With the battle raging above the town, Aunt Bethy would be terrified by their absence. They were already going to be in trouble for not coming in like they were supposed to in the first place. To hide now, afraid, until it all ended?

"I'm going," she said. "Are you coming with me or not?"

Another blast of thunder above. Kael shook his head.

"No," he said. His eyes widened when he realized she was serious about going. "Bree, don't leave me here. Don't leave me!"

"I can't stay," Bree said, the mantra overwhelming her every thought. "I can't stay, Kael, I can't stay!"

She dashed back into the street, racing toward Aunt Bethy's house. As strongly as Kael wanted to remain hiding, Bree wanted to return to their aunt's home. She wanted to be inside, in a safe place with family. Let him be a coward. She'd be brave. She'd be strong.

A boulder crashed through the rooftop of a home to her right then blasted out the front wall. Bree screamed, and she realized she wasn't brave at all. She was frightened out of her mind. Fighting back tears, she turned down Picker Street, where both they and their aunt lived. Five houses down was her aunt's home, and Bree's heart took a sudden leap. Her legs moved as fast as they could carry her.

There she was. Her mother was safe, she was alive, she was...

She was bleeding. Her hand clutched her stomach, and Bree saw with horrible clarity the red gash her fingers failed to seal. She lay on her back, her silver wings pressed against the door to Aunt Bethy's home, a dazed look on her face. Beneath her was a pool of her own blood.

"Bree," her mother said. Her voice was wet, strained. Tears trickled from her brown eyes. "Bree, what are you...what are you doing out here?"

Bree didn't know how to answer. She fell to her knees, felt her pants slicken from the blood. She reached out a trembling hand, wanting so badly to hold her mother, but feared what any contact might do.

"It's all right," her mother said, and she smiled despite her obvious pain. "Bree, it's all right. It's..."

Her lips grew still. She breathed in pain no more. Her hand fell limp, holding back her sliced stomach no longer. Bree touched her shoulder, shook her once.

"Mom," she said, tears rolling down her cheeks. "Mom, no, Mom, please!"

She buried her face against her mother's chest, shrieking out in wordless agony. She didn't want to see any more, to hear any more. Bree wrapped her arms around her mother's neck, clutching her tightly, not caring about the blood that seeped into her clothes. She just wanted one more embrace before the vultures came to reclaim her wings. She wanted to pretend her mother was alive and well, holding her, loving her, kissing her forehead before flying away for another day of training and drills.

Not this corpse. Not this lifeless thing.

A hand touched her shoulder. Bree pulled back, expecting to see her brother, but instead it was a tall Weshern Seraph. Blood smeared his fine black coat. To her surprise, the surrounding neighborhood was quiet, the battle seemingly over.

"Was she your mother?" the man asked. Bree could barely see his face through the shadows cast by the midnight fire. She sniffled, then nodded.

"Then you must be Breanna. I—I don't know how else to tell you this. It's about your father."

His words were a dagger to an already punctured heart. It couldn't be. The world couldn't be that cruel.

"No," she whispered. "No, that can't be right."

The Seraph swallowed hard.

"Breanna, I'm sorry."

Bree leapt to her feet, and she flung herself at the man, screaming at the top of her lungs.

"No, it can't. Not both, we can't lose them both, we can't... we can't..."

She broke, collapsing at his feet, her tears falling upon his black boots. She beat the stone cobbles until she bled, beat them as she screamed, beat them as, high above, the midnight fire burned like an unrelenting pyre for the dead.

CHAPTER

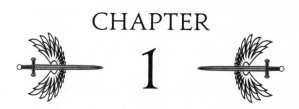

1

I keep telling you," Jevin said as they walked the stone road to the fishing docks. "You aren't ready."

"But you said when we turned sixteen we'd get to go with you," Bree insisted.

"And when is that?" Jevin asked.

"Next week."

The deeply tanned man threw up a hand, as if that answered everything. With his other hand he carried dozens of heavy nets slung over his shoulder. Jevin was a friend of Aunt Bethy's, and he was quick to remind Bree and Kael of how close he'd been to their father as well.

"Peas in a pod," he'd tell them. "Until he joined the Seraphim, anyway."

Bree had used that close relationship to guilt and charm dozens of gifts and favors out of the man, but as they passed through the gathering crowds of fishermen, she decided that connection might now be working against her.

"It's not that long to wait," Kael said, walking alongside her. "I'd rather practice on land a few more times anyway."

Bree had to choke down her exasperated groan.

"Of course you would," she said. "You're terrible at it."

Kael raised an eyebrow at her.

"Yes. That's the point. I'd rather not go crashing headfirst into the ocean because I don't know what I'm doing."

"I'm not sure crashing headfirst into dirt is any better..."

"Enough," Jevin said, interrupting them both. "We're not having this discussion. You want to fly, do it over the island."

Bree had a dozen retorts ready, but she held them in, deciding it was not yet time to wage this battle. Idea growing, she obediently dipped her head and remained silent as they entered the docks. All around her were tanned men, their clothes faded brown and gray. Several long tables lined either side of the street, their surface coated with fish guts and gore as giant cleavers rose and fell, cutting off the undesirable parts as those beside them sliced with long knives, cleaning and gutting the catch of the day. The noise was one of hearty cheers, jokes, and laughter accompanied by thuds of steel and the ever-constant roar of the unseen Fount below.

But most interesting to Bree were the men at the far end, where the docks ended and the sky began. With the morning so young, most were strapping on their wings, buckling belts, and adjusting the connected gauntlet on their left hand. At their feet were dozens of nets and sharpened harpoons. The wings themselves were short and stocky, designed for lift instead of speed. Bree and Kael had practiced with a set just like them, hovering several feet above the ground while Jevin watched protectively. The whole while it drove Bree insane. It was like being a bird with clipped wings.

"Hey, Bryce," Jevin said, approaching a hollowed-out stone block where a bearded man stood within with arms crossed. "Morning going well?"

"No one's died, but the fish ain't catching themselves," Bryce said, deep voice rumbling. "So going as well as one can hope for without wishing on angels."

The big man turned about, scanning rows of wooden shelves inside his structure, each shelf lined with the wing contraptions. He found Jevin's, pulled it off, and handed it over.

"The switch was getting sticky, so I replaced the spring," he said. "Best I can do before sending it off to Center for the theotechs to have a look."

"I'm sure it's fine," Jevin said, hooking his free arm through the two leather loops that went underneath the armpits. As he stepped away, Bree put her hands on the small barrier between her and Bryce.

"Mine, too," she said.

Bryce shot a look to Jevin, who gave a hesitant nod.

"Should start making you pay for this," the bearded man said, leaning down beneath the front shelf and pulling up a smaller set of wings from out of view. "Light elements don't come cheap."

"Thank God you aren't paying for it then," Bree said, accepting the wings. The light element that powered the wings came from Central. Weshern's Archon then allocated a set amount each month to training new fishermen.

"Rate you're using it up, I might have to anyway," Bryce said, but a grin was on his face. Seeing Kael lingering beside Jevin, he called out, louder. "You also going to fly today, kid?"

"Maybe," Kael said, smiling warmly at the man. "But only if Bree doesn't hog it all."

They traveled across the street and onto the wooden planks, Bryce's roaring laughter to their backs. As Bree clutched the wing contraption to her chest, she glanced down. The docks were built onto the side of their island, overhanging the sky, and through gaps in the planks she could see glimpses of the clouds below. The sight gave her shivers of the good kind.

Jevin stopped them at an open spot near the middle, let his net plop to the wood, and then lifted his wings up and over his shoulders. He was a scrawny-looking man, his face long and gaunt, but his arms and chest were corded muscle. The wings could carry only so much weight, and while the stunted version the fishermen were given was designed to carry more than normal, it still had its limits. As a result, nearly all the men around were lean and fit, strong of arm, and thin around the waist. The more fish they could carry each trip, the better their pay at the end of the day.

"Is it all right if I go first?" Bree asked her brother as Jevin began tying the buckles.

"You'd only argue with me if I said no," Kael said, and he grinned at her. "Go ahead. We both know you love flying more than I do."

Bree mussed his hair, then began sliding on the harness to the wings. She'd never understand Kael. They spent every single day of their lives with their feet touching the ground. The clouds, the wind, the world spinning beyond...how could you ever deny the allure? Putting an arm through one side, she shifted the harness onto her back and shoulders, then slid the other arm through. The weight settled comfortably on her shoulders. The wings were a rustic gold, hard and unmoving from their folded position. Everything else, though, was stiff leather and padded cloth. Two buckles went underneath her armpits, a large strip of leather dropped down her back and then latched around her waist, and the last two strips connected to those looped about her thighs before buckling tight. Bree went through the process one after the other, refusing Jevin's offered help.

"How do I look?" she asked when finished, standing tall and thrusting back her shoulders.

Jevin smiled at her.

"Like an angel," he said.

Bree glanced over her shoulder at the small, stunted wings now attached to her back. They were not designed to move, instead remaining perfectly in place during flight. It was the light element that gave the wings the ability to fly, and that element was controlled by the left gauntlet attached to the wings. Reaching over her shoulder, she shifted the wings to rest a bit more comfortably, then unhooked the gauntlet from its side. A slender tube ran from its bottom to the thick stump at the arch of her back, where the wings connected. Bree put her left hand inside the golden gauntlet, then tightened the buckles. It took every hole on the belt to get the wings snug.

"Flex your fingers," Jevin said, having watched her all the while. She did so, showing that the gauntlet fit fine and would not cause issues in flight.

"What next?" Jevin asked, running her through the checklist he'd taught her to prepare for any period of flight.

"Check the element," she said.

She lifted the gauntlet, where along the wrist was an opening covered by a sliver of glass. Inside, protected by the metal of the gauntlet, was a white prism shard: the light element they used for flight. Various tubes and wires understood only by the theotechs connected to the prism, drawing out the energy of the light element and pulsing it through the tube running from the gauntlet's edge to the wings. As Bree flew and the light element was used, the color would slowly drain away, turning the prism gray. Peering through the thick glass, she saw the element was bright white, fully charged.

"Good," said Jevin. "Next, check the switch. Make sure it ain't sticking or being stubborn."

Bree knew all this, and on normal days she'd have grumbled at his belief that he must remind her. Not today. Today she felt a stirring in her stomach. Today, she knew, was different.

Built into the right side of the forefinger was a red toggle switch. Using her thumb, she could tilt it forward and backward, effectively increasing, or shutting off entirely, the push from the light element that was sent to the wings. Back and forth she moved it, quick enough to prevent the wings from gaining any lift. The contraption thrummed, a deep, pleasant sound. The wings themselves shimmered a bright gold.

"Remember, stay above the docks," he told her as he picked up his net. "And try not to fly more than thirty minutes. Bryce gets pissed at me when you do."

He walked toward the end of the docks, and she followed. Jevin paused, and there was no hiding his frustration when he glared at her.

"What are you doing?" he asked.

"I'm going with you."

"No, Bree, you're too young to . . ."

"Josh Hadley is already fishing with his father, and he's fifteen. Do you think he's a safer flier than I am?"

Of course he wasn't, and the argument was hardly a new one for her. Still, Jevin was suited up for work, and with each second he argued, he risked missing out on a good catch.

"Fine," he said. "Your aunt will kill me for this, no matter how many times I tell her it was your idea. Promise me you won't do something stupid."

"Jevin..."

"Promise me."

Bree rolled her eyes.

"I promise," she said.

Jevin hardly looked convinced, but he let it drop.

"Let's go," he said. They walked to the edge of the docks, where the wood came to an end. Peering over, Bree saw only clouds, big white puffy things drifting lazily along. The twisting in her stomach heightened, but her excitement easily overwhelmed it.

"Don't do anything stupid," Kael called out to her, stopping at a groove cut into the wood that marked where those without wings were not allowed to cross.

"I wouldn't dream of it," Bree called back.

"Liar."

Jevin took her by the elbow and guided her closer to the edge, chuckling at her brother's words.

"Remember," he said, "scrunch your shoulders to rotate forward, pull them wide to rotate backward. It'll help a little, but most changes of direction will depend on your own upper body strength."

Her mouth opened, the words *I know* on her lips, but he shushed her with a glare.

"This is serious," he said. "You may think it's all obvious, but when something jostles your wings and you're plummeting toward the water in a dead spin, even the easiest of things can be hard to remember. I've watched good men, fishers all their lives, react wrongly to things they didn't expect. It cost them their lives. So fly slow, fly straight, and stay away from the Fount. Got it?"

Despite the seriousness of his tone, she bobbed her head and smiled.

"Got it."

Jevin took in a deep breath, and for a moment she feared he'd change his mind.

"Well, then," he said, "come along."

With that, his own wings thrummed to life, and he rose into the air, spinning about so he could watch her as he floated away. Bree looked down, off the wood and to the clouds. This was it. Rising above the docks and the nearby buildings was one thing, but now there would be no dirt, no grass, no street. Only the open air. Taking in a deep breath, she stepped back, another step, and then before her rational mind could convince her she was insane she vaulted out into the open space, letting out a whoop as her adrenaline surged. Clutching her left hand into a fist like she'd been taught, she pushed the switch to full. Her wings thrummed, and she felt the belts and buckles tighten as the harness caught her.

The wings pushed only one direction, and that was in the direction she pointed them. Keeping at a forty-five-degree angle, she decreased the throttle until she settled into a comfortable, steady line. Much of the thrust negated the pull of gravity, the remainder pushing her straight ahead. Behind her, the docks shrank. She spun to watch them, shifting so that she was perfectly erect as well as decreasing the throttle the tiniest bit more. Her momentum kept her drifting away from the island, the push of her wings keeping her from dropping.

To her complete lack of surprise, Jevin flew after her, joining her side.

"Remember," he shouted. "Nothing stupid. You promised."

Her smile was her only acknowledgment.

Down Jevin dropped, and though she was excited to follow,

she wanted height first. Remaining erect, she pushed the wings to full power, rising straight up into the sky. The wind blew through her hair, and when Jevin left her, she realized she was alone and free. Only the slowness of her wings, bulky and heavy and designed for carrying fish, tarnished it. Taking far too long, she rose until she could see far along the southwestern limits of her home island of Weshern. Along the outer edges were the fields, great swaths of green and yellow depending on what grew in the fertile soul. From her vantage point she saw Lowville, a tiny little cluster of stone buildings with wooden rooftops, and it thrilled her beyond words. Peering into Weshern itself, she could just barely make out the holy mansion, home of the Willer family that had ruled Weshern as Archon for decades. The building was enormous, with lofty spires and clean white marble walls. So many times she'd viewed it from afar with jealousy, but now she saw it as small as everything else.

Thumbing the switch so it was half pressed, she pushed her shoulders forward and bent her waist. The change in direction of the wings rotated her in midair, and once she was pointed downward she arched her back and spread her shoulders to halt her rotation. Straightening out, her body began to descend, a gentle glide that blew the wind through her hair and spread her smile from ear to ear. She curled the tiniest bit so that her descent sharpened, dropping her through the clouds. Down and down she went, until she emerged beneath not only the clouds but the island of Weshern itself. The soil above her head was thick and brown, a ragged, pointed shape of earth that floated by the grace of God and his angels. And down there, before the Fount, she entered another world.

Beneath her was the Endless Ocean, sparkling and blue. It stretched for miles in all directions, with not a hint of land to be seen. Connecting ocean to island in a great swirling funnel a thousand yards wide was the Fount. The water lifted almost lazily, a roaring mass with a hollow center that gently turned, rising up and up toward the very heart of the island. Through the water Bree saw the faintest hint of the Beam, the mysterious shaft of light controlled by the theotechs that caused the water to rise and the island to float. Once the water reached the bottom of the island, it vanished through enormous grates, was blessed by the theotechs, and then poured out in various waterfalls scattered throughout Weshern. Some of the water went to the fields, some to fountains and decorative ponds, while the rest went to the many lakes Weshern was famous for.

The sound of the Fount, while inaudible on the top of Weshern, was a tremendous roar below, and Bree stared at the swirling waters with her mouth agape. A hundred times she'd read about the Fount and seen its pictures in books at school, but witnessing the true scope of its size was another thing entirely. Swarming about it like bees around a flower were the fishermen. They were brown and gold shapes flitting up and down the great length of the funnel, dragging nets and hurling harpoons. As she watched, she could not deny their bravery and skill. The Fount was always moving, never much, but its size was so great and the fishermen so small that the slightest shift threatened to plunge dozens at a time into the waters, yet with each shift the men were ready, adjusting their circular flights. From the docks to the Fount, she watched a constant flow of men traveling each way, some carrying filled nets to the world above, others hurrying below, eager for another haul.

Jevin must be there somewhere, she thought, and flicking the switch back to full, she flew toward the Fount. Her body lay parallel to the ocean below, but her speed was so slow the strength of the blowing air was not enough to keep her legs lifted. Instead she hung from the straps, needing to use her muscles to keep them straight. It drove her mad, and she pushed harder and harder on the switch, as if to pry the tiniest extra speed from the folded wings. She thought of the aerial stunts performed by the Seraphim during the yearly military parades, and her frustration grew. She didn't want to plod along, feet dangling.

She wanted to fly.

Bree thrust her body backward, altering her course so that the folded wings pointed to the sky. Rising upward, she watched the Fount and the fishermen disappear as she traveled through the clouds and into the space above. Once she was nearly even with the surface of Weshern, she reduced the throttle so that she hovered. Staring at the clouds at her feet, Bree smiled.

"Time to soar," she whispered, and punched her arms forward as if diving into the waters of Lake Pleasance. Her angle dropped, and she pushed the throttle to its maximum. The wings might not have been designed for speed, but with them pointed toward the ground, adding to gravity's pull, she felt the wind blast against her as her velocity rapidly increased. Tilting her head and dipping a shoulder to the side, she shifted her aim, flying faster and faster toward the bottom of Weshern and the Fount below.

For a moment she doubted herself, but the exhilaration was too much for fear. Bree twisted herself parallel to the ocean, and though her descent slowed, her speed remained, and like a shooting star she entered the great shadow cast by Weshern and began circling the Fount. The fishermen were blurs, barely visible from her left eye. Laughing, Bree spiraled downward, looping the twisting waters, feeling the wet spray across her face, her long hair wildly flapping behind her like a cape.

She danced through the fishermen, staying just outside their own steady upward spirals. Harder and harder she pushed at the toggle, willing herself faster, feeling more at home in that moment than she ever had staying at Aunt Bethy's.

And then a fisherman flew in her path.

His back was to her, legs and net dangling as he lifted dozens of fish. He was returning to the docks, and with her rapid descent she was on a direct collision course. Panicking, she felt her mind blank, felt her body lock up. Deep in her stomach she knew it was the worst possible reaction, and as she careened toward the man she forced herself to do the only thing she could think of: she rolled. Shoulder over shoulder she twirled, ending her curved path about the Fount and sending her flying off and away. The roll gained her the few feet necessary to prevent herself from slamming into the fisherman, but her relief lasted only a split second, for as she tried to right herself, she found herself spinning. Head over feet she rolled, and it seemed every twist of her waist and pull of her shoulders was in vain.

She was falling.

Bree's heart hammered in her chest as her stomach looped. She saw the ocean, the island, the Fount, all in a rotating dance as she plummeted. Remembering what Jevin had taught her, she shut off the wings. Without their push, her spinning would slow, increasing her control. She just had to right herself, that was all. The wind on her skin was now a threat, a reminder of how quickly the ocean approached. Crossing her arms, she tried to go limp, to stop fighting the natural pull of gravity. Fear closed her eyes. It was terrifying, relenting control in such a way, but her frantic mind knew it was necessary. Her rotations slowed, and when she opened her eyes she saw water above her, which meant she fell headfirst.

Curling her legs up to her chest, Bree took another deep

breath, then kicked them out as she swung her arms. Her body began to rotate, and she timed it just right, waiting until her feet pointed toward the ocean before setting the switch to half power. Instinct screamed to go full, but she knew doing so could send her spinning once again. The wings shimmered gold, and she felt a pull on her body from the buckles as the contraption attempted to lift her. Her speed was too great, and she steadily increased the power as her heart hammered inside her rib cage. Louder the wings hummed, glowing brighter, but the water was so close now. The buckles about her body dug deep into her skin, the ache her punishment for being torn between the strength of her plummet and the pull of her wings. Eyes wide, she watched the ocean closing in, the waters so blue, so deep. Closing her eyes, she prayed that if she died from impact, it would be quick and without pain.

The impact never came. A hand grabbed her wrist, twisting her about. She opened her eyes to see Jevin spinning her so he could grab her other wrist, and then he looked to the sky as his own wings flared gold. Another strong jolt shook through her body as his wings added to her own. Her plummet slowed, then ceased completely. Face buried into his chest, she felt frightened tears finally release.

"I knew it," she heard Jevin say. "Moment I saw you zooming down like an idiot, I knew this would happen."

"I'm sorry," she murmured.

"Dropped a full net to catch you. Hope you appreciate that."

Bree pushed herself away, and she set the switch to half so she could gently rise.

"I'm glad I'm more important to you than some smelly fish," she said, and despite the tears on her face and the snot she felt dripping from her nose, she laughed. Jevin's glare lasted but a moment before he shook his head.

"Follow me," he said, and he offered her his hand. "Let's get you back on solid ground."

She took it, and together they rose back to the docks, neither saying a word to the other. When near, Jevin let her go, and she drifted down to the wood and landed on wobbling legs. Plopping to her knees, she curled over, cold sweat on her neck. Her palms pressed against the wood, fingernails digging. Kael rushed to her side as the din of the fishermen welcomed her back to her previous life.

"Bree?" he asked, clearly worried.

"I'm fine," she said, not looking at him.

"So how'd it go?" he asked. "What was it like to fly in open air?"

In answer, she vomited all over the docks, bits of it slipping between cracks and dripping down through clouds to the ocean so very far below.

CHAPTER 2

Kael and Bree huddled on the stairs, a door between them and the kitchen. The day was fading, the midnight fire to arrive within the hour, and the twins should have been asleep in their beds. Instead they'd heard a door open, followed by the deep voice of Nickolas Flynn, a longtime friend of their parents who came over from time to time to ensure that they wanted for nothing. They left their soft feather beds and crept down the wooden stairs. Experience acquired over a lifetime allowed them to step exactly where they needed to prevent a creak. Ears to the door, they listened as their aunt and the knight talked.

"Their birthday's days away," Aunt Bethy said, and Kael could hear the anger in her tone. She only spoke in such a snippy, hurried way when she wanted the conversation to move to anything else in existence. Kael imagined her sitting in the rocking chair of their kitchen, just beside the stone fire pit that served as heating for their home and as their oven. "There's no reason to hurry such a thing."

No doubt their aunt refused to look at Nickolas when she said it, instead keeping her long, oval face pointed downward, green eyes locked on whatever she made with her needlework.

"It isn't hurrying," Nickolas said, his deep voice carrying up the stairs. Nickolas was a member of the angelic knights, sworn protectors of Center, the greatest and most powerful of the six holy islands. The theocracy of Center was ruled by the Speaker for the Angels, Marius Prakt, and overseen by his religious servants, the theotechs. Nickolas's folded wings were a gold so pure they were blinding in the daylight sun. His head was smoothly shaven, his armor light and glittering, the two swords secured at his waist razor sharp. Everything about him, including his voice, spoke of control and authority.

"I daresay otherwise," Bethy insisted. "They don't need testing until their sixteenth birthday."

"Their sixteenth is the *last* day to be tested," Nickolas said. "And you owe it to your brother to—"

"I owe it to him to keep his children alive and breathing," Bethy interrupted. "Breanna nearly flew herself into the ocean earlier today, and with one of those fishermen training sets. What do you think she'd do if given a set like yours? She'd break her damn neck."

Kael glanced at his sister, and he saw her face had turned beet red.

"It wasn't that bad," she whispered.

The way she'd reacted when hurling on the dock, or how loudly Jevin had berated them on their walk home, seemed to contradict that, but Kael let the matter drop.

"It only means she needs more training," Nickolas argued. "And I spoke with Jevin about that incident. Bree was going far too fast for her training set to handle. With a set like mine, she'd have been *less* likely to lose control. This is what she wants, and Kael, too. Let them come with me tomorrow to Center. We'll test for their affinity, and after that, the choice is theirs."

Silence for a moment. Kael glanced at his sister, and her eyes were wide. Affinity, as in elemental affinity? That meant one thing, and one thing only...

"Why must they be tested?" Aunt Bethy asked, her voice quieter. "Just because their parents had affinities doesn't mean they will. Besides, there's no reason for them to join the Seraphim. Let Kael become one of the house soldiers if he wishes to serve in the military. And Bree will forget flying in time, once she marries..."

Heavy footsteps moving about the room. The rocking of Bethy's chair ceased.

"Weshern's safety fades each day," said Nickolas, his voice softening, almost pleading. "Your island is yet to recover from the battle that claimed Liam and Cassandra. Both were phenomenal Seraphs, and your niece and nephew might echo their legacy. Don't let them die in obscurity, Kael laboring in plate-mail armor and Bree scraping her hands to the bone pulling potatoes in Lowville's fields. They belong in the sky, protecting those they love. They belong in Weshern's Seraphim."

Both twins tensed, waiting for their aunt's answer.

"No," she said.

Bree was down the stairs in seconds, avoiding Kael's desperate grab at her arm. She burst through the door and into the kitchen, and holding back a curse, Kael followed. If Bree was awake and listening, they'd assume he'd been, too, whether he had or not. The vast majority of the time, it was a safe assumption.

Kael joined his sister in the kitchen, standing tall in his long beige bedclothes. Their home was a modest one, the kitchen cramped by the rocking chair, the dining table, and the many rows of shelves packed with spices, utensils, and bowls. Bethy sat in her rocking chair beside the east-facing window, while on the other side, Nickolas stood before the front door, arms crossed and a frown on his face. His skin was dark as coal, and the contrast made the gold of his armor and the white of his tunic seem all the brighter. While Bethy looked exasperated to see them there, Nickolas seemed almost...hopeful.

"I want to go," Bree said, before either could address her. "*We* want to go."

Bethy looked back and forth between them as Kael shuffled his feet, his gaze more often on the floor than on his aunt's tired stare.

"You don't know what you're signing yourselves up for," she said. "The life isn't glamorous or happy. Most likely you'll die before you reach your twentieth birthday, you know that, don't you?"

"Serving as a Seraph for your island is also a great honor," Nickolas said. "An honor your parents would have been thrilled to witness bestowed upon you."

Bethy rose from her chair. Her hands were at her sides, bones curled from the hours and hours she spent in the fields, fingertips forever stained brown. She walked over so she could address them eye to eye.

"How could you want this?" she asked. "You saw it for yourselves. You saw how terrible battle can be. Do you want to die like your father, lungs punctured with ice and body crushed from the fall? Or would you rather die like your mother, bleeding out across the rooftops?"

"Mother died flying," Bree said. "Don't you dare insult her for it. Better the sky than the fields."

Bethy moved to slap her, but Nickolas caught her hand.

"We all serve God's will, whether in fields of grain or fields of battle," he said, glaring at Bree. "And your aunt only wishes for you to understand the fate I offer. It's bloody, it's dangerous, and it will likely kill you. Both of you. Will you still come to Center for testing, knowing that?"

"You're all I have left of my brother," Bethy said before they could answer, tears in her eyes. "Don't take it from me, please. That life, it'll rip you away, just like it did Liam."

It was almost enough to convince him, and to his surprise, it seemed to sway Bree as well. But Kael knew how much this meant to his sister. Even after she'd nearly died that morning, even while her hands shook as she returned the training wings to Bryce, she'd asked when she could don them again. And if it meant he had to bear the burden...

"I'll go," he said.

Nickolas slowly nodded, looked to Bree.

"I'll go, too," she said, sniffling once. She looked to Bethy. "And I'm sorry."

Bethy wrapped her arms around them both, and she freely let her tears fall. The door creaked as Nickolas pushed it open.

"I'll be here when the morning mist fades," he said. "Dress in your finest, and get some sleep. Tomorrow, we fly to Center."

Come the rise of the sun, the midnight fire was all but smoke. The blessed rays of light pushed it away, banishing it for one more day. The effect was not immediate, though, and for the first hour of morning the sky carried a dark, wispy texture as the smoke gradually dissipated. It was known as the morning mist, and Kael stared at it while standing beside the door to his home. If only the daylight could scatter his nervousness and guilt like it did the mist. Bethy had said little to them after Nickolas left, only held them and told them how much she loved them both.

It hurt, but it wasn't enough. They were committed now. So long as they passed their tests, they would gain entry into Weshern's Academy, established by the Archon of Weshern hundreds of years ago to train and prepare soldiers for aerial combat in defense of their island.

The door opened, closed, and Bree joined him. She wore a pair of brown pants and a long-sleeved white shirt, and around her neck she'd wrapped a deep blue scarf.

"Nickolas said to wear our finest," Kael said as she crossed her arms and leaned against the door. "Shouldn't you wear a dress?"

"We're joining the military, not going to a dance," she said.

Kael shrugged.

"Just thought I'd ask."

He himself wore his finest pair of black wool pants, and his shirt was one that used to belong to his father. It was a light gray, and across his breast was the royal symbol for the island of Weshern, that of a downward-pointed blade drawn with thin blue lines. Kael's boots were black and polished, and he noticed Bree wore a similar pair.

"Good thing we're not dancing," he said. "You'd smash your poor partner's toes."

He grinned, she smacked him in the chest, and he mussed her hair in return. Pointedly turning her back to him, Kael saw her suddenly tense, and he realized Nickolas must have arrived. Clearing his throat, he stood up straight and glanced down the street. Not seeing him, he looked the other way, only to find the knight landing from his flight mere feet in front of him. The morning light gleamed off his polished golden armor. The hum of his wings, so deep and pure, slowly died away.

"Are you two ready?" he asked after inspecting them both. Kael waited for him to berate Bree for how she dressed, but he never did.

"Ready, sir," Kael said, and Bree nodded her head in unison.

"Very well," said Nickolas. "Follow me to the lifts."

He led them down the road, past rows of identical homes with their square designs, stone walls, and thin wooden rooftops. Most were quiet, for where they lived was inhabited mostly by farmers, who had to be out in the fields come the morning mist, rerouting irrigation from the aqueducts, inspecting for bugs, and yanking out the weeds that dared steal precious water and soil from their crops. Aunt Bethy was among them, having headed to the fields earlier than ever. Kael felt certain it was so she didn't have to say a word to them prior to their leaving.

Their home was on Picker Street, just a dead end jut off from Wooden Road, which ran west until it ended at the docks. The other way curled north, exiting their town of Lowville while cutting through the many fields. All along its reach were various shopkeepers, selling wares from Weshern as well as the other outer islands and Center itself. The simple stalls were little more than tents propped up about permanently placed stone tables, and the men and women occupying them quieted their cries as Nickolas passed. Surely the knight had plenty of coin to spend, but it seemed none of the merchants dared harass him while he traveled with a purpose beyond browsing their wares.

"You travel with me to the very heart of humanity's continued existence," Nickolas said as Lowville faded behind them.

"Since you come as visitors, there are a few rules you must know and follow. First, do not leave my side until ordered. Second, keep your mouths shut unless explicitly told to speak. You aren't a native to Center, which means the theotechs can detain you if you're asking questions they don't like or visiting places they don't want you to be in. Is that understood?"

"Yes, sir," they said in unison.

The edge of the island was before them, and with it a chaotic gathering of crates, barrels, and people. They approached the lifts, where ferrymen carried men, women, and their merchandise from island to island. Like the docks, the lifts were a heavy wooden structure built hanging off the side of Weshern, only it looked far sturdier as well as much more crowded.

Nickolas turned so he might address them eye to eye.

"Third," he said, glancing between them, "and perhaps most importantly: do not lie. No matter what you're asked, no matter if you think the truth will cost you your chance at being a Seraph, *you do not lie.* Have I made myself clear?"

Kael had never left Weshern to visit any of the other islands, let alone Center that ruled over them all. He'd thought it'd be no special matter, but Nickolas's tone and warnings made him think otherwise. They were traveling to the home of the theotechs, they of the red robes who gave Kael the creeps whenever he saw one fly by. And everywhere there would be men like Nickolas, strong, controlled, all wielding a similar air of authority. Lump in his throat, he nodded affirmative as Bree quietly whispered the word *yes.*

Nickolas stared a moment longer, then rose back to his feet and beckoned them to follow. Tired and harried men and women parted when they saw him, clearing a way through the craziness. As they passed, Kael heard men arguing over shipments, waving pieces of paper, and pointing at crates that all looked the same to him. Others carried heavy sacks over their shoulders, making their way up and down Wooden Road, toward Lowville or Glensbee to the north. At the lifts themselves gathered a small crowd, waiting for the next to arrive. At the lift's arrival, Nickolas cleared his throat but said nothing.

A man at the back glanced over, saw Nickolas, and then dipped his head and stepped away. Others turned at the commotion, or had people with them tap their shoulders or tug on their sleeves. Soon a path had parted, and Kael and Bree followed Nickolas to the edge of the wooden platform. The crowd grouped back together behind them, sealing them in. So many eyes were on him, Kael felt his neck beginning to flush from the attention. Trying to think about something else, he stared into the sky, where one of the lifts was approaching.

It was a simple enough structure, a large square platform made from split logs that were lashed and nailed together. A thick rope formed its only barrier across the four sides, the rope attached to thick posts built into the corners. From those posts hooked the carrying chains, which in turn were locked to the chest harnesses of four ferrymen, one for each. The ferrymen flew above the structure, thick wings glowing. Though they did not need to carry the chains themselves, their arms rippled with muscle from having to guide the platforms to their destinations. The ferrymen traveled even slower than the fishermen, but their wings could handle far greater weight. Together the four lowered the lift so that it hovered smoothly before the end of the built docks. More than twenty people stood in the center of the lift, forming a circle around a stack of five small crates.

"Welcome to Weshern!" shouted another of the ferrymen who wore a heavy brown robe and remained on the ground, guiding the traffic. He unlatched the rope to allow people to exit. The men and women did, with some of the men carrying two crates apiece.

"Sothren Lift!" the ferrymen called once it was empty.

Nickolas stepped onto the lift, Kael and his sister following.

"We fly to Center," the knight said to the ferrymen. "And we fly alone."

The man in the brown robe nodded, and he looked up to the four carrying the lift, relaying the orders. The men saluted, and once the ferryman had latched the rope, the lift rose from the dock. The sudden lurch startled Kael, and he cried out as he regained his balance.

"Steady," Nickolas said. "You are in no danger."

"Just awkward is all," Kael said, feeling embarrassed.

Attached to the center of the lift was a long, thick rope. Nickolas knelt down to grab it and then offered it to Kael.

"Hold it if you must," he said. Kael stared at it as if it were a snake ready to bite him.

"No thanks," he said. "If I'm about to fly around in the sky as a Seraph, I can't be scared of a slow-moving lift, can I?"

Only a tiny bit of it was bluster. With wings, he could fly anywhere. With a lift, if he fell, well…there was only the ocean below to catch him. Swallowing his nerves, he joined his sister's side. Together they held the outer rope, leaning against it as they took in their surroundings.

All around them were puffy white clouds, nowhere near as thick as those below Weshern but enough to obscure the view after a few hundred yards as well as provide their island with the occasional gentle mist. Their platform rose through them, and Kael's mouth dropped open in wonder once they emerged. The sun seemed to shine brighter, and suddenly he saw the other floating islands.

"There's Sothren!" Bree said, pointing to the nearest of the islands. Unlike Weshern and her many lakes and rivers, Sothren appeared mostly green, her various towns little gray dots amid fields and orchards. The island was their close ally, and Kael remembered hearing their father talk highly of their Seraphim on many occasions.

The platform continued, and Kael craned his neck trying to see the other islands. He could have easily placed them on a map, but to see them hovering in the actual sky made those maps pale in comparison.

"Which nation is that?" he asked, pointing to an island to the far southwest. Her surface was far more yellow than green, covered with fields of wheat and deep canyons carved into the stone. Nickolas joined them at the outer rope and leaned close so they might hear him without need of shouting.

"Elern, the peacekeeper," the knight said. "Those canyons hide the caves where they grow their famous mushrooms."

Bree frowned at him, confused.

"Peacekeeper?" she asked.

Nickolas nodded.

"We have our nicknames for the various islands among the knights. Elern has earned hers through the rule of the Gemman family. They've pledged assistance to any island threatened by invasion from another. If not for their protection, I'd wager Weshern and Galen would have declared all-out war long before you were even born."

Kael stared at Elern's canyons, which looked like deep scars upon the land, and wished he could visit those numerous caves.

"What is Weshern's nickname?" he asked.

Nickolas grinned at him.

"Ice-blooded," he said. "Don't worry, it's a compliment. Your island has never backed down from a challenge, and so long as Isaac Willer is your Archon, I doubt you ever will."

Bree looked about, searching.

"Where is Galen?" she asked. The name made Kael's face twitch. Galen, ally of Candren and home of his parents' murderers. Why would she care to see such an awful place? Nickolas put a hand over his eyes to block the sun, searched for a moment, and then pointed.

"There," he said.

They followed his gaze, but Kael only saw a vague brown dot mostly obscured by the clouds. Bree stared at it, and it seemed like she was trying to send it crashing down with her mind. Kael nudged her side, and when she looked his way, he grinned.

"Just making sure you're awake," he said.

Her concentration broken, Bree rolled her eyes, but she did not return to staring. Not that she could have, anyway. They were passing through a deep stretch of clouds, and even Weshern behind them was hard to spot. The cloud rolled across them, immaterial as mist, and then ended with a brightening of the sun. In the sudden clarity, Kael first laid eyes upon Center, and his mouth dropped open in awe.

If the outer islands were children, Center was the parent. Larger than all five put together, the sight of it made Kael's head spin as he tried to grasp its enormity. Three gigantic founts led up to it, each a tornado of water of frightening size. Fields covered the outer rim, and beside many green and lush forests he saw towns like white dots. Rivers ran throughout, all flowing to the edge and then dropping back down to the Endless Ocean, solid blue lines that eventually became scattered white spray. And unlike the other islands, Center had a mountain at its far side, deep brown rock that rose up like a ragged finger. Built into it were the holy temples of the theotechs, far above and separate from the great cities that spread out near the heart of the island.

It took half an hour for them to cross the many miles separating Center from Weshern. Kael and Bree passed the time by peering down at the ocean or pointing out a new sight or wonder on the surface of Center. As they approached, Kael better saw the many wood structures built along the edge, fishing docks and places for lifts. The very air was crowded with the platforms, forming into long lines. Ferrymen were like birds in a great flock, the air seeming to vibrate to the hum of their wings.

"Where are they taking us?" Bree asked, needing to turn and shout to be heard over the growing din.

"Look to the colors," Nickolas shouted back.

The landing platforms were bunched into groups, and as they neared, Kael saw each group flying a different flag. The ferrymen carrying their lift shifted their angle, joining a line leading to docks flying a flag that was half white, half blue. The colors of Weshern, Kael realized. He looked to the other flags, black and yellow, green and white, red and orange. All guiding lifts from the various islands to their proper place.

It took over twenty minutes for it to be their turn, the ferrymen settling the lift before a platform. Rope pulled away, Nickolas stepped off, only to be greeted by an elderly man with a red robe and a pair of spectacles hanging low off his nose.

"Name and rank?" the man asked.

"Knight Lieutenant Nickolas Flynn," Nickolas answered.

"And the two with you?"

"Kael and Breanna Skyborn, of Lowville, Weshern. They've come for their affinity tests."

"Very good," said the man in red, marking something on the board and parchment he held. "Carry on."

Nickolas led them through, and the bustle there made Kael realize how calm and small the lifts in Weshern truly were by comparison. Everywhere he looked were hundreds of people, carrying belongings, shouting, making deals, and asking questions. Staying close, they followed the gap made by the large knight as he pushed his way from the lifts and to the smooth stone road beyond. Wagons rolled to and fro, the sight of the rare horses pulling them putting a smile on Kael's face.

"The tests are held at the base of the mountain," Nickolas said, not turning to address them. "It is a taxing walk for those not used to it, but I am forbidden to carry you. Consider this part of the test."

Merchants lined either side of the road they traveled, tanned men wearing clothes of all combinations of colors. They held out shirts, pants, glittering jewelry, and exotic pets. There was so much for sale Kael could barely take in it all. Whatever peace they'd known in Weshern for being in Nickolas's presence was absent there in Center. Ahead of them Kael saw an enormous city, its buildings constructed of white marble, and the thought of how many people must live there made his stomach twist. He could not begin to count how many different homes and streets he saw within. Already he felt crowded, and the closer they walked to the city the worse it became. Even the air was filled with knights flitting about. Thankfully the road forked, and Nickolas led them northwest, the road skirting around the city's edge.

It took more than two hours for them to pass the city. A great forest grew to their west, and Kael felt a strong impulse to go running into it to explore. Instead of the broad leaves sported by the trees that grew on Weshern, these had thousands of little needles, and it seemed they did not grow quite as tall, either. They grew so tightly packed that within was dark and mysterious.

"Does anything live in there?" Bree asked at one point.

"Only that which is allowed," answered Nickolas. "And I did not address you."

It was a gentle rebuke, but still Bree frowned and looked away, her gray eyes peering into the woods with a sense of longing he understood well. Deep pine forests were but stories to them, for it was their clear water the people of Weshern prided themselves on. In a brief moment of clarity, Kael realized he looked to the forest the way he sometimes saw strangers from Sothren look at their rivers and lakes.

Steadily the forest withdrew west, and the path followed. Fewer people traveled there, and those who did seemed to more often wear the red robes of the theotechs. Ahead of them the mountain loomed, and the path veered higher and higher. At sight of the mountain, Nickolas suddenly broke the silence.

"We approach the site of the tests," the knight said. "But before we arrive, I want to make sure you two know what it is you are seeking to become, and that you understand the sheer importance of the position."

Nickolas gestured to the forests and mountain.

"For all of Center's grandeur, she is but a splinter of the majesty humankind once possessed. Forests once sprawled for hundreds of miles in all directions. There used to be entire ranges of mountains, peaks upon peaks that a man could spend his entire life climbing and never see each and every one. Plains of grass stretched beyond sight, grazed upon by a legion of animals that now exist only in drawings and paintings. Before the Ascension, humanity counted its numbers not in the thousands, not in the millions, but in the billions. Then came the shadow that swallowed the world. Then the demons of old, the sky of fire, and the Endless Ocean washing over all. We faced extinction, and only God's angels pulling our six islands to the sky gave us one final chance to continue living."

Nickolas paused, and he turned to them and crossed his arms over his chest. His tone shifted, less lecture, more warning.

"As a Seraph of Weshern, you will fight the battles she cannot. Wars between nations once spanned thousands of miles, with the dead outnumbering every single man and woman currently alive. Such instances cannot occur, not with our very existence teetering so close to oblivion. That is why over the years the Speaker for the Angels has set up the many rules of combat you will learn to follow. Each one is to minimize the number of dead while still allowing each of the five outer islands some measure of independence. If you are blessed enough to become a member of the Weshern Seraphim, know that while you serve your island, you also accept an agreement with us here in Center. You will honor that with your very lives, is that clear?"

Kael and Bree nodded in unison. His gaze was so powerful, so intense, Kael wished the man would look away.

"Tell me," Nickolas said, "have either of you spoken with a disciple of Johan Lumens?"

The two siblings glanced at each other, confused.

"We've never heard the name," Kael said, answering for both of them.

The knight frowned.

"Listen well, for this may save your very lives. If you have not heard his name, you soon will, for he is a worm burrowing into the heart of all six islands. He preaches a dangerous dogma, denying the divine wisdom of our Speaker for the Angels, insisting Marius Prakt does not hear the words of Heaven's host. Johan claims the theotechs are not servants of God but enslavers of mankind. It is all nonsense. For more than five centuries we have endured, and it is only through the aid of Center and her theotechs. Only the theotechs know the secrets to create the prisms we need to power our entire societies. Only they know the mechanics of the wings that give us flight. The Fount that keeps each island aloft, the systems deep underground that purify the water you drink, even the divine prayers that protect us from the midnight fire, they are all carefully managed by the theotechs."

Nickolas put a hand on a shoulder of each of them.

"The theotechs are not jailers," he said. "They are the hands of the Speaker, carrying out God's will. Through their sacrifices, we live. Your island of Weshern, your Seraphim academy, your farms and towns…they endure by the hard work of the theotechs, who live and serve among you out of a desire to see all of humanity thrive. Should false prophets or rebels come with poison on their tongues, remember that, and remain faithful."

"We will," Kael said, his sister echoing him. It was strange hearing such a warning. There were those out there who would deny the obvious gifts Center's theotechs gave to other islands? It made no sense. A simple glimpse at the Fount below their island, or a single drink of water that flowed from the many underground caves, should have been enough proof. Sure, the red-robed men were often a rare and strange sight in Weshern, but who was this Johan to make claims about the Speaker and his theotechs? What could he have seen or learned that others before him had not?

These thoughts passed through Kael's mind as they climbed the base of the mountain. At first it was little more than ascending a gentle hill, but soon their steps were labored. The forest closed back around them, hiding the distant city and the sprawling fields about it from view. Should the slope ever become too steep, logs were dug into the ground to form steps. Time dragged on and on, the silence painful, the inability to speak with his sister bothering Kael to no end.

If Nickolas was taxed by the incline, he didn't show it. Even though he wore his elegant set of wings, he never used them to fly ahead or lessen his burden. Instead he led the way, step after step, until at last they arrived at a building with long stone walls and a tall, triangular roof built of wood. Carvings lined the stone, depictions of the elements, roaring fire, pounding rain, billowing snow, and blinding lightning. Two angelic knights stood near the entrance, blocking the path that continued up the mountain.

"Welcome back, Nickolas," one of them said, a man with fiery red hair and a smoothly trimmed beard.

"Won't be here long, Kyle," Nickolas said, saluting. "How many came today?"

"Just nine," Kyle said. "Not counting your two. Any chance we know them?"

"It's Liam Skyborn's kids."

At that, both knights lifted their eyebrows.

"Well, then," said Kyle, "this should be a breeze."

One of them gestured to continue. The door to the building was thick, stained wood with a brass handle. Carved into the wood was the symbol of Center, a great circle with five smaller circles intersected by its perimeter. It seemed Nickolas had no intention of leading anymore, so Kael crossed the grass, his sister trailing after.

"Good luck," Nickolas called from the road. "To both of you."

Taking in a deep breath, Kael looked to his sister, who nodded. Despite his nerves, he smiled anyway.

"After you," he said, pulling open the door and then following her inside.

CHAPTER

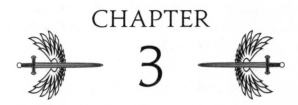

3

Inside was surprisingly dull. Kael had expecting something... different, something imposing. Instead they entered a small rectangular room with white walls and a wooden floor. There were no paintings, no murals, just two windows along the front of the building and a single door leading farther in. A dozen or so wooden chairs lined the four walls, all but one of which were empty. In it sat a girl with long blonde hair and an open book covering the rest of her face. Before the lone door stood a woman in the red garb of the theotechs.

"Your names?" asked the woman.

"Breanna and Kael Skyborn," Bree answered before Kael could even think to. The woman was surprisingly young, her face one of harsh lines and raven hair. Her outfit was different from that of the other theotechs they'd seen. While she wore red robes, they were much tighter against her body, and ended just below the knee. Gold buckles wrapped around her waist, and long black boots covered what was visible of her legs. The look was one of much greater mobility, and had an air of military to it. The woman nodded upon hearing their names, then opened the door and vanished inside without a word. Kael stood there with his sister, dumbfounded, and then a moment later the woman stepped back out.

"Have a seat," she said. "I'll call your names shortly."

Kael glanced around, then chose the seat closest to the door. Bree sat beside him, smoothing her pants and letting out a deep breath. She was nervous, he could tell. Soaring freely over open ocean? That his sister could handle. A meeting with the mysterious theotechs that would decide their fates? Apparently that was far worse.

Their chairs were across from the other girl, and as they took their seats she lowered her book. She looked their age, which surprised Kael, given how late he and his sister were in taking their tests. All his other friends had come to Center two years ago, at first eligibility. The girl wore a brilliant white shirt with a black jacket atop it, and her pants were of a similar dark color as her jacket. Compared to the sharpness of her clothing, her face was rather gentle, and friendly.

"You won't have long," she said, flipping her long blonde hair back over one shoulder. "At most the others have waited ten minutes."

"Thanks," Kael said, and he suddenly felt very awkward. The girl had beautiful eyes, green like grass. That he was noticing this detail only reinforced his sudden feeling of embarrassment. Was that all it took, the presence of a pretty girl, to render him bewildered?

"I'm, uh, Kael," he said, forcing the words to exit his mouth. "This is my sister, Bree."

"Hello, Bree," the girl said, smiling at his sister. Bree gave a curt nod, clearly focused on the tests and not at all caring for conversation. "My name's Clara. So which island are you from?"

"Weshern," said Kael.

The girl's eyes lit up.

"So am I! I hope you do well. It'd be nice to have a familiar face going into training."

If she lived on Weshern, it certainly wasn't anywhere near Lowville. Kael had a feeling he'd have noticed a girl so pretty.

"That so?" he said. "Where do you live? I haven't—"

"Clara," called the woman at the door, interrupting him.

"Sorry," Clara said, rising to her feet. She offered a quick curtsy, then vanished deeper into the building. Now it was just the two of them, and Kael leaned forward, holding his chin in his hands.

"There's no need to be nervous," his sister told him.

"I'm not the one who's nervous."

He glanced her way, winked. She smiled, and he could tell she was hoping he'd help alleviate her nerves.

"You're not nervous either, are you?" he asked, rambling, the one thing he was definitely good at. "I hope not. I mean, I should be nervous, since I'm terrible at flying. You, though? Come on. You're going to fly circles around everyone. You'll be the star pupil, I promise."

"You better be there with me," she told him. "What good is it to be the star pupil without my twin brother there to seethe with jealousy at my accomplishments?"

"Don't worry," he said. "I know my place. Lots of seething and glowering."

She took his hand, squeezed it, and let go. Just like that, she was silent again, but something was different now, her demeanor loose and relaxed. If only he actually felt as confident as he pretended to be...

With a startling burst of noise, the door in the corner opened, and Clara stepped out. Her smile was ear to ear.

"Water affinity," she said. "I knew it, too!"

"That's great," Kael said, grinning stupidly as if her accomplishment were the best thing ever. From the corner of his vision he caught his sister rolling her eyes.

Before Clara could leave, the woman at the door called Kael's name and beckoned him to follow her.

"Already?" he asked as he stood, feeling stupid as he said it. Why in God's name would he question her?

"Already," the woman said, curt, annoyed. Swallowing down the lump in his throat, Kael gave one last look to his sister, offered a crooked smile, and then followed.

"Good luck," Clara called from the exit as the door shut behind him like the sealing of a tomb. Before him was a short hallway that immediately turned right. High windows along the ceiling let in what little light there was. On his left were two doors, and she stopped just before the first.

"You're expected," the woman said.

"Thanks," Kael said, grasping the black iron handle and pulling. Stomach shaking, he stepped inside.

The room was as plain as everything else in the place. A wooden table and two chairs, one on each side, that was all. A thick pane of glass was along one wall, the rest bare and white. An older man sat in one of the chairs, wearing the standard long red robes of the theotechs. He gestured to the other seat, which Kael took, putting his back to the darkened pane of glass. A small box made of old oak and gilded trim lay between them, along with a piece of parchment just in front of the theotech.

"Welcome, Kael," said the man. "My name is Dioso, and I will be administering the tests with you today."

Dioso seemed friendly enough, with a long round face and

gray beard and mustache. He wore a red cap atop his head, which was largely bald. When he smiled, his teeth were clean, his blue eyes disarming.

"I understand," Kael said, unsure how much he was supposed to talk but figuring at least that would be safe to say. Dioso nodded, and he tapped the box that rested between them.

"There are two aspects to this test," he said. "I ask that you give each of them equal care and effort. Remember to stay calm, and keep your mind clear. I also ask that you remain honest with me, and do not try to cheat or purposefully alter the results."

"I will."

"Good," Dioso said. "Then let us begin."

Carefully he opened the box and then removed a heavy black cloth to reveal the contents within. They were five prisms, each of a different color: red, blue, white, yellow, and green. Dioso spread the black cloth atop the table, then one by one removed the elements and placed them atop it. All the while, he spoke.

"This first challenge is a test of your sensitivity to the elements. The order the elements are currently in may or may not change when I have you close your eyes. In the center of your right palm I will make a small cut, just enough to release some blood. That blood will confirm your affinity, as well as aid you in detecting the elements, given your inexperience. When I tell you, I want you to extend that hand and slowly move it above the elements. If it helps, you may touch them, so long as you do not move them or open your eyes. When you are certain, I want you to leave your hand on the element you feel most strongly attuned with. Do you understand?"

Kael nodded.

"Very well," said the old man, removing the last item from

the box: a finely sharpened silver knife. "Now close your eyes and extend your hand."

Kael took in a deep breath. Of the five elements, four of the five would suffice in granting him entrance to the Seraphim. Only light was deemed unworthy of combat. Those with strong light affinity were instead rewarded with the position of ferryman. So long as it was one of the other four, Kael had no preference. But should he have no affinity at all...

Trying not to entertain that terrible idea, he closed his eyes and offered his hand. The old man took it, firm yet gentle, the grip of someone who had performed the cut many times before. The knife moved across Kael's open palm, a quick incision that was finished before Kael could even flinch at the brief but sharp pain. Dioso released him, and Kael felt the tiniest trickle of blood slide down his wrist.

"You may begin."

Kael reached out his hand, hovering it over where the black cloth had been. Almost immediately he sensed something peculiar, like how heat seemed to lift off the stone walkways in summer, only neither hot nor cold, just...there. Familiar. In his mind he saw a single prism as clearly as if his eyes were open. Thrilled beyond measure, he put his hand atop it and offered a nervous smile.

"Here," he said.

"Very good. Open your eyes."

He did, and immediately his smile vanished. In his hand, beneath his fingers, was the light element. At his touch the prism shone bright enough that he had to squint. Upon pulling back his hand, the light faded, the blood upon it rapidly drying and losing color. Kael's hopes faded as quickly as the light. That was it, he realized. His future was set. Any hope of following Bree into the Seraphim had died a brilliant white death.

"Such strong affinity," Dioso said, and he scribbled something onto the piece of parchment on the table before him. "You'll make a fine ferryman, my lad, a very fine one indeed. Now let us finish up this next test."

Dioso took the white prism and put it back into the box, then gestured to the other four.

"This second test is mostly perfunctory," he said. "We shall confirm the accuracy of your sensitivity by comparing the affinity of your chosen element to your affinity, if any, to the other four. Please, place your hand on each one, and ensure some of your blood makes contact so I may see and judge any reactions."

The first was the green one, which at his touch showed not the slightest reaction. Next came the red, and again nothing. As Dioso put those two away, Kael touched the blue prism, and at this one he felt a cold sensation. Frost seemed to grow from nothing around the edges of the prism, creating a thin sheet of ice across it. Kael felt his hope rekindle. Had his first guess been wrong? Might he still be a member of the Seraphim if he bore water affinity?

"Interesting," Dioso muttered as he wrote something on his sheet of paper. "It's rare to see someone with both major and minor affinities."

"Does that mean I may still join the Seraphim?" Kael asked.

"Your major affinity is light, not water," Dioso said, as if that settled everything. "Continue on."

Kael swallowed down his cruel disappointment. Last was yellow, which again did nothing. With that, the test was over, and Dioso put the final prism into the box.

"I pray you are not disappointed," Dioso said, rising from his seat. "Ferrymen are vital to our survival, and Center greatly rewards their gifts. In time, you'll..."

He paused as the door to the room opened, and the woman from before stepped inside.

"Dioso, a moment, if you please," she said.

"Of course," the old man said. "Excuse me," he said to Kael, then left.

Kael glared at the box, trying to decide how he'd break the news to Bree. Maybe she'd change her mind, but he doubted it. She'd not forfeit her chance to become a Seraph only to work the fields instead until he came home at nightfall when the ferrymen rested. More importantly, he'd not dare let her. He'd have to say good-bye is all. A grim smile spread on his face. Well...at least Aunt Bethy would be happy. She'd much prefer him taking the safer work of a ferryman. And Dioso hadn't been lying. Ferrymen were paid well for their long, tedious hours of work.

The door opened, and in stepped Dioso. He said nothing, only returned to the box and pulled out the blue crystal prism, setting it atop the black cloth.

"Let me see one more time," he said.

Frowning, Kael reached out and touched the blue prism. Once more it frosted over, the very center of it seeming to glow with a distant light.

"Major affinity," the old man said. "Congratulations, Kael Skyborn, you are worthy of becoming a Seraph of Weshern. A representative of your ruling family will visit your home to further discuss the details of training and relocation."

Kael stood frozen, refusing to believe his ears.

"I passed?" he said. "But my light affinity—"

"Was not as great as your water," said Dioso, cutting him off. "Or would you like to argue your eyes are better than mine?"

Kael shook his head. Whatever that woman had said to him was clearly influencing his results, but why should he argue?

He was being given everything he wanted, and all he had to do was keep his mouth shut.

"Forgive me, sir," Kael said. "Thank you."

Dioso gave him a smile, and the amount of sadness it seemed to hide was troubling.

"Safe travels, young Skyborn. May God watch over your journey."

And with that, the door opened. The woman with the raven hair beckoned him out, and he left for the lobby, and his sister.

Bree sat with the five elemental prisms laid out before her. Dioso sat in the chair opposite her, watching closely.

"Remember," he said, "even if you feel an attraction toward multiple prisms, you must choose the one that is the strongest. Are you ready?"

She nodded.

"Very well. Close your eyes and give me your hand."

Bree did, and she waited for the old man to shuffle the order of the various colors so she could not cheat. In her chest, she felt her heart thumping despite her attempts to remain calm. This was it. Every hope of her becoming one of the Seraphim rested on her choosing correctly. Dioso took her hand, she felt a sharp pain, and then blood flowed across her palm and down her wrist.

"You may begin."

Bree reached out her hand, and she waited for the slightest twitch or sensation. She'd read it was often like a comfortable aura, an awareness of the element and its potential strength. Back and forth she moved her hand, and after a moment, she dipped her fingers lower, letting the tips brush against all five. With each pass, she felt her heartbeat increase.

Nothing. She sensed no aura. She felt no awareness. No cold, no hot, no radiating familiarity. Everything she'd read, everything a sensitivity to the elements should be, she did not feel. Fighting off panic, she tried another pass, doing everything she could to calm herself. Perhaps her mind was cluttered. Perhaps she didn't know how to listen or feel for it in the proper way.

"You must choose soon," Dioso said, causing Bree's jaw to clench.

It didn't matter. Another pass, and another, and still nothing. Feeling defeat clawing her chest, she finally chose the element in the perfect center.

"Here," she said, and her voice was disturbingly cracked to her ears. "This is the one."

"Open your eyes, child."

She did. Her hand rested atop the blue prism, her blood trickling upon it, and it showed not the slightest change. Bree stared at it, betrayed. That was it, then. She had no sensitivity to the elements, not the tiniest bit.

"Affinity to the elements is uncommon," Dioso said, as if he could sense her frustration. It sounded practiced, a line he'd used a thousand times before, and it robbed all comfort from it. "Do not be upset, Breanna, for there are still many ways to serve your island and your God. Not all are meant to take to the skies."

"I was," Bree said, and she swallowed down a growing lump in her throat.

"Next we test the accuracy of your sensitivity," Dioso said, and he put the blue prism away. "Please, place your hand on each one so I may see its reaction."

The first was the white prism, which contained the element of light. Gently she put a fingertip atop it.

"Not just a finger," Dioso said. "Make sure the blood makes contact."

Bree nodded but remained silent, too upset for words. She placed her palm flat on the prism, smearing it with her blood. Still nothing. Next came the green prism, and as much as she hated it, she dared hope there'd be a change. There wasn't. The disappointment was starting to crash in on her, and she felt tears growing in her eyes. Tilting her head to the side, ashamed of such weakness, she touched the yellow prism, which held the power of lightning. Eyes closed, she did not see the lack of reaction. She didn't need to. After a moment she lifted her hand, then placed it atop the final one.

Immediately she heard Dioso gasp.

"My God…"

When she opened her eyes, her entire hand was aflame. It burst from the red prism, curling about her fingers and crawling up her palm. She felt the heat of it, a distant sensation, more like a rash than the burn she knew she should be feeling. Over two feet into the air the fire leapt, and dark smoke lifted higher to the ceiling. Jaw slack, she stared, baffled, frightened. As the fire continued to grow, the pain heightened until she could stand no more.

With a cry, she let go of the prism. The fire shrank, burning blue a few moments more as her blood upon the prism cracked and flaked away. Tears streaming down her cheeks, Bree held her quivering hand to her chest. Blisters formed from fingertips to wrist, much of her pale skin turning an angry red as if sunburned. From the other side of the table, Dioso slowly pushed back his chair and rose to his feet. Before him was the parchment he'd been scribbling on, and he grabbed the quill and made a single mark in its center.

"God be praised," he said, eyes never leaving hers. "I have never seen a woman so blessed. The Weshern Seraphim have themselves a rare gift."

Despite the pain, despite the tears, Bree smiled. Dioso had said the words that mattered, her burns nothing but a cost she would gladly pay.

The Seraphim . . . the lords of the sky, the masters of flight and battle, warriors just like her mother and father.

And now she would be one of them.

CHAPTER

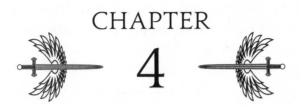

4

Nickolas came with them to break the news to Aunt Bethy, something Bree was very thankful for. They arrived at Lowville as the sun was beginning its descent, though they could have been there earlier if not for Nickolas, who had taken them to one of Center's markets to buy them a treat.

"You're surely famished," he'd said as he handed over two bread rolls stuffed with cheese. "If you're anything like me, you were too nervous to eat this morning, and it's far past lunchtime."

The delay also ensured Bethy would be back from the fields. As they walked down the street, Bree saw her sitting on their porch step, chin resting on her knuckles as she waited. At their approach, she stood, moving as if her entire body were made of stone.

"I don't need you to tell me," she said as they stopped before her. "I can see it in your faces."

"Fire and ice," Nickolas said, nodding and touching the tops of their heads each in turn. "They will do their parents proud."

Bree had expected Aunt Bethy to protest, but instead she very calmly stepped down, dropped to her knees, and wrapped her arms around them both.

"You'll always be my brother's little children to me," she whispered. "I'm scared to lose you, but it's not right of me. It's not fair to hold you two down." She leaned back, smiled at them despite the tears that ran down her face. "You're so strong, so beautiful, so brave. Nickolas is right. You'll do your parents proud."

Such naked emotion made Bree feel awkward and uncomfortable. She hugged back, wishing she knew what to say to calm her aunt's fears.

"We'll be fine," Bree said, stepping back. She tried to force sincerity into each word, to pretend she knew it for a certainty. "Perfectly fine, I promise, won't we, Kael?"

Kael grinned despite his own growing tears.

"Better than fine," he said. "You'll see."

The two turned their attention to Nickolas, who had waited patiently during the exchange.

"This year's class begins in three weeks," he said, removing his left gauntlet from a hook on his harness so he might put it on. "A Weshern Seraph will come for you early that morning. Bring nothing but the clothes on your backs, and make sure those are ready for a long, difficult day."

Nickolas reached out and brushed Breanna's dark hair with his armored fingers.

"And do something about that," he said. "Long hair becomes a danger when making high-speed turns and maneuvers. Better to handle it now than let one of the instructors hack it off with a sword."

Bree nodded but kept silent. As he thumbed the switch, the mechanism of Nickolas's wings thrummed to life. Nickolas saluted, then ran three steps before leaping into the air, soaring away on his beautiful golden wings. Bree watched, and she shivered thinking she would soon wear a set just as powerful.

"Come inside," Aunt Bethy said, gently pulling on their shoulders. "Supper is waiting."

Bree took her seat at the table, her brother opposite her. Bethy did not follow, instead remaining outside.

"Is... is she all right?" Kael asked, glancing nervously to the door.

Supper was a bowl of meat broth and dumplings, and Bree pulled it closer and grabbed the spoon. From the other end, she heard the first of what would be many sobs.

"Bethy will be fine," Bree said.

"But once we leave for our training she'll be all alone."

She set her spoon down and shook her head. Every word made her feel like an awful human being, but they would be gone for nearly a year before they saw their aunt again. If Kael felt guilty and homesick, he might never make it through that year...

"She'll be fine," Bree repeated, louder so that her words would drown out Bethy's quiet sobs. "These are the sacrifices we must make to protect our home. Aunt Bethy will be strong, just like we'll be strong. Do you understand?"

For a long moment he said nothing, only stared at her coldly.

"Yes," he said, clearly lying. "I do."

Bree ate another spoonful, ignoring how cold the broth was. By the time she finished, the crying from the other side of the door had ended, but still Aunt Bethy did not come inside, and would not until the first of the midnight shadow began its crawl from the east.

At the same time as Bethy was coming inside, Bree was preparing to go outside. When she heard the front door shut below, she slid out from her bed, still wearing her outfit from earlier in the day. Not surprising in the least, Kael hadn't fallen asleep either, and she heard his bed rustle.

"Where are you going?" he whispered.

"To take care of something," she whispered back.

"Do you want me to come with?"

She shook her head as she grabbed a slender knife from underneath her bed and tucked it into her belt.

"Stay here," she said. "I want to do this alone."

Bree snuck out the window of their bedroom, hanging from the sill so she might be as close to the ground as possible before jumping. Counting to three, she let go and then dropped. The hit jarred her knees, and she promptly collapsed to her rear upon landing, but that was the worst of it. Standing up, she brushed a bit of dirt from her pants, then checked the blade at her waist. Still secure.

Glancing up and down the street to ensure no night owl might be watching, she turned left and then ran. She ran until the street ended, and she reached the stone barricade beyond. Easily climbing over, she now walked with measured steps across the grass. The dirt always felt different beyond the barricade. Softer. Looser. It should have frightened her, but instead she found it strangely comforting. Looking up to the sky, she watched the midnight fire burning across the darkness. The east was fully consumed, the west soon to be, and in the nighttime glow she walked to the very edge of her world and knelt on her knees.

The clouds were thick below her when she looked down, their white tops colored red. Below them was the Endless Ocean, and part of her wished to see what the rolling waves looked like when painted over by the midnight fire. Perhaps once she was a Seraph and had a pair of wings of her own, she might have the chance to discover for herself.

"Wings of my own," she whispered, and she felt a chill blow through her. Lifting her right hand, she examined the pink flesh, dotted by deeper red circles where the blisters had been. As she'd eaten in Center, Nickolas had taken notice of the burn marks on her hand.

"Don't worry too much about those," he'd said. "It's a funny thing, how our human bodies interact with the elements. Wounds inflicted by what you have a strong affinity for tend to heal at a much faster rate. It won't scar, and by tomorrow, I doubt you'll even have a blister."

Bree had been ready to bear the scars on her hand as a badge of honor, proving her worthiness to join the Seraphim, but the knight had been correct. Not even morning, and already the burns were fading. Her right hand was a little tender, but she could easily ignore that, which was good. She needed it for what she must do.

Drawing her knife, she set it on the grass beside her, then grabbed her hair and began to straighten it with her fingers. Multiple times she combed it, then pulled it all behind her head, twisting it so it might remain in the ponytail. Keeping it together as best she could with her left hand, she grabbed the knife with her right.

It'd been years since she'd cut her hair, and she would not let some unknown instructor be the one to do it. Closing her eyes, she once again counted to three and then sawed through her hair with the knife. It took a few tries, but at last she felt the giant clump in her left hand go limp. Letting out a pained groan as she pulled errant, uncut strands from her scalp, she held the mass before her. So much hair, she saw. She'd been proud of it, of its length, its shine in the morning sun. Shaking her head, it felt weirdly light, and having air blowing against her neck was strange, to say the least.

On Weshern, all waste, no matter the type, was to be reused in some way. Most was buried in the fields, to be broken down and used by crops the following year, but not this time. Not this piece of her. As the sky burned, she rose to her feet and hurled the hundreds of loose strands into the sky, let it cast its black outline across the fire before the wind carried it away.

You have your mother's hair.

Aunt Bethy had told her that once, before her parents' death. Before a large hole had been torn into her heart, ripping out the happiness residing within. No, she'd not cut her hair in years, not since that terrible day, and she felt tears building in her eyes as she watched the last strands fade away. She slumped to her knees before the cliff, fists pressing into the grass.

"I miss you," she whispered. "I miss you so much."

Her tears fell, sobs racking her, but in the privacy beyond the homes and the barricade, she finally felt alone enough to let it all out. She sobbed much like her aunt had sobbed, kneeling before the great expanse of nothing, before fields of clouds colored red by the fire that consumed the sky. *Let it burn,* she thought as she hurled the knife off the side. *Let it all burn if it burns away the hurt as well.*

When she returned home, she was surprised to see Aunt Bethy waiting for her at the door, sitting on the step like when she and Kael came back from Center with Nickolas. Bethy did not watch her approach, only kept her eyes on the roiling sky above. Bree took tentative steps, unsure of what to do or what to say. Finally she stood before her aunt, her head bowed and her arms crossed behind her back, and waited.

"Why?" her aunt asked after a painful silence. "Your mother died in your arms that same night I lost my brother. How could you desire to risk that same fate?"

Bree wished she had a better answer, but she gave the best she could.

"I want to fly," she said. "And not with clipped wings like the fishermen. I want to fly like Mom and Dad flew. Free. Proud. They weren't afraid, and so I won't be, either."

"And when battle comes?"

Bree felt her throat tighten, and she forced out her words.

"And when battle comes, I'll have a chance to make the people who killed Mom and Dad pay for what they did."

Aunt Bethy's gaze finally drifted down from the fire to look Bree in the eye.

"Your father once told me you wanted to fly ever since you took your first step. He was right, too. You were meant for the skies, Breanna, and now you have your chance. I only pray you understand what it will cost. Your peaceful life is gone, gone like the beautiful hair you've cut."

She reached out a hand wrinkled and weathered by untold hours working in the fields.

"Such youth," she said as she gently cupped Bree's face. "Remember it, cherish it, and then say good-bye to it forever. This is the death of the child I knew. Please don't hate me for mourning that, Bree. But when you come home a year from now, I'll be waiting, you understand? I'll be waiting, and I'll be loving you, and missing you, and eager to meet the woman you've become."

It was too much, too naked, too honest. Bree sank into the lap of her aunt, closed her eyes, and buried her face. She made no promises. She offered no assurances. She only enjoyed the embrace, committing it to memory and swearing that, no matter what hardships might come, she would cherish it forever.

CHAPTER
5

Some jobs Kael didn't mind. Others, however, he would not miss in the slightest once he left his life in the fields to become a Seraph. Pulling a wheelbarrow full of pig excrement to shovel onto the cornfields was certainly one he'd be glad to never, ever have to do again.

"Two more weeks," he said as he jammed the shovel into the stinking brown pile. "Just two more weeks."

It'd been six days since their evaluations revealed their water and fire affinities, and Aunt Bethy had spent every one telling whomever would listen how proud she was. For Kael, it was a welcome change from the dour attitude she'd possessed whenever they'd suggested going to Center for testing in the years prior. For all her fears for their safety, and how they might suffer a similar fate as their parents, Bethy truly was proud of them.

One of the few benefits of shoveling the manure (or curses,

depending on the mood he was in) was the solitude it earned him. Bree was with Aunt Bethy and a dozen other men and women, ripping out weeds that lined the entire acre of crops. Kael trailed far behind them, shoveling only when they were done and had moved on. It was tedious, tiresome, and involved multiple trips to the pigpens a quarter mile away, but at least he didn't have to endure the endless gossip of Aunt Bethy and her friends while picking weeds. Bree insisted he was being too harsh, but seriously, did he *really* need to hear the weekly update on whether their neighbor Judy would marry her current boyfriend, Raphael, or instead return to that oh-so-sweet Thomas boy up the road at Glensbee?

Besides, the answer was obvious. Thomas sounded like a complete dick, what with originally dumping Judy after a single argument over...

"Kael Skyborn?"

The voice startled Kael in midshovel, causing him to spill half of it just ahead of his feet. Holding in a curse, he turned to address his surprise visitor. The man had a ratty look to him despite his carefully cut short black hair and his prim, clean robe. He looked similar to the theotechs in that regard, only the robe was brown instead of a bright scarlet.

"I am," he said, pulling down the pale blue rag he'd tied over his face to help against the smell. "Can I help you?"

"Indeed you may," said the stranger. "You can open your ears and mind to what I have to say." Kael frowned, not liking the sound of that at all. "My name is Thane Ackels of Elern," he continued, offering his hand. "Servant of God and disciple of Johan."

Kael left the hand hanging before him in the air.

"Not interested," he said, pointedly putting his back to the man and lifting his shovel. "Now if you don't mind, I have work to do."

"I ask only for a moment," Thane said, looping around. His leather shoes were quickly covered with dirt and pig shit, but Kael wasn't sure he even noticed. "Just a moment, is that truly so great a sacrifice, even when your work is this...noble?"

Kael jammed the shovel into the soft earth.

"Fine," he said. "Say whatever you're here to say and then go."

Thane smiled at him as if they were suddenly great friends.

"They've warned you about speaking to me, haven't they?" he asked. "The knights, or perhaps one of the theotechs in Center?"

Kael thought about lying, dismissed the idea.

"Yes," he said. "I know what lies you'd spread. Like I said, I have no interest."

Thane chuckled.

"Lies? No, Kael, I do not come with lies. I come to expose the lies. The knight who escorted you to the tests, he told you all about Center's grandeur, didn't he? About the noble role of the theotechs? How they serve the Speaker for the Angels, who in his humility relays the angels' wisdom down to us low, pathetic mortals? Did he outright claim theotechs are solely responsible for our survival or merely insinuate it?"

Kael was caught off guard by the sudden barrage of questions, and he wasn't quite sure what to say.

"And you'd what, deny it?" he asked back. "The theotechs are the ones who create the elemental prisms. Without them, our civilization crumbles."

"Indeed, the elements," Thane said. "Their creation is a secret, one they've not shared with the other islands. I wonder why? Do you think it is for our safety, or because that is a power over us they refuse to relinquish?"

Kael glanced about, wishing someone might come join him after all. He hated being alone with this man. He seemed so sure of himself, so confident. But he was a liar, Kael told himself. A careful liar spreading heresy.

"I'm not one to know," he said.

"No, but Johan does. He has seen the truths hiding behind the lies. He has shown the bravery to ask the questions you refuse to ask. The independence of the five holy islands is a lie. We are all slaves to Center, Kael, and willfully blind to the machinations of our jailers."

"Enough," Kael said. "Just... enough. If Center wanted to imprison us, they would have already."

"Not when manipulation is easier. Let a man think he is king of his own prison and he will never leave. The theotechs don't need their knights stationed at every street, forcing us to obey. They just need to carefully ration out the elements. Let the five smaller islands squabble with one another. Let our best slaughter each other in carefully arranged duels and skirmishes. Should someone become too strong, well, it wouldn't take much to cull the herd like the cattle we are."

"They'd never do that," Kael said. His grip on the shovel tightened. "The theotechs are holy men and women, and they serve us as equally as they serve Center. They'd never sacrifice our lives so callously. It goes against God's word."

"Is that so?" Thane asked, and he shook his head sadly. "Ask your aunt about the ghost plague sometime. See if you still think we are anything but animals to them. The Speaker no longer hears the word of God. The angels do not whisper in his ears. Marius Prakt seeks only power, absolute power. This peace we know is no peace at all, for it is built on the backs of demons. The time comes when the illusion will not suffice, when Center's knights and soldiers will cross the skies amid a bloodred sunset. You're soon to become one of Weshern's Seraphim, which means you are one of the precious few who will have a chance to resist. When that moment arrives, promise me this, Kael. Promise me you will fight back. Promise me you will draw your blades and ready your gauntlet to unleash Hell against those who would enslave your family and friends."

Kael wanted to hear no more. He lifted his shovel, holding it like he would a weapon.

"I think it's time you leave," he said. "I'm done listening to the words of a serpent."

"You've listened to the words of serpents all your life," Thane said. "Johan is the true servant of God. The Speaker once served the will of Heaven, but now he is a devil craving power. We must overthrow him. We must return to the true faith." Thane reached into a deep pocket of his robe and pulled out a single sheet of paper with long lines of text scribbled on both sides. "Take this. Read it, cherish it, and keep it close."

Kael would do no such thing. A piece of heretical script like that could get his entire family arrested, if not executed. Doing what he felt was most appropriate, Kael tossed the paper to the ground and used his shovel to dump a layer of manure atop it.

"I won't let anyone die for your cause," he said. "And you know that's what will happen, don't you? They'll find you one day and have you executed."

"Indeed," Thane said. "Right now I scatter seeds, and I do not expect to live to see the harvest. But they will sprout, Kael. The eyes of the people will open. I just pray it is through their own wisdom, and not from the armies of Center storming into their homes with blood on their spears and war on their lips."

The disciple of Johan bowed, and he seemed not at all off put by Kael's dismissal. Kael watched him go, shovel jammed into the soft earth, arms clutching the wooden handle tight enough to give himself a splinter. Once again alone, he resumed his work, but there was no more peace to the isolation, only frustration and doubt as Kael's mind looped the conversation again and again in his head.

When Bree and his aunt brought him his afternoon meal, the two covered with dirt and sweat, Kael couldn't have been happier.

Kael relaxed in a chair at their supper table, but his mind was far from at ease. Aunt Bethy knelt beside the fire, boiling cabbage and carrots. The smell made his stomach rumble, and he hoped the food would be ready soon. Bree sat opposite him, looking tired and bored. She still looked odd to Kael with her hair so short, though it was better now that Aunt Bethy had taken a pair of scissors to it to even out his sister's original ragged attempt. Tapping his feet to relieve his nerves, Kael finally decided to ask.

"Hey, Bethy?" he asked. "What was the ghost plague?"

"Where'd you hear about that?" she asked, not turning from the pot.

"One of the farmers mentioned it while I was filling up the wheelbarrow," he said. "I was just curious what he meant."

He hoped she'd believe his causal demeanor, because Bree sure as hell didn't as she lifted an eyebrow from across the table.

Aunt Bethy stretched her back as she stood.

"It was a terrible illness that struck Weshern years ago, before you two were born," she said, grunting as her back popped. "Nearly claimed your father's life, and would have without the theotechs' help." She lifted a bucket from beside the fireplace and offered it to him. "We need more water. Would you be a dear?"

"Sure," Kael said, rising from his chair.

"I'll go with him," Bree said, hopping up as well.

The door wasn't even shut behind them before Bree started asking questions.

"So where'd you actually hear about the ghost plague?"

"What do you mean?" he asked as they walked down the quiet street. The sun had begun to set, the twilight dark approaching fast.

"Aunt Bethy may not know the difference, but I can tell when you're really after something and not just curious. So, out with it. Why the sudden interest in an old plague?"

Kael debated for only a moment. He had a secret, and now that his sister knew, it'd take the end of the world to get her to stop prying.

"Fine," he said. "You promise not to tell Bethy? It'll only make her upset."

His sister held one hand over her heart and another over her lips. Kael sighed, and he tried to figure out where to start.

"A disciple of Johan came to me when I was alone in the fields," he said.

Bree's eyes flashed with interest.

"As in the disciples Nickolas said to never believe and avoid at all costs?"

"Yeah, them. Seemed like he heard I'd been accepted into our academy and came for a chat."

A worn path of dirt and loose stones marked the exit from the main road, passing through two similar homes and into a field beyond. In the center of the field was a stone well. Once at its edge, Kael held the bucket with both hands and dipped it into the water, which rippled only a few feet below the highest stones. Bree dipped her own hand in and drank, drops of the clear water dripping down her chin.

"One day you'll get in trouble for that," he said.

Bree laughed.

"One day soon I'll be a Seraph," she said. "And then they won't even dare try. So, what did this disciple guy want, and how does that have anything to do with this supposed ghost plague?"

Kael stared into the well as he debated how to answer. Bubbles floated up from the bottom of the well. It was dark, but he could barely see the grate at the bottom, covering the end of a pipe. The water flowed from somewhere deep inside Weshern, where theotechs blessed the ocean water that the Fount pulled up to the island and then pumped to the many lakes, rivers, and wells.

"I'm not sure," he said. "He claimed it was an example of Center's corruption. That's all he really went on about, insisting the Speaker was the devil and theotechs his pet demons."

They started back toward home, Kael carrying the bucket by its thin iron handle.

"So what'd he want from you?" she asked.

"You mean, besides believe him?"

"Yeah, besides that."

Kael chuckled.

"He thought Center would invade us one day. He wanted me to fight back, for all of us to fight back."

Bree laughed.

"A war against Center? We'd be crushed in seconds. He's delusional, Kael. Nickolas was right, there's no point in listening. And you heard Aunt Bethy. Dad would have died in the plague if not for the theotechs. If you really want to spend your time worrying about something, worry about how you'll do on your first day at the academy."

"I'd rather not worry about either."

Bree elbowed him in the side, and he had to twist to keep the bucket from spilling water across their feet.

"Just saying, first day of flight training, you'll be in front of dozens of people you don't know. One tiny little slip up, like when you landed butt first atop Judy Lakeborn's house, and they'll all laugh and laugh..."

Kael glared.

"Tell anyone that story and you die."

"What? Tell people what?"

"Bree, I will dump this bucket of water on your head..."

She flashed him her biggest smile. The blossoming moonlight reflected off her ashen gray eyes.

"You'd have to catch me first."

She dashed off ahead of him, back toward their house. Kael could only walk, lest he lose half the bucket splashing water all over himself. The first stretches of shadow crawled across the western sky. Kael stared at it, fascinated by the way it moved, as if it were a living thing. What caused the darkness? What sparked the fire that followed? Kael didn't know. It was one of many mysteries, and Kael resolved to put Thane's words out of his mind forever. So many things he didn't know, but what he did know was that he wouldn't risk his family and friends on the words of a heretic.

By the time he returned home, the smell of cooked cabbage filled the cramped space, and Bree sat at the table looking as innocent as could be.

One day, Kael mouthed as he set the bucket down and took his own seat. *You wait.*

Bree winked back, blew him a kiss, and then tore into her bowl, not afraid of his vengeance in the slightest.

CHAPTER
6

"Bring only the clothes on your back," Nickolas had ordered, and so Bree and Kael did just that. Kael dressed as if he were to work in the fields, a gray short-sleeved shirt and rough spun pants cut just above the knee.

"Still feel like we should wear something more...formal," Kael said as he came down the stairs. His sister was already eating breakfast. Given how nervous they both were, they'd awoken early enough to catch their aunt before she left for the fields. Unlike the time they traveled for Center, she seemed almost lively, doting over the two of them like a mother hen.

"I should have made you cut your hair as well," Bethy said, rising from her seat at the table to lick her palms and then press down on Kael's head. "You have a cowlick from here to high heaven."

Kael groaned, pulling away from her to wipe it with his own hand.

"There's nothing I can do about it," he grumbled. "Thanks for mentioning it."

"Don't worry about your clothes," Bree said as she ate her oatmeal. "They'll give us uniforms to wear, won't they?"

"They will," Bethy said. "And get used to wearing them. I can count on one hand the days I saw my brother out of uniform after he joined." She grabbed Kael's wrist, dragged him to the sink, and dumped a bucket of water atop his head before he could protest.

"There," she said, wiping his face and hair with a towel. "Glare all you want, but at least you won't spend your first day of training looking like the back of your head's trying to escape."

Kael was too annoyed to say thanks but too grateful to continue arguing, so grumbling to himself, he took a seat beside his sister and began eating.

"Bethy's right, you should have cut your hair," Bree said, finishing her bowl. "It's almost as long as mine."

"There's nothing wrong with my hair," Kael said, running his fingers through its wet strands. "Stop saying stuff like that."

Bree flashed a smile, just quick enough for him to know she was joking.

"I'm only trying to help," she said. "You don't want to be mistaken for your sister, do you?"

Kael was about to threaten violence for her cruel attempt to make him self-conscious the whole damn day when a knock came from the door. All three froze, smiles vanishing. Aunt Bethy rose from her seat at the table and beckoned them close for a hug.

"I'll miss you both," she said. "Stay strong, and make your parents proud."

They hugged her back, then pulled free. Smoothing his hair one last time with his hand, Kael hurried to the door, for some reason feeling like he should be the one to greet the Seraph. Pulling open the door revealed a towering man with gray skin and short black hair. Above his left eyebrow was a long white scar. His armor was similar to Nickolas's, except silver instead of gold, and whereas the knight had worn a white tunic emblazoned with the symbol of Center, this mountain of a man bore the blue sword of Weshern on his white shirt.

"Kael and Breanna Skyborn?" the square-jawed man asked, and he had to bend over slightly so he could peer inside. His voice sounded like it should be coming from a stone statue instead of a human being. "I am Seraph Loramere Wallace. I've come to escort you to your first day at the Weshern Academy. Are you prepared to leave?"

Kael looked over his shoulder to Bethy, who gently nodded.

"I am," he said, turning back. "I mean, we are, yes."

"Yes sir," Loramere corrected. "Always address a Seraph with respect. Now come. I don't want my charges to be the last to arrive."

"Why is that?" Bree asked as they exited their home and shut the door behind them. Kael was surprised his sister would be so bold as to ask why, and it appeared their guide was likewise.

"I mean, why is that, sir?" she asked after the Seraph didn't answer immediately.

"Because whoever arrives last buys drinks for the others," Loramere said, a grin tugging at the right side of his lips. "Long-standing tradition."

Loramere led them down their small street toward Fountain Road, the twins trailing after. Kael did a quick check in his mind on the distance. Fountain Road would take them north to the heart of Weshern, and from there they'd have to travel east until Winged Road arrived at the academy. All in all, close to six miles, and on foot.

"If you're worried you'll be last, you could probably carry us while flying," Kael offered. He had a feeling this serious-looking giant wasn't quite as serious as he let on, and the man's boisterous laugh proved him right.

"No can do," Loramere said. "Another one of those traditions you'll soon tire hearing of. From your home, you walk to the academy. Once there, you'll either walk back a failure or fly back a success." He winked at them. "And don't worry about us. There's a bunch who left yesterday to bring in recruits from the western end of the island. Only way we arrive last is if they fly their kids in."

"How do you know they won't?"

Loramere shook his head as they turned onto Fountain Road, which was still quiet due to the early hour.

"Something you'll soon learn. If you're a Seraph, you don't cheat or lie to another Seraph. Not at nothing, no matter how small. Breaking your word on the small stuff leads to breaking your word on the big stuff, and when you're flying through a goddamn barrage of ice lances and flame spears, you've got to trust your fellow Seraphim. The tiniest doubt, I mean the tiniest little sliver, can get you killed."

It was a sobering reminder to the fate they had signed on for. Kael already felt nervous he'd make a fool of himself on the first day of training. Combining that with the realization that he might soon be dodging elements as other Seraphim tried to kill him? Suddenly Kael felt that a long, quiet walk might be a better idea than joking with Loramere. What was wrong with him? Why in all of Weshern had he agreed to do this?

An elbow dug into his side, and he glanced left to see Bree

staring at him. Her eyes were sparkling, her lips curled into the tiniest of smiles. She'd sensed his apprehension, he realized, and done what she could to shake him out of it. Kael elbowed her right back to show his gratitude.

"Pants pisser," she whispered.

"Crotch sniffer," he retaliated.

Loramere glanced over his shoulder.

"You two better not be fighting like little children," he said.

Kael gave him his sincerest grin.

"Wouldn't dream of it, sir," he said.

The Seraph shook his head as he turned back around.

"You two are going to be trouble, aren't you?"

Yes sir, mouthed Bree, and they both grinned.

True to Loramere's prediction, they were not the last to arrive, only second to last. The gated entrance to the Weshern Academy waited open before them at the very end of Winged Road. For a mile on either side of the gate stretched stone walls marking the limits of the academy and its training grounds. Gathered at the entrance were nearly a dozen Seraphim. The men and women seemed jovial enough, and despite the regal look of their black and blue uniforms and their silver wings they joked with one another as if they were casual friends in a bar. When Loramere reached the group, one of the men clapped him on the shoulder.

"Just in time," he said. "I think I see Garrick down the road not far behind you."

"A good thing, too," Loramere said, smacking the man in the chest with his fist. "The islands will fall to the ocean before I'm buying rounds two years in a row."

"Go on inside," a pretty woman with auburn hair told Kael

when she saw him and his sister standing amid the group, unsure of what to do. "Follow the path until you see the rest."

"Thank you," Kael said, and he felt himself blushing.

"Come on," Bree said, tugging on his sleeve. They entered the gate, following the well-worn dirt path that cut through the enormous green fields. Long, flowing grass grew on either side of them, dancing in the soft breeze. Kael glanced left, then right, seeing very little beyond the rolling expanses and the distant stone wall that enveloped the academy grounds. Up ahead were two buildings split by the path, and between them were several dozen people, mixed together in such a chaotic jumble he had no clue what was going on.

As they neared, a woman stepped out from the group. She was on the short side, her brown hair pulled neatly back from her slender, freckled face. Though she wore a military uniform akin to Loramere's, her shirt was black instead of white, and her jacket a dark blue. Her left hand held a clipboard, her right a silver pen.

"Breanna and Kael?" she asked, eyes flicking to her clipboard for a split second.

"Yes," Kael said.

"Excellent. That's almost everyone. Continue so the ladies can get you fitted."

She gestured into the group, then stepped aside so they might pass. Kael saw about half were his and his sister's age, some in crisp new uniforms, most not. Lining either side of the road were women in blue dresses. Behind them, blocking off the two enormous sheds, were dozens of open crates. Kael slowly wandered into the fray, felt the dozens of concurrent conversations wash over him, and wondered what he should do. Thankfully that was solved by one of the women in blue whistling to gain his attention, then beckoning him over.

"Your name?" she asked as she uncoiled a long, thin strip of white cloth covered with markings.

"Kael Skyborn," he said.

"All right, Kael. Stand still for me, and stretch out your arms."

A second woman joined her from the crates, standing beside the other as the first ran the strip of cloth from his wrists to his armpits, then shoulder to shoulder, hip to ground, around his waist, and seemingly everywhere else imaginable. Kael endured it in awkward silence as the measurer rambled out various numbers to the other woman.

"Ten on the jacket," she said after measuring his arms a second time. "Same for the shirt. Nine on the pants." She dropped down, measured his feet. "Eight on the boots."

It was strange having his body broken down to a series of numbers, but apparently it worked. The other woman hurried to the crates, which he saw were filled with uniforms of all sizes. Returning moments later with a bundle in her arms, she more shoved than handed it to him.

"There's curtained booths to the side of the sheds," the first woman said. "You can change there. Once you have, return your old clothes to me, and I'll have them sent to your room."

Kael followed her instructions, clutching the clothes tightly for fear of dropping something. What if he dirtied his new jacket? Would he get in trouble for something like that? It was his first day, and he hadn't a clue what might be a huge deal, what might be nothing, and he desperately wanted to avoid finding that out. Coming around the left side of the sheds, which looked more like wooden barns to him, he found two booths made of plain wooden stakes jammed into the dirt and covered with thick curtains. Both had lines, and Kael stepped into the one on the left. Moments later, his sister joined the other line, her own arms full.

"Ten, ten, eight, eight?" she asked.

"Ten, ten, nine, eight," he said. "I always told you I was taller."

"They gave no numbers for me," said the enormous recruit ahead of him, turning about with a grin on his face. He had curly red hair, a fat nose, and a jester's grin. His chest and shoulders were broad, his arms thick like a blacksmith's. "They just said 'big' and went to rummaging."

"Maybe they were worried you couldn't count that high," Bree said, grinning.

"They'd be right," he said. "Once I reach ten, I'm all out of fingers."

"That's what toes are for," Kael said, glad the guy had a sense of humor. "And ignore Bree over there. Her mouth tends to run a few seconds ahead of her brain."

The three shared a laugh, and for the first time all day, Kael felt his nerves finally relaxing.

"All yours," said a squirrelly young man who stepped out from the curtain, still tugging at the collar of his new uniform. The red-haired giant ahead of Kael stepped in, turned, pulled the curtain halfway shut.

"Brad," he said, extending his hand.

"Kael, and that's my sister, Bree."

They shook, Kael balancing all his clothes on one arm to do so, and then Brad pulled the curtain shut to change. Kael stood there, still feeling a bit awkward since he and his sister were among the few still not in uniform. As his eyes roamed, he caught his sister staring at him, that devilish smile of hers on her lips.

What? he mouthed when he saw her.

You made a friend, she mouthed back.

Kael rolled his eyes, which she quickly imitated. A few minutes later Brad stepped out from the curtained booth. Bree had already gone inside her booth, and the last of the recruits, no doubt the late arrival that had come with Garrick, waited at hers.

"Got to admit," Brad said, looking down at himself. "It don't look half bad."

"I might go so far as to say it's even half good," Kael said. Brad shot him a wink, then got out of his way.

Inside the booth, Kael stripped down to his underclothes, then started with the pants. The cloth was surprisingly soft despite its sturdy feel. As he buttoned their front, he knew he'd never worn an article of clothing anywhere near as expensive as these. Next came the shirt. Unlike his own, it didn't scratch at his skin, nor did it hang low over his waist. Tucking it into his pants, he found the belt they'd given him and quickly looped it through the hooks in the pants. Inside the booth was a tiny wooden bench, and he sat down on it to pull on his boots. They were finely polished black leather, the interior padded. It felt strange, for everything about the boots spoke of decadence, yet the Seraphim were an order of war.

You're valuable to them, he realized. Only a rare few were born with elemental affinity. If the Seraphim were to maintain their ranks despite their losses in battle, they needed people like him.

Once he finished lacing the boots, he stood, put his arm through a sleeve of his jacket. Like his boots, it was polished black leather. Though it was thin, its interior was soft and warm. The moment it was on his back, he felt something change in him. This jacket...it was a symbol. On its left sleeve was his rank, perhaps the lowest of the low, but it was still a rank. No matter how temporarily, he was a member of the Seraphim, and it stirred a bit of pride in his chest. When he stepped out, he found Bree waiting for him. She wore the same uniform, and seeing her in the jacket, the blue sword of Weshern on her shirt, he couldn't help but smile.

"Hurry," she said. "They're all waiting."

Sixteen recruits gathered not far from the shed. After dropping off their old clothes, Kael and Bree slid in at the back, glancing about at the others. So many strangers, so many names to learn...and then he saw her near the front, quietly talking with another girl beside her. Clara, from their affinity tests in Center. A soft smile was on her face. Her blonde hair, which had hung to her shoulders, was now cut short and curled around her neck and ears. He hadn't meant to be looking for her, but when he saw her he immediately felt his heart skip a beat.

The short woman in the blue jacket waited at the front of their group, and when the apparent last of the recruits arrived in uniform, she looked up from her clipboard and began to address the lot of them. Though she wasn't loud, everyone immediately ceased their conversations. Something about her voice seemed to brook no nonsense, and she spoke with an air of complete and total authority.

"Greetings, recruits of five-fifteen," she said, referring to the year, the five hundred and fifteenth since God ascended the six islands. "I am Rebecca Waller, the over-secretary of Weshern Academy. I'd like to welcome the nineteen of you to our facility. Should you have any needs or questions, you are welcome to come to me, and I will do what I can to address them."

Her voice was hardly welcoming, despite her offer. Not that she was cold, no, just...preoccupied, Kael decided. Like she had a thousand things on her mind, and the new recruits were just one of them.

"Now that you're dressed in uniforms," she continued, "I'll be introducing you to the instructors and teachers you'll be spending the next four years learning from, as well as giving you a tour of the facility. But before that, I'd like you to meet your headmaster."

She turned, guiding their attention to where an older man approached them from down the path toward the gear sheds. His hair was short and white, his skin deeply tanned, his uniform pristine. Instead of a leather jacket he wore a thin blue overshirt buttoned across the front. Its sleeves and chest were covered with patches and medals. All recruits stood at attention as he paused before them, arms clasped behind his back. His sandy brown eyes looked them over, not a hint of emotion on his face. When he spoke, his voice was deep, commanding.

"Welcome to my academy," the old man said. "To those of you who do not know me, I am Jay Simmons. I have been headmaster for twenty-seven years, and if God is kind, I'll be here for twenty-seven more. You nineteen are unique among the people of Weshern, gifted with an affinity to the elements that very few possess. Do not, however, feel that this will ensure you a place among the Seraphim. You are special, and we will treat you as such, but we expect equal return for our efforts. The food you eat, the wings you wear, the elements you use to battle and fly: they all come at a price. That price is the time and effort it will take to become the absolute elite of Weshern's defenses. In six months, we will evaluate your progress, and decide if you are worthy to remain within these walls.

"In my academy, we do not tolerate wastefulness, sloth, or unearned pride. You're here to learn. You're here to become the very best. The protection of our island, the safety of our friends and family, depends upon it. In the weeks ahead, keep that in mind as you sweat and bleed. All we do, we do to help you become something greater than you are now. A warrior. A protector. A member of the Seraphim."

He glanced to the over-secretary, nodded, then departed.

"Thank you, Jay," she said, smiling. The smile died the instant she turned to the recruits. "Now, if you'll all follow me, we can begin our tour of the facilities and meet some of the faculty."

The next hours were a blur to Kael. He met middle-aged men and women, all in various uniforms and with different titles that he struggled to remember five minutes later. His teachers for flight and elemental combat, Instructor Dohn and Instructor Kime, respectively, he met not far from where the headmaster first introduced himself, for the fields the path split were the training fields. After that they followed the path, crossing a white bridge over a stream that split the academy into eastern and western halves.

While the western half was all fields for training, the east was full of buildings. To the north were the apartments, eight buildings, four on each side of a branched-off road. Apparently they all had units assigned to them, two members apiece. South was another road. On its left was the learning academy, inside of which Kael met another cavalcade of teachers. They promised to educate the group in history, etiquette, strategy, and military code and rank. Inside were multiple floors, the walls white, the rooms clean and full of chairs. It felt like the one-room school he'd attended with Teacher Gruden, only far, far larger.

Their next stop was, thankfully, the mess hall. The afternoon was nearly over when Over-Secretary Rebecca brought them inside. "There's something prepared at all times, so never be shy," she told them, and Kael promised to take her up on that offer. The mess hall was enormous, the floor treated wood, the ceiling vaulted. Dozens of long tables filled it in neat rows, with little stools on either side.

"The cooks have worked extra hard today to give you a nice welcoming meal," Rebecca said. "You have twenty minutes before we continue, so try not to tarry while you eat."

A counter closed off the northern stretch of the mess hall, its right half stacked with plates. Grabbing one, they each walked left and handed the plate to a cook in white clothes and blue apron. After a moment, the cook would hand back the plate full of steaming vegetables and a thin slice of fire-roasted ham. Kael took his plate, grabbed a set of silverware from a bucket just left of him, and then looked for a seat. Still feeling like a stranger, he was glad to see Bree had already found herself a table, and he made a beeline toward her.

"I'm never going to remember any of this," he said as he sat down opposite her.

"Don't worry," Bree said. "They'll yell at you enough until you do. Besides, all that really matters is here, the learning academy, and the training fields. I think you can remember three spots."

"Well, four if you count your room," Brad said, setting his plate beside Kael's and plopping down on a stool. "You don't mind if I join you, do you?"

"It's fine," Kael said, mouth full of cabbage.

"Good," Brad said. "Because you're my roommate for the next year."

"How do you know?" Kael asked.

Brad shrugged.

"I went and asked our guide. Sharp lady. I have a feeling she could list how many forks are in this mess hall at this exact moment. So!" He smacked Kael on the back, nearly making him choke. "Roommate! Got any weird habits? Do you snore? Plan on bringing girls over every night? You know, important stuff I should know about?"

"Just that he'll murder you in your sleep," Bree said, glancing up from her plate.

"Well, he wouldn't be the first to try," Brad said, tearing into his ham, and for the life of him, Kael couldn't tell if he was joking or not.

No one else joined the three, so they ate alone, and when finished, they resumed their tour. After the mess hall came the armory, where yet again they endured a barrage of measurements, this time for their swords and wings. Next was the library, and a quick introduction to its head librarian, a bubbly woman with copper skin named Devi Winters. Kael couldn't help but stare wide-eyed at the rows and rows of books throughout the tall three-story building. His previous classroom had fifty, maybe sixty at most, yet here they seemed beyond counting.

"If you should find yourself curious about anything, or needing something to read in your rare downtime, please come and see me," Devi told them. "We're training your mind along with your body, so try not to neglect one for the other."

Finally, at long last, they ended the tour with a trip to their apartments, and the two squat stone buildings that were their showers. "The water is kept in tanks above the stalls and heated with flame elements within the tanks," their guide explained. "There are toilets inside as well. If you haven't figured it out already, we offer only the best, but we also expect the best from you, and that includes hygiene and appearance."

After that, Rebecca dismissed them without fanfare, merely telling them to visit the mess hall if they were hungry, and to expect a wake-up knock on their door come sunrise. The apartments had two levels, and beside the doors were names listing occupants. True enough, Kael's was right beneath Brad's, and together they went inside.

"Don't seem so bad," Brad said.

That was putting it mildly. The carpeted floor felt soft beneath his boots and was colored a blue so deep it was nearly black. The wooden walls were painted white, the curtains sky blue. There were only two bedrooms, each with a bed, a feather mattress, a closet for belongings, and a glass window. Picking a room, Kael plopped down on the side of his bed, leaned back, and groaned with satisfaction.

"Softest bed I've ever had," he said. "I think this one is calling my name."

"After walking around the entire damn academy, that sounds like a fine idea," Brad said, going into the other room. Kael kicked off his boots, then stared up at the ceiling. A sheet of thin paper lay atop his pillow, and curious, he grabbed it and held it above his head. It was a daily schedule, the same each day, apparently. Tactics, history, protocol, all started off with flight training at sunrise.

Flight training...

Kael swallowed. At least he'd get it out of the way immediately, instead of dreading it throughout the day. If only he took to it as well as his sister. If only he wasn't convinced he'd make a damn fool of himself in front of his classmates.

"Hey, Kael?" Brad called from the other room.

"Yeah?"

"You never answered my question. Do you snore?"

"No, not really."

A pause.

"Oh. Well. I do. Sorry about that."

Despite his exhaustion, despite his nerves, Kael covered his eyes with his forearm and laughed.

CHAPTER
7

There was no containing Bree's excitement. When someone banged on their door the next morning, she was already awake and staring at the ceiling. She ate her breakfast in the mess hall quickly enough to risk a stomachache, showered, and then changed into one of many matching uniforms that had been waiting for her inside her closet. Meanwhile, her roommate, Amanda, appeared far less eager for the day to begin as she finished dressing.

"Have you practiced flying before?" Amanda asked, pulling an arm through the tightly fitted leather jacket.

"Plenty of times," Bree said, standing in front of their slender mirror to check her uniform. "A friend of ours was a fisherman, and he let us use their training sets."

Amanda finished putting on the jacket and tugged at its bottom to straighten it. She was tinier than Bree, with pale skin and blonde hair so faint it was nearly white. Contrasted against the dark black and blue of her uniform, she looked like a ghost.

"You're lucky," she said. "I tried to use them once. My parents forbade it. They said I'd just learn bad habits from the fishermen and should wait for proper training at the academy." Amanda glanced her way. "Is it…is it frightening? Trusting your life to the wings like that?"

Bree shook her head.

"Every day we trust the elements to keep Weshern afloat," she said. "Once you realize that, you'll see it's no different from running or climbing a tree. It's only dangerous if you do something stupid or can't control yourself."

Instead of being convinced, Amanda looked ready to shrivel up into nothing inside her uniform.

"You ever lose control?"

Bree smiled at her.

"I'm not sure that's a story I should tell you an hour before your first flight," she said. "I'll tell it after, though, I promise. Now hurry up, before we're late!"

The two were the first students to arrive at the gear sheds. Three waiting mechanics beckoned them over.

"Names?" the biggest of the three asked, thick of arm and heavily bearded. During their tour the day before, they'd been introduced, just one of seemingly a hundred people they'd met. His name was Bartow, and he was the mechanic in charge of all their wings.

"I'm Breanna Skyborn, and this is Amanda Ruth," Bree answered.

The man grunted, then beckoned them to follow him inside the northern shed. The shed was more like a barn, tall and expansive. Covering the walls in columns of three were sets of wings, their silver finely polished, their leather harnesses and buckles freshly cleaned. Bree felt a shiver run through her at the sight. Little wooden plaques hung above each set, the name of the owner carved into them. Grabbing a long pole with a hook on the end, Bartow glanced at a sheet of paper nailed to the wall beside the door.

"This way," he said. Eyes wide, Bree followed him. There had to be more than a hundred sets inside, perhaps more. Each one capable of elaborate maneuvers and incredible speed. Each one capable of taking a man's life. The mechanic stopped at the far end, his eyes finding the proper nameplate far quicker than Bree. From the top row he lifted one of the harnesses with his pole, removing it from a thick iron peg. With easy precision he lowered the harness while sliding the pole behind him so that he could grab it with one hand just before touching ground.

"Breanna," he said, offering it to her. Bree took it, fingers tingling with electricity.

One column over, and he pulled down another.

"Amanda."

Once both held their set of wings, Bartow stepped back and leaned the pole against his shoulder.

"Either of you know how to put those on?" he asked.

"I do," Bree said.

"Good, then you can show her. Head to the other shed when you're done. Sara's got your swords."

And with that he returned to the front. Bree slid an arm through part of the harness, then hoisted the wings onto her back before sliding through the other. The weight of it was incredibly comfortable and evenly balanced. If the fishermen's set she'd trained on was a hard leather gauntlet, this was a silk glove. As she grabbed the first of many buckles, she caught Amanda staring at her, her wings still held in her arms.

"Give me two seconds," Bree said.

She tightened strap after strap, each one more satisfying than the last. The set was tailored for her, of that she had no doubt. There'd be no adding holes to get the buckles tight enough. This set felt like a second skin. When it came to strapping in, though, everything was the same as the fisherman's set. There were only two major differences. The first were the two additional buckles on the heavy loop that went about her waist, which she assumed would be for her swords. The second was a thin circle of soft leather that extended out from the top of the harness by a black cord. She pulled the circle over her head, and as she did, she heard a whirring of a gear as the black cord pulled farther out from the harness. The leather itself was so thin it was like putting on a necklace. She wasn't entirely sure the reason for it, nor the pale crystals woven into it, but she figured she'd learn soon enough.

Finally done, she flexed her arms and pulled her shoulders back and forth. With a soft clatter of metal, the wings shifted with her. So smooth. So easy. The silver seemed to sparkle in the light that shone through the cracks in the wall's wooden planks. Despite being larger than the training set, the new ones felt much lighter, and she wondered if it was due to the significantly lower lift requirements, or perhaps it was made of better material than...

"Bree?" said Amanda.

"Sorry," Bree said, snapping out of her daydreaming. "Here, let me take you through it step by step. Just like a jacket, slide your right arm in here..."

It took a few minutes, but at last Amanda was fully strapped in. Bree made sure to guide her only with words, doing none of it herself. That was how Jevin had taught her, and she had no reason to doubt his teaching methods now.

"There we go," Bree said, tugging on one of the leg buckles to ensure it was tight enough. "How's that feel?"

"Like I'm being hugged by snakes."

Bree grinned.

"That sounds right. Time for our swords."

On the way out, they found Kael and two other boys walking alongside Bartow to get their own sets.

"How do I look?" Bree asked, stopping before Kael and giving him a half twirl.

"Like you were born with them," he said, smiling. Bree laughed, and she had to hand it to him. Every now and then, on very rare occasions, her brother knew exactly what to say.

The rest of their class was filtering in from the east when Bree and Amanda crossed the dirt path to the shed on the other side. Only one mechanic waited there, a burly woman with brown hair and a tan so dark her skin resembled tree bark. She didn't introduce herself, but Bree felt confident she was the Sara they were to meet with next. There were two different doors leading into the shed, one open, one closed, and Sara stood between them with her arms crossed.

"In there," Sara said, pointing to the open door. "Left wall. The swords are named, so find yours and bring them out to me so I can make sure they fit like they should."

"Yes ma'am," Amanda said as the two stepped inside. Bree heard Sara chuckle behind them.

"No ma'ams here," she said. "Just us mechanics."

Although the buildings were of similar size, the interior of the southern shed felt much smaller, and Bree realized it was because it had been sectioned in half. In the half they entered, the lower portions of the walls were covered with pairs of swords set along thin wooden pegs bolted into the wood. As with the wings, little wooden plaques hung above each set, and, starting on the left wall, Bree began scanning for her name.

"Here's yours," Amanda said, pointing. Bree grabbed the two swords (*her* two swords, she realized with a thrill) and examined one closely. Its scabbard was finely sanded wood painted blue, with a decorative steel point on the very bottom. The hilt itself was silver, and she noticed how both had a strange loop upon the top. Also unique was the tight clasp that connected the hilt to the scabbard, and it took a surprising amount of pressure to pop it open. Closing her hand around the handle, feeling its soft leather grip, Bree pulled it free of the scabbard. It made not a noise as it slid out, revealing a thin, razor-sharp blade. Bree stared at her reflection in the blade, and the image gave her goose bumps.

"I guess the swords go here?" Amanda asked.

Bree looked over and saw that her roommate had found her own two swords and placed them into the waist buckles.

"Looks like it," Bree said. Looping each of the buckles shut, she slid her swords into them. Deciding they felt loose, she tightened both of them, then shifted side to side to test. The swords were tilted backward slightly, and when she stepped, the tips hovered mere inches above the ground.

"Let's go see what Sara says," Amanda said. "Hopefully we did this right."

It seemed they did, for Sara took one look at them and then nodded.

"Go on out to the northwest field," she said before addressing another group come for their own blades. "Instructor Dohn is waiting for you."

The fields in the western half of the academy grounds were sectioned into four quadrants, and just off the road in the northwestern quadrant Bree and Amanda waited. Before them were the beginner flight training fields, vast and empty but for the occasional hoop or bar held aloft in the air atop thin wooden poles. With them was Instructor Adam Dohn, the tall man standing patiently with his arms crossed behind his back. His hair was dark and short, his eyes the color of muddy water. He, too, wore a pair of wings. At no point did he attempt small talk, and his silence spread to Amanda and Bree as they waited for the rest of their class to arrive.

At last it seemed they were all gathered in a line before their teacher. Bree stood between Amanda and Kael, and it felt good to be surrounded by that tiny sliver of familiarity.

"I was given nineteen names, and I count nineteen before me," Instructor Dohn said. "I'm sure you had your fill of introductions yesterday, so we'll skip that for now. I'll learn who you are soon enough, assuming you don't crack your head open before the day's end. First off, how many of you have had flight practice before?"

Nine hands went up.

"How many of you have flown out over the open?"

Only two this time, Bree and a red-haired boy on the far side of the group. Dohn looked to each of them, as if making a mental note, and then continued.

"To those of you who've done this before, this will likely be a very boring day. I don't care how good you think you might be, I want everyone paying attention. Whoever taught you might have known what they were doing, or they might have been some fish-brained idiot who thinks himself more clever than he is. So, step by step, you do as I say, no skipping anything, no making assumptions. I hope I've made myself clear. Now, let's start with your left-hand gauntlet..."

Bree was surprised at how closely Instructor Dohn's orders followed Jevin's checklist. Telling herself to remain patient, she went through each bit, inspecting the element, fastening the gauntlet, checking the switch; all of it. Somewhat new was her second gauntlet for her right hand, the apparatus through which they would soon project their chosen elements. As exciting as that thought was, she knew it'd be days, if not weeks, before they moved on to that particular skill set.

After checking the gauntlet came the swords, the only other new part of the routine.

"You'll notice just below your wrist on each gauntlet is a hook-latch," Instructor Dohn said, lifting his arms so he could point to his own. Grabbing one, he pulled on it to show that it came out with a whirring sound, revealing a thin black cord. "The latch is designed to only open inward. Make sure the cord comes out easily and the latch opens and closes without issue. When it comes time to use your blades, you'll jam these against the loop at the top before drawing them. This will keep you from ever losing them during flight maneuvers, as well as injuring yourself or others should you lose your grip."

Dohn smacked his wrists atop his swords to demonstrate, and Bree heard two clicks as the latches secured onto the loops above the hilts. With the ease of a lifetime of practice, the instructor flicked open the clasps and then drew his swords. When he released them, they hung mere inches down from his wrist, the cord built into the thick gauntlets stopping them, the weight of the swords not strong enough to draw the cord out farther. Dohn unhooked one, sheathed it, then the other. That done, he clapped his hands.

"Harness check is over," he said. "Let's get to flying."

Instructor Dohn had them space out at approximately ten-foot intervals, the nineteen of them dotting the field like silver pieces on a game board. Bree's thumb tapped against the switch, for she was barely able to contain her excitement. Today she would discover what a true set of wings could do. At least she hoped so. Dohn's foreboding words about boredom worried her.

"Before we begin, one last change to those who might have used other sets for training," he said. "Push the throttle forward just the tiniest bit until the wings begin to hum. Don't go anywhere, just do this."

Bree obeyed, and as she did, she noticed that her vision seemed to slightly blur, the effect lasting no longer than the blink of an eye.

"Did any of you catch a blurring?" their instructor asked. "Shut off your wings and start them up again until you do. What you see is a shield forming about your eyes, nose, and mouth, created by the little crystal bits built into the harness's neck collar. I don't know how it works, but men and women smarter than I tell me it uses your light element to help protect you from the effects of flying at high speeds. In short, you'll have no problem seeing and breathing during aerial maneuvers. You'll soon stop seeing that blur entirely as you get used to the effect, but make sure you do indeed see it before taking off, because if not, you need to let the mechanics take a look."

Bree turned her wings off and on a few more times, noticing the subtle blur, which never lasted more than a heartbeat. She glanced to her left, curious if she could see the shield on Kael's face, but other than a bit of nervousness, he looked normal.

"That done, time for your first exercise," Instructor Dohn shouted. "I want all of you to rise off the ground." Thrumming his own wings to life, he rose several feet up from the field, then halted. "Once you're off the ground, settle into a hold. Don't go anywhere, not up, not down, and certainly not toward anyone else. Just get comfortable. Show me that you can control the wings by the positioning of your upper body."

Bree felt disappointment sink into her stomach. Boring? God, this wasn't just boredom. This sounded torturous.

Letting out a sigh, she shifted the throttle. While the deep, satisfying thrum of her wings should have excited her, she only felt disappointment realizing she wouldn't get to see a fraction of their abilities. Bree rose several feet, lessened the throttle, and then hovered there with her arms crossed over her chest. Her spot was at the front of the group, and she spun in air to see if the others were as bored as her. To Bree's surprise, several bounced up and down from the ground, using too rough a touch on the throttle, causing them either to fall or jerk upward. Others shifted and twisted their upper bodies to keep themselves from drifting. Her brother, who she'd always thought was slow on the uptake when it came to flight, appeared to actually be one of the better fliers.

Instructor Dohn flew from student to student, shouting out advice, sometimes even grabbing their wings or their gauntlet to correct them manually. Bored, Bree bobbed up and down with a slow, steady rhythm, only partly watching the others. It felt like such a tease. Her wings, they lifted her so easily, and with her barely pushing the throttle past the one-fourth mark…

Bree spotted the instructor approaching her next, and she ceased her bobbing.

"Having trouble maintaining a consistent height?" he asked as he flew up beside her.

"No sir," she said, shaking her head. "My apologies, sir. I'm just eager for the real lessons to begin."

The instructor stared at her with his beady eyes, and he lifted an eyebrow.

"You're one of the two who's flown over open air, aren't you?" he asked. He pointed to the sky above her. "Go up there and fly me a loop. Nothing fancy, and don't go crazy on the throttle. I'm guessing you trained on one of those fisherman sets, and they don't have a fraction of the speed ours do. If you push it anywhere near full, I'll be scraping your carcass off the field."

Bree nodded, heart suddenly aflutter. This was it. Finally she'd have a chance to see what the wings could do...but at the same time, her instructor was watching, as were several of the other students nearby. Swallowing her fear, she rose into the air, her excitement increasing with her elevation. Who cared if anyone watched? She was born to fly.

Once she was a good twenty feet above all the others, she leaned while stretching her legs. The motion rotated her forward and would have brought her into a dive if she let it. Instead she gently increased the throttle. Too fast would jar her body, make her lose control. Bree let her wings gain some speed as she flew, her body parallel to the green training field below, before arching her back and spreading her shoulders. The motion pulled her upward, and she naturally felt her head tilting with it. As the wind blew against her she curled through the air, careful to keep her body still. The sky shifted, dipped, and then she stared at grass. The downward slope increased her speed, and she felt a thrill shoot through her. Still curled, shoulders still pulled back, she watched the ground grow momentarily closer before she was lifting again, staring up at the beautiful blue sky. If not for the blast of wind against her body, she'd have thought the world itself turned, and she was its steady, immovable center.

Before she could stop herself she was curling again, arms out at her sides, a smile on her face as the wind tore through her short hair. The world spun around her as she looped again, except this time when she completed it she straightened her body while simultaneously lessening the throttle. She felt a momentary sense of complete weightlessness as her rise ended, her body floating above the fields, looking down at the silver dots that were her fellow students.

Bree decreased the throttle, steadily drifting back to the grass. Instructor Dohn was waiting for her when her feet touched down, and his expression was difficult to read.

"I asked you to perform only one loop," he said.

"I performed a second in case the first was not satisfactory," she said, knowing full well how stupid it was but unable to help herself.

The instructor shook his head.

"What is your name, Seraph?"

"Breanna Skyborn, sir."

"Breanna, you're dismissed."

Bree blinked, stunned. She'd barely even tested out her new wings, and the instructor was sending her away already?

"Sir, I think it'd be best if I . . ."

"Do not tell me what would be best," Instructor Dohn interrupted. "I asked for one loop, and you gave me two, plus some lip. What we do here today might be too easy for you, Breanna, but it's necessary nonetheless. Go on back to the barracks, and we'll see if tomorrow you're more open to learning. Besides, your boredom will just prove dangerous to the others. The last thing I need is a collision from someone shooting too high while you're busy pulling loops."

Bree lowered her gaze, and it seemed all eyes were on her, not just of those nearby. She desperately wished she could go back in time and follow instructions, but it seemed there'd be no fixing this.

"Yes sir," she said, her voice so soft she worried he'd make her repeat it. Thankfully he did not, the instructor instead lifting back into the air to check the next student. Her wings suddenly feeling heavy, the sky not quite so blue, Bree walked back to the dirt road that split the entire academy. Like a hive of strange bees, the other wings thrummed behind her, their deep sound now a taunt. Slowly, glumly, Bree approached the gear sheds as if they were an execution. She saw Bartow chatting with one of his other mechanics, the two of them leaning against the side of their shed.

"Something wrong with your wings?" Bartow called out to her as she neared.

"No...no, nothing wrong," Bree answered. She knew she should return her wings, but she just couldn't.

Bartow gave her a funny look, but he shrugged and resumed talking with his friend. Bree veered off from the path, turned south, and entered the southeast training field. Like all the other fields, the grass was a vibrant green, and cut ankle high. Unlike the other fields, however, this one had plentiful obstructions. Curious, she walked through them. There were a dozen in fairly close proximity, each one made of thin wood painted white. They had long, slender bases, and at the top they opened up into enormous rings. Each base was numbered.

An obstacle course, she thought, and the realization gave her a chill.

It was terrible. It was stupid. And she was going to do it anyway.

Finding the ring marked with a one, she spotted a solid white line in the grass made from half-buried bricks. Standing before it, Bree surveyed the course. Twelve rings, each successive ring guiding the challenger around in a circle back to the start. A grin on her face, she put her thumb on her switch, tensed her legs, and counted down.

Three.

Two.

One...

Bree leapt into the air, pushing the throttle so that it thrummed to life. The sudden acceleration yanked her harder than she expected, but she recovered quickly enough to correct her angle of elevation. She slid gently through the first ring, found the second. It was to her right, and she rotated her body clockwise while pulling back her shoulders. Her movement curved, but her aim was off, and if she didn't correct it she'd go flying past. With no other choice, she reduced her speed, swung her body the other way, and then slowly passed through. The same happened for ring number three, which was to the left of the second ring. She tried to go a decent speed, yet her path was still far too wide, and she had to kill the throttle so she might twist about and correct her course. Doing so nearly sent her tumbling across the grass, her toes dragging over the ground before she could reverse her momentum.

So it went for much of the course. Bree had to twist and shift her body constantly, and several rings she missed altogether. Not that she minded, not really. Her wings felt like a new friend, one she had to spend time with to get a feel for. Every successive ring was a new challenge, and she met it with a determined grin. When she passed through the eighth ring, she tried flying faster, and this time when she twisted her aim was true. Slicing through the center of the ninth ring filled her with incredible satisfaction. Praying she could continue the streak, she saw that the tenth ring was much higher than all the others. So much higher, in fact, she had no hope of making it. Flinging her legs before her, she reduced her speed while letting her wings cancel out their own speed. Coming to a complete halt before the base of the ring, she slowly rose. Once even with the center of the ring, she tilted forward slightly and drifted through.

Ring eleven was equally impossible, for its bottom was nearly touching the ground. Bree drifted downward, body still erect, as she wondered how to efficiently go from one to the other. Her forward momentum continued from the previous ring, and as she passed through the eleventh ring she straightened out her body and pushed the throttle into a normal flight. The final ring was up ahead, and at an even height. Letting out a whoop, she blasted through its center. Her last ring, and also her best. Spinning in the air, she reduced the throttle. She floated upward, then thrummed her wings back to life when she felt the familiar weightless feeling. The wings kept her at a steady ten feet off the ground as she surveyed the obstacle course. Of the twelve rings, she'd made it through ten of them, all while the rest of her classmates were still trying to learn how to remain aloft in the air...

"You didn't set the timer."

The sudden voice caused Bree to jump, and she felt her neck flushing. Turning, she saw that she was no longer alone in the field. By his age, she guessed him to be one of the older students. His dark skin was in sharp contrast to the white of his shirt, his black hair wavy and as long as hers. He wore his own silver set of wings, and he flew up to join her with a smile on his face.

"I take it you're one of the newbies?" he asked.

"I...yes," she said, the term not difficult for her to decipher.

"Dean Averson," he said, putting his right hand over his heart in a salute while dipping his head slightly.

"Breanna Skyborn," she said, and then realizing she hadn't returned the gesture, quickly tried to replicate it. The movement sent her gently drifting forward, and to her horror, she realized she was going to slide right into him. Dean only looked amused, and he reached out to catch her waist before easing her in the other direction.

"You may take to this like a fish to water, but you've still got plenty to learn," he said.

"I'll keep that in mind."

The young man glanced over his shoulder to the course below them.

"Well, Breanna..."

"Bree. Just Bree."

He looked back, and his blue eyes seemed to twinkle with amusement.

"Bree," he said, "if you're going to do the obstacle course, you should do it right. Follow me, and try not to crash."

"I won't crash," she said, unsure why she suddenly felt defensive.

"I saw you overshooting ring two," he said. "Or did you have a bug on your boots you were trying to scrape off?"

Was he mocking her? Her immediate instinct was to assume as much, but his grin was too wide, his tone far too playful. Knowing he'd seen her goof did little to help the blush that still remained across her face and neck, and, taking extra care with the throttle, she followed the young man down to the road.

Beside the road was a tall wooden box she'd not noticed before. On its front was a large white oval, marked at the edges with thin black lines. The lines were numbered by twenties, starting at zero and ending at two hundred and forty. Its single rotating hand from the center currently pointed to zero. Dean reached behind it and showed her where a corded hook extended out the back, along with a smaller secondary handle.

"This big one winds the timer," he said. "Pull the cord all the way out to the final ring, and once you're there, hook it to the side of the ring. Go on, it isn't hard."

Taking the metal hook in her right hand, she gave her wings a short burst to hop over to the twelfth ring, and she was surprised by the resistance of the cord. From the timer she heard a myriad of gears turning, the mechanisms within winding up and preparing to release. During her approach she felt the cord go taut, and she had to grab it with both hands to pull it the rest of the way. Before she could ask what to latch it on to, she saw that there was a slender groove cut into the bottom of the twelfth ring, and she set it within. Taking a step back, she frowned at it.

"It doesn't seem very secure," she said.

"That's because it's not supposed to be."

Dean gestured for her to return, and she did.

"Now," he said, pointing to the second handle in the back. "When you grab that one, you'll pull it out to the starting line. The moment you let go, the timer starts. To stop the timer, you need to dislodge that hook from the final ring."

"How do I do that?" she asked.

"Smack it with your hand, and it'll come loose. Just try not to be going too fast. Broken hands are pretty common injuries in second-year students. I'll let you figure out why. Anyway, when you dislodge it, the timer stops, and you can come check your time. Once you wind it up, it counts down from four minutes to zero."

"What happens if I take longer than four minutes?" she asked.

"Then it wasn't a time worth remembering. You ready to try again?"

"You promise not to make fun of me when I do terribly?"

Dean grinned at her.

"How about you just not do terribly instead?"

Bree laughed as she grabbed the slender handle and walked to the starting line. Bending over, she tensed her legs, placed her thumb on the throttle. She breathed in, breathed out, and released the handle. It shot from her hand, she pushed the throttle, and with a strong leap of her legs she tore into the air toward the first ring. Her first run through had been calm, patient, but this time she was keenly aware of her spectator. The first ring was easy enough, but just as before she failed to correct herself in time. Shooting past the second ring, she twisted around, the wings fighting against her own momentum to resume the other way.

Up and down, left and right, she weaved and pushed through the rings. She quickly discovered that the strength of her own body would decide many of the turns, for it was the muscles of her back and waist that changed her positioning and re-aimed the thrust of the wings. Every time she thought she had a turn down, she'd jerk too hard one way, climb too steep, or simply not angle hard enough. The eighth ring she had to turn about and try again, and then worst of all came the stretch of nine through eleven. The ninth she pushed through easily enough, but to gain the elevation to reach the tenth she had to kill her entire forward momentum, and at a painfully slow speed she crossed through. Seemingly just as impossible was the ring immediately after, number ten barely ten feet out while still all the way attached to the ground.

Bree tried to speed up the process by falling, and she jarred her neck by flaring the wings just before hitting the ground. Letting out a cry, she gritted her teeth and fought on. The final ring was the easiest, a relatively straight shot. Flying through it, she heeded Dean's warning and slowed down before reaching out her left hand and smacking the thin wood. The ring wobbled back and forth, dislodging the hook. The black cord shot back across the grass, securing into the back of the timer.

Trying to pretend she wasn't in as much pain as she was, Bree flew back to Dean's side.

"How'd I do?" she asked, sucking in air. The exertion had

taken far more of her than she'd expected, and she felt sweat dripping down her neck.

"I'd say the timer ran out at least two minutes ago," he said. "Maybe three. It's hard to keep track after so much time has passed."

Bree laughed despite her pain and exhaustion.

"You're a smartass, aren't you?"

"Indeed I am. What were you doing out here anyway, Bree?"

She really didn't want to mention how Dohn had sent her away, so she instead flipped the issue.

"Practicing," she said, as if it should be obvious. "What were *you* doing out here?"

"Practicing," he said, and when she gave him a look, he shook his head. "I'm not joking. Look behind you, Bree."

She turned, but saw nothing, and told him so.

"Not there," he said. "Higher."

Her gaze lifted, and then she saw them. Hundreds of feet into the air they danced, silver angels diving and twisting in formation. Several separate men and women flew among their numbers, circling, pretending to be an attacker. The twists they made, the rapid climbs and even rapider dives; it was all so fluid. And their speed! Even at her best while making her way through the obstacle course she was a slug compared to those older students.

"Shouldn't you be among them?" she asked as she watched, mesmerized.

"I should, yes, but my switch started sticking," Dean said. "I was on my way to the gear sheds when I happened to spot a crazy girl flying the advanced obstacle course on her first day of training and I just had to come watch the ensuing disaster."

Goddamn it, thought Bree. She felt her neck blushing for what felt like the hundredth time that day. With her pale skin, it'd be more visible than the fire over the midnight sky. Wanting the subject switched to something, anything, she saw a list of times cut into the side of the timer and pointed to them.

"What are those?" she asked.

"Names of the record holders and their times," Dean said.

"What's the fastest?"

Dean tapped at the one on the bottom.

"A minute thirty-seven, by none other than Argus himself."

Bree recognized that name. Argus Summers was a legend in Weshern, having recorded the most ever kills for a Seraphim at thirty-nine, not counting over a dozen more brought down in theotech-sanctioned duels. Now he led the entirety of the Weshern Seraphim as their commander. She'd seen him only once, during one of the yearly parades, and she'd never forgotten those icy-blue eyes of his.

"Minute thirty-seven," she said, staring at the name. "Now I know what to shoot for."

"So you're up for another?"

Bree grinned.

"I am, so be a gentleman and reset the clock!"

CHAPTER
8

Much to Kael's chagrin, they did not start their second day immediately with physical exercise and then flight training. Instead he and Brad were awoken early that morning by a hammering fist on the door to their apartment, calling them to prepare for the seventh-day service. So they marched out, half awake and on an empty stomach, to find an older student guiding the rest south.

"Cross the bridge and head to the advanced elemental training field," the man said. "You'll figure the rest out."

True to his word, it wasn't hard to find where everyone gathered. Students of all four years stood in a massive jumble in the empty field, forming a loose U around a stone pedestal. On one side, Kael spotted several of the teachers and instructors chatting with the headmaster. They all wore their uniforms, freshly cleaned. Kael and Brad hovered near the back, with Kael keeping an eye out for his sister. She and Amanda arrived together, and Kael waved his arm above his head until she noticed.

"I hope this doesn't cut into our flight time," Bree said, sliding up beside him.

"Or breakfast," Brad said, grinning. "They keep us here too long, and no one's going to hear the theotech's droning over the sound of my stomach."

"It depends on who we get," Amanda said, standing on her tiptoes in an attempt to see over the crowd to the pedestal. "They'll send one of the theotechs from the Crystal Cathedral to oversee the ceremony. If it's Vyros, it'll be pointed and short. If it's Jorg, we might be lucky to have practice at all."

"Did you go there often?" Brad asked.

"Every week," Amanda said, and a look of relief crossed over her face. "And yes, it's Vyros. Don't worry, Brad. You'll get your breakfast."

"Awesome, let's get this over and done," Brad said, loud enough for Kael to elbow him in the side. With the theotech stepping up to the stone pedestal, the host of people swiftly quieted. The red-robed man was on the older side, his face wrinkled and the top of his head balding. He projected his voice well as he addressed the crowd.

"Greetings, Seraphim of Weshern and members of the academy," he said. "My name is Vyros Longleaf, and I consider it a privilege to share with you the wisdom of the angels on this fine day."

Kael considered it a privilege to have a place to sit, but the theotechs had strict rules about religious service, one of them being they must take place in open air. The few times a theotech had traveled to Lowville, they'd gathered in the town square to listen. Kael had heard of the fine furnishings of the Crystal Cathedral, built beside the holy mansion, but had never been inside himself. He had a feeling the wealthy and privileged who attended there had nice, cushioned seats instead of having to shift their weight foot to foot to avoid cramping.

"As this is the first service for those of you new to the academy, I would like to address my remarks to you bright and talented children," Vyros continued. "You have much to learn, and for now, I would like you to consider me another of your teachers. The power offered to you here is great, and with it comes a need for responsibility, humility, and wisdom. The first two, your instructors here will handle well on their own, but as for the third, I ask that you listen with open ears and open hearts to my words."

Kael's mood soured as Vyros continued with his sermon. The traveling theotechs from his childhood had far more fire and energy than Vyros, their words focusing on repentance and self-improvement through God's guidance. Kael had enjoyed those sermons well enough, particularly the stirring of emotions in the crowd around him. But this? This wasn't even close. Every listener looked bored. Kael could have handled that, but worse was the message itself. It wasn't about failure or grace, fall or redemption, not even about the sins of the old world that supposedly led to the Ascension.

Instead it was about the role of the Seraphim as protectors of their island nation, and how the theotechs served a similar role to all five islands, plus Center. The constant reminder grated on Kael, and he stole a glance at Bree beside him. She just looked bored, which made him wonder if he was overreacting. That was, until Vyros finally gave away the point of his entire sermon.

"It is the angels who hold our islands in their hands," the theotech said. "It is their wisdom that saved our race, and it is their words we must listen to above all others. Above family, above friends, above nations. Those words, spoken only to one. Those words, repeated to us by the Speaker for the Angels, the illustrious Marius Prakt."

That was it, the message that caused Kael to grind his teeth as he waited for the sermon to end. This wasn't a sermon designed for the betterment of the listener. It was an overly long reminder of the power Center lorded over Weshern. Once aware of it, he couldn't stop hearing it. The many times Vyros referred to the people of Weshern as children. The constant glorification of Center. The reference to how even their Archon, Isaac Willer, also bowed to the will of the angels.

When Vyros asked that they lower their heads and lift their hands to the heavens, Kael couldn't help himself.

"Finally," he whispered, and this time it was Brad's turn to elbow him in the side.

Vyros closed the prayer with a call to obedience and wisdom, then dismissed them to their daily routine. The students scattered, and Kael was all too eager to get some food in his belly and his wings on his back.

At least I don't feel like throwing up anymore, thought Kael as he guided his wings through a set of simple exercises Instructor Dohn taught them earlier that morning. Only his second day of flight training, and already he felt infinitely more comfortable being aloft. The day before, while his sister looped about to the jealousy of everyone, he'd needed all his concentration just to keep his body straight and his speed consistent. As his nerves settled, so too did his flight. Training with Jevin's set had never been a priority for him, instead something he did just because Bree did as well, but now he felt thankful for the friendly fisherman's help.

The clouds were thick above them, puffy and white and very much welcome. In the shade Kael lifted for three seconds, halted, then dropped straight down, the goal to keep his speed the same on the way up as on the way down. For the third attempt in a row he managed it, his feet touching the green grass at exactly three seconds, and he felt a smile blooming on his face. Despite having tried nothing fancier than a few twists and turns in midair, he felt a bit of Bree's excitement starting to wear off on him.

Kael glanced to where his sister practiced nearby. Bree's boredom was clearly evident. She'd rushed through every set of drills, finishing before others had yet to start their second set. While the other students were concentrating hard to fly up, then drop straight and steady, Bree was twirling her body with each rise into the air. On the way down, she'd cross her arms, then twirl again just before her feet touched ground, pirouetting upon the grass before yet another rise.

"Are we bored, Miss Skyborn?"

Kael straightened his back, and his heart skipped a beat. He looked straight ahead, not wanting to earn the instructor's ire as Adam flew over to where his sister trained.

"No sir," she said, hovering a foot above the ground as she faced Instructor Dohn. "I mean, yes sir, I'm sorry. I've already finished, so I thought if I did them again, only more difficult..."

"They're not supposed to be difficult," Dohn said. "That's the point. They're to be learned, and become so deeply ingrained you can perform them even during the chaos of battle."

Bree cast her eyes downward.

"Understood, sir. It won't happen again."

The instructor sighed.

"Fly two quick laps around the field, then return to the sheds. I don't need to babysit a bored natural."

"Actually, I was hoping I could stay and help..." His glare silenced her. "Yes sir. I'll finish and go."

Kael made eye contact with his sister as she turned to go.

It'll be all right, he mouthed to her. She smiled, but he could tell she was upset at being dismissed a second day in a row. Instructor Dohn turned his way, and Kael quickly resumed practicing to spare himself similar wrath.

"Looking fine, Kael, though don't push the switch so fast at the bottom," the instructor said as he hovered nearby. "You want an easy, gentle stop, not a hard yank that might throw off your aim."

"I'll try," Kael said as he rose for another attempt, keenly aware of the instructor's eyes following him. Just before three seconds Kael pulled back the throttle so it was barely pushing power from the light element to the wings, and he dropped as smoothly as he'd risen. Two seconds down, he eased the throttle forward... realizing too late he'd misjudged, and it wouldn't be enough to stop him in time. He struck the ground with a hard jolt to his knees and ankles, and his teeth rattled.

Instead of appearing upset, Instructor Dohn chuckled.

"Now you see why we practice," he said, continuing on to where Brad hovered nearby. Kael felt his mouth go dry. While he'd worried what Dohn might say about him, he worried even more how he might react to his roommate. Brad had struggled all yesterday, with not a single kind word given. Would today be any better?

"Though sometimes it seems even practice won't help," Dohn said as he killed his wings and dropped to his feet before Brad. "What's the matter, Seraph?"

"Having trouble with stopping," Brad said. Defeat was already in his normally cheerful voice.

"And you know why, don't you?" the instructor asked. "You're too heavy for your wings. There's no secret trick to this, Brad-ford, just a plain and simple truth: fat don't fly."

Brad's neck flushed red, and several of the other students snickered. Ignoring them all, Brad dropped, counted to two, and then powered his wings. He overcompensated, his halt sudden enough to jar his neck and jerk his arms. When it happened, Brad eased up in hopes of lessening the effect, which only made his sudden stop turn into a momentary jarring before the second, equally brutal hit upon the grass. Brad cursed as he fell to his knees.

"God almighty, it's like putting wings on a pig," Dohn said. "Your momentum's too great, Seraph. It's going to put a strain on both your body and your wings. Maybe you can learn how to ease into your turns even earlier, but until then, you've got a lot of hard knocks coming your way."

Brad rose to his feet, wiping at grass stains on the knees of his pants.

"I'm sorry, sir," he said. "I can handle the hits, though, I promise."

"Big oxen like you often can, but it won't be enough. Once we start the more complicated maneuvers, you've got a prayer's chance of staying in formation with the rest of your classmates."

Instructor Dohn flew on. Kael began his next drill, which involved tilting his upper body right, flying into the air, then dropping down, tilting left, and flying up to effectively form a sideways eight that had him finishing where he first started. Brad worked on the first, rising and falling, rising and falling, and it seemed each time he hit ground it took a little more out of him. When Instructor Dohn called for them to quit, Kael had done twenty reps of seven different drills. Brad remained on the first, still unable to come to a smooth, painless halt.

All throughout class the rest of the day, Kael caught Brad

moping, his mind clearly elsewhere. When they ended for the day, Kael asked him if he wanted to join him for supper.

"Probably shouldn't," his friend said. "This ox needs to lose some weight, remember?"

Kael didn't know how to respond. When he joined Bree at a table, where she sat alone, she glanced about.

"Brad not joining us?" she asked.

"Doesn't seem like it."

Bree frowned.

"What's the matter? Something happen at practice?"

"You could say that," Kael said, grabbing a sliced apple wedge and biting it in half. "He had trouble controlling his wings, and the instructor rode him pretty damn hard about it."

"If he wants some extra practice, I'd be glad to help," Bree said. "It'd be nice to do some work without Instructor Dohn glaring at me."

"I'll see," Kael said. "I doubt it, but I'll see."

When they finished, he returned to their apartment as the sun was just starting to set. Brad lay on his bed, an open book beside him. His eyes were hidden by one of his beefy arms. Kael pulled off one boot as he glanced at the title. Beginning Aerial Maneuvers (Earth Affinity Edition).

"Sounds like thrilling reading," Kael said.

Brad lowered his arm, rolled his eyes.

"It's not," he said. "Not that it matters. I've been here two days, and I'm already close to failing out."

"Look, you're not going to fail just because the instructor called you a name."

"No," Brad said, sitting up. "I'm going to fail because my damn wings won't work right because of my fat ass."

While Kael had felt uncomfortable during the earlier humiliation, now he felt furious, particularly at Instructor Dohn.

Brad's arms were thick with muscle, as was his chest. If it came to a brawl, Kael would have put his money on Brad over everyone else in his class.

"You're not fat," he said. "You know that. You're big, and you're strong."

"Does it matter what you call it? I'm sorry, Kael, but even after I showed earth affinity, the tester warned me this might happen. I just...I have to accept it. That's all. Not like I ever wanted to be a Seraph anyway."

For not wanting to be one, he looked devastated by the idea of failing out. If anything, he looked ready to cry. Kael put his back to the wall and slid down to the floor, arms resting on his knees.

"If you don't want to be one, then why is it such a big deal?" he asked.

Brad plopped back onto his bed, and he groaned as he stared up at the ceiling.

"It's..." He paused, fighting for the words. "It's my parents. We're fishermen, Kael. Been fishermen for generations. I've been lifting and slinging fish ever since I was five. There's never been a single Seraph in my family, not one. Hell, they almost didn't bother sending me for the affinity test in the first place. But when I came home, and told them I'd been accepted..."

He shook his head.

"My mom started crying. Kept saying how proud she was of me. Same with my dad. So proud. So happy. Someone in our family would make something of themselves, they said, as if what we do means nothing, like being a fisherman is such a damn insult. I don't care one bit about the Seraphim, Kael. Under normal circumstances, I'd have punched Dohn in his mouth to show him the difference between fat and muscle, then marched straight home. But to disappoint my parents like that...it ain't right. Not that it matters at this point, though. *Fat don't fly?* Goddamn, what a prick."

He rolled over, putting his back to him. Kael stared, mind whirring, plan forming.

"I'll be at Bree's apartment," he said, rising back to his feet. "Good night, Brad."

"Good night."

The next morning, before the midnight fire had fully dissipated, Kael flung Brad's uniform onto his chest and then kicked his bed. Brad woke with a start, sucking in air as he looked around.

"What?" he asked.

"Get up," Kael said, tossing Brad's boots onto the bed as well. "We're going running."

Brad glanced at the window, saw how early it was.

"Now?" he asked.

"Now."

"And if I say no?"

Kael kicked the bed again.

"You're not dropping out, you're not giving up, and you're definitely not going back to bed. Now get up, and let's go."

His friend muttered curses under his breath, but he complied. Once he was dressed, the two stepped out into the cool morning air. The very tip of the sun was beginning to appear, the smoky remnants of the fire and darkness starting to thin because of it. Kael's stomach felt like a rock, and his head ached from not near enough sleep, but he ignored it as best he could. Neither in the mood for conversation, they walked to the center bridge. Bree waited there, and unlike them, she had a grin on her face.

"Aren't you two a chipper bunch?" she said.

"Not enough beauty sleep," Brad mumbled.

After taking a minute to stretch, they ran north alongside the stream that split the academy, then curled westward, following the stone wall. Kael kept glancing over his shoulder, and when Brad fell behind, he turned and ran to his side.

"That it?" Bree called back to them. "I guess I'll see you two again when I lap you."

"You going to take that from her?" Kael asked as his friend sucked in air. "Muscle, not fat, remember? Let's see what shape a fisherman's really in."

"We lift, we carry, and we chop," Brad said as he walked. "We don't run."

Kael grinned.

"Well, you do now, *Seraph*."

For the first time that morning, Brad laughed.

"You're a dick, Kael."

"You, too, Brad."

Despite his exhaustion, despite the redness of his face, Brad picked up the pace, running along the edges of the academy, running until the sun rose, the shadows faded, and the true morning rituals and training could begin.

CHAPTER
9

After two weeks of tedious drills, and even more tedious classes on military history and procedure, Bree was finally about to try something new and exciting. In the middle of the southwest field she waited with the rest of her class to begin elemental training. Their instructor, Seraph Randy Kime, appeared to be the polar opposite of Instructor Dohn. Instead of loud and abrasive, he was happy and soft-spoken. He had a narrow face, with pronounced cheekbones, sandy blond hair cut into a bowl, and a small mouth that always seemed to be curled in a smile. Immediately noticeable, despite Bree trying hard to pretend otherwise, was how Kime's left hand was missing from the wrist down.

Beside Instructor Kime was a large crate, which he had yet to open. Once he reintroduced himself, he tapped the top of the crate with the nub of skin and bone at the end of his left arm.

"The first thing I want you all to remember is to have fun," he said. "I mean it, I really do. The elements inside here are... well, they're magical. You're going to wield fire, or ice, or earth, or lightning from the palm of your hand. If that doesn't get you excited..." He made an exaggerated sigh while shaking his head. "Then I don't think you're living."

Bree found herself smiling. His happiness was infectious. When he lifted one of the ice elemental shards, his joy appeared absolutely genuine.

"This is a thing of wonder," he said. "You're here to make it bend to your will, and before today's practice ends, I promise you, you'll see a bit of magic. Yes, magic! So if you would, put on your gauntlets, and then open the element container on the right."

Bree did so, her eagerness growing. The right gauntlet had a similar setup as the left, with a thick base she could open to insert one of the elemental shards. Bree pushed down and in, springing open the lid, then waited to receive her fire element.

"When I call your name, please come and accept your element," Instructor Kime said. "Once you've reached basic proficiency, I'll inform Sara to let you receive your element with the rest of your gear. Now, if you would... Daniel Cloud, up here, please."

Bree tapped her foot as she listened to the names. Daniel Cloud, Brandon Forge, Ryan Keegan... they were going alphabetically, which meant she'd have to wait. More names. Wess Holson. Brad Macon. Saul Reigar. Many she'd met during class, but she'd befriended only Brad and her roommate, Amanda. The others had broken into little cliques since the very first day, and Bree was content to leave things be. Hopefully friendships and camaraderie would come in time. For now, she wanted to remain focused on improving her skills in flight.

"Amanda Ruth?"

Amanda stepped up to Instructor Kime, accepted the offered lightning element, and then patiently watched as he showed her how to place it into the gauntlet and then secure it. Despite her previous worries, Bree's roommate had taken quite well to flying, and Bree had a feeling she'd be just as good when it came to the elemental parts of their training. Beneath her shy demeanor hid a fiercely intelligent mind. Hopefully confidence would soon follow her successes.

"Breanna Skyborn."

Bree hurried to the front. Instructor Kime reached into the crate with his only hand and pulled out a red prism shard. When he offered it, she took it and lifted her right gauntlet so he could observe.

"Slide the shard in right there," he said, watching her carefully as she did just that. When it was inside, she pushed down the lid until she heard a satisfying click. A tiny glass window revealed the prism, which started to pulse a soft red.

"Good, just like that," he said. "Now if you're not in combat, you turn this knob here…"

Just below her wrist was a tiny silver knob, and when he twisted it, the red of the shard ceased pulsing.

"Left for off, right for on," he said. "Keep it off for now, all right?"

She nodded, earning herself a smile.

"Good. Go wait, please, until we're all ready."

Bree returned to her spot, and she stared at the prism through the cloudy thick glass. Deep inside that prism was a wellspring of fire, and soon she would be its master. She remembered her affinity testing, and the shocked look on Dioso's face. Already she'd established herself as the best flyer in her class. If she could do the same with her element...

"Clara Willer."

The last name pulled her from her thoughts, and she watched as the pretty blonde thing hurried to their instructor's side. It'd not taken long for whispers to spread throughout the class about Clara's family. Clara was the youngest daughter of Isaac and Avila Willer, the royal family of Weshern that had ruled the island as Archon for more than ninety years. Despite having two older brothers who would rule ahead of her, Clara was still of royal blood. Bree had been there when Kael discovered this fact, and it'd looked like someone had jammed a knife through his chest.

Finally everyone was ready, and Instructor Kime began ordering them into a single long line.

"You're all new, and while you're having fun, remember these elements are also dangerous," he said. "Never point your right gauntlet at another person, no matter how well you think you have it under control."

Bree stayed with her brother, with Amanda to her left, who tapped her fingers together and grinned when their eyes met.

I'm excited, Amanda mouthed, and Bree smiled.

Good, she mouthed back.

Instructor Kime stood in the center of their line. He also wore a harness and wings, though no left gauntlet, just one on his right. He lifted it up and pointed it toward them with the palm spread open.

"Just below the palm, even with wrist and elbow, you'll see the focal point of your gauntlet," Kime said. Bree glanced to her own, inspecting it as she listened to her instructor talk. The focal point was a clear white crystal. Eight thin silver triangles, like petals to a flower, folded over it when she closed her fist, keeping it protected.

"There are tiny little wires hidden within your gauntlet that connect to the protective casing around the focal point," Instructor Kime continued. "When you close your fingers and start to curl your hand, you'll narrow the opening. Open your hand, and spread your fingers, and you'll pull the focal point open wider and wider."

Bree had noticed this during her flight practices, though she hadn't known the reason for it, only assuming it had something to do with using her element in combat. Instructor Kime opened and closed his hand, making sure all of them saw before he continued.

"The narrower the opening, the thinner and more focused your element will be when you use it. Now, each element reacts differently to these changes, and some elements will use a wide spread far more than narrow. Earth, for example, often uses a wider spread, whereas lightning needs to be kept thin and focused lest you lose control." He clapped his stump into the palm of his other hand. "Now for the important part. The exciting, magical part I promised you. As you've likely noticed, there's no trigger, and it's not because it's hidden. *You* are the trigger. This is the reason a Seraph must have some measure of elemental affinity. Now let me get out of your way..."

Bree flexed her gauntlet as Instructor Kime hurried between them to stand on the opposite side of the line. Before them stretched a massive field of grass, with nearly half a mile between them and the stone wall surrounding the academy.

"Turn the knob on your gauntlets to set your element back to active."

All of them did so. Bree's fire element pulsed like a heartbeat beneath the glass window. Kime paced behind them as he continued talking.

"Now place your right hand out, palm facing the field. Keep your fingers relaxed, and don't worry too much about how wide or narrow the shot is. So long as you don't end up burning your own fingers or cutting them off with a shard of ice, you'll be fine. Now focus on the element. Sense it. The mechanisms within the gauntlet will help, making it feel clearer, stronger..."

Bree held her arm out before her, frowning as she listened. Sense the element? But she sensed nothing. Just like when performing her tests with Dioso, she felt not the slightest presence of the glowing prism mere inches from her skin. Thankfully it seemed no one else was doing any better, with everyone standing about with an arm outstretched.

"Do you sense it?" Instructor Kime asked. "Like it's a part of you? Perhaps another muscle on your arm? A bit of fire burning so close, only cold instead of hot? With most everyone it is different, so try to focus on whatever seems strange and new. Focus on that. Close your eyes if you must. And then...brace your arm. Tighten your fingers. Flex your muscles. Like you were falling and about to hit ground..."

Bree was still listening, trying to imagine what exactly the instructor was asking of her, when a burst of ice shot from her brother's gauntlet. It came out in a thin stream, its point razor sharp, no thicker than a finger, no longer than a foot. The accompanying sound was surprisingly loud, like a hiss of air, only deeper in pitch. Kael's arm jerked backward as it fired, launching the ice shard with such velocity it soared several hundred feet before burying into the grass. Kael looked around as if embarrassed, but his grin was ear to ear.

"Good!" Kime said. "All of you, keep trying! It's startling the first time you harness the elements, but that's what practice is for. You'll learn how to fire nice and steady. I promise, this will soon come as naturally as breathing."

After seeing how much pushback the firing had on Kael, Bree braced her legs and pointed her right arm at the empty field. To her left, she heard Amanda whoop as a flash of lightning burst from the focal point of her gauntlet, tearing across the field without stopping until it struck the distant wall. An afterimage of its yellow and white spear floated before Bree's eyes. When she turned, Amanda laughed.

"I like this better than flying," she said, pushing her gauntlet forward. A second shot out, this one thinner and lasting longer. Its crackle was joined by spears of flame and thin brown chunks of earth flying into the field, tearing apart the grass and blasting up chunks of earth. Bree swallowed hard, trying to quell her rising doubts.

You can do this, she told herself as she outstretched her hand. *Find the element. Focus on it. Imagine it releasing...*

She tensed the muscles in her arm, braced her legs, and widened her fingers. She imagined the fire coming forth. Not just imagining it, but demanding it. For a split second she felt a sharp pain in her head, like a shard of glass breaking inside her skull, and then an intense pressure followed, pushing against her hand. Fire blasted out from her palm, but not a thin stream like Amanda's or Kael's, or even some of the wider sprays of the other students. The fire exploded outward in a torrential blast, enormous in its volume, its heat painful to her skin. The inferno rolled forth, scorching grass and leaving bare earth in its wake. A roar accompanied the release, like that of an angered dragon. Bree cried out in surprise, and then quickly as it came, the fire ceased, fading away into black smoke.

"Holy shit," Kael said beside her, wide-eyed with awe. Though she could tell he was impressed, she felt only exhaustion and humiliation. She hadn't meant for anything like that to happen, and as the fire had roared out of the gauntlet, she'd felt completely powerless to stop it. Sweat rolled down her neck, and her face felt stiff, like when she stayed out in the sun too long and would be burned red the day after. She caught Instructor Kime walking toward her from the corner of her eye, and thankfully he seemed amused by what she'd done.

"Don't fret," he said as he joined her side. His right hand took her gauntlet and lifted it up so he could examine the elemental prism through the glass window. Instead of pulsing red, it was now black with streaks of gray running throughout. "That's what I thought. You burned through your entire element in one single burst, Breanna."

"I didn't mean to," she said.

"Of course not," he said, smiling. "You only need to learn control. Control is an important, and often overlooked, part of being a Seraph. One of Center's rules of war limits all Seraphim to a single prism during a battle. Through focus and concentration, skilled Seraphim can use their element twice as much as others. In lengthy conflicts, this often spells the difference between victory and defeat."

Bree nodded as he talked, though she was barely listening. Her mind was replaying the event, thinking on what it'd been like when she unleashed the element. She couldn't think of any actual decision on her part, any moment where she could exert more control. It felt like trying to use a sleeping limb to tie a knot. Somewhere inside her was a disconnect, and she couldn't figure out why.

"Come with me," Kime said, walking back to his crate. Bree

followed. From within the crate he pulled out a second flame element, and he twirled it in his fingers.

"Always discard the old element in this crate, or at the gear sheds if you're practicing alone," he said. "We send it back to Center at their request, one of the many conditions we must meet if we are to continue receiving more shipments."

Bree popped back open the secure compartment and pulled out the dark prism. Now that it was in her hand she could feel minute cracks running across its formerly smooth surface. She exchanged the prisms with her instructor, sliding her new vibrant red one into the gauntlet and shutting the compartment. When she returned to the line with the rest of the students, Instructor Kime followed.

"This time, I want you to relax," he said. "Don't tense your arm quite so much. Think of a river. You want a slow, steady stream, not a waterfall. Visualize it if it helps."

Bree nodded, mentally telling herself to calm down. She could do this. Hadn't Dioso been overwhelmed by the strength of her affinity? He'd never seen someone so blessed. Extending her arm, she took in a deep breath, then slowly let it out. Kime carefully touched her wrist with his hand, repositioning her elbow as he stood beside her.

"Nice and steady," he told her. "The fire is under your control. You're its master, so make it follow your demands. Imagine a thin spear of flame, then demand it."

All across the line of students, blasts of fire, ice, earth, and lightning shot into the field, some soaring into the air, some crashing into the grass. Nineteen of them there, eighteen capable of mastering their element at a basic level. She would not be the only one unable to handle it. She wouldn't let it happen. Imagining a steady stream of flame, she tensed the muscles of her forearms, pulled back her fingers. Again she felt a mental click, felt heat gather at her palm. Flame sparked, then unleashed, and Bree smiled.

That smile died the moment the fire burst free, an enormous, rolling cloud of black and red. There was no controlling it, no mastering it, no demanding it to her will. The flame roared outward, the heat incredible, the heavy rumbling sound chilling. And within two seconds it promptly ceased, and Bree dropped to her knees, completely out of breath. Again she felt her classmates staring, except this time their stares weren't so impressed, their whispers not ones of awe. No, she heard something far, far worse.

Subdued laughter.

"I see we have some work to do," Instructor Kime said. For some reason, the cheer in his voice only made her humiliation worse.

"I can do this," Bree said. "Let me try again."

"I'm sorry, Breanna, but each student is allotted only two prisms a day. We have to buy them from the theotechs, and they don't come cheap."

"Please," Bree said. "I know I can control it, just give me one more chance."

Instructor Kime shook his head again, his smile fading just a tiny bit.

"These aren't my rules, but those of the academy," he said. "If you'd like excess element allotted to you, you must discuss that with Headmaster Simmons." He put his hand on her shoulder. "Wait until tomorrow, and we'll try again. Until then, you can watch the others practice. Wess seems to have figured out his fire element fairly well, perhaps you could pay attention to him?"

He was just trying to be nice, Bree knew that, but she couldn't help but feel patronized. Biting her lower lip, she nodded.

"I might," she said softly.

"Good," Instructor Kime said, patting her shoulder once before removing his hand. "Don't let this get you down, Breanna. Sometimes first steps result in stumbles. I'm sure you'll figure this out in time."

Bree wished she could share his optimism. She badly wanted to stay, but her humiliation was stronger, and she couldn't shake her desire to flee. Crossing her arms, she walked back to the path that separated the northern and southern halves of the training fields, then turned around. Instructor Kime flitted about, going from student to student, repositioning their arms, offering advice as they continued to unleash more and more impressive blasts of their element. Kael seemed to be doing well, at one point firing three successive blasts so close together they looked like a single barrage of razor-sharp icicles. Those on either side of him started leaning closer, asking him questions, and he answered back with a huge grin on his face. All of them appeared to be having fun, plenty showing off to the others. Bonding. Laughing.

Feeling ready to cry, Bree turned away and hurried east toward the gear sheds. The idea of turning in early made her sick, and she veered south, thinking perhaps a run through the obstacle course would improve her mood. Except unlike most mornings, this time the field wasn't empty. Bree frowned as she neared the advanced flight field. A group of seven gathered between the road and the obstacle course, where the grass wasn't quite so high. Instead of flying or practicing their element, they had their swords drawn. A couple shifted from stance to stance, performing drills, she guessed, while the rest dueled one another.

Bree veered back onto the path, her pace slowing. From the

road she watched them practice, listening to the steady clang of steel hitting steel. Something about the sight of their shifting and parrying calmed her, and though her chest felt hollow, at least she was no longer on the verge of tears. Dean was among them, and she watched as he fought another, much bigger student. Though he wasn't stronger, Dean was faster, and he shifted side to side, using one blade to parry incoming attacks and the other to thrust and stab for openings. Bree could hardly believe it, but they seemed to be sparring with only their wings and harness, and no other armor beyond that.

After their sparring ended, Dean's opponent said something, then tilted his head Bree's way. Dean turned, saw her, and it seemed his eyes lit up for a brief moment. He said something back, then sheathed his swords and came her way. Bree crossed her arms and looked away, suddenly feeling guilty, as if caught doing something wrong.

"Come to fly the obstacle course again?" he asked her, using his sleeve to wipe at a line of sweat built up across his forehead just beneath his dark hair.

"I..."

What had she come for? She'd thought about taking a few runs on the course, but with so many older students nearby, she felt too intimidated. Flailing for an answer, she finally shrugged.

"I just wanted to watch," she said sheepishly.

"I see." He glanced west. "Shouldn't you be at elemental practice, or are you too good for that as well?"

Bree's eyes flicked to the dirt road.

"I'm no good at it," she said.

Dean cocked his head.

"I find that hard to believe."

"Well, it's true." She gestured to the others as they practiced. "When do we learn how to use swords?"

"Not until your second year. Our blades are considered a last resort, to be used only after a Seraph has drained all of his element. It's better to learn how to fly and use your element before trying something you may never use."

Only once an element is drained? thought Bree. *Well, that won't take long.*

"Feel free to watch, and don't be a stranger," Dean said. "We've organized this practice ourselves, a nice warm-up before we start flying around in those tedious formations."

Dean smiled, dipped his head, and then turned to rejoin the others. Bree felt panic shoot through her, and before she could stop herself, she called out to him.

"Can I practice with you?"

The older student stopped, and when he turned about, his left eyebrow lifted in curiosity.

"You want to sword fight with us?" he asked. "We're all third and fourth year. We don't use practice blades anymore. You're likely to get hurt."

"I'll be fine," she said.

"No, you won't," he said. "Not unless someone actually teaches you."

Whatever hope she'd felt promptly died. Swallowing down a rock the size of her throat, she nodded.

"I understand," she said.

Dean shook his head, smile growing.

"Good. So I hope you understand how privileged you are to be trained by the soon-to-be legendary Seraph Dean Averson. Now come on, let's join the gang."

As he headed into the grass, Bree's feet felt made of lead.

"Well?" Dean asked when he noticed she wasn't following.

"Sorry," she mumbled, hurrying after.

She hung back half a step, and she tried not to stammer or blush as Dean introduced her to the rest.

"Hey, all, this is Breanna Skyborn," he said. "She's wanting to get a head start on mastering swordplay, so she'll be joining us for...well, until she gets sick of us, I'd wager."

"The more the merrier," said Dean's previous opponent. "Most consider this a waste of time."

"A lost art, even," chipped in a second.

"Skyborn?" asked a thin woman with dark red hair pulled back into a tight ponytail. "My parents flew alongside your father. They never had anything but kind words to say about him."

"Thanks," Bree said, feeling embarrassed by the attention.

"This way," Dean said, stepping aside. "Where you'll be safe from everyone else's incompetence."

"Yours is the one she needs to be afraid of," the red-haired woman called, and the others laughed.

"Ignore Sasha," Dean said. "She's just jealous that in a few minutes you'll already be better than she is."

"Eat a dick, Dean."

"You first, Sasha."

The camaraderie, the casual banter...Bree felt herself growing jealous. Would her class ever be like this? Right now, she could barely even list everyone's names.

Once safely away from the rest, Dean stopped before her, and he pulled his swords from their scabbards.

"Draw your blades," he said.

Bree undid their latches, jammed the wrist locks onto the loop at the end of their hilts like Instructor Dohn had shown them, and then pulled the weapons free. Dean nodded, pleased she'd done so without problem.

"Keep your grip firm but not too tight," he said. "Same goes for your whole body. Relaxed but ready to react, that's your goal."

"I'll try."

"Perfect," he said. "You ready?" He gently tapped her right sword with his left. The clang echoed in her ears, the barely perceptible vibration of her blade traveling down her wrist, up her elbow, and to her chest. Something about it gave her a thrill, and she felt herself smile for the first time since she'd humiliated herself at the elemental practice field.

"I am," she said.

"All right, then," Dean said, repositioning so that he stood a few feet to her left. "Nice and slow. Mimic everything I do the best you can, got it?"

He held his swords out before him, and Bree placed her own in the same basic manner.

"We're going to learn formations, as well as practice fluidly moving between these formations. We'll start with just two, nice and simple."

He pulled his right hand back while positioning his left sword before his chest so that it was parallel to the ground. Bree watched, then recreated the motion with her own arms. Dean checked, nodded in approval, and then moved to a new stance, this one with both weapons at the ready before him. Bree did the same, and she felt a strange recognition to it all. It was like flying, in a way. She was master of her body, of its positioning and movements. Total control. Perhaps fire would be beyond her, but if she could master this...

"Faster," she said as he moved back to the initial stance. "I only have a few minutes to be better than Sasha, remember?"

Dean laughed.

"Aren't you cocky," he said. "So be it. Faster we'll go."

True to his word, he began shifting stances faster, watching to see if she correctly followed. She always did, the swords growing comfortable in her hands, her body fully her own, fully in control. All but her eyes, which lingered far too long on Dean's handsome face, his shining smile. Only once did she think he noticed, but if it bothered him, he never showed it.

If anything, he smiled all the wider.

CHAPTER
10

It was their third week of elemental training, and to mark it, Instructor Kime separated them into groups.

"For now, you'll work closely with those of the same element," he said. "We're also going to start more formalized drills, but don't worry, they won't be as tedious as your other drills, I promise. It might be just me, but I think they're actually kind of fun."

Kael tried to hide his excitement when he realized what the pairing would mean. Of the nineteen, three besides Kael had ice affinity. Daniel Cloud was one, short, thin, and with darting eyes as if he expected to be attacked at any moment. Kael had tried chatting with him a few times, never getting far. The second was Saul Reigar, a man who seemed perfectly suited to ice affinity. He came from a wealthy family, and while Kael had actively gone out of his way to befriend others in his class, Saul

seemed to do the reverse, brushing aside any perceived friendliness and mentioning multiple times how he wasn't there to
make friends.

And then, of course, there was Clara...

"Looks like it'll be the four of us," Clara said, the last to join
their little circle. Despite how short she'd cut her hair, she'd
still pulled it back from her face and into a tight little knot.

"Looks like it," Kael said, feeling lame even as he said it. But
he wanted to say something, lest she think he was ignoring her.

"What do you think the new exercises will be?" she asked.

"Just more of the same," Daniel said. "That's all this place
is, more of the same. We'll learn how to shoot smaller shards
instead of bigger shards, I'd wager."

Clara stood to Kael's left, and when he saw her frown, he
shifted closer to her, painfully aware of her proximity.

"It'll be more fun than that," Kael said, and he grinned.
"After all, Kime said so, and he doesn't seem the lying type."

Saul's sarcastic chuckle showed what he thought of that, but
it made Clara smile.

"I'm not sure he's capable of telling a lie," she said. "It's a
wonder he became a Seraph."

"Certainly doesn't seem like the fighting type," Kael said.
"Maybe he smiled people to death?"

"Well, it looks like you found me out," Instructor Kime
said from behind Kael. His heart immediately stuttered, and
heat rushed to his neck and cheeks. "I saw just one battle,"
the instructor continued, "and I thought, Randy, maybe you
should just teach these wonderful children coming into the
academy instead?"

Kael turned about, feet kicking the grass as he struggled to
meet the instructor's eye.

"I'm sorry, sir," he said.

Instructor Kime patted him on the shoulder with his hand.

"I've heard far worse from experienced Seraphim," he said. "Now, here."

From a pouch strapped about his waist he pulled out four ice prisms, and he handed one to each of them before moving on to the next group. As he walked away, Kael glared at Saul, whose smug smirk was infuriating.

"Why didn't you warn me he was coming?" Kael asked.

Saul shrugged.

"And miss out on you eating your own foot?" he said. "I can't imagine why."

Kael rolled his eyes as he loaded the element into his gauntlet. From the corner of his vision, he watched as Instructor Kime approached his sister, who'd remained separate from the other two fire users.

"I'm not sure there's a point," she said as he offered her the fire prism. "It just feels like a waste."

"Your element has already been allotted," he said. "And every day is a new day, and might be the one where you finally experience a breakthrough."

Bree accepted the elemental prism with a frown. Jamming it into her gauntlet, she turned, stepped a few feet away, and then lifted her right arm. Fire exploded out of her gauntlet with such force she had to brace her legs against it while holding her arm with her other hand. The flame cloud rolled forward, and Kael winced at the sight. While the rest of the class had steadily mastered their element, Bree showed not the slightest hint of progress. The first time she'd unleashed such a blast, he'd been stunned, convinced that, as she had with flying, she'd prove herself superior. But now that Kael had more practice with ice, he saw it for what it was: the infantile flailing of someone completely unable to control her element. It was like a blind person trying to draw, or a deaf one trying to sing.

There was no hiding the defeat in Bree's voice as she removed the emptied prism and handed it back to Instructor Kime.

"Three weeks without progress," she said. "If I can't learn by now, I doubt I ever will."

Instructor Kime held his wrist stump with his other hand, and he looked so sad.

"I know you won't learn when you're convinced of failure," the instructor said.

Bree dipped her head in respect.

"I'm sorry," she said. "May I be dismissed?"

"Yes, you may."

Bree passed by him as she left, and Kael patted her shoulder in an attempt to cheer her up.

"Just give it time," he said. "And see you at lunch?"

"Sure," she said, offering him a half smile before trudging north. Kael watched her go, wishing there was something he could do. Each passing day seemed to take that much more out of his sister when it came to elemental training. She couldn't join in the new exercises or games Instructor Kime taught them. She couldn't even work at simpler tasks at the same time. Two blasts, draining both her prisms, and then done. For the first week she'd lingered about, talking with others, putting on a pleasant mask as if the failures didn't bother her. Now she didn't even try.

"Your sister's going to fail out if she doesn't improve," Saul said, interrupting his thoughts.

"Why's that?" Kael asked.

"She's a Seraph who can't use her element," he said, as if it were obvious. "What good is she to anyone?"

There was a painful amount of truth to his words. All their

formations, their exercises and drills: it was leading them toward group battle tactics. If Bree's fire was unreliable and used up within the first few seconds of battle, then she couldn't fulfill her duties. She couldn't scare off attackers. She couldn't defend her fellow Seraphim.

"She has her swords," he argued, the only weak defense he could offer.

Saul smirked.

"Yes, her swords, which she'd need to break formation and enter close proximity to use. Spare me, Kael. Your sister won't last beyond the six-month evaluation. Worry more about yourself. At least you've got a chance to stick around."

Finished with the last group, Instructor Kime stepped a few feet ahead into the field.

"Line up," he shouted. Before anyone could ask where, he lifted his gauntlet. Though he couldn't fly, given his missing left hand, he still wore wings and had his own element. With a flick of his right hand, he unleashed a blast of fire. It curled like a whip, lashing into the grass before rapidly dissipating. In its wake it left a long black line of ash and char. Saul headed for the line, Daniel at his hip. When Kael went to follow, he felt a hand gingerly touch his elbow.

"I'm sorry about your sister," Clara said. "Even if what Saul said is true, he shouldn't be so rude about it."

"He's just saying the obvious," Kael said, not sure why he was defending Saul.

"No, he's enjoying how great it feels to be superior to someone else," she said. "It's selfish and juvenile."

No bitterness in her voice, no anger, but she spoke with such authority it left Kael's jaw slack. At all their training sessions, Clara had been the happy, smiling girl without a single cruel word to say about anyone. To hear her tear apart Saul so matter-of-factly was stunning to say the least, and his surprise did not go unnoticed.

"Bugs will fly in there if you leave your mouth open long enough," she said, and her green eyes seemed to sparkle. "Now come on, we have pointy shards of ice to throw."

Together they joined the rest at the line Instructor Kime had burned. When Kael took his spot, he caught Saul staring at him from the corner of his eye, though he said nothing. Kime paced before them, calling out his instructions.

"We're going to play a game," he said. "It's one thing to fire wildly out into a field, but another to hit a moving target. This should help you learn how to gauge distances, as well as the speed of your own attacks. Pick one of your group to start with, then take turns as challengers. The person starting is to fire a burst of their element into the air, and then the challenger must try to hit the first shot with their own. If they do, swap places. Otherwise, it's time for the next challenger. Those of you with lightning affinity, we'll tweak the challenge a little, so don't fret."

Instructor Kime moved to join the five with lightning. With the rules given, Saul shrugged and gestured for them to give him space.

"I'll start," he said. "Who wants to challenge?"

"Kael does," Clara said before anyone else could speak up. Saul lifted an eyebrow as Kael shrugged.

"I guess I do," he said, stepping up to the line.

"You ready?" Saul asked as he lifted his right arm.

"If you are."

With no other warning, Saul shot a long icicle from his gauntlet, keeping its aim low to minimize its time in the air. A cheap shot for a silly game, Kael thought as he lowered his own gauntlet, but by keeping its arc so low Saul made it far easier to track and gauge distance. Letting out a low breath to steady his aim, he sent the mental impulse to his arm to fire. His fingers tensed, as did the muscles in his forearm, but he noticed with each day of training the physical reaction lessened, and he had a feeling it might one day vanish altogether. A similar shard of ice shot from his gauntlet, jerking Kael's arm back with its recoil. The sound of air tearing accompanied the shot, like a miniature cannon.

The shard flew across the field, its path just below that of Saul's. When the two shards connected, Kael pumped his fist into the air.

"Lucky shot," Saul said, stepping back from the line.

"I doubt I'll hit another all day," Kael said, grinning ear to ear. It was a lie, of course, but he had a feeling false modesty would drive Saul crazy. "Who's next?"

"I'll try," Daniel said, stepping up.

"All right," Kael said. "Let's do it."

He lifted his gauntlet, aiming a lobbing shot much higher than Saul's. He paused a moment, watching two distant chunks of stone the size of his head miss each other by a foot, then let loose the shard. Daniel tensed, eyes to the sky, and then flexed his arm. A shard of ice raced across the field, just barely missing.

"Shit," Daniel muttered.

"The height was right," Kael said, trying to be encouraging. "Little bit to the left and you had me."

"I'm next," Clara said.

Kael fired an even higher lobbing shot, purposefully easing up on its speed by pulling back his arm at the moment of firing.

Before it could even reach its full height, Clara whipped her arm up and intercepted it with her own shot. Instead of a thin shard, hers was far, far greater in size. Kael opened his mouth to protest, caught himself when he saw the amusement in her eyes.

"Kime never said what size to shoot," she said. "And it serves you right for giving me an easy one."

Kael laughed as he stepped back and gave Saul his turn. They alternated for the next half hour, each scoring multiple hits. By the time Instructor Kime joined their group, it was rare for any of them to go longer than three tries before a challenger snagged their shot.

"Good," Kime said after watching Kael blast Daniel's shard of ice into tiny clear pieces. "All of you are doing very, very well. After tracking a target so small, you'll find hitting a full-grown Seraph an easy target. Soon you'll be ready to do this while flying. For now, I want you to group in twos. Spend more time with each shot, and help critique your partner whenever you miss. Experiment with different sizes of ice, different angles, until you get a nice feel for all of them."

The instructor left them to pair up, and Kael exchanged looks with the other three. He knew exactly whom he wanted to group with, but how the hell was he going to propose it without...

"Kael, care to be my partner?" Clara asked.

Kael blinked.

"I'd love to," he said. Surprise was the only thing that kept an idiotic smile off his face.

"Are you sure about that?" Saul asked, and he stepped between her and Kael. "He's worse than I am at ice. I'd be happy to help you learn instead."

Clara smiled at him so sweetly, there wasn't a hint of her earlier private thoughts she'd shared with Kael.

"Come now, Saul, act like that and you're bound to hurt Daniel's feelings."

The wiry Seraph stayed back from the other three, and he shrugged when eyes turned his way.

"Anyone's fine with me," he said, mumbling.

"See?" Clara said. "So we'll go over there," she gestured to the side, "and you two stay here, that way no one's interrupting or interfering with the other."

Saul's face hardened as if into stone, but he did not argue. Clara hurried farther down the firing line Instructor Kime had burned into the grass. Kael moved to follow, but Saul grabbed the sleeve of his jacket and held him still.

"You should really trade partners with me," he said, a hard edge to his voice. Kael pulled free, his own stubbornness rising.

"Worry more about yourself," he said, echoing Saul's earlier words. Putting his back to him, he hurried over to Clara, who was preparing to release a lance of ice. She lifted her gauntlet, a thin shimmer of blue growing from the firing prism.

"He tried convincing you to switch anyway, didn't he?" Clara asked. Kael nodded. "I thought he would. Just like his type."

Pieces clicked together in Kael's head.

"You're doing this to annoy him," he said. "So why me over Daniel?"

Clara turned his way and feigned a gasp, her gauntleted fist closing to seal away the unfired ice element.

"I would never," she said. "I'm just a clueless little princess who lucked her way into the academy. But if I *were* to do something like that, I'd have picked you over Daniel because Daniel would have caved to Saul's pressure. That, and you seem like a nice enough fellow. Am I right?"

"I have no idea," Kael said, lifting his own gauntlet. "But I'm more than happy to be with you. Practicing, of course."

Kael silently begged she didn't notice his awkward flub as he shot a shard of ice into the air.

"Of course," Clara said, grinning mischievously as she blasted his shard to pieces, grinning as, across the field, Saul watched and glared.

CHAPTER
11

Do you know what he wants?" Kael asked Bree as the two walked the dirt road toward the elemental practice field. Bree had donned her wings and obtained an element from the mechanics, per Instructor Kime's request.

"My guess would be another attempt at fixing my problem with fire," she said. "A trick or gimmick, most likely. Did you see me shooting fire while standing on my head yesterday? It was humiliating."

"It wasn't that bad," Kael said. Bree glared at him.

"Oh, it wasn't?" she asked. "So the snickers I heard, all in my imagination?"

"I just said it wasn't that bad," Kael said, shrugging. "Not that no one laughed. So what if a few did? Grab a sword and challenge them to a duel. That'll shut them up quick."

Bree smiled and elbowed her brother in the side. "If only

it were that easy," she said. "So, you going to stay and watch Instructor Kime's latest attempt at fixing the unfixable?"

To Bree's surprise, her brother blushed.

"Actually, if you don't mind, I've got somewhere to be."

She raised an eyebrow at him. Their classes were over, as were their drills. The two had exited the mess hall after eating supper prior to Bree grabbing her wings from the shed, which left them only an hour or so before dark began to fall. For him to be embarrassed about how he was to fill his free time narrowed the possibilities significantly.

"Is Clara waiting for you?" she asked, a grin spreading ear to ear on her face. Kael's blush brightened.

"Teacher Gaughran's tactics test tomorrow," he admitted. "Clara was wondering if I'd study with her."

Bree paused a step and gestured back toward the apartments.

"Well, why the hell are you with me, then?" she asked. "Go. Have fun. I'll be out here throwing fire with my eyes closed and counting backward from one hundred or something."

"Hey, if it works, it works," Kael said, and he waved. "Good luck, Bree. I'll see you tomorrow."

He jogged off, leaving Bree alone. Since she didn't have her brother tagging along, she powered on her wings, taking pleasure in the deep thrumming sound they made. She lifted into the air, flying the remaining distance at a gentle pace. She didn't need to soar, only wished to feel the wind through her hair and leave the weight of her body momentarily.

Instructor Kime stood alone in the practice field, and Bree gently eased the throttle so she might land beside him. The sandy-haired man smiled at her and patted his left arm's stump of bone into his palm. He, too, wore his wings and gauntlet.

"I'm so happy you're here," he said. "I was worried you'd forgotten about me, and I'd be standing out here alone until night fell."

"Never," Bree said, smiling.

"Good, that's good, because I've something special for you to try tonight. Follow me."

He led her to the firing line he'd burned weeks ago. Bree overlooked the training field, which after a month of abuse was mostly blackened dirt, much of it uneven due to ice and stone constantly slamming into it day after day. Though the elements themselves faded away into mist, the same could not be said for the damage they caused.

"This might seem strange," he said, "but I'm going to try something that I don't usually have students work on until their second year."

"I can't do the absolute basics, so we're going to try second-year skills instead?" Bree asked. "You're right, Instructor, it does seem strange."

"Randy is fine," he said, and his optimism was unfazed by her doubts. "It's just you and me, and right now, I want you as relaxed as possible. You see, I wonder if, despite focusing so much on controlling your element, you are simply in the wrong mind-set to do so." Instructor Kime took her right gauntlet in his hand and lifted it up. "Spread your palm wide. Don't worry about the size of the burst. That's for later. For now, I want you to *imagine* the fire exiting your gauntlet as a solid spear of flame."

"Imagine?" Bree asked, frowning.

"Yes, yes, imagine," Randy said, bobbing his head as if excited by his own creativity. "Do you remember when I said how this connection between prism and Seraph is magical? I wasn't exaggerating. There is something truly special there, something we don't much understand. What I do understand, and what I want you to now understand, is that it goes beyond just activating the element so it might release. Your mind, if trained and focused, may manipulate the element into a great variety of shapes beyond the simple variations achievable by widening and closing the focal point."

To illustrate his point, he stretched his arm, palm open and facing the battered field. A burst of fire shot out. Instead of in a spray, or a quicker, tighter projectile, it widened out in a rectangular wall, growing for dozens of feet before becoming so thin it dissipated in a puff of black smoke.

"This manipulation is difficult," Randy said, turning back to her. "General consensus at the academy has always been to ensure Seraphim learn the basics of elemental manipulation before moving on to this, but right now you're floundering in the dark, Bree, so I'm willing to do all I can to shed a bit of light."

Bree tried to wrap her head around this new idea. Her imagination could shape it, control it, not just release it from her gauntlet? Part of her wanted to be excited, but part of her was afraid to get her hopes up after a solid month of failure.

"This is fascinating, it truly is, but I don't see how this helps." Bree frowned and looked away. "When the fire pours out of me, I feel...helpless. Completely lacking in control."

Randy stepped closer, and he held her wrist and aimed it at the field.

"You have a natural affinity to fire, Bree, one that your entry tests described as unprecedented. But all that is irrelevant if you do not work at it, learning how to use that potential. A hawk may have eyes better than my own, but it matters not if it never opens them. Should you ever make that connection and learn to harness the fire in your prism, you'll be a truly wonderful sight. Now, let's see if we can trick your mind. Imagine the fire releasing as a spear, and then when you see it happen, imagine it stopping. My hope is, through such persuasion, you will gain a feel for how to control the element instead of blindly activating it, then failing to halt it until the prism is completely spent."

Bree swallowed her frustration and worry. Out here, alone and with dark approaching, she felt so much more vulnerable than with her classmates surrounding her. If this failed, there'd be no shrugging it off, no acting like it was no big thing. Instructor Kime would see through it in a heartbeat.

That and, more than anything, she wished him to be right.

"Imagine," she whispered as she breathed in and out. Instructor Kime stepped away to give her space. Focusing her concentration on the prism connected to the gauntlet, she imagined a spear of flame bursting from the palm of her gauntlet. While she hadn't made much progress, the one thing Bree had gotten better at was activating the fire ability on demand. The moment she imagined the spear, she made the mental connection, willing the fire to release. Like all previous attempts before, she felt a crack in her mind, but for once, something was different.

Fire gathered at her gauntlet, then burst outward. Exactly as she'd imagined it, it came forth as a spear, except unlike in her imagination, it lacked a defined end. The spear arced across the field in a narrow beam, crossing several hundred yards before striking dirt. Bree tightened the muscles of her hand and arm, her teeth clenched tight. For once, she felt a connection, however vague. Her fire…she could detect it, just like Instructor Kime insisted. She sensed it in the space before her, sensed the release of power draining from her prism.

The problem was, she still had no control. Less than a second after release, she felt the fire growing from a narrow beam to a tremendous, wide explosion. Concentrating as hard as possible, Bree tried to keep it together, to force it back to a beam, but it was like scattering rocks into the air and then demanding they remain still. There was nothing for her to focus on, nothing to keep the fire restrained. The fire burst wider, harder, and she screamed as she felt her energy draining with it. It was as if she couldn't control her own arm, and she had to brace her legs to withstand the force of the release.

The fire ceased, the prism drained in less than five seconds.

"Damn it!" Bree screamed, dropping to her knees and slamming the gauntlet into the dying grass. She gasped in air, feeling completely out of breath. Why was it so hard? Why must she be so incompetent at what everyone else grasped on their first day? And to feel like there'd been a chance of improving, only to have it yanked away, made it that much worse. She caught Instructor Kime looking down at her, and she started to apologize, then stopped. She'd expected pity in his eyes. Instead she saw hope.

"That was wonderful," he said. "Truly wonderful."

If there'd ever been a time Bree had felt more baffled, she couldn't remember it.

"How?" she asked. "I lost control like I always do."

Randy knelt beside her, and his smile was nearly ear to ear.

"But I also saw the spear," he said. "For four weeks you've made no progress, but today I saw your first true step forward. No matter how tiny, a first step is still a first step. This means you'll make another, and then another. I don't care how much time it takes, Breanna, but I assure you, one day we will have you walking."

Bree felt her insides being torn. Part of her wanted to believe him so badly, to think she might one day zip through the skies with bursts of flame roaring from her palm. Another part of her, a part fed by a month of failure, refused to believe such a thing might ever happen. Today was a fluke, and nothing more. Most frightening of all was her belief that another attempt would reveal the truth: that she'd learned nothing, gained nothing, and never would.

"Are you up for another try?" Randy asked, and he offered her a hand. She took it and stood, unable to meet his eye.

"Not for a bit," she said. "Doing…that always leaves me tired."

The instructor nodded, seeming to understand.

"I've talked with Headmaster Simmons," he said. "He's agreed to increase your daily allocation from two prisms to four, if you're willing to put in the extra time. I'd still like you to attend my training sessions, listen to my lessons, and give your best effort. Come before training, or after, like tonight, and see if you can master your element. Will you do that, Bree?"

Every training session with fire element left her drained, and she thought of doing more immediately following her morning jog with Brad and Kael. The prospect was exhaustion, as was coming in late, when her body was sore from spending hours in the skies twisting and turning to complete Instructor Dohn's drills. To do it twice, along with Randy's own practices…

"Baby steps," Bree whispered, then stood up straight and thudded her fist against her chest in salute to her instructor. "If this is what it takes, then yes, I will."

Randy smiled at her, and then tapped the stump of his hand against his palm again.

"Don't let this get you down," he said. "You'll make us all proud one day, Bree, I promise."

Bree opened the cover on her right gauntlet, removing the blackened, expended prism. She handed it to Instructor Kime, then glanced at the charred crater where her spear of fire had slammed the ground.

"I pray you're right," she said softly, swearing one day to leave the training field with her elemental prism intact, instead of dark, clouded, and broken.

CHAPTER 12

Bree took her seat beside Brad at the lunch table, having grabbed only an apple from the front. She felt too exhausted for anything else. Brad, who had a massive plate of potatoes slathered with butter and steamed vegetables, gave her a frown.

"That's all?" he asked.

"That's all," Bree said, biting into her apple. "I'll be heading back to the practice course after eating. The last thing I want to do is vomit a bunch of potatoes while flying."

"You're making a mistake," he said.

"How so?"

"Have you ever thrown up apples before? They taste terrible coming back up. Potatoes are way better."

"The point was to prevent throwing up, Brad, not make it easier when I do."

The mess hall was full of students from all years, the lunch hour rush just starting to pick up. Because of it, they'd had to find a table all the way in the corner. Bree caught Kael wandering near the middle of the enormous room, searching for them, and she stood and waved once so he could join them. Kael sat opposite her, and he, too, had a plate filled with potatoes and mixed greens.

"See, this guy knows how to eat," Brad said, pointing.

"I don't think anyone here can challenge you in knowledge of eating," Kael said.

"Hey, now," Brad said, leaning back so he could smack his stomach. "The pounds are dropping like mad from this here belly. Even Instructor Dohn's noticed, though I swear it just pisses him off even more."

"Yeah, because he knows he'll be stuck with you," Kael said, and he flung a tiny piece of broccoli across the table, aiming for the stomach Brad had so proudly patted. His cheer was the polar opposite of Bree's sour mood. For nearly two weeks she'd snuck off to the training fields both morning and night to make yet another attempt at mastering her fire. So far, no matter how basic or exotic the shape, each try went the same. The fire would erupt, it'd vaguely resemble her desired effect, and then it would continue outward, wild, untamed, uncontrolled, a reckless explosion that lasted until her prism was completely drained. The toll was wearing on her, and it seemed she suffered a headache at all times.

"I take it training went well?" she asked Kael, deciding that needling her brother might improve her mood.

"Went great," he said, shoving a forkful of potato into his mouth as if that might spare him from clarifying further. Not that Bree needed him to elaborate. Nearly every single day over the last few weeks he'd been paired with Clara at practice, and even a blind dog could have seen how badly he was starting to crush on her.

"The practice, or the flirting?" she asked, earning the desired blush. She laughed, but before she could rib him further, she saw Kael glance over her shoulder, and his body immediately tensed. Bree frowned, confused, and then turned to see a group of three heading their way. Saul Reigar was one of them, but the other two she didn't recognize. Both appeared to be much older students, one tall and dark-skinned, the other with the same dirty blond hair and square jaw as Saul.

"These seats taken?" the one who looked like Saul asked. Bree glanced at Kael, who had put on an emotionless mask.

"Nah, they're free," her brother said.

Bree scooted over as Saul sat next to her, the other two setting down plates beside Kael.

"I don't think we've met," the man continued. "I'm Saul's brother, Jason. It's good to meet you two. Believe it or not, I've heard plenty about you twins."

Jason offered his hand, and Kael shook it. When he shook with Bree, she noticed how firm it was, how forceful. Dominant. Her mood soured even more, and she couldn't shake the awkward mood that had descended upon the entire table. Only Jason seemed jovial, his grin ear to ear.

"Hopefully it's been all positive," Kael said, eyes focused on his plate, as if eating was suddenly the most important thing in the world to him.

"Mostly," Jason said, and the way he glanced at Bree, a gleam of mockery in his eye, made her stomach sick. This wasn't good, not at all, but what did they want?

"So you're an ice thrower, just like my brother," Jason continued. "Been having fun training? Saul told me you're the lucky son of a bitch who always gets to practice with Clara Willer."

Bree's sick stomach suddenly felt a whole lot tighter. Clara...

this was about Clara? If so, then things were about to get far uglier.

"Yeah," Kael said, eyes still on his food. "It's no big thing."

"No big thing?" said the man beside Jason. "She's Isaac Willer's daughter. Royalty, man, she's like a princess. Might even be Archon one day. Aren't you having fun throwing ice around her? Don't be telling lies."

By now Brad had figured it out as well, and he tried inserting himself into the discussion in an attempt to defuse the growing tension.

"Throwing ice doesn't seem that much fun to me," he said. "Hurling boulders the size of a man's body? That's where the fun is."

The other three laughed, the only acknowledgment they gave him.

"So, tell me more about you," Jason said. "Your family. Where you live. What you do."

"They're farmers," Saul said. "Just poor dirt farmers."

"Something wrong with being a farmer?" Kael asked, finally willing to confront the older student.

"Not at all," said Jason. He put an arm around Kael, gripping his shoulder. The act looked comforting, but Bree could see how tense it made her brother, how uncomfortable. "It just makes me wonder what a poor farmer might have in common with royalty."

"They're both Seraphs," Bree interjected. "Is that not enough?"

Jason squeezed Kael tighter, completely dwarfing him.

"Maybe, maybe," he said, staring down at Kael as if daring him to meet his eye. "Still, my little brother here thinks it's about time you give it a rest. A poor little dirt farmer shouldn't be spending so much time with royalty, you know what I'm saying? So starting tomorrow, pair up with someone else instead, and let Saul be the one with Clara."

Bree glanced at Saul, and she was surprised by how uncomfortable he looked. Jason was clearly the one in charge. Question was, how far would he go?

"If you have a problem with the pairings, Instructor Kime's over there in the corner," Kael said, carefully measuring every word. "If you have an issue with who Clara spends her time with, go tell her yourself...or are you worried she won't be scared of your veiled threats?"

Jason's grin seemed to be all teeth, belying his lighthearted words.

"Threats?" he said. "No threats here, none at all. It's called advice. Nothing wrong with advice, right? And I'm thinking it's a good idea for you to find other people to train with. Think of it as a lesson in learning your place. Don't you think that's a good idea, Alex?"

"I do," said the muscular man beside him. "I think that's a great idea."

"See, a great idea," Jason continued. "We may all be Seraphim, but we still need to know our place. A piece of shit like you doesn't belong next to an Archon's daughter. Someone like my brother does. You got that, Kael?"

Before Kael could answer, Bree stood from the table.

"I should return to practice," she said, though she had no such plans. Kael had mentioned where Instructor Kime sat, and she had every intention of going to him for help.

"Taking a few more runs at elemental training?" Jason asked, but the mockery in his tone and the sickness in his grin, told her he already knew the answer.

"She's not much for elemental training," Saul chipped in. "Flying's more her thing."

"Oh, that's right, I heard about her...issue." Again that nauseating grin. "One-shot Bree. I think you're in the running to be the worst elemental student this school's ever seen."

Bree froze, every muscle in her body tightening. Jason's grin faded and was replaced by something hard. Something eager.

"What's wrong, Bree?" he asked. "Can't take a little good-natured ribbing?"

Clenching her jaw hard enough to hurt, she shook her head. *Walk away,* she told herself. No reason to let them rile her further. As she left the table, heading toward Kime's corner, she heard Jason start laughing.

"With how fast you blow your load, be glad things aren't worse," he called after her. "You could have been born a man."

Her neck flushed red. From the corners of her eyes she saw people watching her, heard their laughter. Many didn't even bother trying to hide it. Was that what they thought of her, even her own classmates? It felt like the entire mess hall was staring at her, and part of her wanted to shrivel into a ball and vanish. Humiliated, she turned instead toward the trash buckets set near the sinks. At the buckets, she paused, her half-eaten apple still in hand. A broom lay propped against the wall to her left. Trying not to think, she walked over to it and grabbed the handle. Twirling it once with her fingers, she started back toward her table, apple still in her other hand.

Jason and Alex had risen to their feet, preparing to leave. Still smiling, still feigning friendliness. Both their backs were to her, and as she closed in, she flung her apple.

"What the hell?" Jason said as the apple connected with the side of his head. He turned, a hand clutching his ear, and that's when Bree swung the broom handle, cracking him across the mouth. Blood splattered from his busted lip. Before he could react, she struck his right knee hard enough to drop him. Alex swore as he swung a meaty fist for her face. Bree ducked underneath, spun two steps to gain space between them, and then came out of the spin with the broom handle lashing outward. The bottom cracked Alex across the forehead, just above his left eye. Alex grabbed at the swelling bruise while stumbling into the table.

Bree heard people calling her name, but she blocked it out. Saul was coming around the table, running as fast as he could given the little distance he had to gain speed. Taking her makeshift weapon in both hands, she thrust it outward, just like she would with her sword. The rounded top jammed into his stomach, and she saw the surprise in his eyes as he suddenly halted, the air blasted out of his lungs.

A fist struck her across the face. Hands reached for her. Rolling with the blow, Bree came back up swinging at her attacker, catching Jason yet again in the face. By now Alex had regained his footing, and he rushed around the table while flinging his plate. Unable to dodge, Bree cried out as it struck her chest. Staggering, she avoided Jason's first punch, felt the second hit her stomach. He moved to take the wooden handle from her, but she stopped that attempt by flinging the broom straight up and into his crotch.

It seemed the selective silence that had enveloped her faded, and the noise of the rest of the mess hall came flooding in. Students were grabbing Bree's arms, pulling her from the other three. Kael and Brad stood between her, Saul, and Alex, pushing them away when they tried to continue after her. As instructors came rushing in, shouting over the chaos, Bree felt herself being led away.

"Still glad *you* were born a man?" Bree screamed at Jason, who knelt surrounded by students, one hand clutching his crotch. Blood dripped from his lip, one of his eyes was blood-shot, and already purple welts grew on his face.

"Fuck you, Bree," Jason shot back, and Bree took immense satisfaction in those muffled, pained words.

After two hours of waiting, Bree entered into the headmaster's office. The room was small, the walls covered with paintings of forests, rivers, and waterfalls. Behind Jay Simmons's desk were plaques and medals showcasing his long, storied career in Weshern's Seraphim. His desk was empty but for a single sheet of paper, on which he'd scrawled a massive list of notes. An empty chair waited before the desk. The headmaster nodded to the Seraph who'd escorted her in, and the man bowed in respect before leaving, shutting the thick door behind her.

"Have a seat, Breanna," Jay said in his deep, commanding voice.

She did so. The chair creaked as she leaned back, and that noise felt thunderous in the tiny room. The headmaster glanced over his notes for a few long seconds, then crossed his hands and set them on his desk. His brown eyes looked into hers, and as much as she tried, she could read nothing in them to help her out. He opened his mouth to say something, seemed to reconsider, then shook his head and let out a long sigh.

"Assaulting three of your fellow students with a broom?" he asked. "What the hell were you thinking?"

Despite knowing better, she couldn't help it.

"That I would lose if I just used my fists," Bree said, then added, "sir."

The headmaster exhaled loudly through his nose.

"Now is not the time for joking," he said, leaning back in his chair. "Confrontations between Seraphs are hardly rare, but I am not going to turn a blind eye to such a ridiculous brawl in the middle of the mess hall. You, and all your fellow students, are here to become disciplined soldiers, not wild animals biting at each other for every little insult."

Bree looked to her feet, trying to fight down the steadily growing guilt she'd felt over the past hours.

"Have you talked with the others?" she asked.

"I have. I've spoken with the three you fought, plus your brother, Bradford Macon, and your instructors. I've gone over your introductory evaluations, your attendance records, and even your initial affinity tests. The result is a picture that is far from flattering for one with such promise."

"If you talked with everyone, then you know I gave those three what they deserved."

"Did you, now?" The headmaster crossed his arms over his chest. "Perhaps you think so. Believe it or not, Jason told me the reason for the fight. Seraphim don't lie, and he knows I'd have expelled him the moment I caught him in one. I know why he came to your table. I know of his disapproval of Clara Willer's association with your brother." He hunched closer, his voice dropping in volume. "Breanna, I know you thought you were helping Kael, but he needs to be the one to handle this. Having you protect him makes him look weak and unable to defend himself. That's a difficult position for anyone to be in, one you've now made worse."

"You're wrong."

His brow furrowed.

"I assure you, I've witnessed this sort of group dynamic many times over the years."

"No," Bree said, finally looking up and meeting his gaze. "About why I did it. It's not because of Kael. I did it because they insulted *me*."

Jay leaned back as if he'd been slapped in the face. Bree felt her anger growing. Of course he'd thought it'd been about Kael. His entire investigation was based around the idea that she'd lashed out to defend her brother's honor. But now he looked down to his notes and softly grunted.

"What you shouted to Jason as you were taken from the mess hall," he asked. "Was that in relation to the insult?" She nodded. "What is it he said?"

Bree felt embarrassed to repeat it, and she looked back to her feet.

"That it was a good thing I wasn't born a man," she said. "Because I... because I'd blow my load too fast."

The headmaster's fingers tapped against the sheet of paper before him.

"This referenced your difficulties with flame element, correct?"

Again she nodded. Jay fell silent, and Bree waited, tired, bruised, and wishing she could go to her room and hide from the world. Would he expel her for this? Take away her ability to train? The idea of losing access to her wings, of spending her life grounded, filled her with such terror she thought she might leap off the edge of Weshern instead. There was nothing she could do. Feeling thoroughly helpless, she waited for the headmaster to condemn her.

"My talks with your instructors were very interesting," he said, his deliberations seemingly over. "Instructor Dohn was glowing in praise, at least in his own way. You're often bored due to a lack of challenge, and your times on the obstacle course have already surpassed those of many second-year students. Yes, I know about your constant runs, Bree, and have even watched you myself. In some aspects, you have more potential than any recruit I've seen in a very long time. But then I talk with Instructor Kime..."

He shook his head.

"Your tests at Center showed the strongest fire affinity Weshern has ever had in a Seraph. Yet you have no control. No restraint. It's such a disappointment."

Such a disappointment.

The words stabbed into Bree. Was that all she was? One giant disappointment because of her fire element?

"I've tried," Bree said. "Every day I try, far more than anyone else. It's not my fault that no matter what I do, no matter what Instructor Kime has me try, nothing works."

"You sound as if you've given up hope."

The stress of the day was too much. Bree wiped at her eyes, banishing the betraying hints of tears, and then faced the headmaster.

"No," she said. "But I'm close."

The headmaster rubbed his upper lip with his forefinger as he stared at her, thinking.

"To bully your brother, and then insult your own skills in such a crude manner, has those three boys crossing the line," Jay said. "But while they may have stepped over the line, you went sprinting past it like a madwoman. Without considering a single alternative, you immediately resorted to violence. No matter what they said to you, can you accept your fault in that regard?"

She nodded weakly.

"Good. You'll be punished, and more severely than the other three, but I won't have you expelled. I've turned the most troublesome students into fine warriors for Weshern, and I'm not ready to give up on you, either. You'll be given a heavy allotment of manual labor around the academy, though none of it will interfere with your classes and training. We'll start with the execution tomorrow. You'll be in charge of the burial afterward. Miss Waller will give you the information you need as to where and when."

Bree tried to hide her relief. She'd accept any punishment so long as she didn't lose her access to the skies.

"Thank you, Headmaster," she said, rising from her seat. "Am I excused?"

"Not yet," Jay said as he also stood, smoothing out his shirt and jacket before opening the door to his office for her. "Bree, don't be surprised if the attitude of certain students turns a lot colder toward you. I'll do my best to ensure you suffer no retaliation, but I cannot be everywhere at all times."

"I'm not afraid of them," she said, standing tall.

"Are you afraid of anything?"

She swallowed.

"Just the ground," she said, then shut the door behind her.

CHAPTER 13

You don't have to be here," Bree told him, but Kael shook his head. They were in the center of a throng of people gathered for the execution held in an expansive field of grass. The morning was young, and hot, and the men and women on all sides did little to help as Kael wiped away beads of sweat from his forehead. Thin clouds drifted above, and Kael wished they could have been puffier, thereby offering a far better respite from the sun. For him, winter couldn't arrive fast enough.

"Maybe not," he said. "But I'm here anyway. Least you could do is appreciate it."

Bree rolled her eyes as the murmurs around them increased. They'd come from all across Weshern, the people eager to witness the execution. Kael had only gone with Aunt Bethy once to see an execution several years before. It'd been a long, boring affair, and only sparsely attended. This time, though? The atmosphere was electric, this crowd ten times the size, and he wondered what might be the cause.

"How many today?" he asked Bree, leaning closer so she'd more easily hear him.

"Just one."

"Lots of people here for just one."

Bree shook her head.

"This one's different. Listen to how they talk."

Kael did just that, and there was an undeniable anger rumbling throughout the crowd. The field they stood in was just off the main road leading from the Seraphim training grounds to the heart of Weshern. Even now, more people came walking, jogging, and riding carts from the city. Kael crossed his arms, wondering how long until the Seraphim finally arrived with the prisoner. Beside him, Bree stood on her tiptoes, then plopped back down to her heels.

"I won't see from here," she said, and without waiting for him, she began pushing through the crowd toward the front.

"Bree!"

She didn't stop, and muttering curses, he began pushing after her, offering apologies to everyone he bumped. Some glared, some cursed him right back. Feeling his neck flush midnight red, he rejoined Bree, now at the innermost ring. The crowd was formed into circles around a well, halted by thin stones shin-high that had been laid down hundreds of years before. Kael stared at the well, feeling mildly uncomfortable. Bree would be the one in charge of filling it with dirt once the execution was done, and the body dropped within.

"I hope beating the snot out of those three was worth it," he muttered.

Bree shot him a wink, a smile tugging at the left side of her mouth.

"Trust me," she said. "It was."

Despite the heat, he laughed.

Time trickled along, and Kael spent it listening in on the men and women on either side of him.

"Things haven't been this bad since the ghost plague," said an old man beside him. Kael turned, confused.

"The ghost plague?" Kael asked, frowning. The old man shook his head.

"Before your time, young one," he said. "Best you not worry about the past."

The man pointedly put his back to him, frustrating Kael to no end. He hated when adults treated him like such a child. He was sixteen, and a member of the Seraphim. Surely he deserved better than that. A tug on his sleeve turned him back to his sister, who was pointing upward.

"They're here," she said.

From the sky came four men. One was a theotech, held aloft with a thin set of gold wings. His red robes flapped in the wind as he landed in the open space left for him around the well. Clutched to his chest was a leather-bound tome, which he immediately opened. Above him remained two angelic knights, come with the theotech from Center to aid in the execution. Their gold armor was finely polished, shining brightly in the morning light. What little he saw of their tunics underneath was startling white. Last, hanging from two separate chains clamped to each of his wrists, was the prisoner.

"It's Thane," Kael said, recognizing the ratty-looking man with short black hair stuck to his face with sweat. Naked from the waist up, his body was thin, his skin bruised in multiple places. "The disciple of Johan who approached me in the field after the affinity tests."

"And that's what they'll kill him for?" Bree asked, eyes locked on the prisoner. "Simple words and pamphlets?"

"It seems they will," Kael said.

"I hope it was worth it, then," Bree said, frowning. "Johan must have Center terrified."

Johan, Kael thought, and he chewed on the inside of his lower lip. Whoever this Johan was, he must carry a powerful presence to convince so many people to turn against Center and her theotechs, especially with the severe penalty awaiting those who committed such heresy.

"Why aren't our Seraphim holding the chains?" Kael asked. It seemed odd that Thane had been captured in Weshern, yet two knights from Center had flown over to aid in the execution.

"Thane's not from Weshern," she answered. "That means he's not ours to kill."

"If *they're* killing him, why are *we* burying him afterward?"

"A theotech and his angelic knights dirty their hands?" she said. "What world do you live in, Kael?"

"Apparently not one where people clean up their own messes."

As the rumble of the crowd rose in volume, the two knights lowered the prisoner until he hovered just above the stone well. Despite his impending fate, Thane showed no fear, nor did he keep his eyes to the ground. Instead he stared at the people with a strength that Kael found fascinating.

"People of Weshern," the theotech shouted, holding his leather book up before him and clearly reading from a prepared script. Immediately the crowd quieted. "This man has spoken heresy in the eyes of our Lord, promoted treason against the Speaker, and attempted to stir rebellion amongst the people of your holy island. He is a vile criminal, and fully unrepentant of his crimes. For this, your Archon, Isaac Willer, has asked us to deliver a sentence of death. As a representative of Center, I come to tell you that we accept this request."

So far the prisoner remained silent, challenging none of the claims. The theotech turned, now directly addressing him.

"Thane Ackels of Elern, you have been sentenced to death. In the rock of our land, you will be broken. In the dirt, you will be consumed. In our fields, you will be made anew, granting life where you once brought death. Have you any last words?"

Thane looked to the crowd, and at first Kael thought he would go to his grave without protest. He was sorely mistaken.

"Slaves of Weshern!" Thane screamed, with a voice that surely could not be coming from such a starved, beaten body. "Open your eyes and witness the masters who hold your chains! Already you bow before the Speaker and his dogs, but the time approaches when that will not save you. His armies come! His knights will soar across a bloodred sky, descending upon you with swords, thunder, and fire. In the name of God and his angels, you will be butchered like the sheep that you are!"

The reaction from the crowd was swift and vicious. People cursed him, calling him dozens of names, not one of which Kael would feel comfortable repeating in Aunt Bethy's presence. The theotech frowned, and he motioned for the knights to begin the process. Steadily the two lifted, carefully rising equal with the other so that Thane remained centered over the well's opening. Upon hearing the theotech's order, the two would release their chains. Thane would fall into the well, out of sight from the people, and land on the stone floor six feet belowground. His body would be crushed by the fall, then covered with dirt so that the well was ready for the next execution, whenever it might be.

Given Thane's feverish intensity, Kael feared it might be much sooner than normal. The man pulled on his chains as the knights lifted him, fighting even when facing certain death. Higher and higher they rose, at least thirty feet up by Kael's best guess.

"We are the disciples of Johan!" Thane screamed. "We are the eyes with the bravery to see, the tongues with the courage to speak, the hands with the strength to act. Your freedom is an illusion. Your independence is a lie. The time comes, Weshern, the time comes. Will you lie down and die?"

At fifty feet, the mandated height of all executions, the knights stopped. The strong men looked down to the theotech, waiting for the final signal. The crowd's anger dipped, seeming to collectively hold its breath at the impending drop. The theotech's right arm lifted. Still Thane struggled. Still he cried out.

"The only will that leaves the Speaker's tongue is his own. God is not with him. Open your eyes, damn fools, open your—"

The theotech's right arm dropped, and so did Thane. Kael's eyes widened, immediately sensing something was wrong. Distracted by Thane's screaming, and fighting to control his flailing movements, the knights had not released their chains simultaneously. The delay wasn't much, just a half second at most, but it was enough to cause Thane's body to swing slightly to one side, and that movement continued as he fell, rotating him through the air.

The aim was off. Thane's body was sideways. Instead of disappearing down the well to die unseen, Thane struck the stone lip with his waist. His body folded immediately as if made of cloth. Momentum continuing, his upper body whipped downward, head propelled toward the side of the well. Kael looked away just before impact, but though he could shut his eyes, he couldn't prevent his ears from hearing the sound, like that of a melon breaking open. When he recovered the strength to look, it seemed the broken mess that had been Thane had slid down the well, vanishing from sight. Kael thanked God for small mercies.

"Wonderful," the theotech grumbled as the two knights drifted to the ground. All around, Kael heard the crowd gasping in shock, some even turning to vomit. He didn't blame them, either. The contents of Thane's head were spilled across the grass beside the well, with a wide splatter of blood painting the stone side. Kael still couldn't get the sound of the breaking bones to stop echoing in his head. Kael turned to his sister, trying to block out the repeating images of the death. Mere moments before it'd all been so impersonal, the vanishing of a life he'd met only briefly. Now he saw the blood upon the stone, saw the shovel waiting for him and Bree beside the well, and he couldn't shake a sudden queasiness gripping his stomach.

"You all right?" he asked, turning to Bree. His sister stared straight ahead, her face a stone mask. If not for the twitching of her cheeks and trembling of her lips, she could have passed for a statue. When she didn't respond, he grabbed her shoulder, and she startled.

"Sorry," she said. "What is it?"

"Just wondering if you're all right," Kael said, frowning at her. "Did you watch the whole thing?"

Bree pulled free of his grasp.

"I did," she said. "And I'll be fine."

Nearby the knights tried to explain what had happened to the theotech, their words drowned out by the din of people angrily shouting at being forced to witness such a gruesome display. The whole atmosphere was uncomfortable, but other than show impotent anger, there wasn't much the crowd could do. Kael and Bree remained where they were as the people began to disperse. A few lingered behind, shouting to the theo-tech in case he'd listen, which he never did. His back remained to the crowd at all times, his focus only on the knights and their bungled execution.

"I guess we should get started," Bree said, reluctantly approaching the well. Beside the shovel was a bucket of water and a large rag. Kael followed his sister across the thin stone markers, doing his best to keep his eyes ahead instead of on the arguing trio. One of the knights caught him staring anyway, and his glare was chilling.

"So do we just toss dirt in the well until he's covered?" he asked as Bree grabbed the shovel and stuffed the rag into her back pocket. A morbid part of him wanted to look down the well and see the remains, but the moment he felt the impulse, shock and repulsion slapped it down.

"That's a start. I also need to get rid of"—she gestured to the smear of gore—"this . . . and then clean the sides of the well."

She jammed the shovel into the dirt beside the well, where the brain matter had pooled together. It jiggled atop the metal, and Kael spun aside and clenched his jaw tight to fight back a sudden need to vomit. His back to the well, he watched knights and theotech fly off into the air, the theotech still berating them. He heard the shifting of the shovel, a thud of wood hitting stone, and he assumed it was safe to turn about.

"You don't have to stay," Bree said, eyes to the ground as she worked.

His neck reddened, Kael embarrassed by how weak he seemed compared to his sister. Multiple times he wanted to vomit, yet she kept right on going. The bruise to his pride added a bite to his words he never intended.

"Sorry," he said. "Just give me a moment for my stomach to settle. Not everyone's made of stone like you."

Kael was not prepared for the anger in Bree's eyes when she looked up and glared.

"I'll be fine without you," she said. "Just go home, Kael."

The casual dismissal only further upset him. He reached for her shovel and grabbed the handle.

"Stop being so cold," he said. "I'm not buying it for a second."

"You know me that well, do you?" she asked, staring him in the eye. "Then you should know you're pissing me off."

"Good. At least it's a reaction."

She tried pulling the shovel from his grasp, but he held on tight. When that failed, she let go and slammed her foot into the bucket, knocking it over.

"What?" she asked, nearly screaming. "What do you want from me?"

"I want you to stop acting like this is normal. You're scooping up a man's brains with a shovel, for God's sake. At least don't be pissed at me for being upset. So what that you watched him hit ground and I didn't? It doesn't mean shit."

She flung an arm in the direction of the well.

"You think I wanted to watch that?" she asked. "You think I *want* that sight giving me nightmares for weeks?"

Kael took a step back, his temper starting to subside. His sister's tone... he could read it well, and the sudden hurt leaking into her voice convinced him he was missing something obvious, something important.

"If you didn't want to, then why?" he asked.

"I don't have a choice," she said. "Everyone looks down on me because I can't master my element, as if it's my own fault. I'm so exhausted, Kael. Every single day, so exhausted trying to control my fire, and it never happens. And yet they sneer, and talk, and act like I'll be useless in battle. If I don't want to be expelled, I have to convince them they're wrong. If I want to stay with you, if I want to remain a Seraph, I have to be better than everyone. I have to be the best."

Her legs buckled, and she sat, her back purposefully to the blood on the well.

"My swords are all I have," she said, staring at her hands. "I won't get to kill from afar. I won't get to look away. I have to learn to handle this. I have to become stronger, so much stronger..."

Kael stared down at his sister. Though her voice had cracked, there were no tears in her eyes. Just a thin mask of calm, one he no longer believed. When Thane's body had hit, Kael had nearly vomited and quickly looked away, yet she'd forced herself to watch because she thought it would make her a better Seraph. She felt the same shock, the same revulsion, but she hid it beneath a cold facade that was steadily breaking before his eyes.

"I'll be right back," he said, trudging north and taking the empty bucket with him. A small stream lined the field, part of its irrigation system, and Kael used it to fill the bucket. When he returned Bree was in the process of covering the body with dirt. All the others had left, which suited Kael just fine. Grabbing the bucket with both hands, he splashed the fouled side of the well while Bree watched.

"Rag," he said, holding out his hand.

"You don't have to help," she said.

"And that matters why?"

Bree pulled out the rag, hesitated, then handed it over. Kael scrubbed on his knees at the wet stones, making them clean, removing every last remnant of the death. Beside him, Bree tossed shovelful after shovelful of dirt until the body was buried and they could leave. When at last they were done, Kael wrapped his arm around his sister.

"I'm sorry," he said. "I never should have said you weren't normal."

Bree leaned her head against his shoulder.

"I can think of worse insults. And thanks for helping."

"Well, I mostly did it so you wouldn't hit me with the handle of your shovel. You do have a reputation for that, I hear."

She elbowed him in the side.

"You're lucky we're related," she said. "Now let's get out of here. If I have to endure that smell for another second I'm going to lose it."

When they returned to Bree's apartment, they found Amanda sitting on the floor of the entry room, arms crossed over her knees. She looked up, clearly shaken.

"It was like this when I came back," she said softly. "I...I forgot to lock the door. I'm sorry, Bree. I'm so sorry."

Kael stepped past her into Bree's room, felt the hairs on his neck stand on end. Writing covered every single wall, calling her a wide assortment of names that would have felt right at home while the people chanted their hatred toward the now-deceased disciple of Johan.

"Should we tell someone?" Kael asked, fighting to keep his voice even.

Bree stared at the walls, silently soaked in every curse, every foul word, with the same steely look she'd had after Thane's death. All her pain hidden. All her sadness walled away, as if it didn't even exist.

"No," she said. "If they're too afraid to say it to my face, then I've already won. Hand me a rag. It looks like we're not done cleaning after all."

CHAPTER 14

The best part of Kael's day was practicing his ice element with Clara at the training field. The second best was escaping Miss Woods's dry, boring lectures. Kael's desk was by the door, and he was the first one out every time. At least in Mr. Gaughran's class they learned something that felt useful. They'd started with basic tactics used by each elemental type, then moved on to the intricate hand movements squad leaders used to relay orders while flying in formation. But history? When would he ever, ever need to know about the Elern-Weshern War of 117 A.A., or the names of all the Archons prior to the Willer family taking over?

Kael waited beside the door as the rest of the class filed out, meaning to have a chat with Bree, but Clara came out first and grabbed him by the elbow.

"Do you think we could have a word?" she asked him. "In private?"

"Sure," Kael said. They started down the hall, opposite the rest making their way toward the other exit and the mess hall. He kept glancing over his shoulder, caught sight of Bree, and he waved at her so she'd know where he went. She waved back, winked at him when she saw Clara, and then jogged to catch up with Brad.

"So what's so important?" Kael asked. He kept his hands crossed over his chest to keep from fidgeting. Being around Clara made him self-conscious, and the last thing he wanted was to be snapping his fingers or repeatedly cracking his knuckles while she tried to talk to him.

Clara stopped, peered over his shoulder to make sure no one was watching, and then pulled out a piece of paper from her pocket. It'd been folded multiple times into a small square, and she handed it to him.

"Sorry, I was hoping to do this sooner, but I only got my hands on this today."

Kael frowned, confused, until he opened it up to reveal a familiar list of scribbles.

"Are you insane?" he asked, handing back the pamphlet of dogma written by one of the disciples of Johan. "You can't carry that around. You'll get in trouble."

"Who, me?" Clara asked, and she put a finger to her lip and hunched as if she were a model of pure innocence. "I found this on the floor of the hallway, and I was just on my way to turn it in to the headmaster, I swear. Surely you wouldn't dare accuse the daughter of the Archon of being a traitor now, would you?"

Kael rolled his eyes.

"Fine. Whatever. I've seen it before, and I've got no interest."

"It's not for you," she said, snagging it out from his hand. "It's for Jason and Saul."

The gears in Kael's head turned, and it didn't take much imagination to figure out her intentions.

"Clara," he asked carefully, "what are you planning?"

"The two share an apartment," she said. "And trust me when I say it wouldn't be difficult for me to obtain a key. After that, I mention to Headmaster Simmons that Saul was saying some strange things to me during training, things about Johan and Center. They'll do a room check, find the pamphlet, and the rest will work itself out from there. Nothing serious will happen to either of them, not with how wealthy the Reigar estate is, but it'll be a nice black eye on their family honor. Most importantly, Saul and Jason will be sent home during the investigation, which if we're lucky will last at least six months."

Clara smiled at him.

"So how about it? How does six months free of Saul sound?"

It sounded tempting was how it sounded. Saul refused to say a word to him during elemental training, and just being in his presence filled Kael with tension. Not that Kael believed he'd try anything. Expulsion was too likely a punishment. Chewing on his lip, Kael tried to decide if he was comfortable with such underhanded tactics, and as much as he'd love to see Saul humiliated in retaliation for humiliating Bree, he knew it'd never sit right with him.

"Look, I'm ... I'm thankful, but this really isn't that big a deal," he said, trying to downplay how much the whole affair actually bothered him. "It was one fight, that's all, and now it's over."

"No, it's not over," Clara said. "Amanda told me what they did to your sister's room. It's awful, and it's cowardly."

"And it's our problem, not yours," Kael said.

"No. It's not. You think I don't know what started that fight between Bree and Jason? That…lowlife thought he could control who I spend my time with. I grew up sequestered in the holy mansion. Now I'm finally out here, on my own, and people still want to play games while claiming it's for my own good? I won't allow it. I won't."

Kael could hardly believe the growing fire in Clara's green eyes.

"They decided you weren't worthy of my time," she said. "I beg to differ."

Lost as to how to respond, Kael stammered for a moment, struggling for an answer.

"This will work," Clara said. "All you need to do is trust me."

"I do trust you," Kael said. "And I do think it'd work, but that's not the point. We might have peace now, but it will only make things worse when they return. They'll believe Bree and I were responsible in some way, no matter how little proof they have. They'll know, and they'll act on it. Worse, they might figure out your part if they hear you were the one claiming they spoke about Johan. Besides, I can deal with Saul's ugly looks. It really isn't that hard."

"And why's that?" she asked.

"Because I'm with you, and he's stuck with Daniel."

Clara laughed, and she visibly relaxed.

"Are you sure about this?" she asked, holding the pamphlet with two fingers and waving it before him. "You have to admit, they deserve it."

"That they do," Kael said, snagging it from her fingers and promptly ripping it into several pieces. "But I also know we're better than that."

Clara stared at him, and Kael would have given anything to know what thoughts were racing through her mind.

"You're right," she said. "We are better than that."

A playful smile spread across her lips.

"I think those two brothers should be in the mess hall right about now," she said, and she offered him her hand. "Would you please escort me there?"

Kael wrapped his fingers around hers, the touch making his entire hand tingle as if it'd fallen asleep.

"It would be my honor. Shall we also walk by Jason's table on our way to pick up our meal?"

"We shall," Clara said, smile now ear to ear. "A shame you weren't born to royalty, Kael, because I think you'd have been better at it than I am."

Kael doubted that, but he wasn't going to say a single word otherwise while he walked the hall, hand in hand, and heart ready to explode in his chest. Not a single damn word. They stepped out, crossed the path to the mess hall, and went inside.

The look on Jason's face was everything he hoped.

CHAPTER
15

Bree knelt, rag in hand, as she cleaned the floor of the women's showers. The floor was smooth stone, long since faded a pale gray from whatever color it might have once been. Bree scrubbed and scrubbed with her brush, scattering lye every few minutes.

It could be worse, she told herself. *I'm not sure how, but it could be worse.*

Cleaning the showers was one of several additional tasks Over-Secretary Waller had assigned to her for the past few days as punishment for giving Jason Reigar what he deserved at the mess hall. She almost preferred burying Thane's body after the execution over this. Awful as it was, at least that had been over fairly quickly. The constant scrubbing and cleaning of the tiles was so time-consuming, so tedious, it left her body aching, and even worse, kept her from practicing flight in her off hours as much as she preferred.

Bree sat on her haunches, and she groaned at the pain in her back. Sweat dripped from her forehead, and she wiped it away with her forearm. It was always uncomfortably hot inside no matter the time of day, a normally welcome aspect of the wondrous showers. Academy servants kept tanks above them filled with water, and a theotech from Center came once a week to change the flame elements stored somewhere inside. The ceiling had a dozen grates with thick covers you could pull off with a chain, pouring out water like a warm rain.

The extravagance of it, the cost associated with giving the Seraphim recruits such an unnecessary perk, would have turned Bree's stomach if she didn't love it so much, especially compared to the far colder baths she'd taken in Lake Pleasance growing up. Bree consoled herself with the idea that everyone should have at least one guilty pleasure. But counter to what Bree would have believed, the constant hot water didn't keep the floor clean. Somehow, it made it worse, which meant day after day she was stuck on her hands and knees, scrubbing at the dirt and scum that refused to go down the floor drains.

How long until my punishments are over? she'd asked the over-secretary earlier that day. Rebecca had dismissed her with a wave of her hand.

When they're over, was the only answer she'd been given. Far from satisfactory, to say the least. Worst was how it kept her from spending time with Dean. Over the past few weeks they'd begun shamelessly flirting with each other, much to the chagrin of the rest of the group. Joining him in practice, moving their bodies together in a dance of steel, had easily become the highlight of her day, even more than flying. And now she couldn't, because she had to scrub showers.

Bree didn't regret hitting Jason with the broom handle. She just regretted not hitting him even harder. If she was going to be miserable, at least she could have taken out a tooth or something...

After what she'd guessed to be half an hour, Bree rose from the floor, stretched her arms and legs in a vain attempt to prevent further cramping, and called it quits. She'd scrubbed two thirds of the floor; surely that'd be good enough for one day. Her stomach rumbled, and she couldn't wait to get changed and grab some supper from the mess hall. Dumping the rest of the water in her bucket down the drain, she piled her supplies inside and carried it out.

"Hey, beautiful. How's the work going?"

Bree froze in terror at the sight of Dean leaning beside the door, arms crossed over his chest. Her hair was pulled back from her face in a knot, then covered with a rag to help keep sweat out of her eyes. Her hands were filthy and raw from the lye, her entire body coated with sweat. She wore an oversize white shirt and brown pants she'd been given by Rebecca, the same clothing the academy servants wore, and the knees and sleeves were wet and covered with muck. The only thing Bree could imagine being worse was if she'd strolled out of the showers completely naked.

"It's...going," Bree said, debating an escape plan.

Dean chuckled.

"You've missed sword practice the past two days. They must be working you to the bone."

Bree shrugged, unsure of how to act. She might not have regretted what she'd done, but she still felt embarrassed every time the topic came up.

"It's what I deserve," she said, deciding to play it safe.

"No," Dean said. "It's not."

Bree had started for her apartment, but his pronouncement

halted her in her tracks. Dean wasn't just being sympathetic. She could hear it in his voice, see it in his eyes. He was angry.

"What do you mean?" she asked.

Dean pushed off from the wall.

"Jason's in my class, and I can assure you, you're not the only one who's wanted to hit him upside the head. And after what he said to you..."

Bree's face flushed beet red, her gaze drifting down to the grass.

"You heard about that, did you?"

Dean cupped her chin to force her to look at him.

"If you hadn't gone after him, I would have, once I found out," he said. "Jason's an entitled bastard. After the humiliation you've given him, you don't deserve punishment. You deserve a damn award, so I'm going to do what I can to make up for all this hard work. Do you still have any of your civilian clothes?"

Bree shook her head.

"Your uniform will be fine then," he said. "We're not going anywhere fancy. I'll come get you just after dark, so be ready, and try not to tell anyone. Sound like a plan?"

Bree's panic and excitement warred with each other, making it suddenly difficult to form words.

"Wait, what?" she asked. "Where are we going?"

Dean winked.

"My secret," he said. "See you in a few hours."

He hurried off, leaving Bree standing there with a baffled look on her face while holding her bucket of cleaning supplies. She glanced down at herself, dirty, sore, and stinking of old water and lye, and then went right back into the showers, this time to use instead of clean.

*   *   *

"Is it dark yet?" Bree asked, glancing out the window of her apartment.

"It's getting dark," Amanda said, sitting in their chair and looking entirely too amused.

"Yes, but the sun's almost gone. Or by 'after dark' did he mean the midnight fire? Or maybe just the dark before the fire that blots out the stars..."

"Bree, stop pacing. You're only working yourself up more."

Bree hadn't realized she was pacing, and she fought down a blush as she forced herself to stand still.

"Sorry," she said.

Amanda laughed.

"I'm not sure I've ever seen you so nervous. You can strap a hunk of metal to your back and fly at high enough speeds to get yourself killed, but *this* is what has you biting your nails? You must really like him."

Bree tugged at her jacket, her fifth time adjusting it so.

"I don't know," she said. "Maybe? Please don't say a word about this to Kael, all right? He'd never let me hear the end of it."

Amanda twisted her thumb and forefinger in front of her lips as if locking them, then tossed away the imaginary key. Before she could thank her, a knock at the door paralyzed her body.

It's a date, she told herself. *A stupid little date. Snap out of it.*

But was it even that? She didn't know. Dean just said it was a secret, but they were sneaking out at night to go somewhere together. Surely that met the definition of a date, right? Of course, this was such a stupid time to be debating that question, what with Dean standing outside her apartment, knocking for the second time. Bree grabbed the door handle, breathed in and out to steady herself, and then opened the door with a pleasant smile on her face.

"Finally," she said. "You've kept me waiting."

Dean was also dressed in uniform, wavy hair pulled back and face recently shaved. He lifted an eyebrow at her.

"I'm pretty sure I'm early," he said. "You ready to go?"

Bree nodded. She stepped out the door, turned to give one last look to Amanda. Her roommate winked at her, then waved good-bye.

The world was approaching its darkest, the sun fully set and the sky half covered with the crawling shadow. Side by side Bree and Dean hurried along the path running through the center of the academy, heading toward the main entrance. The midnight fire would light up soon, but Bree guessed they'd be out by then.

A single Seraph stood on guard at the front gate, dressed in uniform and wearing her wings. Bree wondered how they would sneak past, but Dean strolled up unafraid. As they neared, she recognized the Seraph as Sasha from their little sword-training group. Bree wondered if it was her normal schedule, or if Dean had engineered her being on duty just for tonight.

"Have fun," Sasha said as she opened the gate for them. "Just not too much fun. If you don't get back before sunrise you're on your own."

"Understood," Dean said, and he flashed her a winning smile.

"Thanks," Bree said, even though she felt silly saying it. She had no bloody idea where they were headed, but the simple act of sneaking outside the walls of the academy had her heart hammering in her chest as if it were trying to escape. They passed through the gate and onto Winged Road, following it west.

"So where are we going?" Bree asked as they paused momentarily. The sky was completely covered in shadow, the pitch-black too deep to walk without potentially stumbling off the path.

"How many times do I have to say it's a surprise?" Dean asked as the first flicker of flame lit up the western horizon.

"At least three more."

Dean took her hand, easily his boldest move since they first met. Bree could tell by his sudden silence that he was nervous, so she squeezed it to show she didn't mind.

"Surprise, surprise, surprise," he said, relief palpable in his voice. "Now let's go."

They walked a quarter mile down Winged Road, passing fields on either side. Bree said little, instead content to enjoy the electric feeling that tingled up her left arm from Dean's touch. They turned north at a crossroads, toward a familiar sight. It was Lake Serene, one of many Weshern was famous for. Its edge was surrounded with tall oak trees, the midnight light making it seem as if their broad leaves were aflame. Most impressive was the cliff the lake jutted up against, along with its waterfall. There was no apparent source for the water, for it emerged from a cavern halfway up the cliff, pouring out into the lake to keep it forever full. There was no river above, just dry land and a town tourists from other islands were keen to visit due to the view.

Aunt Bethy used to take her and Kael to the lake as children, though the one place she'd not taken them to was the tavern built alongside the water's edge. Dean pushed the door open for her, then followed her inside.

The tavern was lit with slender candles whose yellow glow was far more welcoming than the outside fire. The spacious room was surprisingly cramped, with at least thirty men eating and drinking at various tables, on the rug before the fire, and at the bar. The barkeep, a friendly-looking bearded man in a long apron, waved Dean over as he greeted them.

"Always glad to serve our noble Seraphim," the barkeep said. "What can I do you for?"

"Two half-pints of ale," Dean said, handing the man a single silver coin. The barkeep stuck it into one of several pockets in his apron, exchanging it for pieces of bronze with such practiced ease he never had to look down.

"This your first time here, milady?" the barkeep asked as he grabbed two cups from a shelf behind him. Bree nodded. "Well, you're in for a treat. Most places can only afford the slop we brew here in Weshern, but I've got the finest ale from Elern herself."

Bree had no idea what the difference between them might be, but she assumed the barkeep knew what he was talking about. She accepted her cup, and together she and Dean found a table in the far corner. It was tiny and square, propped up high on worrisomely uneven legs. Dean took a gulp from his cup, and he laughed when he set it down.

"I honestly think this stuff's brewed in Weshern," he said as Bree tasted her own. It was strong and bitter, but not overpoweringly so. "He probably claims it's from Elern to justify the cost. Not that he needs to. It's still the best ale in Weshern. Supposedly the Willers order a barrel or two every year for their servants. Should probably ask Clara about that. I bet she'd know where it's brewed. The Willers know everything, or at least they pretend they do."

"Dean?" Bree said.

"Yeah?"

"You're rambling."

"Oh. Sorry."

Bree smiled as she took another drink. The liquid burned her throat, but it felt so pleasantly warm in her stomach she did her best to ignore it. Dean shifted his stool nearer to the rickety table, and he leaned in close.

"So, what all is the evil over-secretary making you do besides scrubbing the showers?" he asked. "Cut grass? Change sheets? Clean rooms?"

"Mostly the showers," Bree said. "Everything else gets closely attended by the academy's servant staff, but apparently the showers tend to fall pretty low on their priority list. Plus I had to bury that disciple of Johan. That was unpleasant, to say the least."

Dean's eyes scanned the tavern, and his mood dampened.

"I wouldn't say that name too loudly here," he warned.

Bree frowned.

"It's not like Johan's name is illegal. What will someone do, turn me in as a traitor?"

"Quite the opposite," Dean said, and he nodded to the far wall. "See the dartboard over there? Take a peek at what the max point is."

Bree took another sip, then turned to glance over her shoulder. She found the wooden dartboard, six darts jammed into scattered locations. In the very center was a circular formation cut and painted in a very familiar way.

"Center," she said.

Dean nodded.

"Say 'Johan' loud enough and you'll soon have someone joining you in your seat, curious if they'll have an ear. Johan's name may not be illegal now, but it wouldn't surprise me if it soon is. His disciples are like roaches. No matter how hard the theotechs try, they can't seem to get rid of them."

The alcohol was starting to affect her, loosening her mind. Leaning in closer, she dropped her voice to a whisper.

"So what about you?" she asked. "Think they have a point?"

Dean downed the rest of his drink.

"Honestly, I haven't a clue," he said, cup thudding down upon the table. "It's not like the relationship between Center and the outer islands has always been rosy, but still... I think I'd rather worry about the enemies I know we do have over the enemies that may not be real." He gestured to her cup. "You finished?"

She set it down, half full, and nodded.

"Probably not a good idea to have any more," she said.

Together they rose from the table, Dean once more grabbing her hand. Instead of leaving, he returned to the barkeep and dropped two coins onto the bar.

"The key to the falls," he said.

The barkeep reached into a shirt pocket and pulled out a large iron key. Bree stared at it, suddenly nervous. A key? What did Dean need a key for? After scooping up the coins, he handed it to Dean.

"Make sure you bring this back," the bearded man said. "Otherwise I'm telling your headmaster what all you've been up to here."

"You have my word," Dean said, smiling.

They exited the tavern, the din of music and conversation fading as the door shut behind them. Land lit red by the midnight fire, Dean led her around to the back of the tavern, following a pathway in the tall grass alongside Lake Serene toward the waterfall. When the path split in two, they went right instead of keeping beside the water. The path steepened, and quickly ended at a brick wall with a single gate. A metal plate was bolted to the center, declaring it off-limits. At the bottom of the plate was the circular symbol of Center. Dean pulled out the key the barkeep had given him, unlocked the gate, and then pushed it open.

"After you," he said.

Bree passed through the gate and started up the rocky path. She guessed Dean was taking her to the cliff face, but she wasn't sure why the way to the path was locked. There had to be other ways up, for on her approach she'd seen a multitude of homes built along its edge. Trusting him to have a good reason, she continued the climb, Dean trailing just behind her, having stopped only to shut and relock the gate.

The closer to the top, the more Bree realized they weren't quite heading to the cliff face. Instead, the path ended at the entrance of a cave. Bree hesitated, for inside was so dark she could not see a thing. All she could hear was the tremendous roar of the nearby waterfall.

"You're not scared, are you?" Dean asked as he joined her side.

"There's a difference between being brave and being stupid," she said.

"Good thing I'm both." Dean offered her his hand. "Just walk with me, and keep your other hand touching the side of the cave. It'll be fine, I promise."

Bree swallowed her apprehension, took his hand, and followed him into the cave. Her left hand brushed along the cave wall, which was surprisingly smooth. They disappeared into the cliff, into darkness as complete as it'd been on their trip to the tavern. The roar of the waterfall grew with each step. After a long minute the wall began to curve to her left, and she saw the first hint of red light.

"Where are we?" Bree asked.

"You'll see soon enough."

They curled more, and suddenly they stepped out into another cave. The light of the midnight fire illuminated it from the wide opening to her left. Before her an enormous stream of water flowed toward that opening in a deeply carved groove. They were inside the cliffs, she realized, at the actual waterfall itself. A stone path ran alongside the water all the way to the edge, where the water crashed down into Lake Serene. Bree stepped closer to the water, which seemed to come up from nowhere. At the bottom she could barely see an enormous grate, similar to the one at the bottom of the well nearby their old home on Picker Street.

"This is where the water for the falls is pumped out," Dean said, still holding her hand. "Care to see the view?"

They walked the stone path, stopping just before the edge. The water plummeted off the side, foaming white as it fell. The lake spread out before them, along with the trees that formed its border. The lake's surface reflected the burning midnight fire, making it seem as if a great stretch of flame flowed beneath her. Bree sat upon the edge, taking in the awesome view.

"It's beautiful," she said, nearly shouting due to the roar of the falls.

"I thought you'd like it," he said. "Something about the water makes the fire seem...gentler."

It was true, in a way. The sky above was a burning scar, but the water below seemed more magical, almost inviting. Dean sat down beside her, and deciding it worth the risk, she leaned against his body. His arm immediately wrapped around her. Bree's smile spread ear to ear. She said nothing, only enjoyed the moment, enjoyed the closeness of his body. The water flowed on and on, seemingly endless, and Bree dipped her fingers into its surface, felt its cold resistance.

"So have you ever jumped?" she asked.

Dean glanced at her, doing a fine job of masking his true thoughts.

"Jumped?" he said. "Are you joking, or serious?"

"Serious," she said.

"Well, then, seriously, no, I have never jumped. Never wanted to break my neck, either."

Bree slipped free of his grasp and stepped back from the edge while removing her jacket.

"My aunt took us here every summer," she said. "Kael and I used to swim beneath the falls, taking turns trying to touch the bottom. We never did."

She set her jacket down on the stone, removed her belt, and then untucked her shirt. Dean watched, calm mask not quite so calm anymore. As if in protest, he remained seated by the edge.

"You're insane," he said. "You know that, right? Completely insane. I'm not jumping."

Bree kicked off her boots and set them beside her jacket.

"Is that so?" she said, pulling off her socks next.

"Absolutely."

Bree felt nearly drunk from excitement. Never mind sneaking out of the academy and trespassing in a cave blocked off by the theotechs. Being alone with Dean, sitting so close, his eyes unable to linger on anything else but her? Intoxicating.

"Fine then," she said. "Close your eyes and turn around."

He blinked.

"What?"

Bree crossed her arms and frowned at him.

"You made me trust you, so now it's your turn. Eyes closed, and no opening until I say."

Dean threw his hands up in surrender.

"As you wish," he said, turning back around. Bree hesitated, debating whether to continue. Fear and doubt bubbled up in her stomach, and she shook her head to clear them away. To hell with it all. Bree stripped to her underclothes, then walked barefoot to Dean's side. Kneeling down, she curled against him and pressed her lips to his. She felt his body stiffen, but true to his word, he kept his eyes closed. Bree let the kiss drag on, relishing every second of it. When she finally pulled away, she felt out of breath, and her heart was completely aflutter.

"Follow me if you want another," she whispered into his ear, then dropped her shirt and pants onto his lap.

Before second thoughts could paralyze her, Bree turned and dove off the edge. The spray of water blew against her skin, mixing with the air. She felt as free as when she'd leaped off Weshern's edge using the training set with Jevin. The heavy mist forced her eyes shut. She kept her hands together, kept her breath held. The fall lasted only a moment, but it felt like forever, giving her a rush akin to looping about with her wings. Then her hands pierced water, and she broke its surface with a sudden shock of cold. Bree's body curled as she sank deeper, slowly angling herself back toward the top.

Her lower lip was already shivering by the time she gasped in a lungful of air. Treading water, she let the current push her away from the falls. From down below, she could only see a bare shadow of the cave she'd jumped from, the falls obscuring much of it with their wide white spray. Teeth clenched, she waited and waited.

Dean's muscular body leapt out from the cliff, and just like Bree, he left the pants and shirt of his uniform upon the rock. It took only a moment for him to drop, but in her mind he hung forever. He was jumping down for her, just for her. That alone pushed away the chill of the night. Bree's cheer pierced the calm, welcoming his arrival. Arms leading, he knifed into the water like a hunting bird of prey, kicking up a wide splash.

"Goddamn, that's cold," Dean shouted upon bursting back to the surface. He smoothed his hair back from his face as he sputtered, momentarily dipping down below the water.

"See?" Bree said, floating with the water up to her chin. "Was that truly so bad?"

"Yes, it was," Dean said as he swam toward her.

"Oh really?"

"I hated every second."

Bree splashed at him, but it did not deter his approach. His arms wrapped around her waist, and they both kicked to stay afloat. He leaned in close, and Bree let him. After all, a promise was a promise.

"Every...single...second."

They returned to the academy a few hours before sunrise. Both were shivering when Sasha opened the gate for them, their uniforms cold and wet.

"Swimming?" Sasha said, looking at both as if they were out of their minds. "Hope it was worth it."

"Worth every second," Dean said, and Bree had to bite her tongue to keep from giggling the entire walk back to her apartment.

CHAPTER
16

Bree soared over the training field, a grin on her face as wind blasted through her hair. After several more weeks of boring drills and tedious exercises, Instructor Dohn had finally given them chances to truly test their wings. They flew in two groups of eight, with Adam Dohn making up for their odd number. One group flew east, the other west, keeping in *V* shapes with one person leading, the others trailing. Those going east would remain high, while those going west were to drop beneath.

"We need you to learn what it's like to see an army approaching," Instructor Dohn had explained. "More importantly, we need you to realize just how fast it can be, and how little time you'll have to react."

Bree was just to Amanda's right, her roommate currently in the lead position. The grass below them was a faded yellow blur as they zipped along, careful to keep their speed matched with Amanda's. Ahead of them, the other group was a bunch of silver and black dots. Bree kept Amanda in the corner of her eye, waiting. It was their turn to drop, but only after their leader did so.

The dots became solid shapes, thrumming wings and black windblown jackets. Bree tried to envision what it'd be like if the two groups unleashed their elements during their approach. Balls of flame exploding between them, shards of ice flying in, all while thick blasts of lightning picked Seraphim off one by one. Bree imagined herself calmly flying through it, deftly dodging each shot...but suddenly she felt her sides hitch as she realized she didn't have to imagine it. She'd seen it before, the night her parents died in battle. The excitement of it, the allure, quickly faded.

The memory stole her concentration away, so when Amanda dropped, curling in her stomach while lowering her head to point her wings downward, Bree was the last in formation to rejoin. Like a flock of birds they dove, while, high above, the other formation thundered past. Perhaps she imagined it, but Bree swore she could feel the wind of their passing, like a wave rolling over her back.

They reached the end of the field. Bree heard Amanda call out an order, but even with her so close it was still muffled. At such speeds, speech was all but hopeless, hence the rapid hand signals they'd begun learning in Teacher Gaughran's class. It was also why Instructor Dohn harped on them so strongly to follow their formation leader without the slightest hesitation. Bree's grin grew. At the end of each field, their positions shifted one to the left, with the very end sliding around to the right. This put Bree in the lead position, and she had every intention of enjoying it.

"Come on," she shouted as they turned around and raced

across the field, not caring they couldn't hear her. She pushed her switch harder, increasing the throttle beyond what the others had risked. Too many were afraid of speed, she felt. Time to give them no choice. A check left and right showed that while the formation had spread a little long, they still kept pace. Good. She might have worried that the second group would react too slowly, but Kael would be in the lead position coming from the other direction, and she trusted him more than anyone else to dive down in time.

The thrumming of her wings increased, and she outstretched her hands on either side of her, tensing the muscles so they remained still despite the wind. The powerful gusts should have made seeing difficult, but the faint shield of light protected her. It was as though she wore goggles and a mask that ended at the edges of her cheeks, for the wind tore through her hair and across her ears at full strength. She still felt the air on her eyes and mouth, only it seemed...weaker. Slowed, somehow.

The distant dots that made up the other group rapidly approached, and Bree felt her heart pound. Again she imagined explosions of fire, of weaving between boulders flying through the air with enough force to shatter bone and wings, only this time she retaliated, hurling blast after blast of perfectly aimed flame. The group closed in, and as she expected, the eight dove, following her brother. They passed underneath, the combined volume of their wings a shiver-inducing thrum that made Bree's smile all the wider.

When practice ended, Instructor Dohn gave them permission to fly about, practicing whatever drills they felt they needed, or to do similar flybys in smaller formations. Bree floated over to where Kael hovered, and she twisted so she could kick him with her heels, sending him drifting.

"Must you be so childish?" Kael asked as he turned about and gave his wings a single burst to kill his momentum.

"Must you be so easy to torment?"

Her brother grinned.

"Speaking of, you had your group fly much faster than they had earlier, didn't you?"

"You know me so well."

Kael laughed.

"I knew you would before we even turned around," he said. "I almost had us drop down the second we started, just to make sure we got out of the way in time."

"What, afraid you'd react too slowly?" Bree asked, smirking.

"Me? Of course not. It's all those other slow people in my formation I was worried about."

"Slow people like me," Clara said, hovering over from beside Instructor Dohn. "Which is why I need some extra training. Kael, would you do me the honor?"

Kael lifted an eyebrow.

"Honor of what?"

The blonde girl grinned.

"Of chasing me."

Just like Bree, she kicked Kael in the chest, simultaneously pushing him away while giving herself separation so she could rotate about and then flare her wings. She tore into the air, and letting out a playful cry, Kael gave chase. Not to be outdone, Bree punched the throttle to her own wings. All three soared into the air, each in chase of the other. There'd be no tagging, of course, nor even any real attempts to make contact. The goal was simply to mimic a person's path, then get far enough ahead to cut them off and force them to chase instead. Of all the games and drills Instructor Dohn had taught them, this was far and away the most dangerous. It was also Bree's favorite, likely for that very reason.

Bree gave no real effort in taking the lead, for during the past week she'd shown no difficulty in doing so. After all her practice on the obstacle course, she could pull off maneuvers the rest could currently only dream of. Only Kael stood a chance of surpassing her, and only because he spent so much time flying with her at the end of every practice. Bree tailed the couple perfectly, staying back so she could watch and see how well she predicted each turn or juke. Their path took them high into the air, far above the others lingering down below. The only ones nearby were Gavin and Brad, who chased each other while doing tall, wide loops.

Clara weaved left to right, nothing particularly fancy. Bree had a feeling she wanted to be caught. The stupid grins on both her face and her brother's certainly gave credence to Bree's suspicion. Kael pulled up alongside Clara, weaving in the same left-to-right pattern instead of trying to pull ahead. Bree twirled a few times as she trailed, and she realized she watched a dance, not a game. The two were in their own little world, and they never noticed when Bree fell back a bit more and took stock of the training field.

Beneath her, flying side by side, were Amanda and a waifish girl with red hair named Lily. They were practicing flying in formation, with their arms outstretched so that their fingers were just barely touching. They weren't flying particularly fast, and Bree thought to join them instead of playing third wheel to Clara and her brother, who clearly only had eyes for each other. Shifting direction, she started to close the distance. Looking ahead, she saw that they approached the far west side of the field, the same side as Gavin and Brad, except for some reason she couldn't find the two.

Feeling the first tinge of worry, she looked around, then finally up, where she spotted them. The two were nearly side by side, and at the peak of another loop. Bree finished the loop in her mind, and suddenly that worry was full-blown panic. Amanda and Lily would be flying right through their path at the bottom of the loop, and unless they looked up, they'd have no idea of the danger.

Stay calm, she told herself as she drastically increased her throttle. *Don't lose control now.*

Diving down, she set herself on a path for intercept. As her hair danced around her face, she did another mental calculation, trying to judge if she'd make it in time. Maybe, but she'd have to go faster, faster than she'd ever flown before. Her thumb pushed the throttle even farther forward.

Brad led the way, Gavin just barely behind. Any other time, she'd have been impressed by their coordination during such a stunt. Not now. Knowing she had only seconds, she descended upon the women from behind, pulling back the throttle so she wouldn't go flying past. Amanda was on the right, Lily the left. Flying beside Amanda, Bree shot out a hand to grab her arm, and then with all her strength, she pulled while twisting her body to put her wings on a path away from the incoming collision. Amanda followed, but Lily released her grasp of Amanda's fingers. Bree spun, repositioning her wings to fight against her momentum as Amanda flew on ahead, clueless as to what was going on.

As they pulled up from their loop, Brad still in the lead, they headed straight for Lily. Bree felt her heart stop, felt her breath catch in her throat. Lily saw them come in from above, and panicking, she twisted right. Both men saw her as well, and they attempted to avoid her in the same way. Brad turned and veered correctly, but Gavin curled right into Lily's path, his split-second reaction one of instinct, and one he could not escape out of.

The sound of their collision would haunt Bree for months to come. The initial contact was marked by a loud, forceful crack, followed by the earsplitting sound of metal scraping against metal. Bree felt paralyzed as she watched both bodies fall, Gavin's spinning wildly, Lily's dropping straight down. Blood sprayed above them like a cloud.

"Lily!" she heard Amanda cry. Bree turned to see her roommate standing in the air, hands to her face, her wings powered just enough to hover. Tears streamed down her cheeks. "Oh my God, oh my God, oh my God."

The bodies hit ground, bouncing limply across the yellow grass. Brad, having recovered from his dodge, raced past Bree toward the mangled body of his dead friend. Others joined, including Instructor Dohn, but Bree just stayed where she hovered. She didn't know what to do. She didn't know how to react. Feeling strangely numb, her mind muted, she watched as other students flocked over, accompanied by the constant sound of Amanda's shocked cries.

"Oh my God, oh my God..."

After the bodies were taken away and the rest of the class dismissed, Instructor Dohn came over to where Bree stood on the road, watching. He ran a hand through his dark hair, and she noticed he walked the long distance across the field instead of flying. Dimly she wondered if he walked on purpose. When he reached the road, he crossed his arms over his chest.

"Are you all right?" he asked her.

Why wouldn't I be? she thought. *I wasn't the one in the wreck.*

The collision flashed in her mind, and she felt her insides scraping raw as her heartbeat hammered the way it had for the past ten minutes.

"No," she admitted. "I don't think I am."

He put his hand on her shoulder, and she brought her gaze back up to him. Gone was his stern face, his constant judging. It seemed his demeanor had cracked, revealing a surprising tenderness.

"Bree, what you did out there was amazing," he said. "If not for you, Amanda might have been caught in that collision. You saved a life today, perhaps Brad's as well." He leaned down so he could stare her in the eye. Something about it left her uneasy. It was as if he understood everything about her, and it made her feel strangely naked. "But you're not remembering that. I can see it on your face, see it in how you're out here alone, watching. Saving Amanda's life wasn't enough. You're convinced you could have saved Lily's as well, aren't you?"

Bree felt her lower lip quivering, and angry at herself, she swore not to cry. Not to break.

"Maybe," she said weakly.

Both hands on her shoulders now.

"Listen to me, Bree," he said. "You risked everything, and because of it, you saved lives. Never, ever feel guilty for that, do you understand me? Sad as it is, this sort of thing happens every year at the academy. Cry over it. Pray for them. Mourn for their loss, but do not blame yourself. If you do, you'll never survive as a Seraph. No matter how good you are, no matter how hard you try and how skillfully you fly, you *will* see your friends die. Sometimes you could have done things better. Sometimes there's nothing at all. If you let either eat at you, it'll carve you hollow, leaving nothing but a frustrated, burned-out husk of the girl you once were."

Bree sniffled, and she took a step back so he would release her shoulders.

"May I be dismissed?" she asked, proud of how firm her voice sounded.

"You may," Instructor Dohn said. "Please, go do whatever it takes to grieve. Don't rush yourself back into training until you're ready. We'll all understand."

Bree put her back to him and began walking east. Do what it took to grieve? She didn't know what that was. She felt restless, on edge. Her skin crawled with invisible worms, and it seemed every breath she took was too small, too empty. More than anything, she wanted her mind off the sight of Gavin and Lily slamming into each other, to purge that awful screeching sound of metal scraping metal that somehow echoed on and on in her ears. So she went to where she felt the freest, where her mind felt most at ease.

"There you are," Dean called from the advanced flight-training field. He sheathed his swords, dipped his head toward his opponent, and began walking across the grass toward her. Bree stayed on the road, feeling strangely nervous about joining their sparring group despite having trained with them daily over the past month.

"You're late," Dean said, and when he reached her, he bent over to kiss her cheek. "Where've you been?"

"I was…delayed," she said, part of her wanting to tell him everything, part wanting to pretend it'd never happened. Normally any contact with him, even a simple kiss on the cheek, should have set her nerves aflame, but today she felt cold and numb. "We can still practice, right?"

"Of course," Dean said, glancing over his shoulder, as if afraid of being caught. "But, before we do…I've been meaning to ask you something."

Not now, she thought. *Whatever it is, not now, ask later, ask when I can handle it...*

"What?" she asked, the word rising flat off her tongue.

"Well, the solstice celebration's coming up soon," he said, rubbing at the back of his head with his left hand. He was nervous, she realized. Blushing, even. "I was wondering if you'd like to attend the Willer family's ball as my guest."

It was too much. A single sob escaped her lips, and she crumpled and sat in the dirt road. Dean dropped with her, his face a perfect portrait of worry.

"Not quite the reaction I was hoping for," he said, wrapping an arm around her.

"It's not you," she said, wiping at her face while sniffling. "There was an accident today during practice."

"Was anyone hurt?"

She nodded.

"Gavin and Lily. They...they didn't..."

He pulled her against him, and she melted into his chest.

"I'm sorry, Bree," he whispered. "It's always rough the first time you see it happen. It'll hurt less over time. You're strong, stronger than I am."

She closed her eyes, hands on his shirt, head tucked underneath his chin. The tips of their wings clacked against each other as he snaked a hand around her waist to keep her close.

"I don't want to be strong," she whispered. "Can't I be like everyone else?"

She heard him chuckle.

"I think, right now, you are."

Bree slowly breathed out as the last of her tears ran down her cheeks. Her numbness was wearing off, and though she felt raw, it was so much better than before. She heard footsteps on the grass, but she kept her eyes closed, not yet ready to return from the enveloping darkness to the bright daylight world.

"She all right?" she heard Sasha ask Dean.

"Accident during flight training. Two-person collision."

That appeared to be answer enough.

"I'm sorry," Sasha whispered, and quick as she arrived, her footsteps retreated.

Dean seemed willing to let her remain forever, but at last she pushed away, pulling wet strands of hair from her face and sniffling again.

"Oh God, I'm a mess," she said.

"I'll pretend not to notice," he said, earning a broken laugh. She kissed his cheek, having to stand on her tiptoes to do it, and then wiped at her eyes.

"Now what was this about a ball?" she asked. She wanted to push the tragedy of the morning away, to think about something, anything, besides the loss of her friends.

"Nothing important," he said. "It can wait until you're feeling better."

Bree shook her head.

"I'll be fine, really."

Dean kissed her forehead.

"If you insist. It's a dance the Willer family throws every year at the holy mansion to mark the winter solstice. All the various big shots of Weshern are invited. I wasn't planning on going, but now that I might actually have a date to make everyone jealous..."

"I doubt I'll make anyone jealous," she said, shaking her head. "But if you want me to go, I will."

His smile stretched ear to ear.

"If they're not jealous, they're fools who should be," he

said. "Thank you, Bree. This means a lot to me." He glanced over his shoulder, to where the rest were practicing with their swords. "So, are you still up for some training?"

"After all that?" she asked. "Hell, yes. I need to hit something." Dean furrowed his brow as if deep in thought.

"You know," he said. "Maybe for today, you should practice with Sasha or William instead..."

CHAPTER 17

Kael reclined in a stained oak chair with padded cushions on the second floor of the academy's library, an open book in his lap. Absently he flipped through the pages, only halfheartedly reading the words. It was the pictures he stared at mostly, incredible drawings by artists long dead. They showed the rise of the islands, the burning of the stars, and the age-old battle of angels against demons, the reason for their cities fleeing into the safety of the skies.

Is that us? Kael wondered as he stared at one of the winged warriors. Instead of metal wings, his were made of beautiful white feathers, and they unfurled in an enormous wingspan that the Seraphim's harnesses could never match. His armor was golden bronze, his arms bare, his face covered by his narrow helm. In one hand he wielded a spear, the other a circular shield, which he used to ward off the strike of his opponent, a demonic figure made of pure flame and shadow whose very

arms had turned into sharpened blades. An army of such creatures swarmed the ground, helpless to follow the islands rising
into the sky as the waters of the Endless Ocean came crashing
in to drown them all.

"Kael?"

He glanced up from his book to see Bree emerge from the
stairs. Clenching his jaw, he bit back a rude retort. It'd be childish to berate his sister for ruining his privacy when she was so
clearly worried about him.

"Yeah?" he asked, pretending he wasn't upset.

"I thought I'd find you here," she said. "You weren't with us
for our run this morning."

Bree took a seat opposite him in the other chair, settling into
the brown cushions. She wore her uniform minus the jacket,
which she'd grab prior to flight training, when its comfort
would be needed as protection against the buckles and hard
metal of the wings connecting to the back of the harness.

"It's not like I'm needed," he said. "Brad can run for longer
than I can now."

Her face darkened, and she narrowed her eyes.

"What's wrong?" she asked. "I know something is, so please
just tell me instead of bickering."

Kael sighed and closed his book.

"It's nothing," he said. "I've got it handled."

"You're moping in the library. I beg to differ."

"Like you're always a bastion of happiness, Bree."

He'd gone too far, and he saw it immediately. His sister
flinched as if slapped, and she ceased the gentle rocking of her
chair.

"Forgive me for trying," she said, standing. "I'll see you at
practice."

"Wait," he said before she could leave. "It's not you, it's…

it's Clara." She paused, arms crossed over her chest. Waiting for him to continue, he realized. Either that, or to apologize. Kael decided both might be the proper action. "I'm sorry. I didn't mean to snap at you. This morning Clara asked me to come as her guest to her family's party or dance or whatever it is."

"Did you accept?"

He shook his head.

"I told her I couldn't."

Bree sat back down in her chair and leaned forward in it, hands clasped before her, eyes locked on his face. He recognized that look. She was analyzing him, reading his emotions, her sharp mind racing through reasons and solutions.

"Why did you turn her down?" she asked him.

Kael took in a deep breath, tempted to refuse. The answer was humiliating, with Bree the worst one of all to reveal the reason. But she'd hound him until he cracked, or even worse, go to Clara for more clues.

"Because it's pointless to keep this going," he said. "Better to stop now before we both get hurt worse."

Bree frowned.

"If this is about Saul . . ."

"It's not about Saul," he snapped. "At least, not directly. But he was right, Bree. Look at us. We come from tiny little Lowville. No parents. No other family, just an aunt who works the fields the Willers themselves own." He looked away, and swallowed as if something foul were in his mouth. "I'm nothing, not compared to her."

Bree's chair creaked as she leaned closer, her eyes hard as stone.

"You are not nothing," she said. "You're a Seraph."

"I'm a glorified soldier," he said. "She may one day rule all of Weshern. I just . . . I can't do this, Bree. I'm not like you. I'm not."

Kael rubbed his eyes as he felt his chest tighten. With his

other hand he clutched his book tightly, fingers digging into the leather covering.

"What do you mean by that?" Bree asked, her voice so soft.

"Everyone who sees you fly knows you're special," he said, his own voice dropping. It felt shameful even admitting this. "You work so hard, you're the best flier, and now because of Dean, you'll soon be the best swordfighter, too. But me?" He looked up. "I'm not even close. When it comes to flight, I'm not the best. When it comes to elements, again, not anywhere close. I've got nothing to offer, no reason to think I'm worthy of someone like her."

"You're wrong," Bree said. "You may not be best at flying or ice element, but you're close at both, and you get better every day. I can see it, and so can everyone else. For how special you think I am, I might not even last through the six-month evaluations, but you're a lock, and we both know it."

Kael shook his head, feeling angry despite knowing it was ridiculous. Why should he be mad at Bree for insisting he was wrong, especially in this?

"Just drop it," he told her as he stood. "Clara deserves better than me, and one day, she'll figure that out."

Bree stood as well, and she grabbed his arm to keep him from leaving.

"You don't get it," she said. "Do you know who decides if you're worthy? *She* does, just like you decide if she's worthy of you." She released his arm. "Is she worthy, Kael?"

"I'd rather be at her side than anywhere else," he said, his throat horribly dry.

"Then be happy she sees something in you, and don't insult her by pretending nothing's there. Who cares if you're a farmer or a lord? Be happy. Go with her to the party. You do want to go with her, don't you?"

Kael felt his jaw quiver, felt his throat tighten.

"I do," he said. "I'm terrified, but I do."

Bree took his hands in hers, and she smiled at him.

"Then go with her," she said, "and to hell with anyone who disagrees."

Something in the way she said it made it seem so easy, so obvious, and Kael laughed as he felt the pressure in his chest break.

"Still may not be that easy," he said. "I did tell Clara no. What if she's already asked someone else?"

"Then you'll be kicking yourself for the rest of your life," Bree said, pushing him toward the stairs. "It also means you should be running to find her before that happens."

Kael grabbed her instead, pulling her close so he could hug her.

"What would I do without you?" he asked.

"Mope in a library, I'd wager," she said, grinning.

He hugged her again, kissed her cheek, and then rushed down the stairs.

"Hey, return that book for me, will you?"

His sister shouted a rude name down the stairs in response, but he laughed, feet flying out the door, the last of his nerves long gone.

CHAPTER

18

"Thank God for sensible Amanda," Bree said as she and Dean approached the mansion while high above them the sky burned with fire. "Those things look horribly uncomfortable."

"Those things" were the elaborate dresses the many women lined up on the stairs were wearing. They were all of a solid color, most of them blue. The bottoms were flared out in wide circles, and at both their waists and shoulders were big poofy ribbons and tassels and other things she didn't even know the names of. No matter the size of the women, their midsections were covered with laced-up corsets cinched so tightly it made Bree wince just looking at them.

"Is yours that much better?" Dean asked, holding her hand.

Bree glanced down at her borrowed dress. When she'd informed Amanda of her plans to wear her uniform to the dance, the girl had nearly lost her mind. She'd practically begged Bree to let her borrow a dress from her parents, to at least see if one fit. Bree relented after two days, Amanda hurried home the night before the dance, and then returned with not one but three. After trying them all on, Bree's favorite had been a fairly simple white gown that once belonged to Amanda's grandmother. The sleeves ran all the way to her wrist, the dress clung to her hips instead of pushing out like a giant bell, and best of all, there was no need for a corset. The only frill was a single blue bellflower Dean had carried with him when he arrived at her apartment, and which he'd pinned just above her left breast.

"I can breathe in my dress," Bree said. "I'm not sure the same can be said for them. Or is breathing an act of commoners the wealthy have learned to do without?"

Dean tugged her closer so he could whisper in her ear.

"I'd say the suits are worse, but they're not. And for the love of all that's holy, at least pretend like you're trying not to insult anyone."

Bree muffled her laugh with her hand. Sure enough, one of the women directly in front of them had turned about and glared, though the balding man holding her hand seemed oblivious.

Sorry, Bree mouthed to her. It didn't seem to help. An excellent start to the evening, she decided.

As they walked, Bree took in the sights of the mansion, which she'd never been anywhere near this close to before. Tall, broad-leafed trees formed a perimeter, evenly spaced out every ten feet or so. Their branches were immaculately trimmed so that each one created an enormous half-circle of leaves at the tops of their trunks. The mansion itself was built of stone, which on its own would have been rare, but rarer still was the white marble that made up many of its columns and cherub statues. While the building itself was a towering two stories, the windows and doors themselves were short and narrow, the stained-glass windows laced with bars.

Protected from the air, Bree realized as they approached the front door. *Any Seraph seeking entrance would have to come through the doors and face the military guard.*

Eight such guards flanked the reinforced oak doors that were currently flung wide open. They carried enormous shields the size of their own bodies, their free hand holding a long, sharpened spear. They wore shining steel armor, accentuated by black tunics and blue sashes. While the Seraphim were the Archon's elite battling in the air for pride and power, the military were the ground troops, Weshern's second line of defense against invasion. In the narrow corridors of the holy mansion, where no Seraph could fly, their shields guarded their bodies from the elements, and their spears gave them reach no Seraphim blade could match.

"What's with the tattoos?" Bree asked. Several of the guards bore tattoos on their faces, lines of thin blue dots shooting in seemingly random directions from their eyes.

"That means they're personal bodyguards of the Archon and his family," Dean said. "It also means you shouldn't bother trying to chat with them. In the olden times they used to yank out their tongues, but now they just swear vows of silence."

They reached the top of the stairs, and staring in through those wide doors reignited Bree's nervousness. So far she saw only a long hallway, and it was surprisingly dark and claustrophobic. The noise from beyond it reached her, a deep hum of many intermixed voices. This would be worse than her first day at the academy, worse than their visit to Center. Hundreds decked out in their finest, wielding power, wealth, and influence, and here she was, a Seraph in training wearing an old borrowed dress. As the guards stopped them and one without tattoos reached out for their invitation, Bree thought that maybe, just maybe, Kael had been correct to shy away from such a world.

"Straight on through, then right at the hallway," the guard said after glancing over the invitation and then handing it back.

"Thank you," Dean said, pocketing the invitation and then dipping his head in respect. Bree clutched his hand in a death grip as they walked into the dark entryway.

"How did you get invited again?" she asked. "Are you secretly rich and never told me?"

Dean laughed.

"I'd wager I come from a family even poorer than yours, Bree," he said. "Truth is, all third-year classmen and up are invited. This way the Willers can say they knew us from the start should one of us become a big war hero."

"You make them sound so devious."

Her date flashed her a cocky smile.

"The royal family's beloved for a reason," he said. "And it's not just for their looks."

They reached the end of the entryway and stepped out into a hallway twice as tall and lit with softly burning torches hanging from steel braziers. Bree examined one, surprised to see that at the end was a fire prism much like the ones she used during training. The torch itself wasn't wood at all, but painted stone, and Bree wondered what ancient technology the Willers used to harness the fire in such a way, not to mention the simple cost of doing so. Obtaining elements from Center was expensive, and much of Weshern's harvests and trade went toward obtaining them.

Amid the torches were dozens of portraits of various family members, and quick glances at the dates showed they would be long dead by now. Most bore the familial trait of blond hair and fair skin. Amid the fine suits and dresses, the occasional member bore the uniform of the Seraphim, and for some reason it made Bree feel proud knowing their ruling family still devoted itself to service in the defense of their island. The ceiling high above them was covered with glass stained a deep blue, and Bree found herself staring at its swirl of purples from the light of the midnight fire shining through.

"You nervous?" Dean asked as they traversed the blue carpet toward the larger ballroom where the rest of the party gathered.

"Just a little," she said, turning to her date. "You won't laugh if I stumble while dancing, will you?"

"You won't stumble," Dean said. "You took to it as well as you did flying."

"Not even close, and you know it."

Over the past week, they'd started spending their nights together in the advanced flight fields, with him teaching her how to dance. Well, among other things…

"Stand up straight, smile wide, and pretend you belong," Dean said as they reached the end of the hallway. "And if you're not sure how to respond, just smile and laugh softly. You'll be surprised by how many sticky conversation topics you can escape unscathed using that trick."

Bree did just that, standing up straight, pulling back her shoulders, and smiling as if the Willer mansion was the most amazing thing she'd ever seen. That done, she accompanied Dean to the end of the hallway, where the ruling couple, Isaac and Avila Willer, greeted their guests. The Archon was an imposing man with a large nose, squinty eyes, and a blond beard closely trimmed so that it covered only his mouth and chin. He stood as if his spine didn't know how to bend, and he wore a pair of white gloves. Beside him, Avila was a picture of noble beauty, her dress in many ways as plain as Bree's, its fabric lacking any frills as it hugged her body down to her ankles. Of course, such frills were unnecessary when your dress appeared to be made of the finest silver ever dug from the innermost pits of the land. Her long blonde hair split into elaborate twin ponytails that fell to either side of her chest. Dozens of black ribbons kept the hair in place, each ribbon decorated with diamonds.

"Dean Averson," Isaac said, reaching out and shaking the Seraph's hand the moment he neared. "Glad to see you again."

"Thank you," he said, bowing low in respect. "I wouldn't miss this for the world."

"And who is your date?" Avila asked, and sensing she couldn't hide forever, Bree stepped forward and performed the best curtsy she could manage.

"Breanna Skyborn," she said. "I am honored to be in your presence, your majesties."

"No formalities here," Isaac said, motioning for her to rise. A wistful look overcame his firm stare. "I knew your parents, honorable Seraphim the both of them. My eldest perished that same day. I fear even now we suffer from the echoes of that terrible battle."

Avila smiled, very smooth, very practiced. Her teeth were white like pearls, and despite her age, her skin still shone with life.

"Now is not a time to dwell on the sadness of the past," the royal lady said. "Tonight, we celebrate the future. Dean, Breanna, please enjoy our food, our music, and our company."

They dipped their heads slightly, and Bree and Dean accepted the dismissal, stepping farther into the ballroom so the next couple behind them could begin introductions anew.

The ballroom was easily the largest construction Bree had ever been in. If she'd been wearing her wings, it'd have felt more appropriate to fly from one side to the other instead of walking. The walls stretched heavenward with a gentle inward curve, all sides covered with elaborate paintings of Weshern's forests and lakes. The ceiling itself was painted black, and arched to form a gargantuan dome. The black paint seemed odd to Bree, and she wondered why they chose such a singular color given the lively greens and blues throughout the paintings. Near the ground were more than a hundred torches similar to the ones in the hallway, and the sheer amount of fire element involved was staggering. The floor beneath her was white marble, again adding to the incredible wealth of the holy mansion. To her surprise, gold swirls covered the floor, forming intricate patterns connecting various circles. At the far side, a band of seven played soft, soothing music with an assortment of stringed instruments both great and small.

Everything was so elaborate, the amount of people so overwhelming, Bree felt her nerves flaring anew. She didn't want to be here. She'd make a fool of herself, say something stupid or . . .

"Stay with me now," Dean said, squeezing her hand, and the simple gesture pulled her out of her mental spiral. "I know it's a bit overwhelming in here, but you get used to it."

"I take it you went last year?" she asked as they wandered toward the center of the general assembly.

"I did," he said, his mind clearly elsewhere as he surveyed the people.

"I thought you said only third year and up received invites?"

"Sasha took me as her date," he said.

Bree's eyes widened. "Sasha? You mean you two were . . ."

"Not dating in the slightest," Dean said, and he nudged her. "I wanted to rub elbows with the fancy folk. Sometimes the right connection can mean the difference between being a squad leader and being the tail end of a formation."

"So did you make any good connections?"

Dean laughed.

"Let's just say I'm going to have to rely on skill and good looks instead."

As Bree weaved through the massive congregation of people, the sound of their discussions like the waves of the ocean beneath Weshern, she spotted her brother. He wore his uniform, and he stood beside Clara Willer, who wore a sparkling silver dress similar to her mother's. At least seven older men and women gathered around her, politely chatting. Bree tugged on Dean's hand so he'd realize she stopped, then weaved closer to Kael until she finally managed to catch his attention.

"How's it going?" she asked her brother once he separated from the crowd and came her way.

"I've never been so miserable in my life," he said. "Everyone pretends I don't exist. It's like I have fleas or something."

"Well, Clara looks happy," Bree said, gesturing to his date. Kael glanced over his shoulder, and he chuckled.

"She does," he admitted. "Which means I'll continue to grin and bear it. It's only one night, right? I can handle one night of this."

Bree poked him in his ribs.

"You grew up with me," she said. "You can handle anything."

"No argument here." He lifted a glass, half filled with a dark red liquid. "The drinks help as well. Shame I didn't have any of this while growing up stuck with you."

He smiled, this one far more authentic than the grin plastered on his face when she first spotted him. It made her feel much better, and she decided he was smarter than he looked.

It's only one night, she told herself, echoing his own words. *And he has far more eyes on him than I do.*

Kael returned to his date, and Bree did the same. Dean guided them to the long buffet table, its surface covered with a thin white cloth, its silverware polished to a sparkle. Dozens of empty glasses waited beside an enormous bowl of wine, and taking a ladle, Bree scooped herself something to drink. When she tasted it, she was surprised by its incredible chill. Glancing back to the crystalline bowl, she saw bits of frost collected around the edges, and leaning closer, she realized three prisms of ice element were bound together by a silver chain and then set inside the hollow upraised center.

Drinks, she thought. *We use it to defend our nation, yet the Willers chill their drinks with it.*

Part of her wanted to be filled with righteous indignation at such an extravagant waste... but part of her keenly remembered the pleasure she took in the hot showers at the academy, the water heated by flame elements. Bree took another sip, swallowing down both anger and embarrassment for her own mental hypocrisy.

"Good idea," Dean said, pouring himself one as well. "Getting drunk will make the night fly by."

"I won't get drunk," Bree said.

"A few more cups of that and you will," he said. "Let's see what wins tonight, your self-control or your boredom."

"How could all this be boring?" Bree asked as they drifted away from the table. She gestured to the paintings, the people, the musicians. "I can barely take it all in."

Dean sipped his own cup, shook his head as he swallowed.

"Do you know anyone here besides Clara and your brother?" he asked.

Bree frowned.

"Not really," she said.

"Neither do I. So prepare to make small talk with people you don't know, and will never meet again."

"It can't be that bad," Bree whispered, dropping her voice as they made their way to one of the walls. The painting was of Lake Pleasance, where she'd swum often while growing up. She wanted to see how well the painter captured its blue waters, its border of towering trees, and the many geese that lived upon its shores.

"We'll see."

Before Bree could reach the painting, she spotted two familiar faces far less welcoming than her brother's. Saul and Jason Reigar, both of them wearing fitted black suits with blue shirts. That they wore those instead of their Seraphim uniforms irked Bree to no end. The two Reigar siblings looked bored as they stood beside an older man she guessed to be their father, who was busy chatting with a balding man in a faded Seraphim uniform.

"Hold up," Bree told Dean. Her date paused, caught her looking at Saul and Jason, and immediately started to protest.

"Bree...," he said.

"I'll behave," she promised as she headed their way.

"I don't believe you."

"Doesn't matter if you do."

She circled about a gathering of older men, weaved between a trio of women, and then flashed the two brothers the biggest smile of her life.

"I didn't know you two would be here," she said as if they were best friends. "I'm having the most wonderful time. Aren't you?"

Jason rolled his eyes and ignored her. Saul seemed more embarrassed, as if he felt obligated to at least acknowledge her presence.

"It's just a ball," he said. "Been to plenty like it before."

"You're so lucky. Who is your lovely date for this evening?"

The splotch of red around his neck was answer enough, and he mumbled something about not having bothered to ask anyone. Dean, meanwhile, had finally caught up to Bree, and she grabbed his hand and yanked him to her side.

"Dean was kind enough to invite me," she said. "I'm so glad, too. I'd not miss this for the world. Oh, did you see Clara and Kael?" She turned and pointed to the crowd. "They're over there, just in case you didn't spot them. Make sure you say hello. I'm sure they'd love to see another familiar face."

Saul's entire neck was red now, and he glanced about as if seeking a method of escape.

"Let's not bother the nice people," Dean said, pulling her away toward the painting. "I think they're trying to talk business."

"All right," Bree said, and she winked at Saul before nodding toward Jason. "Have fun with your date!"

"She's just a different girl once she gets a drink in her," Dean said, laughing off their glares as best he could. Bree giggled as they walked away.

"That was fun."

"You're insane."

"You say that as if you didn't love that about me."

Dean kissed her cheek.

"You're right," he said. "But let's not push the limits too often while we're amid the rich and powerful. I'd rather not go from being a Seraph to someone's lavatory cleaning boy."

She laughed.

"If you insist," she said. "And very well. If it will make you feel better, I'll behave."

Bree finished her first glass, wisely decided not to have a second. She felt a soft loosening of her mind, and her smile came much quicker to her lips than normal. Nice as it was to feel relaxed instead of nervous, she didn't want to risk humiliating Dean any further than she potentially already had. Older men and women drifted over to the corner in which they lurked, usually just long enough to find out their names and ask simple questions, such as whether Bree enjoyed life in the academy. The sameness of it, the steady murmur of voices and droning of the music, soon made her wish she could be out practicing with her wings instead.

"About time," Dean said, setting aside his own glass after at least an hour.

"What?" Bree asked.

In answer, Dean pointed to where Isaac Willer had walked to the center of the room. Lifting his hands above his head, the Archon clapped four times, slowly gaining the attention of the rest of the room. The din quieted, the musicians having halted their playing, and in the sudden silence, Isaac shouted out in a deep, booming voice that easily filled the entire hall.

"I thank you all for coming tonight," he said. "The winter solstice is upon us, and Weshern has thrived for yet another year. I pray we continue to endure as we always have, overcoming whatever obstacles and trying times may come. But for now, we celebrate. For now, we dance beneath the stars."

One more clap, and then the fires on the many torches instantaneously extinguished, plunging the dance hall into darkness. Bree frowned. In such dark, how were they supposed to . . .

And then the lights twinkled into being, first one, then ten, then hundreds. Soft and white, like hovering diamonds in the darkness above. Bree felt her jaw drop. Stars. The ceiling was a great field of stars. Their light shone upon the paintings, and Bree spun, taking it all in. Their world...at last she could see it as the books described. Soft blue hues tinted the trees and lakes like God's own paintbrush. The water seemed to sparkle, welcoming, mysterious. Even the frozen animals, geese and deer she'd seen a hundred times before during visits to the lake, took on a new sense of majesty in the twilight. The sight was so beautiful, so pure, and nothing like the harsh red glow of the midnight fire. Looking back up to the field of stars, she felt tears building in her eyes. The stars were false, she knew, likely using light element as the mansion had in the other furnishings, but she didn't care. It was a glimpse at a world denied to her, a world she'd always wanted to see. Now at last, she could.

"Milady," Dean said, offering her his hand. "Would you give me the honor of a dance?"

"Of course," she said, blinking away the tears and hoping he hadn't noticed.

The musicians began anew, and at a far greater volume. Bree took Dean's hands, and just like they practiced, she stepped back, then forward, following Dean's lead as he shifted gently side to side. It was a simple enough dance, asking very little of her. She'd thought it'd be silly to do so in a room full of people, but when hundreds of others danced the same, it felt like she was a part of something, a ritual binding her to the strangers in a way she'd never understand. Dean smiled at her with every step, and the false starlight sparkled in his blue eyes. Even with all the people, the darkened room felt far more intimate.

Bree heard a humming sound beneath them, and then the gold swirls on the floor started to glow.

"I have a surprise for you," Dean whispered into her ear. "Follow my lead."

Without further explanation he guided her through the slowly waving chaos of dancing couples. Bree noticed how there was a very slight order to it, as if the dancers were a funnel gently rotating. Dean actively danced against it, though where and why, she couldn't tell, but at last he reached one of the golden circles on the floor and put themselves within it, refusing to budge despite the flow of the room.

"What's going on?" Bree whispered.

"Let's just say I paid attention last year," he said, pulling her closer to him. "Hold me tight."

The gold shone brighter, and then to her shock, the floor began to rise. Glancing about, she saw that all of the golden circles were floating, and she could only guess at the machinery involved. Dean kept her twirling as they lifted, two dozen circles in total rising up as the rest of the guests continued to dance below. His right hand moved to her waist, pulling her even closer. One by one, she saw the various platforms stopping, yet theirs continued to rise.

"Dean," she said, realizing what was happening.

"Shush," he whispered. "Just dance."

And so she did, this time even slower, their feet merely shifting side to side. Of all the platforms rising to the ceiling, theirs was the very last to halt. Couples at all heights danced and moved, and those on the bottom floor peered up at them all, taking in the wondrous sight. Being at such prominence made Bree's heart hammer in her chest, while Dean seemed quite at ease as he leaned down and kissed her lips.

"People are watching," she whispered when he pulled away.

"Let them," Dean said. "You belong among the stars, Bree. I've known it from the very first moment I saw you."

She smiled, then leaned against him, her face on his chest. Back and forth they rocked, and she closed her eyes, imagining them not on a platform but in an open field, the stars, the real stars, shining above. And in that moment, she was happy, and would not trade it for the world. Not even for her wings. The music played, their bodies swayed, and on their platform of gold and marble, Bree and Dean danced and danced.

CHAPTER 19

When people warned Kael not to drink too much at the ball, he'd always assumed it was out of fear he'd act like a fool should he become intoxicated. Now, as he met with Loramere at the entrance of the academy, he realized his splitting headache might be more the reason.

"You look like you had a great time last night," Loramere said, the giant Seraph crossing his arms and grinning down at him. "You also look like you're paying for it, too."

"I'll be fine," Kael murmured. It was still early, the last remnants of morning mist still dissipating. He and Loramere both wore their uniforms and wings, with the other also carrying a large, rolled scroll capped at both ends with bronze. A thin steel chain looped around his neck, the ends connected to the bronze caps to keep the scroll secure during flight.

"Everyone says their first night drinking is a night they never forget," Loramere said. "That's a lie, of course. The first night's the easiest to forget. It's that first morning you'll always remember. Like goats are butting heads just behind your eyeballs, am I right?"

"You could say that."

Loramere laughed as he slapped Kael across the shoulder.

"That's a good man. Next time, drink some water along with your wine. It'll help, I promise. Now, are you ready to accompany me on my official duty to Center?"

Why else would I be out here? Kael thought.

"Lead the way," he said instead, not daring to say such disrespectful thoughts out loud no matter how hungover he might be.

Loramere gave him a quick salute, then clenched his left hand into a fist, thumb on the throttle. Kael did the same, and together they powered their wings and rose into the air. When the older man flew north at a gentle slope, Kael followed alongside him at such an easy pace, Kael could almost talk normally, so long as he stayed elbow to elbow with the bigger man.

"Who's your civics teacher?" Loramere asked as the lakes of Weshern passed beneath them.

"Miss Woods."

"Ah yes, that old iron nail. She tell you what we're doing?"

Kael shook his head.

"I was to be here at dawn, and do what I was told. That's all."

"Leave it to her to make us do the teaching," Loramere grumbled.

They approached one of Weshern's towns, and Loramere banked higher to ensure they were far above any of the square buildings. Kael overlooked the city, strangely fascinated by how the streets, which would have felt aimless and winding on foot, divided the place into neat little segments with exits at all four sides.

"Every four hours from dawn to dusk, we send two Seraphim carrying a message to Center to deliver to the theotechs," Loramere explained, and he tapped the capped scroll that was chained about his neck. "One is experienced, one tends to be younger, but always two, and always every four hours. I'm sure you'll come on plenty of these in the next few months, and no matter how impressive this first one feels, trust me, they'll get boring fast."

"What happens if you don't have a message to deliver?" Kael asked.

"Never happens. Sometimes the message you carry is as simple as 'I bear no message,' which is a conundrum I'd recommend you not dwell on too much, especially given your current mental state."

"Why go if there's no message?" Kael asked.

"Because if we're to declare war against an island, we need Center's permission," Loramere said. "Trust me, on our flight we'll be spotted by men and women of all four other islands. It's hard to take anyone by surprise if you only send out messengers when there's an important request. That's why we keep it nice and steady. Routine, Kael. You can disguise a lot of things by making them part of a boring old routine."

They were nearing the northeast end of Weshern, and Kael could hardly believe how quickly they'd crossed the expanse of the island, starting in the far east at the academy. End to end, Weshern was approximately thirty miles wide. What might have taken him an entire day on foot they'd crossed in half an hour with their wings. Being so high made it hard for him to realize how great a speed they flew, but seeing the roads twist and turn below him, the villages passing one after the other, was illuminating. The docks where he and Bree had flown with Nickolas months ago to have their affinity tests rapidly came into view. Kael remembered how nervous he'd been to ride the platform to Center. Now he zipped along high above the bustle of the docks, and he barely gave them a second thought.

It'd been wearing on his mind for a while now, and Loramere's words only brought it up again. After the long silence, he finally worked up the nerve to ask.

"Why do we do all this?" he asked. "One elemental prism per Seraph, permission for duels, having the theotechs oversee battles...what's the point?"

"The point is keeping the death tolls to a minimum. Battles end quicker if people can retreat and may only bring a single prism. Duels grow rarer if both need permission. Theotechs ensure that when a side retreats, no one ignores that call."

"Yes, but we shouldn't need to come crawling to them for permission for every little thing we do. We're independent nations."

"Are we really, Kael?"

It sounded borderline treasonous, and Kael frowned at the Seraph.

"What are you saying?" he asked.

"What I'm saying is the whole reason we have water to drink and food to eat is because the theotechs manage the Fount beneath Weshern," Loramere said. "Theotechs loyal to Center, not our Archon. They also supply us, at a ridiculously high cost I might add, the elements we use to power our wings and arm our gauntlets. We may not be under the direct rule of Center's theocracy, but we're hardly independent."

There was no denying what he was hearing, not with how similar the two arguments were.

"You sound like a disciple of Johan," he said.

Loramere's face immediately darkened.

"Johan preaches that the Speaker doesn't hear the words of

the angels, and we should overthrow Center's control completely, forcing the theotechs to reveal the secrets of the elements and those operating the Fount to hand over control. Don't confuse me for one of his disciples just because I'm willing to admit the complicated nature of our relationship with Center."

Loramere increased the speed of his wings, and Kael did likewise. The harsh response left him quiet, and he decided not to press the issue further. They passed the edge of Weshern, leaving nothing between them and the sparkling blue ocean far, far below. Kael's stomach tightened, and he was surprised by his sudden exhilaration. Despite all his hours flying, this was his first time over the open water. Even when he was performing some of the trickier aerial maneuvers, the ground was a few hundred feet below him at most. Now? Now, there was only a distant, rippling blue blanket. It reminded him of just how high they were, how free of the world they flew even when walking upon the grass and rock of Weshern.

Kael flew as close as he dared to Loramere and shouted to be heard.

"So what message are you carrying for us?" Kael asked, wanting to remove the silence that had come over him after the mention of Johan and push their conversation back to safer waters. "Is it one of those boring no-message ones?"

Loramere shrugged his shoulders, the motion causing him to dip a little in the air.

"Can't say for sure," he said. "We don't open these scrolls under any circumstances once they're sealed, understood? This thing could request a death duel between members of different islands, it could be numbers and rates related to trade, or it could be a request for all-out war. If it's opened, the theotechs will assume it was tampered with and not honor the request.

Trust me, Kael, you don't want to mess up some trade treaty because you got a little curious." Loramere tapped the scroll again. "Oh, and based on my experience, the odds are pretty damn good that, yeah, this is another one of those boring no-message days."

Loramere shifted a little to correct his course, and Kael followed. Up ahead, already looming large despite such distance, was Center. Its cities were white dots among the countryside, the forests dark green splotches, the rivers thin blue veins. Above them all towered the mountain, its lower half dotted with forests, its upper a deep brown. Scattered throughout were the holy temples, though from so far away they were still invisible. Flying one after the other like a trail of ants were the ferrymen, coming to and from all five directions. Instead of joining the line of ferrymen flying toward Center from Weshern, Loramere kept them far to the right, and he slowed his pace considerably.

"We're not going to the docks?" Kael asked.

"And endure all that mess?" the Seraph asked, and he gestured toward the docks with their colored flags and layers of platforms full of ferrymen. At such distance, it looked to Kael like the buzzing of a beehive. "No, we're heading straight to the source."

Kael shrugged, figuring he'd find out when they arrived. Given how Loramere flew at a leisurely speed with the throttle barely halfway full, the minutes crawled by. A few times Kael dared look to the ocean below, mesmerized by the sparkling surface, but he couldn't do so for long before his stomach started to tighten and his breaths began to feel shallow.

"So tell me about last night," Loramere said, so relaxed he might as well have been relaxing in a hammock beside a cool pond.

"Not much to say. Was pretty boring."

The older man glanced at him, eyebrow raised.

"Did you not have a date?"

"No, I did," Kael said, suddenly thinking he'd prefer silence. "Clara invited me."

"As in Clara Willer?"

When Kael nodded, Loramere laughed.

"No wonder you were bored. You spent the whole night hobnobbing with royalty, I take it? Been to a few of those myself. The elites spend so much time kissing ass they never say anything interesting for fear of developing a personality. Makes for long nights. Did yours end well at least?"

Kael felt his neck suddenly flare with heat, and he struggled to find the right words.

"What do you mean?" he asked, attempting to stall.

"I mean did you get a kiss from Weshern's most eligible bachelorette?"

Face and neck now in full blush, Kael shook his head.

"No," he said.

"She shoot you down?"

Kael felt there should be a million other things more proper to discuss as they flew toward Center, but it seemed Loramere was having far too much fun to let the topic drop.

"I, no," he stammered. "I mean, I never . . ."

The giant man let out a deep, rolling laugh that was easy to hear despite their flight.

"So you lost your nerve? I'm disappointed in you, Kael. You can fly loops in the sky, but can't work up the nerve to kiss a girl? Not even a good-bye kiss?"

Loramere was making it seem so simple. But it wasn't, Kael told himself. Was it . . . ?

"I don't think she wanted me to," he said.

The Seraph twisted so he could grin at Kael.

"Where'd you say good-bye to her, at the door?"

"Yeah."

"Did she linger around afterward, maybe tell you how great a time she had before you could go?"

More heat burning in his neck and face.

"Yeah."

"Then you're as clueless as you are cowardly. A fine combination, Kael, and one you need to start fixing as soon as possible."

"I'll keep it in mind," Kael grumbled. "For now, how about we stick to our duties?"

"As you insist, little Seraph," Loramere said.

The southern edge of Center was almost upon them, the buzzing chaos of the docks several miles to their west. By now, Kael had an idea where they flew. An enormous fortress surrounded by forests, like a castle from the old fairy tales Aunt Bethy used to tell, loomed at the southwest edge of Center. Dozens of stone towers rose up from various corners, for the fortress had multiple wings stretching out in all directions. Its rear was built into the very beginnings of Center's mountain, its walls and towers melding into it as if the fortress were a natural extension of the stone. There was no mistaking the fortress's entrance, not even from afar, for it bore twin wooden doors bolted together with iron, the doors more than ten times the height of a man. Two long walls angled out at either side of the entrance, and armored men with long spears and shields patrolled its surface. In the skies all about the fortress hovered golden-armored knights, at least two dozen by Kael's count.

"We're heading into the belly of the beast," Loramere said. "This is Heavenstone, the theotechs' private fortress and home to their angelic knights. Keep your mouth shut and do nothing that might draw attention. When it comes to the theotechs, the worst thing you can do is get noticed."

Kael bobbed his head as they flew across soft rolling hills leading up to the entrance, effectively following a winding road of stone bricks. Despite the early hour, he saw more than a dozen heavy carts pulled by donkeys traveling the road, and he wondered what they brought with them. Goods to barter? Tribute, perhaps? He knew so little of Center, only that its power was absolute, that power wielded by the Speaker for the Angels, the man responsible for sharing and protecting the word of God since the Ascension.

As they flew closer to the fortress, Kael saw one of the knights split off from the castle and zip toward them. He didn't join them, only hovered above, following like a shadow.

"Don't let it unnerve you," Loramere said. "They're a careful lot, that's all. Speaking of..."

Though the castle looked at least a quarter mile away, Loramere dipped low to the ground while righting himself. The glow of his silver wings faded, and Kael mimicked the maneuver. The wind blew against their upright bodies, killing their speed, and with practiced ease Loramere dropped to the ground, legs pumping for just a second or two as he slowed to a walk. Kael let himself float a bit longer, not wanting to misjudge and topple face-first onto the brick road, then let his feet touch down. Shutting off his wings, he stretched his arms and legs. He'd been far more nervous than he realized, for the muscles in his back felt incredibly tight.

"Never fly straight into any building owned by the theotechs," Loramere explained as they walked side by side down the road. "Always land so they can get a good look at you, as well as confirm you're not a threat."

Sure enough, the knight who had been shadowing them flew

overhead, accompanied by the thrumming sound of his wings. Kael almost wanted to wave at him, to show they weren't dangerous, but he remembered what Loramere said. The last thing he wanted to do was get noticed, for any reason. Best to pretend he'd done this all before.

Falling silent, the two strode toward Heavenstone, which looked even more imposing from ground level. Ahead of them was a covered cart driven by a young man, and the sound of its wheels upon the stone clattered in a constant chorus. Despite the heavy cloth covering, Kael spotted wicker baskets full of apples underneath, and his stomach rumbled.

"Should have eaten something before we left," he said.

"We can swing by one of the markets afterward if you'd like," Loramere said.

"I didn't bring any coin with me."

Loramere clucked his tongue as he shook his head.

"I'll be nice and pay for today," he said. "It's not your fault you're young and stupid."

"Thanks," Kael muttered.

When they reached the edges of the two walls on either side of the road protecting the entrance, Kael snuck a look at the tops. At least fifty men patrolled either edge, with another ten positioned at even intervals, staring down carefully at all who passed. On the road itself, ten soldiers stood guard on either side of the door. The traffic had bunched into a line, for each cart was thoroughly checked, and those who walked carrying baskets or bags had to set them down so the soldiers could riffle through them.

Kael and Loramere waited patiently in line for their turn, and Kael realized how strange that was. At the Weshern docks, Nickolas had commandeered a lift for them to use, but here on Center? Here they would wait, no different from a farmer or baker. Whether deliberate or accidental, either way it made him realize of how little importance they were to Center when compared to the prestige they carried back on Weshern.

After several minutes, it was finally their turn.

"What business brings you here?" asked one of the soldiers, who stepped out from the line to address them. Like the angelic knights', his armor was tinted gold, though paler, and instead of a white tunic, his was a dark crimson.

"I bring news from Weshern," Loramere said, standing upright and speaking in a rigid, formal tone. "It is for the eyes of the theotechs only."

The soldier nodded, and he beckoned them on through the doors. Kael did his best to stare straight ahead, but he cheated at the last moment when they stepped through the enormous doors that looked like they belonged to a giant. Though they were opened only a sliver of the way, there was still enough room for two carts to enter side by side. Four enormous black iron chains were bolted to the interior side of each door, and they stretched up to the ceiling and then vanished through gaps in the stone, connecting to various hidden machinery. Kael doubted he could lift even a single link without aid.

The entry room was enormous, the ceiling as tall as the doors. The floor was bare stone, much of it covered with dirt, straw, and excrement from the animals pulling the many carts. Twin rows of pillars formed a natural walkway, but instead of following it to what appeared to be an enormous market, Loramere took an immediate right, passing between two pillars. On the other side was a red carpet running parallel to the pillars, and Loramere led them down it to the end of the room.

"Just follow the red carpet," Loramere whispered. Given the

rattling of wheels, the clop of hooves of the horses and donkeys, and the hundreds of voices bartering back and forth, Kael had to slide even closer and strain to hear him.

The carpet turned right, to where two angelic knights stood guarding a curved archway leading deeper into the fortress. Their armor gleamed in the light that came in through the many slender windows. One man had two swords strapped to his waist, while the other held an enormous black ax, its head painted with swirling red runes. The handle alone was as tall as Kael. He couldn't imagine the strength required to lift and swing it in combat, but the knight appeared to hold it with ease. Standing at a lectern behind the two knights was a robed theotech, all red cloth and gold chains and white hair. On his lectern was an enormous open tome, and at his side was a wooden box filled with at least twenty scrolls tied shut with a simple bit of string.

Loramere clasped his hands behind him and bowed low, and Kael hurried to do the same. Neither said anything, only waited to be addressed by the theotech.

"Weshern?" the man asked, his voice groaning as if marbles were lodged deep in his throat.

"We are," Loramere answered.

The theotech outstretched his hand.

"Well, let's have it."

Loramere stepped between the knights, careful not to move all the way past them, and handed over the scroll before stepping back. The theotech removed both caps, broke the wax seal, and unfurled the scroll. His watery eyes skimmed over the message, and he chuckled softly.

"How interesting," he said. "I believe this is a first for me, Seraph, a request for a duel where I already have the answer waiting."

He bent down to the box, grabbed one of the scrolls almost

immediately, and then held it out. The knight with the ax took it and handed it to Loramere, who accepted it with another low bow of his head.

"We will administer the duel tomorrow at sunrise," the theotech said. "You may go."

"Many thanks, kind theotech," Loramere said. Spinning on his heels, he marched away, and Kael followed.

"A duel?" he asked as they trudged down the red carpet. "Between whom?"

"If you want to know, then go ahead and see for yourself," Loramere said, tossing him the scroll. Kael caught it, and he stared at the Seraph with his eyes wide.

"We're allowed to look?" he asked. After all the care to ensure the delivered message was secret, it seemed bizarre that the response would be so carelessly handled.

"If the theotechs give us a scroll, it's common knowledge of the least importance," Loramere explained. "If it was something important, or needed to be kept secret, it'd never be in our possession. A knight would fly over with it instead. Besides, it's just a duel. Word of it will be announced the moment we land back in Weshern anyway."

It made a little sense, Kael supposed. When he tugged on the string, the scroll easily slid open. As they exited the enormous double doors, Kael unrolled it so he could read the already-prepared acceptance.

Eric Drae, of the holy island of Galen, accepts the proposed duel offered by Dean Averson, of the holy island of Weshern. As this is a matter of honor, the duel is to the death, and bears no other terms or consequences.

Kael's feet felt frozen to the ground, and it was only when Loramere called his name harshly that he forced himself to continue moving away from the fortress entrance.

"Well, what is it?" Loramere asked. "What's the matter with you?"

"I need to get home, now," Kael said.

"Don't you want to grab something to eat first?"

Kael shook his head.

"How far until I can safely fly?" he asked, thinking of the security and paranoia surrounding Heavenstone.

"About where we landed," Loramere said, gesturing into the distance. "If you're in a hurry, you'll need to run."

Kael rolled the scroll up and gave it back to the Seraph.

"Then I need to run," he said.

Legs pumping, he raced past the many carts continuing to travel his way. A shadow flashed over him as one of the knights followed, perhaps curious as to the reason for his run, but he paid it no mind. He had to find Bree. He had to tell her. Perhaps it wasn't too late. Perhaps they could still cancel the duel, and even if they couldn't, she still deserved to know.

When it seemed he was far enough away, he leapt into the air, jamming down on the throttle and paying no mind to the painful jerk on his body from the sudden shift in speed. Soaring over rolling green hills, Kael pushed the throttle as high as he dared.

Dean Averson . . . duel to the death . . .

"I'm sorry, Bree," he whispered as he soared over the island's edge, giving not a thought to the expanse of blue water roiling far beneath him.

CHAPTER

20

Bree walked through the field, the morning dew wiping off the grass and onto her pants.

Why didn't you tell me?

She'd screamed it at Dean the day before, screamed it as she struck his chest with her fists.

I didn't want you worried, he'd said. As if that helped. As if that mattered. A mere day before, the six-month evaluation had loomed like a bear on her back, but now it meant nothing compared to her current terror. Dean had told her to meet him at the field south of the academy, just before sunrise. In the red hue, she hurried to where Dean already waited. He wore his wings, his large swords strapped to his waist. He'd drawn one sword, and he lazily weaved it through the air. When he saw her approach, he sheathed it and smiled.

"You're almost late," he said.

"I almost didn't come."

She wrapped her arms around him, settled her head against the leather straps of his chest harness. He kissed the top of her head and ran a hand down the side of her face.

"I'm glad you did," he whispered.

Bree pulled away and put on a brave face. She didn't want to be a distraction, not when Dean's life was on the line, so she smiled and pretended all was fine.

"Don't you dare get hurt," she said. "I'd hate to lose my sparring partner."

"I don't plan on it." He turned to face the direction of distant Galen. Weshern was the easternmost of the five outer islands, Galen the westernmost. Bree followed his gaze, and like a gold dot in the smoky sky, she saw Dean's opponent flying in alone.

"Who is he?" she asked. Dean had said little the night before, promising to explain only the following morning.

"Eric Drae," Dean said, staring at that approaching gold dot. "Three years ago, Eric killed my older brother in a duel. Three long years I've waited, until the theotechs would finally accept my request when I turned eighteen. This is everything I've prepared for, Bree. I won't lose."

"You don't have to do this," she said. "It's not worth your life."

"It's not worth my life," he said. "But it is worth my brother's. He deserved far better. I won't let him go unavenged."

He reached out and brushed her dark hair away from her face, then smiled such a sad smile.

"I love you, Bree," he said.

"I love you, too."

Dean turned, put his thumb on the throttle, and then softly rose into the air. Alone, Bree watched him fly toward that gold dot, now barely perceptible as a pair of wings on a red-colored jacket. Bree glanced over her shoulder toward the academy, and she saw that several of the Seraphim had gathered to watch from atop its walls. Among them was a pair of theotechs, and as Eric closed in, they took to the air. Bree watched them fly over her head, red robes and sashes billowing. The pair split, one flying toward each duelist.

"You can do this," Bree whispered as Dean floated in the blue morning sky. The two theotechs raised their arms, the groups three hundred yards apart and at even height with one another. Bree clutched her hands together, her chest tighter than a fisherman's knot. Eric was close enough that she could almost make out his features. She didn't know what she'd expected, but he looked rather plain, his hair dark, his body lankier than Dean's. He looked like Kael, she realized, a tanner, older version of Kael. The realization made her even more uneasy. Dean was supposed to kill a monster. That's what Eric was, right, a monster who'd killed Dean's brother? Not a student just like her. Not someone who resembled her own brother.

The theotechs shouted something too far away to hear, then dropped their hands in perfect synchronization. And just like that, the duel began.

Dean tilted his body forward and then burst into motion, his right arm outstretched. Thin balls of flame no larger than his fist shot at Eric, leaving thin black smoke trails. Instead of charging, Eric turned about at the signal and fled. As Dean chased, the two theotechs flew to the safety of the academy, remaining hovering in the air to watch.

The fireballs missed, all three too far to the left due to Eric's sudden veering to the right. Dean chased, and Bree realized how similar it was to the game she played with Kael. Eric weaved back and forth through the air, flying at an incredible speed. Dean followed like a shadow, twisting himself left and right with careful movements. Occasionally he flung another ball of flame, but with Eric consistently dodging, it looked impossible for Dean to get a clear shot. When Dean closed in, Eric suddenly killed his speed and spun about, bracing his right arm with his left. Bree felt her heart freeze as a boulder twice the size of a man shot out from Eric's gauntlet, the stone seeming to start out no larger than an eye before rapidly increasing to its full size.

Dean may not have been prepared, but he reacted quickly enough to save his life. Shoving his upper body downward, he dived underneath the boulder while increasing his speed. As smoothly as he'd spun, Eric rotated another hundred and eighty degrees, flaring his gold wings with power. Just like that, he was now chasing Dean instead of being chased. Thankfully Dean had maintained his speed, while Eric had not, which meant he had a large degree of separation. The two zipped across the skies above the field, Dean pushing his wings harder than she'd ever seen him fly. Eric did everything he could to shrink the gap, hurling slender stones the size of a fist to force Dean to weave and dodge. Doing so cost him speed, and with steady determination, Eric closed the distance.

As the stones came flying in, Dean looped upward, then twisted halfway through so he could charge straight at Eric. Again Bree felt her heart skip a beat as the two unleashed their elements at each other, fire and stone connecting in midair. Neither harmed, they looped back around for a second pass. Instead of small projectiles, Dean attempted a single spray, lashing his right arm to cover a far larger area. Eric seemed to have anticipated the tactic. He flung a large stone straight at it, and as the projectile cleared a path, he dove through. Two smaller stones followed, one clipping Dean across the leg, the other flying just above his head.

"Just a little longer," Bree whispered. The man from Galen had used far more of his element than Dean. If he could endure a few more minutes, he'd gain the advantage, with Eric forced to use the last of his element for defense. And if he ran out completely, and had to resort to blades...

It seemed Dean had the same thought. Abandoning the headlong charge, he veered away, flying in Bree's direction. He weaved and twirled, and when Eric started firing stones, Dean pulled up and shot straight into the air. Eric failed to anticipate, and as he shot underneath, Dean unleashed a barrage of six balls of flame. Five missed, but one caught the top of a wing. Bree held her breath, hoping it'd damage the mechanics, but that appeared to not be the case. Unhindered, Eric plummeted toward the ground to force Dean back into the chase.

Except Dean didn't chase. He kept the height advantage, hovering in place as he steadily rotated, watching Eric fly about.

"What are you doing?" Bree whispered. Dean was letting Eric get away, and once safely out of reach of his fire, Eric rose back into the air. Looping about, he charged headlong, and it seemed like that was exactly what Dean wanted. The two raced toward each other, subtly weaving and shifting to make any potential shots more difficult. Bree watched the distance between them shrink, her eyes bouncing back and forth between the two Seraphim. Dean must have seen something, or learned something from their previous charge, but what?

Eric unleashed a barrage of razor-sharp spikes, and Dean twirled his body as he knifed through them. Now close, he straightened up and braced his arm with his other hand. Fire burst out of it, again in a wide wave. Just like before, Eric shot a stone to blast a hole through it. That was it, Bree realized. That was the maneuver Dean had anticipated. Dean sent lances of fire into the exposed gap, except Eric never tried to fly through. Instead he dove low, beneath the fire, and then curled upward. Bree saw his gauntlet reaching, and she let out a cry.

"No!"

Eric flew skyward, passing mere feet away from Dean. A single stone fired, just a blur of gray reflecting the morning sun. Bree couldn't see the connection. She didn't have to. Dean's body tensed, and his wings lost their silver glow. Arms and legs suddenly limp, Dean began to drift to the ground. Bree's mouth hung open, and her mind refused to accept what she saw before her.

This isn't happening.

Eric looped back around at a more careful pace, and he drew a sword from his belt. On his second pass he slammed straight into Dean's body, his sword leading. It buried into his chest, and as they spun from the impact, Eric guided them toward the ground. Toward *her,* Bree realized. When he was twenty feet away, he shoved the body off his blade, dropping it at Bree's feet.

"A fine battle," Eric said, dipping his head as if in respect. Bree stared at him in shock. *Respect?* This man killed her lover, dumped his body at her feet, and then pretended to have respect? As Eric flew away, Bree rushed to Dean's body, fell to her knees. There was no hope, no delusion of his survival. His eyes were lifeless. A shard of stone was embedded halfway into his stomach, and his chest bore a vicious puncture. When she put her hands to his chest, smearing them with blood, she felt no heartbeat.

"Dean," she whispered, tears trickling down her face. "Why, Dean..."

She looked up and saw that Eric was calmly flying back toward his home island. Whatever life he'd known, he'd resume, but there'd be no such thing for Bree. Her afternoon training sessions, her swordplay, their nights sneaking out to watch the midnight fire... gone. Something snapped within her, and she looked back to her friend's body with growing rage. She had to hurry. The theotechs were on their lazy way. Her hands flew across the buckles, undoing one after the other. She dared not think of the consequences, dared not doubt her actions, anything that might persuade her from her revenge. Instead she focused on her fury, let it fuel her movements. Faceless, nameless Seraphim of Galen had taken her parents, and now Eric had stolen Dean from her as well. She wouldn't let him get away with it, no matter the cost.

The last of the buckles undone, she pulled the wings off his body and slid her arms into the harness. Dean's was obviously fitted for his much larger frame, and she tightened the straps as she buckled them on her own person. That done, she grabbed the sword belt, wrapped it about her waist, and then cinched it tight. Her eyes scanned the sky. Eric had shrunk to a distant dot, likely with no idea of what she was doing. The theotechs, however, looked like they understood, and they flew with sudden urgency. Not that it would matter. They were too far away. There'd be no stopping her now.

"Come back here," Bree whispered. She burst into a run, then leapt into the air. Her thumb pushed the switch to its maximum, the first time she'd ever done so. Her wings flared, catching her and then yanking her skyward. Air blasted about her, tugging at her hair and clothes. The sensation of speed was incredible, and it seemed her launch was accompanied by a rumbling shock wave. She flew straight at Eric, no dodging, no weaving. Just speed.

Bree was halfway there before Eric realized he was being followed. The Seraph glanced over his shoulder, saw her, and then temporarily cut the power to his wings. As his momentum carried him, he spun about so that he faced her, braced his arm, and then unleashed a torrent of stones. Bree reacted on instinct, shifting left before twirling her body as she rolled right, lances of stone knifing beneath her. She kept the throttle pushed to its maximum, refusing to slow.

Mere seconds away, she lifted her right gauntlet and opened her hand. Eric saw it, and instead of fleeing, he countered it with his best defense. It was a wall meant solely to protect him, flat and broad and moving with hardly any speed. But Bree didn't fire quick balls of flame, nor did she send out a fan like Dean's. Palm wide, fingers stretched back, she unleashed every bit of the power within the fire prism. There'd be no other chance, no second shot. The fire burst out of her, draining her, erupting in a massive explosion that rolled through the air. The power of it jarred her arm backward, and she had to push against it with all her strength to prevent losing control entirely.

Eric had not expected such a display, and his wall was meager protection against it. He banked to the side while trying to dodge, and he was only partially successful. The fire washed over half his body, charring his skin and melting parts of his left wing.

There in the sky, she heard him scream.

Eric hovered, trying to regain control of his wings as he fought against the pain. Bree gave him no chance. She drew one of Dean's swords, not bothering to latch it to her gauntlet. It was longer and heavier than hers, so with two hands she gripped it as she flew toward Eric. With a single swing, she opened him at the stomach, just like he had Dean. He gave another cry, the golden hue around his wings fading, and then he began to plummet. Bree looped around, still not satisfied. Angling lower, she caught him halfway to the ground, slashing one of his legs. Blood splattered upward, leaving a trail in the air. Bree twisted, righted herself, and then cut the power to her wings. She fell just above Eric's body, the handle of her sword gripped tightly with both hands, the blade pointed downward.

When Eric hit ground, Bree followed. The sword tore into his chest as she slammed onto the field, the impact jarring her entire body. Her weight gave the blade power, and it pierced to the hilt, pinning Eric to the grass field. Bree gasped, and it seemed all her rage poured out through the weapon, leaving her with a sudden numbness in her hands and chest. She leaned on her knees, still clutching the sword, her forehead pressed against the hilt. Her eyes closed. Finally, in the silence of the field, she released her sorrow, let it tear out of her from the very pit of her stomach as she screamed and screamed.

At last she quieted. Tears sliding down her face, she rose to her feet and looked to the academy. The theotechs approached, coming for what was theirs. Bree yanked at the buckles, and she felt so tired, so defeated.

"Take it, you vultures!" she screamed as she hurled the harness toward them. "Take it back!"

The two landed in flanking position, their faces stone masks. One she recognized as Theotech Vyros from their seventh-day services. The other was a stranger.

"On your knees," Vyros ordered.

She obeyed, not that she had any choice in the matter. The other theotech pinned her arms behind her back before slapping cold steel manacles about her wrists. They gave no reason. They asked for no explanation. Silent, they lifted her up and carried her away.

For several hours, Bree waited on the bench outside Headmaster Simmons's office while the theotechs summoned a representative from Galen. The time crawled by like a wounded animal.

Her face was dirty and wet from her occasional tears, and her right arm and shoulder were sore from when she unleashed her fire. No one talked to her, nor offered to remove the manacles that trapped her arms behind her back. Over-Secretary Waller swung by once to speak with Jay, and when she came back out, her look was calm as ever.

"The theotechs will be here soon," she said, tightening the band that held her brown hair away from her face. "Say as little as possible, and let Jay do the rest. And for your sake, pray the theotechs are in a good mood."

Bree nodded, said nothing. She felt too empty and drained to discuss anything. There was no excuse she could offer, no debate to be made. She'd killed Eric Drae in full view of two theotechs and a number of Weshern Seraphim. The only thing left to resolve was her punishment. So she stared into nothing, reliving the two deaths. Eric's should have given her satisfaction, but each time she imagined the sword plunging through his chest, she felt increasingly numb. Dean's, though... that singular moment ached every single time.

She heard a door open, and she glanced to her left. Coming down the hall were the two theotechs who had attended the duel. They'd removed their wings, which revealed more of their long, flowing red robes and their golden jewelry adorned by the symbol of Center. With them was a man she did not recognize, and she assumed him to be the Galen representative. He wore white pants and a white jacket, black boots, and a deep crimson shirt. Sewn into the fabric on either shoulder were burning torch emblems. His dark hair was pulled back into a ponytail, and while the theotechs completely ignored her as they stepped into Headmaster Simmons's office, this man glared as if she were the most disgusting thing he'd ever seen.

The door to the headmaster's office had barely shut before it opened again.

"Come," said Vyros. Standing with a groan, Bree ignored the ache in her legs and walked inside.

Jay sat in his chair, his face an unreadable mask. When she entered, he acted as if it were beneath him to even look at her. The two theotechs flanked either side of his desk, and Bree had a feeling they would be moderating this meeting, not her headmaster. The Galen representative stood beside the door with his arms crossed over his chest. A lone chair waited for her, and she sat on its front edge so there was room for her bound hands.

"We're all here," Jay said. "Shall we finish this meeting so I can return to my students?"

"In time," Vyros said. He ran a hand over his balding head, as if smoothing hair that was no longer there. "But first, let us hear her confession. Breanna Skyborn, I want you to address all your answers to myself, and no one else. Do you understand?"

"I do," she said.

"Good." Vyros tilted his head, his green eyes drilling into her. "Then let us get straight to the point. Did you steal Dean Averson's gear and use it to kill Eric Drae?"

Bree swallowed a rock the size of an apple.

"I did," she said.

"Then I see no point to this discussion," the Galen representative blurted out. "She has admitted to the murder. Combat between islands is expressly forbidden without Center's permission, and it carries only one penalty, death."

"Patience, Luke," the other theotech told him. "Have you somewhere else to be?"

Luke frowned but said nothing.

"Indeed, unauthorized combat is a serious crime," Vyros said, turning back to her. "We cannot let the islands descend into anarchy as they act out their petty grudges. Permission for a duel was given only for Eric Drae of Galen to fight Dean Averson of Weshern, not for Breanna Skyborn. I see no other way to interpret these events."

Headmaster Simmons cleared his throat to gain their attention.

"What you saw was a woman initiating a duel against the man who killed her lover," he said. "As such, it is a perfectly defensible reason for a duel, a duel that Eric clearly accepted by turning about and attacking Bree with his element."

Luke looked like he'd been sucker punched.

"Is that true?" he asked, whirling on Bree.

"I...no," Bree said, making sure she addressed Vyros and not Luke. "Dean and I weren't..."

"Breanna," Jay said, his deep voice brooking no argument. "Tell the truth. Were you and Dean lovers?"

Dean had always insisted they keep their relationship private, to avoid any possible punishment from the academy administration, but that seemed pointless now. Without Dean, there was no secret left to keep. Bree looked to the floor and fought down a wave of embarrassment at admitting such a thing to four older men.

"Yes," she said. "We were."

"Valid reason as it may be," Luke said, "it still doesn't justify this farcical duel. No permission for their fight was ever given by Center."

"Permission doesn't need to be given," Jay said. "The practice began as a courtesy, and has now become tradition. All duels must be willingly accepted by both parties, begun on fair terms, and watched by a neutral third party. Those are the only rules we must abide by, and Breanna followed all three."

"That's ridiculous," Luke said, and he sounded completely baffled. "Even if that were the case, Center never accepts any duels involving a Seraph below the age of eighteen."

"Again, that is policy, not law," Jay said, turning to Vyros. "And the punishment for breaking it is my responsibility, not yours. With two theotechs as witnesses, Breanna Skyborn engaged the murderer of her lover and defeated him in fair combat, having issued her challenge by flying after him, and he clearly accepting by being the first to use his element. Can you deny any of this?"

"It does indeed match what we witnessed," Vyros said, looking to the other theotech, who nodded.

Luke looked ready to explode, and he clearly saw his opportunity for retribution dwindling.

"If you accept this, you spit in the face of all of Galen," he told Vyros. "Eric was a good man who fought and won a fair duel against a family that has tormented him for years, only to be attacked and killed without warning or preparation."

Bree frowned at that. Tormented? What did Luke mean by that?

"Eric dumped Dean's body at his lover's feet," Headmaster Simmons interjected. "I think you and I disagree on what it means to be a good man."

"It was an act of respect, not mockery!"

"Enough," Vyros said, stepping between them. "We have reached our decision, and it is final. By killing Dean, Eric provided ample reason for another duel, the nature of which was clearly spontaneous due to Breanna's use of Dean's old harness. The battle was fair, and Eric's actions showed he had every desire to partake in it."

"This is shameful!" Luke shouted.

"Then look to the man who brought you that shame," the

other theotech said. "Put it on the shoulders of your own Seraph, who lost to a first-year student lacking a single minute of combat experience."

Luke flung open the door, but before he left he turned and pointed a finger right at Headmaster Simmons.

"This will not go unanswered," he said. "Our people will cry for justice, and our Seraphim will give it to them."

Luke slammed the door behind him. Bree watched him go, and while she knew she should feel relief, she just felt drained. She'd cried her tears, first over Dean's body, then the body of his killer. Now she only wanted rest. Vyros walked to her side, and at his beckon, she leaned forward and twisted to give him access to the manacles. Pulling a key from his pocket, he unlocked them, and Bree groaned with relief as she pulled her arms before her, stretching muscles that were now terribly sore.

"I would strongly recommend not performing such a stunt again," the theotech said. "The extenuating circumstances here are all that protect you. Should this offense be repeated by *any* Seraph of Weshern," he said, glancing at Headmaster Simmons, "then we will consider this a purposeful slight toward Center's authority, and will react accordingly."

"I assure you, it will not happen again," Jay said.

"Good."

The two theotechs dipped their heads in respect and then stepped out. The door shut behind them, leaving Bree alone with the headmaster. The older man crossed his arms and stared at her, his lip and jaw twisting as if he were chewing on his own tongue.

"What did Luke mean, about Dean's family tormenting Eric's?" she asked when he did not speak.

"Dean's father was a skilled Seraph," Jay said. "He died in battle against Galen, but before he fell he killed both of Eric's parents. The siblings have challenged each other to duels ever since, an unfortunate tradition I've been forced to witness over the past six years. I daresay when Eric dropped Dean's body at your feet, he thought that tradition finally come to an end."

Bree winced at the memory, wishing she could somehow push it away, pretend it never was.

"What Luke said…he's threatening war, isn't he?" she asked. "Why would you risk so much for me?"

"Because I watched two good students die at that man's hands," Jay said. "And when you flew after him, I thought I was about to watch a third. For that alone, I refuse to let you drop to your death in a Galen well."

Bree nodded, still feeling unworthy of such a gamble.

"Thank you," she said, her voice cracking.

"That doesn't mean you will escape this completely," he said. "I have not decided your punishment, and I won't without speaking to the Archon first. Until further notice, you are confined within the academy's walls and skies directly above. You are also banned from all training sessions and classes. Know that if you fly beyond our walls in an attempt to flee or hide, I will have you executed the moment you are found. And you will be found, Bree. Weshern is not big enough to hide you forever."

"Yes sir," Bree said, her mouth suddenly feeling like it'd been stuffed with cloth.

The headmaster stared at her a moment longer, then shook his head.

"Maintaining your presence here in the academy will be seen as an additional insult to Galen. Combining that with your recklessness today, your earlier outbursts…Bree, unless you can get your flame element under control, I suggest you start contemplating a life outside these walls."

There was no other way to interpret such a statement. Fighting back tears, Bree clicked her feet together, put her arms behind her back, and then bowed.

"Sir, if that is the case, I'd like my additional allotment of fire element canceled."

There was no hiding the sadness on the headmaster's face.

"I understand," he said. "And I'm sorry, Bree. You'll be missed."

Bree hurried out from the office, wishing for nothing but solitude. To her surprise, Theotech Vyros stood waiting beside the door, arms crossed.

"Oh," Bree said, unsure of what else to say as he stared at her with frightening intensity. He loomed above her, and she felt so small, so insignificant as she stepped away. This was not the dull man from the weekly sermons. This was a man with a purpose, whose eyes seemed to see far more than should be possible.

"Try harder to stay safe, Breanna," Vyros said. "Gifts can only be repaid by the living, not the dead."

He offered nothing else, only stared at her as she hurried away, each step quicker than the last as she fled his chilling words.

CHAPTER

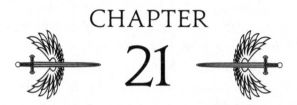

21

For the second time that year, Bree knelt before the wall surrounding the academy and touched the names of the dead. Her fingers looped over the name of Gavin Welker, slid past Lily Welsh, and then stopped on the most recent name carved into the stone. Her entire body froze as she stared at it, wishing she could scrub it away, leaving the stone bare and clean. Only former Archons were buried in permanent graves beside the holy mansion, a small tombstone marking their passage from life to death. All others, no matter how rich or poor, were buried in communal graves, their bodies to be broken down and reused in the fields. Those who were members of the academy were given a single remembrance: their name, carved in stone upon the wall, coupled with the year of their death.

Dean Averson, 515 a.a. It was all she had left of him.

Bree's finger dipped into the *D*, slowly circling through its smooth indent. They'd held the burial earlier that morning at the communal grave north of the academy, Theotech Vyros presiding over the service. Hundreds had attended, and she wished it was because they'd loved Dean like she had. But no. Dean's death was just another rallying cry against Galen, a prism for the people of Weshern to shine their hate through.

More fingers brushing the letters. She pretended she didn't touch stone, but instead his smooth skin, his soft lips, his smiling face. Lost to her. Bree pulled back her hand as if the stone burned her, then struck the wall with her fist, beating it until her hand bled as she sobbed. Lost to her, and for what?

"Was it worth it?" she screamed. "Was it worth losing me for your pride, your damn family pride?"

That'd been the worst of it, the absolute worst. She'd hovered at the back of the congregation, chewing on her tongue to hold back sniffles as Vyros droned on and on about the glories of heaven. She should have gone unnoticed, but Dean's mom had spotted her before she could leave. Ignoring the others wishing to comfort her, the woman had rushed to Bree and clutched her hands in a vise grip. Her eyes were solid red, her face permanently wet.

"Thank you," this grieving mother had told her. "Thank you for avenging both my sons."

Thanking her? Bree should have cut the wings off Dean's harness, should have latched onto his arms and demanded he never leave her side. Killing Eric had been selfish. Killing him had been mindless hurt and rage. She didn't want to be thanked. She didn't deserve that, not from a woman who had just lost everything. It left her sick and confused and fleeing the funeral before the first shovelful of dirt fell across Dean's carefully wrapped body.

And now this name on the wall. There was nothing she could do to wash it away. Even if she unleashed all her fire from her gauntlet the fire would blacken the stone but not fill in the gaps. DEAN AVERSON, 515 A.A. Never changing. Never coming back. She pressed her forehead against the name and closed her eyes.

"I loved you, Dean," she whispered, imagining him hearing. "You knew that, right? Because I'd have told you more often, I'd have done more, I'd have...I'd have..."

She cried against the stone amid the cold wind and silence, let the sorrow bleed out of her until her pride forced her to regain control. She'd always considered herself strong. She had to be if she wanted to follow in her parents' footsteps. But sometimes when the prying eyes were gone, when lost in solitude, she felt like nothing more than breaking, breaking and screaming as she raged against a world she could not strike with her swords nor burn with her fire. A blunted blade. An impotent flame. Perhaps that was all she was, but it didn't matter. The ghost of Dean would not tell her how to go on. She'd have to do it herself.

Wiping her face clean on her sleeve, she backed away from the wall, giving Dean's name one last touch. Needing to be doing something, anything, she hurried to the gear sheds and retrieved her swords and wings. Headmaster Simmons had banned her from official practices, but that didn't mean she couldn't train on her own. Once outfitted, she flew to the field not far south of the road where Dean's group had practiced. Long before she reached there, Bree knew something was wrong. Only one person remained, Sasha, a frown locked on the lanky woman's face as she moved through her stances.

"Where is everyone?" Bree asked, gently landing on her feet.

Sasha spun on her heel, her swords weaving in a jagged, rushed pattern.

"Already done for the day," she said.

Bree frowned. It was far too early in the morning for them to be finished, especially since most had attended the funeral prior to starting. The group could have worked for half an hour at most, a paltry amount compared to when Dean had kept them going sometimes for hours at a time, swapping dueling partners until they were all exhausted.

"Do you want to spar?" Bree asked. She felt too drained for it, but she craved anything to get her mind off the name carved into the outer wall.

Sasha twirled her swords, then jammed them into their sheaths.

"No, I think I'm done, too."

Bree felt another wave of tears coming, and she fought it down. Sasha refused to meet her gaze, and the curt way she answered her questions made it seem she were angry. But why?

"You're mad at me, I get it," Bree said before Sasha could leave. "Could you at least tell me why?"

Sasha released her ponytail by ripping off the band, then shook her head to loosen her red hair. At last she met Bree's gaze, and her eyes were bloodshot.

"This was Dean's group," she said. "He was the only one who thought swordplay could be something more than a final desperation tactic in battle. The past three years he learned what he could from books, trainers, and Commander Argus himself. And do you know what he gained from all that?"

Sasha tugged on the buckle of her sword belt. When it came loose, she flung the swords to the grass.

"Nothing," she said. "Dean died, because we don't fight with swords, we fight with lightning and ice and stone. You, the worst fire user in academy history, managed to kill the person the finest swordsman could not. Yes, Bree, I'm mad, but not at you. I'm mad at myself for wasting my damn time."

A trail of tears trickled down her cheeks, but Sasha kept her voice controlled. She moved to leave, reconsidered, then picked up her swords and tucked them underneath her left arm. Sasha's face softened a bit as she put a hand on Bree's shoulder.

"Go home," she said. "There's no place for you in battle, and we all know it. I think you do, too. The time of meeting blade to blade in the skies is gone."

Bree had no heart to answer. She could barely form words in her tired mind. Sasha's fingers squeezed her shoulder, an act meant to be comforting, but it felt like she was driving nails into her flesh. No place. Go home. Was that what they wanted of her? Was that what they all wanted?

Bree, I suggest you start contemplating a life outside these walls.

There was no fighting off the tears now. She let them flow as she drew her own swords, pointedly putting her back to Sasha as the woman walked away. Hands shaking, she put her left foot forward and readied her blades. Lips quivering, she shifted, one stance to another, the ghostly image of Dean smiling beside her, urging her on.

Kael was soaking wet when Amanda opened the door to let him in.

"Has Bree come back yet?" he asked, ducking inside.

"No, I'm sorry," Amanda said, frowning with worry.

Thunder crackled, and as the light flashed over them, Amanda peered over his shoulder at the storm.

"Damn it," Kael said. "If she does, let her know I'm still looking for her."

Amanda bobbed her tiny head.

"I will," she promised.

Taking in a deep breath, Kael tugged at the bottom of his jacket to straighten it and then stepped back out into the storm.

It had rolled in on a cold wind an hour before, deep black clouds shockingly close to the surface. Lightning crashed within them, the thunder at a constant rumble, but so far the strikes had not hit Weshern. Not that that made Kael feel particularly safe as he ran across the street toward his own apartment. The rain beat down on him, huge drops that stung like insect bites. Any sane person would have found shelter, lit a candle or two, and passed the time. Apparently Kael was not sane, and he blamed his equally insane sister.

She'd come to his room hours after yesterday's battle. She'd said little, refusing to discuss the fight or her conversation with Headmaster Simmons and the theotechs that followed. He'd expected her to cry, or be furious, something, anything. Instead she sat there, as if his presence was all she wanted. When she left that night to sleep in her own room, Kael couldn't shake the feeling something was terribly wrong. And then she'd not been there for their morning run, or practices in the fields, or at their classes. As the storm came rolling in, he knew he'd never sleep that night without confirming she was all right. But Bree wasn't at the library, nor the mess hall, nor her room.

As Kael stood before the door to his room, he rubbed his forehead, realizing there was one place he hadn't checked.

"I'm going to kill you if you're out there," he murmured as he turned away from safety and instead ran west to the training fields. Another stroke of lightning lit up the night, the power of its thunderclap making Kael's heart jump. Frightening as it was, the lightning gave him his only light to see amid the deep cloud cover and torrential rain. Keeping to the path so he didn't get lost, he crossed the bridge at the very heart of the academy.

Wind gusted, causing his jacket to billow behind him. Kael kept his eyes down and hands raised in a vain attempt to shield his face against the rain.

When he ducked inside the gear sheds, he ran a hand through his wet hair, then flung his arms to shake off some of the water. He was still a dripping mess, but at least he tried. Though it was empty, the shed wasn't locked, and he walked through the wide spaces, waiting for a lightning strike. When it did, and light flashed through the thin cracks of wood, he confirmed his fear.

Bree's wings were gone.

The mechanics had begun letting the students fetch their own harnesses after their third week, and Kael was thankful for the practice. Normally retrieving them with a pole was no difficult matter, but the darkness complicated things. Telling himself to be patient, he carefully set the hook, waited until another lightning strike, and then lifted the harness in its fleeting light. Sliding it down, he grabbed it and began buckling on the wings. Light was hardly necessary for that, for he, like all the others in the academy, could practically do it in his sleep. That done, he flicked on the switch, powering the wings. From his left gauntlet faint white light shone out from the thin window. The element he'd used earlier in the day was still inside, and he sighed with relief. At least he could use it for light if he absolutely had to.

A vicious gust of wind greeted Kael's exit from the shed. He squinted his eyes instinctively against it but was surprised to see how the rain seemed to slow as it neared his face, its contact against his skin much more gentle.

"Well, that's neat," he said, heading back east. "Get to learn something new every day."

Such as why his sister would need her wings during such an angry thunderstorm.

"Bree!" he screamed, fighting for his voice to be heard over the crash of thunder. "Bree, where are you?"

He jogged down the street, his head on a swivel. If Bree was using her wings, then they'd be glowing a soft silver, and in such darkness he should be able to—

And then he saw her, not far off the road by the obstacle course. As the rain beat down on her, she swung both her swords in a rapid shifting of stance to stance. Pulling her swords back, she leapt forward, flaring her wings so that she flew a good thirty feet before thrusting. A twist of her waist, and she turned about, dashing forward again for another strike. Kael watched her, feeling strangely saddened. Her skill was incredible, and he'd seen few students of any year performing actual combinations of aerial maneuvers and swordplay during practice. Yet her every twist, every cut, looked born of a mad desperation. It was as if she fought a foe she could not harm, no matter how viciously she slashed the midnight sky.

"Bree!" he cried out to her, finally gaining her attention. She spun, and when she saw him, she sheathed her swords.

"Leave me alone," she shouted.

"Not happening."

Another stroke of lightning, this one finally hitting ground a mile or two in the distance. As its light washed over them, followed by the crack of thunder, Bree turned away and flared her wings. Before he could stop her, she soared into the air.

"Bree!" he screamed, and despite his own terror, he flew after her. Rain whirled all around him, and though its sting on his face was lessened by the harness, he still had to squint against the impact. Flying into the raindrops was disorientating, even more so when thin streaks of white lashed through the clouds, as if the storm was insulted by his very presence. Ahead of him,

Bree's silver wings were a beacon, and he followed it against all rational sense suggesting otherwise. Higher and higher they flew, until they were amid the very clouds themselves. The wind was incredible, buffeting him side to side so that flying in a straight line was all but impossible. He couldn't see Bree anymore, could barely tell up from down.

The next thunderclap sounded as if it came from inside his own head, and it struck him like a physical blow. Screaming, he closed his eyes and pushed his wings to their limits, desperately praying he flew in the correct direction. The thunder rolled and rolled, like the growl of a vicious lion the size of the world itself. And then, all at once, he was free. The rain ceased. The wind calmed. Kael opened his eyes, and he saw that he had emerged above the thunderstorm. Farther beyond was his sister, and the sight took his breath away.

Bree hovered with her arms at her sides and her head tilted backward. The midnight fire consumed the heavens above, rolling in chaotic fury as far as the eye could see. Lightning flashed through dark clouds beneath her, colored red by the burning skies so they appeared a firestorm of Hell itself. Bree's eyes were closed, and if she could remain lost there forever, Kael feared she gladly would. Above was fire, below a storm, and it seemed she hovered in the only place in all the world where she knew peace.

"Bree," he called again, gently guiding his wings toward her. "Bree, please, come back down."

"I killed him," she said, eyes still closed.

"You did what you had to do," Kael said carefully.

"Not Eric. *Dean.* It's my fault, Kael, all my fault. How do I live with that?"

He frowned, confused.

"How could that possibly be your fault?" he asked.

She finally looked his way, tears sliding down her face.

"He should have been practicing," she said. "He should have been learning to fly, or throw his fire. Instead he spent all his time teaching me swordplay. Pointless, stupid swordplay. If he'd spent more time training, if he'd been that much better..."

"Bree," he said, lessening the thrust of his wings so that he hovered beside her. "What happened to Dean wasn't your fault. You can't let that guilt eat at you, not when there's nothing you could have done. Dean spent all those hours with you for a reason, and it was because he enjoyed every single one. Don't take that from yourself. Don't taint his memory that way."

She sniffed, and she wiped at her face with a hand.

"It doesn't matter," she said. "It was all for nothing. They're going to expel me."

"You don't know that."

"I do," she said. "The evaluations are tomorrow, and I still can't use my element. I thought...I thought if I tried hard enough, if I improved in everything else, it would make up the difference. But it won't. It never could. I've been fooling myself, wasting everyone's time..."

Kael reached for her hand, but she pulled away. The motion sent her drifting, and he had to tilt forward to slowly chase.

"They'll see how good you are," Kael argued. "They have to. Everyone else can see it."

Bree crossed her arms over her chest, and her gentle drift made it seem as if she was retreating in fear.

"They'll see a girl who in six months is still worse than most were on their very first day," she said. "They'll see a girl who injured three other students for a single slight in a mess hall. A girl who recklessly engaged a Seraph of a foreign nation without permission. A girl who's an insult to her parents' memory."

Kael gritted his teeth, and he felt his own tears starting to build.

"They'll also see the best flier Weshern's had in a generation," he said. "They'll see the very first member of our class to score a kill. For everything you've done, for how hard you've worked, Mom and Dad would have been proud, and you damn well know it." He offered her his hand. "It's not hopeless, Bree. Please, come back down. Get out of this storm."

She stared as if his hand might bite her. A thunderclap rolled beneath them, and in its red light, she closed her eyes.

"You're so good to me," she said. "But my time here is done. The headmaster made that clear as day. I'm scared, Kael. What do I do when I'm expelled? What do I do when I lose the skies? This is all I've ever wanted, and now that I've had it, how do I go back?" She looked at him, pleading, seeking some sort of hope. "Do I wear my hands to the bone digging weeds and planting crops? Do I take a chisel and hammer and learn to carve? Or do I haul nets of fish day in and out, just to pretend the skies are still mine?"

Kael wished he knew what to tell her. He wished he had some guarantee of happiness to offer, something that wasn't a condescending lie.

"I don't know," he said. "But I know you're strong enough to endure. You always have been, and you always will be."

Again he offered her his hand. This time she took it, and he pulled her close for a hug. When she wrapped her arms around him and buried her face against his shoulder, he felt her entire body collapse like a taut string finally cut in half.

"I'm sorry I dragged you up here," she whispered, barely audible over the storm.

"I'd chase you to Hell and back if I had to," he said, and he gently separated from her. "Speaking of which, we need to get back down through all that..."

Bree sniffled, and she grinned at him.

"I'll lead the way if you're scared."

Kael mussed her hair before she could retreat.

"If you insist," he said, and when she flew downward with a sudden burst of silver light, he followed her readily into the storm.

CHAPTER 22

After Gavin and Lily's deaths, two others had withdrawn from the academy, leaving just fourteen of them to wait together in the large classroom not far from Headmaster Simmons's office. All across the walls were drawings of the various floating outer islands, each meticulously detailed, showcasing their fields, forests, rivers, and cities. Bree had spent the first twenty minutes analyzing each one, Galen in particular. It seemed so normal, so similar to Weshern. Farmland lined the exterior edges, and in its heart was an enormous lake with eight winding rivers flowing in all directions toward the edge. Of all five, Galen had the most forests, and part of her wished she could one day walk among them. But she never could, not with tensions as they were, and certainly not after what she'd done. After killing Eric Drae, she'd likely be arrested on sight, the theotechs' wishes be damned.

Next door was a second classroom, inside of which the

six-month evaluations were held. There were no exams to take, no trials or tests of flying prowess. It was simply a meeting of their teachers who revealed their assessments, handed down as a lengthy critique to each student and ending with a simple yes or no as to whether the student could continue at the academy. Those given a yes would return to their apartments. Those who were told no would be immediately removed from the academy grounds, without so much as a good-bye. The students were being called alphabetically by last name, which left Bree plenty of time to prepare for the inevitable.

Four chairs formed a semicircle, and together they waited, Bree and Brad on one side, Kael and Clara on the other. They'd laughed and joked as the other students left one by one, but as the numbers lessened, so too did their conversation. By the time Rebecca Waller entered, looking stately as ever, they were down to six.

"Bradford Macon," she said to the quiet room.

Brad hopped to his feet, and he flashed the rest a smile.

"See you all back at my apartment," he said. "We four can celebrate with drinks that may or may not be allowed on campus."

"Your evaluation may still be changed," Rebecca told him as he walked toward her at the door. "Perhaps you should say such boasts more quietly?"

Brad blushed, and he looked to his feet as he passed her by. The door shut, and then they were five. The only other two were Saul and Amanda. Saul stood in a corner, arms crossed and eyes closed as he waited. Amanda, meanwhile, had been the only one with the foresight to bring a book, and she sat on the floor not far from their semicircle, slowly flipping page after page.

"Sometimes it's nice being a Willer," Clara said, staring longingly at the door. "But not now."

"I'm just before you, so you shouldn't be alone too long," Kael said. "I mean, how much time does it take to say 'you're terrible, get out of here'?"

"I don't know," Clara said. "We'll find out by how long it takes them to finish Brad's."

Bree laughed despite her nerves.

"That's terrible," she said.

"I'm a terrible person," Clara said, flipping her short blonde hair with a flick of her hand. "But being pretty and wealthy seems to disguise it well enough."

"It's what won me over," Kael said, looping an arm around her waist and nearly pulling her out of her chair. Bree smiled at the two, and she felt happy that her brother would have someone to rely on after she was gone. Some people, like Amanda and her book, could endure troubles in solitude. Kael certainly could not.

Time passed, and finally the door opened again.

"Saul Reigar," announced Over-Secretary Waller.

Saul pushed off from the corner, showing no signs of having slept despite remaining quiet and with his eyes closed the whole while. Standing ramrod straight, he smirked as he passed Bree's chair.

"To a wonderful evaluation," he said, facing her so he could bow with an extravagant wave of his hand. "And to never seeing you again."

Kael looked ready for a fistfight, but Breanna shrugged it off. She'd hurt Saul's pride numerous times now. What did it matter if he had one last moment to gloat? The door shut, and when it did, Kael gave it a rude gesture.

"What an ass," he said. "He's going to be so pissed when he finds out you're staying."

"No, he won't," Bree said. "I'm finally at peace with this, Kael, I really am. You don't need to worry about me."

She could tell Kael didn't believe her, and part of her could hardly believe it herself, but at last the moment was here. There'd be no more dreading it, no more struggling impotently to master her fire. She'd had her taste of revenge, of loss in battle. If she must move on, then she'd move on knowing she gave it her all.

"Don't give up yet," Clara said, putting on a cheerful face. "You don't know you'll be removed."

Bree shook her head.

"I do know," she said. "Headmaster Simmons practically told me so. I don't blame him, either. I'm of no use to a formation if I cannot control my element. There's no way to get around that simple fact."

"No use?" Kael asked. "You're the only one of us who's killed an enemy in combat. How could you *not* be of use?"

Bree had no desire to argue the point, and she said so. She'd cried her tears above the storm, and come the morning, she'd awoken with a new determination. No matter what happened, she'd face her future without fear. Given her skills with a blade, a position in the military guard remained possible. And as much as she'd despaired over being a fisherman, she would not deny the dignity of working for her daily bread, nor the skill involved in looping around the Fount without harm.

Time drifted on. Bree briefly fantasized that Saul would be expelled from the academy as well, but she'd seen his skill with ice. He'd clearly be a dangerous threat to the enemy.

The door opened, another name called.

"Amanda Ruth."

Amanda's book closed with a thud, and she quickly rose to her feet. She headed for the door, paused, and then suddenly dashed straight at Bree, wrapping her arms about her.

"I'll miss you," she said.

Bree felt a lump growing in her throat, and for a moment she let a bit of her sorrow leak through.

"I'll miss you, too," she said, squeezing the thin girl back.

Amanda smiled her waifish smile, then followed Over-Secretary Waller out the door. Clara stared after them, obviously troubled.

"I hope they fail her," she said softly.

Kael's eyes widened, and his mouth dropped open.

"What?" he asked. "Why? She's the best with lightning by far."

Clara shook her head, and while Kael didn't understand, Bree did. She'd experienced it firsthand not so long ago, wrestled with it many sleepless nights.

"Her skill with flight and lightning are excellent," Bree said. "But that's not all it takes to be a Seraph."

Clara nodded in agreement.

"You have to kill," she said. "To look at a man or woman and decide to end their life. I don't think that ability is inside her. At least, I don't *want* it to be. If they fail her now, she'll never have to find out. I hope the teachers see that in her as well, and do what's right. Sending her into battle will only get her killed."

Bree felt her respect for Clara growing more and more. With all their practices in empty fields, it was easy to see flying and using elements as part of a game. Kael had learned the truth when they watched the knights drop the disciple of Johan into the well. As for Clara? Bree stared into those green eyes, and she had a feeling Clara, as a child of the ruling family, had never been allowed to forget the number of lives in her hands.

"Amanda's stronger than you two give her credit for," Kael said. "She was closer than anyone when Gavin and Lily wrecked. No one would have blamed her for leaving the academy then and there, but she stayed. She knows this is life-and-death, just like you two do. She'll be a fine Seraph, just you wait."

"Make sure you write me a letter telling me how wrong I was," Bree said.

Again her certainty of her own failing flustered Kael, but thankfully he didn't argue.

"Fine," he mumbled. "You watch. She'll be a killing machine of the skies. She's so small, no one will be able to hit her. Tiny little Amanda, like a hummingbird with lightning."

"Truly, the enemies of Weshern will quake with fear," Clara said, and they all smiled.

The door opened, but instead of Rebecca, it was Brad who ducked his head through it.

"I'm in," he said, grinning ear to ear. "Instructor Dohn even complimented my progress. I'm stunned the islands haven't crashed into the ocean."

"There's still time yet," Kael said, laughing. "Now get out of here before Miss Waller catches you."

Brad shot them a wink, then ducked out, slamming the door shut behind him. Kael shook his head, and he gestured toward the door.

"If that oaf gets to stay, and you don't, then there's no justice in this world," he told Bree, who rolled her eyes. Thankfully Clara pinched Kael in the side, saving her the trouble of doing so herself.

Time rolled on, and though she was next, Bree was surprised

by how calm she felt. When Rebecca opened the door and called her name, it seemed Kael was more upset than she was.

"You'll be fine," Kael said, rising from his seat and hugging her before she could leave.

"I know," Bree said, hugging him back. "Make Mom and Dad proud."

She stepped away, he mussed her hair, and then Bree followed the over-secretary out the door and into the nearby room.

The classroom, one in which Bree learned history from Teacher Lechek, had been cleared in preparation for the evaluations. All the desks were removed but for one, a long oak desk at which sat Headmaster Simmons, Instructor Adam Dohn, and Instructor Randy Kime. Bree wasn't surprised by the absence of her other teachers. As much as they insisted that history, protocol, and strategy were important, it would be on the basic mechanics of flight and elements that they would be judged.

All three wore their pristine uniforms, and it was weird to see the two instructors without their wings. A single chair waited on the other side of the desk, and Bree took her seat. As she did, she analyzed the faces of her superiors. Instructor Dohn's black hair was smooth and combed, and that made him look far less intimidating for some reason. Instructor Kime was smiling at her as he always did, every student seemingly a great friend to him. Headmaster Simmons, however, looked troubled, and he refused to meet her eye.

"Breanna Skyborn," he said, glancing over a single sheet of paper before him. "This is an evaluation of your talents and weaknesses, as perceived by your instructors as well as myself. This is not a time to defend yourself, nor argue things you disagree with. Please remain silent, and listen with an open mind. Do you understand?"

Bree nodded.

"I do," she said.

The headmaster shifted to his left, and he waved for Instructor Dohn to begin.

"Bree, I'm not going to mince words," Adam said, folding his hands before him and leaning on the desk. "You're supremely confident, almost arrogantly so, and doing anything you consider beneath your skills wears on your patience and bores you tremendously. Because of this, you tend to focus on improving yourself instead of helping your fellow students learn. It may not be my field to critique, but you're a terrible leader, and not much better at being a follower, either. All that said, you're a damn fine flier. In only six months, your times on the obstacle course are better than most graduate students'. I don't say this lightly, but you're the most natural-born flier I've seen in a decade."

Bree felt taken aback by the incredible praise.

No matter what happens, at least I will always have this, she thought. Hearing such praise put a chink in her emotional armor. To think she'd never realize her full potential...

"Instructor Kime?" Jay said when Adam settled back into his chair.

"Yes, of course," Randy said, and he drummed the fingers of his right hand on the table, while his left arm tucked up against his chest. The man cleared his throat, then reluctantly forced his blue eyes to meet her gaze.

"Breanna," he said hesitantly, "despite all my months of effort, you have shown no progress whatsoever at mastering your fire element. The moment you initiate a connection between yourself and the prism through the use of the harness, you lose all control. I have tried everything, and while I would normally accept the blame for a student's difficulties, I cannot do that here. I'm not sure how to best explain it, but let me try.

If the use of an element is like playing music, I fear you are tone-deaf. Nothing will change that. It's not your fault. It's not from a lack of effort or skill. I believe, and this makes me so sad to say this, but I believe you were simply born this way."

Tone-deaf, thought Bree. That wasn't a bad way to describe how she felt when attempting to control the fire bursting out from her gauntlet. In many ways, she felt helpless as it happened.

Instructor Kime drummed his fingers again, and he nodded at Jay to show he was done. The headmaster cleared his throat, and again he looked over the sheet of paper.

"I will keep this succinct," Jay said. "Bree, you are reckless, temperamental, and give in easily to anger, even going so far as to attack fellow students. You also show little regard for tradition or protocol. Your willingness to go after Eric Drae after Dean's death illustrates a worrisome tendency to think of yourself over others, and it makes me question how reliable you would be in battle, when staying in formation is of the utmost importance in keeping a squad protected. In short, you have a lot of room to grow."

It was such a thorough drumming of her character, Bree almost laughed, and she would have had the atmosphere of the room not been so somber. Whatever regrets she'd started to feel after hearing Instructor Dohn's evaluation were completely stomped and done with after the other two. However much she belonged in the skies, it wasn't as a member of the Seraphim. In battles waged with fire, stone, ice, and lightning, battles that relied on tight, controlled formations, there was no place for a reckless girl wielding only swords.

"With all that said..." Headmaster Simmons paused, as if debating. "All that said, these evaluations are to judge not just what you have already accomplished, but what you may accomplish with enough training. This decision was not an easy one, but I have been convinced that because of your skills in flight you should be given another chance to properly develop mastery of your element."

The statement hit her like a sledge. They weren't expelling her? But why? *I have been convinced?* The way he said it felt wrong, and she lurched to her feet.

"What is going on?" she asked. "You said earlier I would be expelled."

"I said nothing of the sort. I merely warned you it was a possibility."

Except that wasn't the case at all. She knew what he'd meant. Jay was hiding something, lying perhaps, but for what possible reason? It didn't make sense. Loramere insisted no Seraph would lie, which meant if Jay was, it was under extreme circumstances.

"Headmaster...," she said, trying to find the proper words. It felt like she was at the heart of some giant prank. She'd made peace with leaving. She'd accepted returning to Aunt Bethy and living a life outside the academy knowing she'd given it her all. But this...this felt wrong. It felt forced. She wanted to be happy, but how could she when she knew, without a shadow of a doubt, that she didn't belong? Bree stared at her instructors, and now they all looked upset, even Randy.

"I don't understand," she said weakly.

"You don't need to. As of now, you may resume attending classes and participating in drills. Archon Willer has declared no additional punishments necessary for your duel with Eric Drae."

It was too much. Nothing for that, either? She'd suffered worse for attacking Saul with a broom handle. But what else was she to do? Demand punishment? Something else was at play, but it seemed she would not be given an explanation. Doing her best to smile, she turned to leave, and that's when she saw them. Her blood froze. There in the corner, hidden from view of the entrance, stood two gray-haired theotechs in their red robes. A fire lit in her breast, and she stormed their way as Jay and Adam leapt from their seats.

"You're not supposed to be here," she said.

The two men stared back, refusing to say a word. Their arms remained crossed over their chests, each hand tucked into the sleeve of the other. As if they didn't care. As if they hadn't watched every single minute of her evaluation. Vyros's earlier cryptic words came back to her with a vengeance.

"Is this your gift?" she asked, her face mere inches away from theirs. "Is it?"

They started toward the door, but Bree jumped in front of them, refusing to let them pass.

"What am I to you?" she asked as Adam grabbed her arm. "Why do you even care?"

She struggled, trying to free herself, but Jay joined him, the two wrestling her away from the theotechs so they could leave.

"Tell me!" she screamed, lunging one last time toward them. "What do you want from me? What do you want?"

The door shut behind them. The theotechs gave no answers. They never made a sound.

CHAPTER
23

Kael felt ready to give up ever understanding his sister. When he'd come back to his apartment, he'd found Bree already inside, Brad having let her in.

"She's pretty upset," Brad had whispered.

"Figured she would be," Kael had whispered back as he went into his room where she waited.

Except she hadn't been removed. What should have been the greatest news possible, that she'd remain a member of the Seraphim, seemed to only frustrate her. Yet when he asked why, she gave no answer.

"It's not right," she kept saying, never clarifying. "It's not. Something's wrong."

When she finally left, the midnight fire consumed the sky. Kael watched her cross the street toward her own apartment, wishing he could understand. Knowing she'd still be there every day as he trained filled him with relief and elation. Why could she not feel the same?

The next morning, he woke, dressed for his run, then ducked his head inside Brad's room. To his surprise, Brad remained in bed.

"Wake up, lazy," he said, kicking the side of the bed with his foot. Brad rolled over, ran a hand through his curly red hair as he yawned.

"I'm not going," he said.

"What?" Kael asked. "Why not?"

"Not feeling well," Brad said. Kael frowned, not liking the way his friend seemed hesitant to meet his gaze.

"Are you sure?"

"Am I sure I don't feel well?" Brad gave him a look, as if the question were the stupidest thing ever, but Kael didn't buy it. After a brief moment, Brad gave up. "Fine. Bree told me to stay here instead of going on our morning run, and to just pretend I was sick or something."

Kael crossed his arms and leaned against the wall.

"Did she say why?" he asked.

Brad shook his head.

"Something spooked your sister, and bad," he said. "And I have a feeling she isn't the kind to get spooked too easily."

It was true, not that he'd admit that to Brad.

"I'll find out what's wrong," he said. "Enjoy your extra sleep, you lucky bastard."

"Will do."

Alone, Kael walked to the bridge in the center of the academy grounds, enjoying the crisp morning air. It was normal for Bree to be upset, he told himself. She'd convinced herself it was for the best for her to leave. To suddenly be wrong, and have to readjust mentally to the day-in, day-out training, well . . . surely that couldn't be easy.

Bree waited for him at the bridge, stretching her legs. The weather had steadily grown colder, and unlike for their earlier runs, she wore her jacket. Kael crossed the bridge, and he smiled at her as if it were any other day.

"Ready?" he asked, not bringing up Brad's absence. He was curious if she'd mention it herself, but it seemed even pretending was beyond her. She looked tired, with deep black circles underneath her eyes. Her hair, which she normally straightened with near religious consistency, was still tangled from sleep.

"Ready," Bree said after glancing about, though for what, he had no clue. They began a jog north, following the stream. Neither talked, and Kael wondered if he just needed to wait it out before things returned to normal with his sister. It wasn't like this was new. She'd gone through foul moods before, particularly after their parents died. When they reached the north wall, Bree suddenly slowed to a walk.

"You all right?" he asked, slowing so she could catch up with him.

"I'm fine," she said. "We need to talk."

Kael hid his frustration, telling himself this was a good thing. Whatever was bothering her would now be out in the open.

"That's what I'm here for, I guess," he said. "So let's talk. Is this about your evaluation?"

"Mostly. Kael, was there anyone else in there with you during your evaluations? Besides the instructors, I mean?"

Kael frowned, confused by the question.

"Yeah, there was," he said. "Two theotechs from Center were in the corner near the door. I didn't see them when I first came in, only when I left."

Bree nodded, as if that confirmed...something.

"They were there for me, too," she said. "But I talked to Amanda. They weren't there for hers. I'd bet if you asked Brad, he'd say the same thing."

"I don't get it, Bree," he said. "If that's true, why would the theotechs have any interest in us?"

"I don't know," Bree said, and she glanced around the field as if fearful of hidden ears. "But it's because of them I've had special treatment. Think about it, Kael. I should be dead after what I did to Eric, but I was let off without even a slap on the wrist. Headmaster Simmons made it perfectly clear in our meeting I was to be expelled, but a theotech was waiting for me outside the room, and told me I should be careful so I can repay them for their 'gift.' One day later, the headmaster changes his mind, and I get to stay. That doesn't seem odd to you?"

"It could just be coincidence," Kael said, but even he didn't believe it. Bree sensed his hesitation, and she leapt on it like a starving dog on a dropped bone.

"You know something," she said. "What is it?"

Kael took in a deep breath, then let it out.

"I never wanted to tell anyone," he said. "It's...well, it's kind of embarrassing, but I was worried it might get me in trouble, too. Back during our tests, I didn't have water affinity, Bree. I was light."

Bree didn't look the slightest bit surprised, which made him feel better for some reason.

"You should have been a ferryman," she said. "Yet you're not. Why?"

By now they'd reached the curving northwestern edge of the academy's surrounding wall, and Kael stopped before it and leaned against the brick as if he were tired. The beginner flight field stretched out before him, the grass a faded yellow.

"A theotech came and spoke with Dioso," Kael said, thudding his head against the wall. "After that, he came back in and changed the results so that my minor affinity with water was labeled major instead."

Kael looked to his sister, and he felt a worm squirming around inside his chest.

"What does this mean?" he asked.

"It means they're watching over us," she said. "Making sure we become members of the Seraphim."

"But why? It doesn't make any sense. We're nothing to them."

Bree pulled at her lower lip with her fingers, a nervous quirk he hadn't seen her use in years.

"I don't know," Bree said. "Maybe something involving our parents?"

Kael shrugged.

"Maybe," he said. "But what could either Mom or Dad have done to explain why theotechs from Center would meddle in Weshern's affairs, just for us? I think a better guess is they were close with the Willers. Isaac knew our parents, and they flew with one of his sons. He might be able to influence the theotechs to some degree, and he certainly has the power here to ensure you don't fail out."

"It's possible," Bree said. "We need to find out for sure."

"How do we do that?"

She shook her head.

"I don't know. But we need to try. If we're involved in something, I want to know. Yesterday will be the last time those theotechs catch me by surprise."

She started walking south along the wall, and Kael pushed off so he could follow.

"It could be nothing," he said, trying to rein in her recklessness. "Just some coincidences and politics we don't know about. Maybe someone's repaying a debt to Mom and Dad, and we'll never—"

He stopped as a horn suddenly blared to life from the center of the academy. It gave three long blasts, paused, then another three. Beside him, Bree tensed as if expecting a punch.

"What's going on?" he asked.

"The horn's calling all Seraphim to gear up," Bree said. "We're under attack."

Under attack? Kael felt a cold sweat building on his neck.

"Does that mean we..."

"No," his sister said, shaking her head, and there was no hiding her disappointment. "Not us, Kael. Not until Argus says we're ready."

In the far southeast corner of the academy just opposite the armory were the graduate barracks. As they watched, distant silver shapes rose into the air above, gathering into formation.

"Come on," Bree said, grabbing his hand and pulling. "We need to climb."

Every six hundred feet or so, ladders had been built into the surrounding wall, and the twins ran south until they found one. Bree scampered up, then turned to face the gathering forces of the Weshern Seraphim. Kael joined her, and for some reason it amused him how uneasy he felt given the lack of rail or protection on either side of the wall. He could fly thousands of feet into the air, but standing on a flat wall maybe ten feet high still made him nervous? Instructor Dohn had insisted some fears were rational and could be conquered, while others were irrational and never would be. Heights, according to him, were a rational fear, though Kael's current unease seemed to argue otherwise.

For several more minutes they watched the number of Seraphim steadily increase in the sky. Not since last year's parade had he seen so many gathered in flight at one time. The horn continued to blare at least once a minute, three long notes that seemed to grow more ominous with repetition. Starting to wonder if they'd ever move out, Kael spun on his feet, scanning the horizon.

"Oh my God," he whispered, and he grabbed Bree's shoulder so she'd turn to look.

Flying in from the west, like a swarm of golden wasps, came the enemy Seraphim.

"Red," Bree said softly. Each island used a single color for their jackets to help distinguish themselves in the confusion of battle. Weshern's was black. As for red, that color jacket was burned into Kael's mind five long years ago.

"Galen's attacking," Kael said. "But for what?"

"They're coming for me," Bree whispered.

"You don't know that."

Luke's haunting words said otherwise. Kael watched as the army flew closer. The Seraphim were broken into *V*-shape formations, each seven strong, and Kael began counting up the total number of such groups. Twenty-one in total. Almost one hundred and fifty strong. Sparing a glance at their own forces, he feared they had maybe a hundred and twenty at most. But they had Argus Summers leading them, and he alone counted for at least twenty. Despite his fear, Kael wished he could be with them, but with so little training, he'd fall out of formation, and a lone Seraph was easy pickings for a well-trained squad.

"Look there," Bree said, pointing. Kael traced the line of her finger until he saw them, a trio of theotechs flying in from Center. As for all battles, Galen had requested the attack, outlined their reasons, and then launched upon receiving permission. The theotechs would oversee the battle, reporting the results to

Center as well as guiding the fleet of vultures, younger members of their order who served on reclamation teams to recover the technology from the dead. Seeing them hovering there, mere observers to the coming bloodshed, made them appear so much more frightening. It was as if they had hearts of stone and condoned the coming death.

"They're launching," Kael said, glancing to his right. The Weshern Seraphim were also dividing into V formations, though theirs were nine strong instead of seven. Kael counted fourteen of them, which meant they were as outnumbered as he feared. One after the other they charged the Galen forces, the Seraphim maintaining their tight formations with brilliant control. Kael spun as they flew overhead, accompanied by a deep thrumming sound, the combined volume of more than a hundred wings pushed to their maximum. He wondered if they'd be safe on the wall, but before he could voice his question, the battle erupted.

Massive chunks of stone flew from the lead Seraphim on each side, forming walls, disrupting formations, and colliding into each other with cracks like thunder. Walls of ice joined the stone, flying outward for brief moments before falling. Both sides dove beneath blasts and above hurled earth, and as the distance between them shrank, the fire and lightning were unleashed. It was like a great storm in the sky, and the sound of its rumble took Kael's breath away. In those first few moments, he saw Seraphim from each side go tumbling to the ground, bodies smashed by stone or struck dead by fire and lightning.

Despite the battle raging above the field to their west, it was still impossible to follow individual Seraphim, only formations. Now that the head-on exchange was finished, the forces began to weave and circle one another, seeking out advantageous positions. Kael watched one group of five Galen Seraphim dive low, shooting lances of fire and ice into the path of one of Weshern's formations below. Instead of fleeing, the other formation banked hard and rose, a barrage of boulders forcing the five to veer away... and right into the path of Argus Summers's formation. It was the only one Kael could identify from such a distance, for Argus's wings and those of his elite had black stripes painted across the sides to distinguish them from the rest. Two blasts of lightning tore into the squad of five, followed by thin spears of fire aimed directly into their path of evasion. Galen's formation scattered, several fliers dying in the vicious barrage.

Bree reached for Kael's hand, and he took hers gladly. As they both watched the battle, it seemed time rewound itself, and they were eleven years old, watching the battle that would claim both their parents.

Kael spotted Seraphim from both sides veering off and then hovering in place. They were snipers, men and women who lurked on the fringes of the battle, watching for an advantageous moment to strike. Sometimes they were spotted and had to flee a counterbarrage, while other times they'd swoop in behind and kill a Seraphim before he or she realized they were in danger. Kael watched one Galen sniper knife up from far below the battle, shards of ice shooting from his gauntlet at stunning speed. Two of Weshern's Seraphim died as the shards tore into their stomachs. Two of the remaining three of the formation fled, but one remained behind, diving toward the sniper. Kael saw dots of fire and ice fly between them, and he had no clue who might win.

When it was the Weshern Seraphim who veered back to the sky, and the Galen sniper who plummeted to the ground, Kael breathed a sigh of relief.

"This is wrong," Bree said softly. "So many dying, and for what? For me?"

The sky was filled with shards of ice and bursts of flame, punctuated by blasts of lightning that shot with frightening accuracy throughout the entire chaos. The sounds merged together as a constant rumble, one so deep Kael felt it in his teeth. His earlier desire to join in was long gone. He couldn't imagine how he'd react in such madness. Likely he'd have already been one of the many dropping to the ground, wings broken, bones shattered, flesh burned and ripped open.

Though it felt like an eternity, the battle ended as quickly as it began. Two long blasts came from a horn somewhere in the mess, and just like that, both sides veered away from each other. It was the horn of surrender, which both twins immediately recognized. The theotechs, who'd remained still all throughout, sprang to life, flying between the recovering forces.

"Which side?" Kael asked, trying to decipher where the horn had come from. "Which side surrendered?"

Bree stared a moment longer, watching the theotechs.

"They did," she said, not hiding her relief. "We won."

The Galen Seraphim flew west, now scattered and spread out instead of in tight formations. Kael counted, and of their initial hundred and fifty, it looked like they'd lost more than twenty. A devastating loss, certainly, but when he turned to their own number, he saw similar losses. At least Galen had surrendered. If Bree *had* been the reason, a surrender by the Weshern forces would have meant immediately handing her over for torture and execution. The thought chilled him to the bone, and that he'd watched the battle for even a moment like it was some sort of game flooded him with shame.

"Let's go," he said as their fellow Seraphim fluttered back to the ground near the armory. Bree reluctantly followed him down the ladder and across the field. By the time they reached the shacks in the center, the academy was abuzz with movement. A steady stream of Seraphim flew overhead, some bringing wounded, others bodies to bury once the vultures had picked them clean. Kael found several of his classmates gathered together not far from the bridge, Brad among them.

"Hey," Brad said, jogging over the moment he saw them. "Look, now is not a good time. Bree, maybe you should go back to your room."

Bree pushed past him, and when he reached for her arm, she broke out into a run.

"Shit," Brad said, and together he and Kael chased after her. They crossed the bridge, passed the mess hall, and then turned south toward the armory and apothecary. In the open space between the buildings the wounded were gathering, for there were too many to fit inside the tiny building. Bree slowed, for mingling about were the rest of the Seraphim. Kael caught up and grabbed her wrist.

"Bree, stop," he said.

"I have to know," she said, glancing over her shoulder. "I have to."

Wishing there was another way, Kael let her go. She wandered into the Seraphim, some removing their wings and swords, others remaining armored. After a moment, Kael reluctantly followed. People made room for her, and Kael saw the way they looked at her. Few seemed to recognize her. Of those who did, the reaction was split between pity and disgust. Her steps slowed, as if she realized for the first time she had no idea where to go.

"Was this for me?" she asked, in a voice so soft it was barely a whisper. No one heard. Hands clenched into fists, she leaned back and shouted it again. "Was this for me?"

The gentle buzz of conversation halted, and now all eyes

were upon her. No one said a word as Bree spun, meeting their gazes. So many were unreadable. Did they hate her, Kael wondered? Pity her? Willingly protect her?

"Yes," said a familiar voice. Kael turned to see Loramere pushing his way through the crowd. He bled from a cut across his forehead, and blood soaked through a bandage tied around his left bicep. "They wanted you for an execution, and we gave those Galen bastards a good lesson on what happens when they try for one of our own."

Halfhearted cheers rose from a nearby few. Bree clenched her fists as if in pain.

"So this is my fault?" she asked the giant man.

"Of course not," Loramere said, sliding beside her and putting a hand on her shoulder as he tried to guide her away from the wounded. Bree, however, would have none of it. She pulled away from him, spinning to stare at the many lingering eyes.

"How many died?" she asked, and when no one answered, she shouted it louder. "How many died!"

"Seventeen."

Kael and Bree turned to see a man push through the crowd. Black stripes were on his wings. His hair was dark and cut short, his smooth skin tan, his eyes an icy blue. Across his forehead was a single scar running up from his left eyebrow and vanishing into his hair. Though he had seen him only at parades, Kael immediately recognized Commander Argus Summers, leader of all Weshern Seraphim. An escort of two came with him, muscular men with stripes on their wings as well.

"Seventeen," Bree said, tears building in her eyes. "Seventeen dead, and for what? Why didn't you ask? I could have turned myself over. I could have stopped this!"

"It wasn't your decision to make."

"I don't want this," Bree cried, the tears falling. "I don't want any of this. I'm not worth it. Seventeen? Goddamn it, seventeen..."

Argus put his hands on her shoulders, and he leaned down to look her in the eye.

"We don't hand over one of our own," he said. "We'll die for you like we'll die for any other Seraph of Weshern. One day, Bree, I pray you'll fly into battle ready to do the same for us."

If any had disagreed with the decision, they didn't anymore. Kael couldn't believe the respect Argus commanded, the sheer authority every word he spoke carried. He remembered his fear of combat, and he realized that if he could follow a man like Argus into battle, he wouldn't be afraid. If anyone could guide him safely, if anyone could lead them to victory, it was him.

Bree sniffled, and she lowered her head.

"May I be dismissed?" she asked.

"Of course."

She pulled away, eyes to the dirt. When she reached Kael, she brushed right past him, ignoring his pleading for her to stop.

"Let her go," Brad said beside him. "I think she needs to be alone."

Kael watched his sister emerge from the other side of the crowd, then break out into a sprint. His throat felt tight, and tears were forming in his own eyes. She'd looked broken, torn to pieces inside. She looked like she had when Dean died.

Turning about, Kael saw that a theotech had flown in from the west, landing beside Argus. The two were conversing quietly, and the sight made Kael's hands shake.

"Brad," he asked. "Were there theotechs at your six-month evaluation?"

"What?" Brad asked, confused. "Of course not. Why?"

Of course not. As if it was obvious. As if it was ridiculous to conceive.

"I thought so," Kael said, putting his back to the two and weaving out of the group of gathered Seraphim.

"Where are you going?" Brad asked, hurrying after.

"To the library," he said.

"The library? But why?"

Kael almost answered but caught himself. Looking once more to the theotech, he shook his head.

"Too many ears," he whispered, suddenly wondering if Bree's paranoia might be well-founded after all.

CHAPTER

24

The next day, Bree walked the path to the obstacle course, fighting to remove the echoing number in her mind. Seventeen. It'd haunted her long, sleepless night. Seventeen dead, all for her. No matter how hard she tried, she couldn't justify it. Her life for so many? It was ridiculous. Damn Weshern's pride and Argus's insistence. Seventeen lives for her own was seventeen too many.

A lump grew in her throat as she reached the obstacle course. Nearly every day she'd made at least one attempt to break the record. Nearly every day, Dean had been her witness in case she accomplished it. Now there was no one, just an empty field.

Bree shook her head. She didn't need a witness, for she'd never beat it anyway. Her fastest was always five to six seconds off Argus's record, and she'd made no gains on it for two weeks. Perhaps it was a small defiance, but she'd make the run, resuming a normal part of her day despite the absence of the smiling young man who once waited for her at the very last ring.

Lining up at the start, she released the cord to begin the timer and then dashed forward, her wings thrumming to life. Bree could do the course blindfolded by this point, each twist and turn coming perfectly naturally to her. A gentle curve to the right shot her through the first two rings. Before she'd even passed through the second, she was already twisting left and killing her speed for a split second. Once straightened out, she flared her wings back to life, diving through the third ring while rolling to correct her aim for the fourth. The next few rings she dipped and weaved through, losing hardly any speed.

It was only when she reached the ninth ring that she debated how to respond. The ring was fairly close to the ground, and she slowed as she approached it. Dipping low, she arched her back so that she was rising even as she slipped through. The tenth ring was so much higher, and mentally cursing, she saw she hadn't lost enough speed and ended up overshooting the ring. Bree shut off her wings completely, twisted so she faced the other way, and then rose back up. She passed through, dropped down so she could arc through the low eleventh, and then shot through the final ring, angrily smacking the side with her hand to dislodge the hook to stop the timer.

Bree looped back around to the start to check her time.

Not even close, she thought, and she faced the course with her hands on her hips while she recovered her breath. It was that terrible stretch of nine through eleven, she knew. With how close together nine and ten were, she had to kill too much of her speed to climb from the low nine to high ten. If only there was a way for her to slow down faster without sacrificing her positioning...

An idea sparked in her mind based on her previous run, and Bree dared to smile. Maybe, just maybe, she had a shot. She hurriedly reset the timer, then returned to the start position, cord in hand. Before starting, she saw that she had a spectator, a lone Seraphim without his wings watching her from far down the road.

Good, thought Bree. *I'll have a witness.*

She stretched her back and shoulders one last time, bent at the waist, and released the cord.

Bree streaked through the initial rings, pushing herself even faster than before. This would be it, she decided. The last real idea she had to beat Argus's record. Wind flew through her hair as she curled left and right, knifing through the rings with perfect precision. As she crossed eight, she lowered her angle and pointed herself straight at nine. Unlike before, she did not slow her speed at all. Instead, just before passing through, she twisted her body, putting herself feet forward and face to the ground, and then shoved the throttle to its fullest.

The wings thrummed nice and heavy, and with Bree pointed the opposite direction of her movement, they killed her momentum almost instantly. Bree screamed, feeling as if her body were being torn apart. She used that scream to focus, continuing it as she pulled back her shoulders and neck. Her new path caused her to fly a loop, and head first she flew through the high tenth, her body already on a downward dive. She twisted, banked through the eleventh, and then shot toward the twelfth. Most Seraphim slowed down to strike the final ring lest they harm their hand, but this time Bree did no such thing. Grabbing her left sword, she flew closer to its edge and then flung the scabbard out to the side so that her blade smacked against the thin wooden ring, dislodging the timer.

Bree cheered as she looped back toward the start. Her witness had moved beside it as well, and as she flew close, she felt her heart suddenly halt upon realizing who it was: Argus Summers himself.

"How'd I do?" she called out to him, trying hard not to be intimidated.

"Come see for yourself," he said, gesturing to the timer.

Bree landed, and as Argus stepped aside, she stood before it and checked the hand. One minute thirty-five seconds. She'd beaten him by a full two seconds.

"I did it," she said, and she felt torn on how to react. At last she'd taken down the record, but Argus was right there. Would he be upset? She glanced his way, trying to judge his reaction, but his face was like a statue's, those blue eyes of his analyzing her every move.

"Well done," he said. "It took me until my third year to realize that backward trick at the ninth ring. Adam's reports do not exaggerate when they call you a prodigy."

Bree smiled, and she wiped sweat from her brow. Before she could thank him, he offered her a rolled piece of paper he'd been carrying in his left hand. Curious, she took it and unrolled it. Whatever happiness she'd felt immediately vanished.

Drawn in charcoal was a crude mockery of herself. Her face was narrower, her eyes slanted, and her lower lip far larger than the upper. Thin lines along her eyes and neck made her look emaciated. Written above in bold letters was her name, while below was a single word: *unpunished*.

"What is this?" she asked.

"This was brought to us by one of our traders," Argus said. "Similar ones are posted throughout Galen. You're the face of every lie they've ever told about our people, and forgive my boldness, but this one here is the kindest of the lot. The others bear far crueler words."

Bree felt her pulse begin to race.

"I told you I should have been handed over," she said. "How many people will continue to die for my sake?"

"And how many times must I tell you we do not hand over our own?" Argus said. "Besides, if it wasn't you, it'd be someone else. They wanted a battle, Bree, and you were merely the excuse. While we fought Galen's forces, they sent a small division alongside Candren Seraphim to attack our allies in Sothren. While we achieved a hard victory, Sothren suffered a massive defeat. Whatever balance we had, it's now been lost."

Bree frowned, trying to think over what she knew. Weshern and Sothren were allied together in a mutual defense pact against Candren and Galen. As for the fifth island, Elern...

"What about Elern?" she asked. "Won't they protect us?"

Argus shook his head.

"Elern's promised to aid any island against invasion, but Sothren's Seraphim are all but decimated. Even with Elern's help, we still might lose. The uneasy peace we've had for the last sixty years is coming to an end. These aren't skirmishes anymore, Breanna. We're not squabbling over trade rights or political prisoners. This is war. If Galen secures another victory against us, they'll begin carrying over ground troops, and we'll have no way to stop them. The fighting won't remain in the skies. It'll be in our streets, our homes, and our fields, and they'll all be bathed in blood."

Bree thought of soldiers with wide shields and tall spears smashing in the door of their home to kill Aunt Bethy, and she felt panic rising inside her chest.

"Center won't allow it," she said. "That's the point of us, of our Seraphim, to fight those wars so the rest don't have to."

"Center will allow it because they don't care about us, Bree. They don't care about our lives, our traditions, our very independence. So long as the trade flows, and they receive their food and wine, they'll not bat an eye, and I'd wager Galen's Archon has been whispering more than enough promises in the ears of the theotechs about how they'll share in our spoils."

Their commander made everything seem so dire, so beyond her control, Bree had to fight down a shiver. Bree stared at the drawing of her, the implied guilt. Unpunished. To the people of Galen, she was already condemned, and for what? Slaying a man who'd murdered her lover and dumped his body at her feet? A man from the nation that had killed her parents when she was only a child? Knowing nothing of her, they'd insult her and smear her name?

Bree crumpled the crude portrait in her fingers, a silent vow on her lips. If they wanted to plaster her name throughout their island, then she'd make it one to remember. Somehow, some way, she'd make them dread her name. Not mock it, not despise it. *Fear* it.

"Why are you telling me this?" she asked, throwing the paper to the grass.

"Given our desperate situation, we need Seraphim more than ever," Argus said. "Your skill in flight easily qualifies you in that capacity, but then when I speak to Randy, I hear a far different tale."

Bree withered under his steel gaze and looked to her feet.

"When it comes to my fire element, I have...trouble," she said.

"So I heard," Argus said. "It's such a shame. If only your skills weren't so poor, you'd be an excellent soldier. God knows we're in sore need of them."

"I'm sorry," she said, feeling incredibly guilty for some reason. "I've tried so hard, but it never seems to matter."

"Then you're not trying hard enough."

He said it with such dismissal, such distaste, Bree found herself taken aback.

"Yes I have," she insisted. "I've tried harder at becoming a Seraph than anything else in my life. I spend twice the hours in the sky than anyone else in my class. While others sleep, I run laps around the academy. For weeks I used four fire prisms a day, when just a single one exhausts me. I have done *everything* I know to do, Argus. I want this. I want to fly at your side, to show you I'm ready to fight instead of letting others die for me. How can anyone not see that?"

Argus crossed his arms and frowned at her.

"You mention your extra allotment, yet Jay tells me you've stopped accepting it. Care to explain why?"

"I don't see the point, so why waste everyone's time?" Bree said. "I can create a dozen shapes, from spears to walls to spheres, but it never lasts. I drain the prism, and then it's over. No matter what I do, I always lose control."

"That's it exactly," Argus said. "Control. It's the one thing you lack. Everything I learn of you shows this key failing. Disrespecting Instructor Dohn, the fight in the mess hall, using Dean's harness to chase after Eric: it is all action without thought to consequence. That manifests into your flame as well."

Bree felt too exhausted and mentally raw for such a dressing down.

"Then what do you want from me?" she snapped. "What should I do?"

"I want you to *focus*," he said. "Pour your anger and frustration into a single aspect. Your element is your weakest skill? Then work at it above all else until you finally succeed. If two extra prisms daily wasn't enough, then ask for four, and then six, until the breakthrough comes. Don't come out here and try to break a meaningless record. Whatever limits you know, push beyond them until you get the damn job done, no matter the toll the struggle takes."

Despite Argus's rank, despite his legendary skill, Bree couldn't bear to remain silent under such an attack.

"What would you know about struggles?" she said. "You're Argus Summers, the most gifted Seraph we've ever had."

"You're wrong," Argus said. "I wasn't even the best in my class. Randy Kime was."

Bree's mouth dropped open. *Instructor Kime?* But that didn't make any sense. Argus ran a hand through his short dark hair, and he glanced west, to where Randy flew drills with the second-year students above the training field.

"You should have seen him," he said. "When it came to fire, he was an artist. The speed of flight meant nothing to him. He could anticipate distances and velocities as if they were the easiest things to master, and when he let loose his flame, he rarely missed. An enemy would weave and dodge, and he'd play with them like you or I might play with a child."

Bree tried to imagine kind Instructor Kime in battle, but she couldn't. It seemed too weird.

"I trained day and night to reach his level," Argus said, turning back to her. "I begged and harassed the headmaster until he allocated me a double ration of both light and ice element to practice with. Those first two years, I slept four hours a day at most, all so I could improve. All so I could spend more time in the skies, or at the practice fields flinging ice. There were people more talented than I was, Bree, people who took more easily to flying or to their element, but none worked harder than I did. And you know what? It still didn't matter. Randy was better than I was. I was an apprentice struggling to overcome a master."

Bree was shocked by such admissions from their commander. How could he say someone was better? Everyone knew he was the best. No one even came close.

"What happened?" she asked. "If he was so much better, why doesn't anyone know?"

"In our very first battle together, Randy killed a man above him, then turned to fire at another. The man he'd killed had drawn his swords, and as he dropped, one blade fell wildly. It struck Randy on the wrist, and it cut down to the bone. He ignored it, and by the time the battle was finished, he'd torn it even worse. The apothecaries did their best, but the wound grew infected, and after two days they had to cut off his hand."

Argus lifted his own left hand and stared at it, as if imagining it'd been him.

"Simple bad luck," he said. "That's all it takes. I've worked harder than anyone alive because of that. Luck is a fickle demon to be warred against. The more time you take, the more effort you put in, the less power luck will have in your life. And even then, you still might lose. People wonder at my three kills in that first battle, but they ignore how Randy had four. Listen to me. Randy was one of the most gifted men alive, but instead of actively dodging the dead body, he ignored it and continued fighting. Ninety-nine times out of a hundred, that body falls past him without so much as a scratch. But it didn't, and that tiny little mistake cost Randy dearly. Try harder, Bree. Do everything you can. Perfection will be beyond you, but to give up is to invite the same demon that cost Randy Kime his hand."

Bree felt like she'd been judged and found wanting, and

her face flushed as she clenched her teeth, unsure of what else there was to say. Argus cleared his throat, and his tone changed somehow, growing more formal, more distant.

"Of the students I have observed from your class, I consider three currently worthy of joining us in battle: Saul Reigar, your brother Kael, and you."

"Me?" she asked. "Are you sure?"

"Honestly? No. I wish I could say it is because of your skill, but it's not. Given your incompetence with your fire element, you will be of limited aid during battle. The reason you'll be with us is because you're the current face of the conflict. You've been labeled a coward and a cheat by the Galen people, and Archon Willer wants you flying into battle to defend both your name and your nation as a direct counter to these claims."

"I understand," Bree said with a voice that was suddenly hoarse.

"I don't expect much. With your skill in flight, I believe you're capable of surviving, which is all we really need from you. From now on, you will join the third- and fourth-year students with their formation practices. You have a lot to learn in very little time, so expect to spend many hours in formation instead of performing simple drills and pointless obstacle courses."

"As you wish, Commander."

Argus dipped his head, then walked away. She watched him go, anger rumbling in her belly. Teeth grinding, she looked to the timer, still marking her record attempt. Drawing out her sword, she knelt before the wooden contraption and used her gauntleted left hand to safely hold the blade near the tip for greater control. Beneath Argus's name she began to carve, digging the tip of her sword into the wood. It was awkward using the weapon for such a purpose, and she had strain to form the jagged letters. After what felt like forever, she stepped back and surveyed the results.

1-35 BREE SKYBORN

That done, she flew across the grounds and landed before the learners' academy building. Not bothering to remove her wings, she shifted sideways so she might fit through the door, then hurried down the hall to the headmaster's office. Over-Secretary Waller wasn't at her desk, so Bree knocked on the door, then hesitated.

"Come in."

Bree stepped inside, put a fist across her breast in salute, and then bowed to Jay Simmons at his desk.

"Headmaster," she said. "I've come to request my additional allotment of fire element be resumed."

The older man leaned back in his chair, arms crossed over his chest.

"Does this mean you've regained hope at progressing?" he asked.

"I don't know," Bree said. "But I'm going to keep trying until I do."

A smile blossomed on Jay's face.

"Good enough," he said. "Consider your request happily granted. And might I add, Bree, it's about damn time."

CHAPTER 25

More than anything, Kael wanted to return to his room and sleep. The past few days he'd spent so many hours practicing formations he'd used triple his normal daily allotment of light element. Every muscle in his body felt sore from the constant twisting and pulling of his wings to dive, climb, and turn. Sadly he had no plans to retire just yet, not when he had his investigations at the library to continue. After grabbing an apple from the mess hall, he tore into it as he crossed the street, passing the squat armory to the far taller library behind it. Before he could enter, he found a surprise waiting for him.

"I thought I'd find you here," Clara said. She stood on the top step, arms crossed as she leaned against one of the four pillars that marked the library front. Her face appeared to be made of the same white stone as the pillars. Kael's tired mind grasped wildly for an excuse.

"I, uh, was just coming here to relax," he said. It sounded painfully false to his own ears.

"Just like last night, and the night before?" she asked. "Should I point out that I haven't seen you at all since you started combat training with the older Seraphim?"

More tired mental scrambling. He didn't want to lie to her, not in the slightest, so he tried to find some way to at least tell a bit of the truth. Kael shifted his weight from foot as she towered over him to foot halfway up the stairs.

"I'm sorry," he said. "My mind's been kind of…occupied lately."

"Do you have a few moments to spare right now?"

There was no way to tell her no without explaining why, and truth be told, he did miss spending time with Clara. Since Argus chose him as one of the three to be elevated to full combat duty, his schedule had rarely intersected with hers.

"Sure," he said. "I guess I do."

Just like that, her stony facade dropped, and she was all smiles as she grabbed his hand.

"Good," she said. "Now hurry up, or we'll miss it."

"Miss what?" he asked as he nearly fell down the stairs from her pulling him after her.

"You'll see," she said, green eyes sparkling.

She guided him onto the road, then turned west at the intersection. He caught her glancing at the sky a couple times, but he saw nothing in particular to explain her sudden hurry. Her steps turned to a sprint. Across the bridge they ran, hands still locked, and she slowed only upon reaching the gear sheds.

"Get your wings on," she said, once more scanning the sky. "And make it quick."

By now his curiosity was piqued, and he did not argue. Rushing inside the empty building, he found a pole and pulled his set of wings down from the wall hook. Part of him groaned at the thought of putting them back on after so many hours of training, but he had a feeling Clara wasn't interested in performing more boring drills. So what did she plan?

He didn't know, but his heart sped at the possibilities.

Outside the shed, he found her already waiting, her silver wings strapped comfortably onto her back.

"Follow me," she said without checking to see if he was ready. Her wings hummed to life, taking on a soft glow. Twisting her back to him, she soared into the air, and flicking the throttle forward, he followed. She rose at a steep angle, flying toward seemingly nothing in particular.

"Where are we going?" he shouted, hoping she'd hear.

"You'll see," she shouted back over her shoulder.

Higher and higher they rose into the evening sky. The sun was just beginning its descent, and it was painful to look directly at it. The academy steadily shrank beneath him as they climbed far higher than they ever would during drills. Still baffled, he had to veer a bit to the right when she spun to face him while reducing her speed to a hover. Coming to a stop beside her, he looked up to see a ceiling of puffy white clouds stretched out as far as their training fields.

"Figured it out yet?" she asked him, a devilish smile on her face.

"Not in the slightest," Kael said.

"So disappointing. Come on up and look, and you finally will."

She offered him her hand, and he took it. Together they hovered higher into the clouds. To Kael's surprise, they were thin, maybe two feet thick at most, and they emerged immediately. Coupled with that surprise was how the sun colored the clouds due to its initial descent. Instead of being soft white like the bottom, the top seemed to shine a vibrant pink. Hovering upon it, Kael felt like he stood upon a pink cotton carpet, and the silliness of it put a smile on his face.

"It's beautiful," he said to Clara as she pushed him away.

"I thought you'd like it," she said as she fell through the clouds. Kael followed her, then flared his wings to chase her as she immediately rose back up. The two reemerged as if they were fish leaping in and out of the ocean, only instead of blue waters they had their own private pink pool. Kael twirled as he veered himself up and down through it, having never seen clouds so thin and thoroughly enjoying the chance to explore. It felt so good to relax, to play. Clara ceased diving, instead skimming along the surface of the cloud, her right hand hanging down so her fingers could tease the surface. The pink shifted at her touch, not much, just enough to mark her passage, like a hand waving through the smoke of a dwindling campfire.

Kael spun about, spread his arms, and dropped down into the clouds as if falling into a layer of snow. Once beneath the clouds, he righted himself, burst ahead, and then rose in front of Clara, catching her extended hand on his way up. Her body began to swing, and he grabbed her other hand to lock themselves together. Swirling, they rose above the clouds, angels on a heavenly dance floor. Kael lessened his wings to a hover, and Clara did likewise as she peered up at him.

"Kael?" she said.

"Yes?"

He expected a question, but instead she pulled herself closer and pressed her lips to his. Panic struck him, a primal fear of knowing absolutely nothing of what to do next, nor how to do it. If put off by his sudden freezing, she didn't let it show. She kissed him again, soft lips brushing his, and he opened his own

the slightest bit as he finally kissed back. Just like that, everything felt natural. She held him tightly, eyes closed. His hands
drifted to her waist, keeping her close as the kiss continued on
and on.

At last she pulled away, and she gave a playful push so they'd
separate.

"Was that your first kiss?" she asked him as she slowly
drifted away.

"Not counting moms and sisters?" he said, heart still hammering in his chest. "Yeah, it was."

Clara smiled, scrunching her nose as she did.

"You're adorable."

He reached for her arm, caught her wrist, and yanked her
closer. Clara laughed as it sent them into another spin. He
kissed her again, quick, relaxed, and suddenly he couldn't
believe it'd been two days since he'd spent time with her. What
the hell was wrong with him? Clara kissed back, but this time
when she pulled away, she didn't try to separate, instead leaning her head against his chest.

"So what brought this on?" he asked as they continued to
slowly twirl above the clouds.

"Nothing," she said.

"Nothing?" he asked, letting his obvious disbelief creep into
his voice.

Clara shook her head as she gently pushed him so he'd let
her go. As she drifted, she twisted her waist to straighten out.

"It's . . . it's just what I'm hearing at home," she said, her right
hand clutching her left elbow. "I don't think we're going to
wait for Galen and Candren to make the next move. If we're to
fight, my father wants it on his terms."

Kael immediately filled in the rest on his own. Reaching
out, he took her hand in his and squeezed it tight.

"I'll be fine," he said. "I promise."

"You can't make that promise," she said. "I've read all the books. I've heard all the stories. The first battle is always the worst. It's the one that claims the most lives."

She was right, of course. What else could he tell her? With his other hand he brushed her short blonde hair, for the first time seeing how it shone pink from the sun as well. She was so beautiful, and it killed him to see her afraid. But that fear was of losing him, and whatever he was to her, it was far more important than he'd ever realized. Knowing that gave him the strength to say what he never thought he'd have the nerve to say.

"I love you, Clara," he said. "I can at least promise you that."

She smiled, and he knew for the rest of his life he'd do whatever it took to see her smile that way at him again.

"I love you, too, Kael," she said.

Unable to pass up such an opportunity, he pulled her close for another kiss. Up there, with the whole world sealed away by a carpet of clouds, her wealth, her family, her power, and his own meager background didn't matter. In the sky, they were Seraphim, they were equals, and he relished every second of her touch, her closeness. Despite wishing it to never end, the kiss did, and Clara shut off her wings.

"I'll see you tomorrow," she said as she fell through the clouds.

"Same place and time?" he asked as he shut off his own wings. When he reemerged beneath the clouds, Clara had gained distance between them, and with air blowing against them from their increased speed, she had to shout to be heard.

"I was more thinking your room."

Kael's heart nearly stopped. Clara clearly saw the effect on him, and she laughed as she turned about, flared her wings to life, and shot toward the gear shed.

Kael looped through the clouds a few more times to clear his head before returning his wings and harness. He found he was still breathing heavily despite using a fraction of the effort he'd expended throughout the day during training. He'd often heard men, including his own father, talk of how their loved ones cast a spell over them, and for the first time Kael had a taste of how true that was.

Shaking his head as if to rattle his mind back into functioning order, he traveled back to the library.

Task at hand, he told himself as he crossed the bridge. *Keep your mind on the task at hand.*

Instead of remembering every single second of each kiss. Instead of wondering what Clara meant by his room tomorrow. Instead of...

"Focus, damn it," Kael said, rubbing his eyes.

By the time he entered the library, the sun was half an hour from setting, and he almost felt like a normal human being.

"Back again?" Devi the librarian asked. She stood on a stool left of the door. Books lay atop a nearby table, and she replaced them one by one on a top shelf. As she asked, the stool wobbled, and Kael felt a tiny moment of panic, but Devi didn't seem bothered in the slightest.

"Just browsing still," he said when certain the diminutive woman wouldn't fall and break her neck on the table.

"Well, if you need help finding something, or some good recommendations, I'd love to help."

She resumed reshelving books. Kael started to walk deeper into the library, then stopped himself. He'd been reluctant to reveal his reasons in case word might trickle back to the theo-techs, but so far he'd made pitiful progress. There were simply too many books. But maybe if he could come up with a convincing reason...

"Actually," he said, spinning around, "there is something you could maybe help me with."

Devi looked thrilled, and she beamed down at him from her wobbling stool.

"Great," she said, hopping down despite several books needing to be shelved remaining on the table. She wiped her hands on her black pants, a simpler version of the uniform the rest of the Seraphim wore. "What are you looking for?"

Kael judged his words carefully before he spoke them.

"I was hoping to learn more about my parents. They never talked much about what they did as Seraphim, but now that I'm here, and I might better understand…"

Devi bobbed her head, and he was thankful she didn't offer the standard pity and apology he often received when discussing his dead parents. Instead her bubbly smile vanished, replaced with a rather frightening amount of concentration.

"What were your parents' names?"

"Liam and Cassandra Skyborn."

"What was your mother's maiden name?"

Kael had to think for a moment, for it wasn't something that came up often. Their mother had been an orphan who snuck her way over from Center to Weshern, which had rendered her side of the family nothing more than stories she sometimes told at bedtime.

"Jennings," he said. "Cassandra Jennings."

Devi tapped her lips as she thought.

"I can't think of anything off the top of my head, but that doesn't mean much. Follow me."

She led him past rows and rows of thick wooden shelves, each one packed tightly with leather-bound tomes of varying age. They passed her desk, then turned to a corner of the library Kael had not been to before. Along the wall was an enormous set of thin shelves, tiny copper plates nailed into their fronts. The writing on the plates looked like gibberish to Kael, but Devi seemed to understand as she scanned them, tapping them occasionally as she searched.

"Here we go," she said, settling on one and pulling on a groove carved into its top. The shelf slid out with a groaning of wood, revealing a slender box full of hundreds of thin yellow cards. Devi shifted it to one arm, searched again, and then grabbed a second box much lower. Carrying both back to her desk, she set them down and began to thumb through the first.

"Even if your parents were the most boring Seraphim ever, we'll still have a few records of them," Devi said in a half-distracted sort of way. "I may not be the best at this sort of thing, but the librarian before me was a bald giant named Kolten, and I swear he'd describe the way the clouds looked if he thought it might be of later importance."

"Why would he do that?" Kael asked, chuckling.

Devi glanced up from the box, peering out from underneath her long dark hair.

"During the Ascension, we lost nearly everything about the world before," she said. "We've learned from that, and work hard to never let that happen again. The position of a librarian is a very important one." She sighed as she returned to thumbing through the cards. "Even if it's lost a bit of its...glamour over the past century."

Her short fingers resumed searching, flicking through cards with remarkable speed. Kael watched, shifting his weight from foot to foot as he waited. Searching on his own had been slow, and carried a feeling of impossibility to it. But now? Watching Devi, he realized that there would be no more delays and wasteful browsing. If there was a truth to discover, now he'd find it, and he couldn't decide if that was frightening or a relief.

"Skyborn...Skyborn...hah!" She tore the card out as if it were the heart of a vanquished foe. "Skyborn. Let's see, Liam Skyborn, safe to say not the Liam from 312 A.A., unless he fathered you at the ripe old age of two hundred. Ah, there we go."

She set down the card, stared at it with her walnut eyes as if burning every word into memory, and then hurried away. Kael followed, surprised such a tiny woman could move with such speed. Near the front door she turned down one aisle, finger waving as she checked titles written on spines in either white or gold. Kael noticed that that aisle in particular had similar books with similar titles, all containing a year. Grabbing the one titled *S Class—494*, she pulled it free and handed it to him. Kael grunted, surprised by its weight. Returning to her desk, she gestured for him to put the book down before her. Devi opened it, rapidly flipping pages until coming to a sudden halt.

"Here," she said, pointing. Kael turned the book so it faced him, took a seat in an uncomfortable wooden chair, and began reading. The script was written in incredibly tight and neat handwriting, and though the ink had faded a little, he still found it an easy read, other than the occasional need to squint given the tiny size. It took him a moment, but at last he realized what it was he read. It was a list of all members of the Seraphim class of year 494 A.A. Minor traits and marks were listed in shorthand with artless brevity. Kael read over his father's entry, which looked to have been slowly added to throughout the following years.

Liam Skyborn. Blck hr. Brwn eys. Admttd 494. 6-month eval pasd. Rnk 5 in class.—Grad to yr 2.—Mrrge to Cassandra Jennings, May/497.—Srphm Honors, 498.

Birth to twins: Breanna, Kael, Jly 2/499. Battle (Wshrn v Gln, April 18/501). Battle (Wshrn v Cndrn, Spt 2/503). 2 kills. Bttle (Wshrn v Gln, May 22/507). 1 kill. Bttle (Wshrn v Gln, Aug 9/510). 2 kills. Deceased.

Kael found himself fighting back tears. That was it. His father's entire life, summarized into all that was important to those in charge of history. His fingers brushed the text, and they hovered over that damning word, *deceased*. Abrupt. Heartless. Ending the writing with such simple, immediate finality. If only he could erase that final word, returning his father to him instead of leaving him and Bree alone at the age of eleven.

While he was reading, Devi vanished, then returned with another yearbook, this one for 496.

"Cassandra Jennings, page one hundred thirty-nine," she said.

Kael wasn't sure he had the strength to read it. Wouldn't it just be more of the same? Her entrance to the academy, her marriage to their father, a list of the battles she fought... and then at the end, that same terrible word. Yet he'd sworn to learn all he could, and so he did, flipping to page one hundred thirty-nine. He skimmed his finger over the words, trying to pull in memories to match the dates, to pour life into the history. His fingertip touched that last battle, hovered, unable to move on to the final pronouncement of her life.

"Devi," he said, looking up. "This battle... I've never asked before, but I think I'm ready to know. The battle my parents died in, what were they fighting for?"

Devi leaned closer, lips moving as she read the date.

"August five hundred ten," she said. "There was a shortage of fire element that year. Galen put in a trade offer to Center we couldn't match, so we challenged them to battle for it instead."

Kael slumped in his chair. That was it? That was the reason his parents had died? He'd always assumed they were protecting their home, or their island's honor.

"They died for nothing," he whispered.

"Not nothing," Devi said, taken aback. "The elements are our lifeblood, Kael. Without fire element, our Seraphim forces are greatly weakened. We must protect ourselves, and your parents sacrificed their lives to ensure the people of Weshern would remain safe."

The librarian was trying so hard, but Kael couldn't shake that nagging doubt. Their Seraphim had killed and died to ensure they had the elements necessary to kill and die? What was the point? And why was there a shortage of fire element in the first place? Everything about the process was carefully guarded by the theotechs. Thane's words haunted him, reminding him of his claims. Had Center callously engineered the battle that cost him his parents by falsifying a shortage? Before joining the academy, Kael would have dismissed the entire notion as conspiratorial nonsense. Now?

Now he wondered just how much truth had been in Thane's words. And since he was already in a library, perhaps he could look into something else the disciple of Johan had claimed...

"Do you have anything about the ghost plague?" he asked.

Devi frowned at him.

"You shouldn't call it that," she said. "It might land you in trouble if anyone from Center hears you. The proper name is the Weshern plague."

"So what was it?" he asked, still confused. Instead of answering his question, Devi did as he should have expected and went to fetch another book. Moments later she returned, lugging a tome even thicker than the two volumes he already had. It thunked down onto the table, and Devi let out a gasp of air.

"Whew," she said. "There you go. So why such interest in the plague?"

Kael pulled the book closer and read the title. *History of Weshern, 496 A.A.*

"Just something my aunt once said," he explained, hoping to deflect further curiosity.

"It was a rough time," Devi said. "Turn to March. You'll find the plague easily enough."

"Thanks," he said, and he started flipping. Devi hovered a bit more, then tapped her fingers on the desk.

"Let me know if you need anything else," she said before returning to the filing that he'd interrupted earlier.

"I will," Kael said, eyes not leaving the pages. He found March, written in the same tight script. It didn't take long to find what Devi meant. Dominating the page was the story of an illness ravaging Weshern, and as he read it, he felt his blood chill. Hundreds of men and women had been sent to Center for treatment. At the very end of the article, it listed those who had returned alive, all two:

Cassandra Jennings and Liam Skyborn.

Kael read over the entire page a second time, committing everything he could to memory, and then shut the book and went to find Bree.

"So, what was so special about the ghost plague?" Bree asked as they walked the path running through the center of the academy. Kael had found his sister eating supper, and he'd convinced her to go on a walk with him across the grounds so they could speak in private. The midnight fire would soon burn across the sky, and in the late twilight it was easy to be alone out near the training grounds.

"The people of Weshern called it that because they never saw any signs of illness," Kael explained. "Theotechs came and took people by the dozens, claiming they could detect the first signs in people's eyes or on their teeth. After a few months of this, people threatened to riot, and the Willers demanded we be allowed to treat the sick instead. Eventually Center relented, and the plague, if it ever existed, ceased to be."

"What does this have to do with our parents?" Bree asked.

Kael shook his head, remaining silent as they passed the gear sheds. It didn't look like anyone was about, but he didn't feel comfortable answering. It wasn't until they were several hundred yards past and had grass training fields on either side of them that he answered.

"They sent almost two hundred for treatment," he said. "But Mom and Dad were the only ones to return alive."

Bree shuddered, and she crossed her arms over her chest as she stared at the path they walked.

"What does it mean?"

"I don't know," Kael said. "But there's something else I don't like. Remember how Mom and Dad said they met?"

It was a common story they'd heard, for their father in particular loved to tell it.

"At the year's end festival," she said.

"What year?"

Bree frowned as she thought.

"Four ninety-seven, right?"

Kael nodded, for he'd remembered the same.

"They went to Center for treatment earlier that year," he said. "The only two Weshern survivors...but they never met prior to the year's end?"

Bree paused, and she finally looked over to meet his gaze.

"They went to the festival together because they were introduced by mutual friends," she said. "That's what Dad always told us."

"Friends," Kael echoed, and he nodded. "I'd love to know who those friends were, wouldn't you?"

Bree glanced back to the academy, and she shivered.

"The theotechs took an interest in our parents," she said. "And now they've taken an interest in us. Why?"

"I don't know," Kael said. "Worse, I'm not sure we can even find that out, not without giving away our search in the first place."

Bree reached out to grab his hands, and she squeezed with frightening strength. In the sky above, the first slivers of deep shadow crawled from the west.

"Keep your eyes open," she said. "Keep your ears listening, and no matter what happens, you be careful. We're in the dark, Kael, and that's a dangerous place to be."

Kael squeezed her hands back.

"Until we know more, we tell no one, and trust only each other," he said. "Promise?"

"Promise."

Before the night shadow could light up with fire, the twins hurried back to the safety of their rooms, vows of secrecy on their lips.

CHAPTER
26

Bree knew something was wrong the moment the doors to the mess hall opened, and in walked three fully armed and armored Seraphim of Weshern. With them was Instructor Kime, and for once he wasn't smiling.

"Kael," Bree said to her brother across the table.

At her words he turned to see the Seraphim crossing the hall. Randy spotted them and said something to his escorts. One nodded, and then they approached, stopping just before their table. All around, the other students quieted down, confused by what was going on.

"Bree, Kael, you're needed for training lessons," the instructor said.

Bree shared a look with her brother, knowing that was clearly not what they were actually being summoned for.

"May we finish our breakfast?" Kael asked.

"No, you may not," said Randy.

"Both of you, come with me," one of the Seraphim said. Bree vaguely recognized him from her evening formation training sessions. In the mornings it was just students, but the later half of the day they were joined by the entirety of Weshern's Seraphim forces for tense, tightly controlled drills. They'd had a lot to learn, but over the past two weeks Bree, Kael, and Saul had made vast strides. As they were led out of the mess hall, Bree had a feeling she was about to be grateful for those lessons. Of the three Seraphim, only one remained inside the mess hall with Instructor Kime.

"Give me your arms," said one Seraph to Kael once they were outside the building, and the other requested the same of Bree. The two stretched out their arms, the Seraphim grabbed them by the wrists, and without any warning, they rose into the air. Hanging beneath them, Bree suppressed a surprised shout as she flew backward across the academy. Moments later they set them down at the gear sheds. Sara and Bartow were already waiting outside, Bree's and Kael's wings in their arms.

"Suit up," they told them.

"What's going on?" Kael asked as he slid an arm through the harness.

"Now is not the time to discuss it," was the Seraph's answer.

Bree strapped on her wings, her mouth dry and her heart starting to race. A lot of things could be happening, but she knew what this was, what it had to be. Air starting to feel thin around her, she tightened the buckles and gritted her teeth to ignore the sudden discomfort. Before she could finish, she saw the third Seraph fly in from the mess hall, Saul hanging by the wrists. When they set him down, he nodded to Kael and Bree, an unspoken message traveling between them. They were the three chosen for combat. The horns had not sounded warning of an attack, but they wouldn't if Weshern was the one going on the offensive...

"Where to now?" Bree asked as she tightened the last of her buckles and did a quick check of her elements. Both fire and light shone brightly underneath their protective shields.

"The armory."

The Seraphim led the way, the twins following. At the armory, the entire Seraphim forces gathered, every one of them in their silver wings and combat uniform. Sunlight glinted off the metal of the wings and the decorated points of the sheaths belted to their waists. As her feet touched down and she shut off her wings, Bree offered a silent prayer that her brother would endure the day even if she did not.

The men and women gathered in loose groups, and Bree scanned their faces wishing to see someone familiar. She saw several from the swordplay group Dean had invited her into, but they were scattered about, and for some reason it felt wrong to bother them. Sasha noticed her, however, and she gave her a soft smile.

You'll be fine, the woman mouthed.

I hope so, Bree mouthed back.

Feeling a little better, she stayed beside Kael, arms crossed over chest as she waited. She didn't have to wait long. Like a comet flying across the sky came a man with black stripes on his silver wings, and he barely slowed down before slamming into the ground at their center.

"Seraphim of Weshern," said Argus Summers as he stood to his full height. "Your Archon made the formal request, and Center has given us our permission. This morning, we fly to the island of Galen. This morning, we bring justice for their aggressions. They have stirred their people against us and done all within their power to break the peace our five islands have known for a decade. Good men and women, our friends, our family, have died because of their pride and recklessness."

Argus put a fist upon his breast in a salute, and he turned so he could look upon them all.

"Such evil bears a price," he said, voice quieter yet somehow easier to hear in that crowded gathering. "This beautiful morning, we will make them pay."

The hundred gathered men and women lifted their arms in a cheer. Bree mimicked the action, wishing she were as confident and excited as the bellow escaping her lips. *Act it until you make it real,* she told herself, one of the things Instructor Kime had told her in an effort to master her fire element.

"My Wolf Squadron will maintain point," Argus continued. "I want Scorpion on our left, Hawk on our right. The rest of you, follow your squad leaders. Trust them to choose the proper paths of battle. Nothing fancy or experimental today, my friends. Surprise is on our side, as are skill and bravery. I trust those qualities alone to lead us to victory."

Another cheer, and then everyone began to rise into the air, drifting toward their squad leaders as they formed up. While Saul was in Coyote Squad, Kael and Bree were together in Fox. Their leader was an experienced woman named Olivia West, the most beautiful of all the Seraphim Bree had met. Just being around her made her feel awkward and uncomfortable, but Olivia's attitude seemed strict and professional at all times. In terms of learning how to fly in formation, Olivia was about as good a teacher as Bree could hope for. Even better, Sasha was also a member, giving Bree another friendly face besides her brother's to whom she could ask questions when necessary.

"We'll be hanging back for a counterpunch," Olivia said as

the nine grouped together. "Ideally a formation that thinks they can get the jump on Argus's Wolves. Garrick, try to scatter them downward, and I'll do the same with my own stone. The rest of you, stay in formation, and pick your shots wisely. As for the newbies..." She spun to face Kael and Bree. "Kael, use your ice defensively. Unleash Hell on any group you think is about to draw a bead on us. As for you, Bree...stay close. Maybe if we get into the thick of things, you can get off at least one good shot."

Bree nodded, feeling embarrassed by such condescension. It was deserved, of course, but it still stung knowing how unreliable she was in the grand scheme of things. One good shot. Despite the tiny progress she'd made in shaping the initial blast of fire, she still drained her prism within moments. Her increased daily allotment only helped reinforce that fact as she tried in vain to rein it in.

"Form up!" Olivia shouted as other squads did the same. Olivia kept point, Seraphim on either side flying in matching lines. The farther back, the less experienced and skilled you were considered, for the closer you were to the front, the less time you had to react to your squad leader's maneuvers. Unsurprisingly, Kael and Bree were the very last two in the formation. Wolf Squad spun once around the academy, then streaked west, and the rest of the squadrons followed. Fox remained near the back and above the others, so much so that they had to pierce through occasional tufts of clouds. The island of Weshern passed beneath them, little more than a distant blur as her Seraphim flew to war.

Given their location, Bree had ample view of the others gathered before her, and she imagined the chaos she'd witnessed earlier when Galen had attacked in an attempt to win her over for execution. Her imagination lit up the formations with balls of flame and lances of ice, and she felt her stomach suddenly tighten. She coughed twice, dry and painful, and before she could stop herself she tilted her head down and vomited up what little breakfast she'd eaten.

Please don't land on someone, Bree thought as the vomit sprayed out beneath her to the island below. In front of her, Sasha lessened her speed until they were nearly side by side.

"Don't worry about it," she shouted, her red ponytail flapping behind her head. "Nearly everyone throws up the first time, either before or after."

"Did you?" Bree asked.

Sasha bit her lower lip, and she grinned.

"Well, I said *nearly* everyone."

Bree laughed, and she caught Kael grinning at her as well. A bit of her nerves lessened, and she did her best to breathe normally. Sasha's wings flared brighter as she pushed herself back into formation. Spitting out the last foul taste of bile from her mouth, she focused on the task at hand. Her actions in battle would be close to the games Instructor Dohn had them play, where they chased after one of their classmates. Bree would keep an eye on Olivia at all times, doing her best to remain in formation whenever she turned, dove, or climbed. There were a few signals Olivia could make with her arms, particularly for the more difficult maneuvers, but for the most part they had to trust one another and have a feel for their squad leader's reactions. All the hours of drills and mock combat helped, but Bree felt certain true combat was going to put all of that to the test.

The ocean passed beneath them, Weshern a steadily fading image behind. The five outer islands created a semicircle around Center, their positions drifting only minuscule amounts each year. Weshern was the farthest east, and nearest to it was her ally, Sothren. Even at their rapid pace, it took an agonizing amount of time, fifteen to twenty minutes by Bree's estimate, to reach Sothren's edge. Argus guided them alongside the island, using it as a screen of sorts against the much more distant Galen. Just before they might fly over, they banked right, and suddenly Wolf Squad gained speed, causing the rest to follow suit. As Bree pushed her throttle, she saw they were at nearly ninety percent.

Argus really wants surprise on our side, she thought.

Sothren passed to her left, and Bree spared what glances she could. Just as Weshern had the most lakes and indigenous fish that could not live within the ocean's waters, Sothren's pride was its great orchards of fruit. They had multiple types of apples, some even green and yellow, while the soft red type were the only ones that grew on Weshern. She'd heard of the other fruits, of their bitter pears and juicy oranges, even melons that were so enormous they grew out of the ground instead of from a branch, but she'd never had the chance to try any of them. One day, she decided, she'd take a trip to Sothren just to eat all the different fruit it offered. Assuming she lived, of course.

Once Sothren was beyond them, and Center far to their right, they bypassed the nearer Elern to the south and took aim for Galen. Seeing the distant green and brown island, its Fount a slender line of pale blue barely distinguishable from the clouds, reawakened every bit of her stomach's discomfort. This was it. Battle was coming. Bree thought of her single-mindedness when she attacked Eric Drae, of how it'd felt so instinctual, and she prayed that feeling would return. She couldn't fight like this. She couldn't fight afraid, and doubting, and worrying over every little detail. That wasn't how she flew. Minute after minute clocked along as they crossed the miles, until at last Olivia shouted something at the front. Two

Seraphim halfway down the formation repeated it so all could hear.

"Galen forces approaching!"

Even if she never heard, Bree would have understood. Tiny red and gold dots swarmed up from Galen's edge like gnats, quickly falling into *V*-shape formations, each seven strong. As always, a cluster of theotechs hovered nearby, watching, waiting. Terror clawed at Bree's heart with thin, hooked nails. There was no turning back, no escaping this. A year of training, of flying, of flailing with her element and twisting through each ring of the obstacle course, had led her to this. She looked to Kael, and she saw he'd already turned her way. He knew her too well, and he also knew exactly what to say.

"Bet I kill more than you," he shouted, shifting closer to ensure she heard him.

Bree shook her head, fighting off a smile as her competitive spirit took over.

"You wish," she shouted back.

"We'll compare afterward then!"

Because they would, Bree told herself. They would both endure. They would survive.

Wolf Squad began to weave side to side, just gentle enough that the nearing army could not fully ascertain their angle of approach. Olivia lifted a fist, then opened it, their signal to spread out. Bree fell back farther as their formation elongated. With the increased space, they would be less vulnerable to the incoming projectiles, though it'd be harder to also hide behind their defensive countermeasures of stone and ice. Given their role in the far back, the evasive formation made sense. Wolf, Scorpion, and Hawk, however, kept tight formations as they led the way, trusting their leaders as well as their fellow Seraphim to provide adequate defense.

For a long moment, the only sound was of the whooshing of the wind and the thrum of their wings. The white noise was comfortable, another form of silence to Bree, but that silence was broken when enormous boulders shot upward from both sides. As they fell, they crashed into one another, shattering into pieces, and that sound seemed to awaken a chaotic chorus. Lances of ice slammed into more stone, these wide and flat and lofted in protection. Fire crackled as it burst into the center of their formations, punctuated by blasts of lightning streaking through each side's numbers. Bree watched the opening salvos crash and burn into one another while striking down Seraphim wearing both black and red jackets. So far in the back, she had the briefest moment to take it all in, the sudden fury and splendor of all four elements unleashed, before Olivia curled downward and to the right, leading them into the battle.

Twin streaks of lightning flashed above Bree, but she was too focused to wince despite her terror. A barrage of ice lances whirled before them, unleashed by a Galen squadron chasing after Wolf Squad, and then Olivia led Fox Squad right onto their tail. Wide flat stones lashed out, Bree heard a crack as one Galen Seraph had his wings ripped off his back, and then their foes dove, exactly as Olivia had said she'd try to force them. Fire and lightning erupted into their path, catching two more and sending their bodies plummeting to the ocean. Bree started to twist, expecting Olivia to have them follow as the battered squad banked a hard left, but instead she began a near vertical climb. Bree obeyed despite her confusion, which lasted only a second before a trio of fireballs exploded directly in the path they'd have taken if keeping chase.

There were no clear sides now as the battle erupted into a whirling, vicious dance. Olivia had them continue to climb as elements shot through the air all around them. It seemed she was trying to gain them some separation so they might make another ambush, but two different Galen squads chased after, one from either side. Olivia banked side to side, and Bree mimicked the evasive maneuver. The two Galen squads opened with a salvo of stone, and despite her best efforts, Bree closed her eyes as she juked to one side. She felt the distortion of the air as the stones flew past, heard a loud nearby crack. When she opened her eyes, she saw one of their squad dropping, his body struck with a bolt of lightning on the way down to ensure his death.

Her panic lasted only a moment before she looked right and saw Kael still with her. A lance of ice knifed a few feet to his right, and he turned around, bracing with his gauntlet. True to Olivia's command, he unleashed more than a dozen lances right back, six to either side. The act had him falling behind, and Bree screamed his name as the chasing Seraphim returned fire. Kael flew as fast as his silver wings could carry him, fire and stone hurtling through the air about him. Before she could realize what had happened, thin shards of stone flew past Bree on each side, and she winced in surprise. Olivia had turned Fox Squad about-face, diving straight down toward the ocean and their pursuers, and she'd not seen it due to her attention being on her brother. Several others flew past her, and Bree turned and dove, punching her throttle to full so she might rejoin the formation.

Such a head-on meeting was considered the most dangerous possible attack, but it was better than letting the two groups slowly pick them apart. At least gravity was on their side, giving them far greater speed, and Olivia used it for all it was worth, extending her gauntlet and creating a dizzying layer of five boulders careening at different angles and speeds. Bree clenched her gauntlet, thinking maybe to use her fire, but then the Seraphim they attacked pulled into a hover. Two died, their bodies crushed by Olivia's stone, but the survivors lifted their right arms and unleashed all they had. Olivia banked left, but Bree noticed far too late. Seven lances of ice, each thicker than her torso, shot up into the air. On instinct she twisted her body and veered right, barely avoiding their aim. Sasha in front of her wasn't so fast, nor so lucky.

"Sasha!" Bree screamed, trying to crane her neck to see as she spun wildly away from their formation. The woman plummeted headfirst toward the water, showing no control over her wings. She'd been struck right in the chest, and a stream of blood trickled after her as she fell. Telling herself not to cry, Bree weaved side to side as the cacophony of battle overwhelmed her ears. She didn't know where she was. She didn't know where her squadron had gone, what she should do. Fighting off panic, she swooped low and away from the battle, hoping she might have some chance to recover.

After a few moments she turned to see if anyone chased. No one did. The battle raged on in front of her as she hovered in place, silver and gold wings curling and twisting as elements filled the air between them.

"Where are you?" Bree whispered, searching. Her eyes lit up when she finally spotted Fox Squad. Their numbers were down to five, but Kael was still one of them. That joy immediately faded when she realized where they were. Olivia had them curling at the very edge of the battle, seeking another target. Beneath them, though, was one of Galen's snipers. He'd been lurking close to the ocean, waiting for an opportune time to strike, and it seemed he'd found it. In less than a minute, he'd be in position to attack.

"No," Bree whispered. She'd seen the damage a sniper could

cause at the last battle, but what could she do? Bree lifted her hands, and she hated herself for her total lack of control. All around her elements raged against each other, and she could only dodge and weave, praying to survive. Her brother was in danger, but at such speeds and distance, what would one reckless blast of flame accomplish? Nothing. Her fire was her own enemy, uncontrollable and wild. When she tapped into its fury, nothing kept it restrained and focused. All she had were her swords. Having now experienced the chaos of battle, its air filled with powerful elements and her foes racing at incredible speeds, she understood how worthless her blades truly were. She'd be lucky not to have her arm taken off should she ever connect a single swing.

Worthless. Was that what she was? All her training, all her skill in flight? Worthless?

Bree stared at the encroaching sniper, and she felt rage overwhelm her mind. She jammed her wrists down, connecting the sword hilts to her gauntlets, and then drew them from her scabbards. So tightly she clenched them, it seemed her vision went red. No, she would not be worthless. She would not watch her brother die.

Her body tightened, her arms flexed, and her fingers tensed. *Focus,* Argus Summers had told her. *Pour your anger and frustration into a single aspect.* And so she did. Connection with the prism made, the fire began to release from the gauntlet. Her mind shaped it, molded it, bent every bit of her sheer will into demanding it obey. All her training, all her skills, she'd poured so much of it into her two swords, and now she stared at the one in her right hand with frightening intensity. Instead of burning wildly into the open air, the fire swirled up the hilt, enveloping the blade. Bree clanged her left blade against it, and the fire leapt to it as well, bathing the weapon in flame. In her mind, she felt a soft tug, the faintest of strain to keep the fire burning, and burn it did, surrounding but not consuming the metal of her swords.

For months, Bree had struggled to rein the fire in, to halt its flow after establishing connection with the prism in her mind. No longer. Let it burn. Let it consume. Steady. *Controlled.*

Eyes back to the sniper, Bree pushed the throttle to its absolute maximum. Wind tore against her, but she didn't care. She needed speed, craved it. Twin trails of flame dripped off her swords as she held them out to either side of her. She tried not to think about what it meant, and instead on flying at such incredible velocity. The only other time she'd pushed her wings to their maximum was when she'd attacked Eric Drae, and something about the sensation of the air billowing against her, the harness pulling tightly on her entire body, felt perfectly natural as she reentered the carnage.

The sniper never saw her coming. His right arm extended, but only a single shot of lightning escaped before Bree came crashing in. She pulled both swords back, then swung as she flew past. Just before contact, the fire on her blades flared brightly. Bree felt resistance for only the briefest moment before her swords cut clean through, slicing his wings as if they were made of cloth. As the man tumbled to the ocean, Bree twirled through the air, righted herself, and overlooked the battle. She didn't dare think, only act. Two Galen Seraphim flew nearby, and one spotted her alone and broke off for a head-to-head assault.

Grinning, Bree gladly accepted, her wings thrumming so loudly it was as if they were screaming. Her foe shot blast after blast of fire, but Bree shifted left, right, then twirled while rising slightly so she cleared the third explosion's reach. Then they were too close, their paths ready for a collision. Bree pulled up at the last second, arms outstretched as she spun like a dancer. On the third revolution she felt a brief jerk as her sword cleaved her foe in half. Ending her spin, she looked about, saw several gold wings flying behind her on a course a hundred feet below. Diving as if into a lake, she zipped into an intercept course, then rotated so she fell feetfirst. With all her strength she plunged both her blades downward just before the moment of impact. Her knees curled to her chest upon contact, and she screamed in pain, but her swords plunged true. The dead Seraph's body rotated wildly before she kicked off, separating so she might chase the rest of his squad.

Having realized they'd been ambushed, the remaining two righted their bodies and turned so they could brace their arms and fire. Bree danced through the shards of ice and stone, imagining the gaps of safety between them as rings on the obstacle course. Her two foes realized they could not hit her and turned to flee, but she had far more speed than they. Wings screaming, she cut one of them off, lashing out with her left hand as she flew past. The flaming blade sliced through his thigh, not lethal but enough to force him into a panicked dodge. Wrenching her waist to the right, she looped about at a sharper angle than the remaining member, cutting the woman off at the very end of her turn. Dipping downward, she chopped with both swords above her head, opening up the woman's stomach and chest. Her foe's body collapsed, the buckles of her harness broken, her wings careening wildly toward the ocean.

The vultures will be busy today, Bree thought as she watched her fall. To her left she spotted a vicious exchange and gave chase, arms back, fire trailing after her in twin streams for several hundred yards before burning out into black smoke. The battle had calmed down, for dozens of Seraphim had died on each side, but in some ways it had grown even more chaotic.

With so many squadrons having lost members, and many more falling out of formation, the barrages of elements were more random and scattered. Bree weaved through it all as if right at home, giving no thought to the random blasts of ice or lightning that tore through the air. Never before had she pushed herself to such limits. Every single muscle in her body ached, but what did that matter compared to this? For once, she was free. Limitless. A bird on the winds.

It was Wolf Squad, Bree noticed as she neared. Of their initial nine, six remained, though three had their swords drawn. They must have been out of their element, not a surprise given the continued length of the battle. Argus guided his six as two separate squadrons of four chased, one on each side. When he tried to veer one way or the other, a squad unleashed fire and lightning, guiding them back, penning them in. Despite it, Argus weaved through the danger with incredible ease, but even he would fail in time. Pushing the throttle harder as if to squeeze every last bit of speed out of it, Bree shot after the closer of the two groups.

Like a comet she crashed into their center, catching them completely unaware from behind. She sliced upward through one man's legs, twisted her body half a rotation, and then plummeted back down next to his squad mate, fire flaring about her blades as she cleaved the Galen Seraph's wings in half. Neither hits were fatal, but they'd pose no threat as they both plummeted toward the ocean. The remaining two began evasive maneuvers, but she could tell they were baffled as to how to react. One drew his blades. The other lifted his right arm to fire. Bree charged the one with swords, praying the closeness would prevent the other from taking a shot with whatever element he was proficient with.

Her gamble proved right. Bree slowed down to half speed as she engaged the enemy Seraph. The man crossed his swords and moved to block, and she almost felt insulted. With all her strength she swung her own. She felt another tug on her mind, a steadily increasing strain as the fight wore on, but she would endure. Her burning blades cut straight through the man's block, each one crushing a collarbone before continuing downward into ribs. Her momentum carried her into his body, and she put her feet against him, knees to her chest, before leaping off.

The last remnant of the squad unleashed his element as his former squad mate fell, dead, to the ocean waters. The man wielded fire, and he let it out in a wide stream, far too wide for her to dodge. So instead she circled him faster than he could turn, staying just outside the reach of his fire. He turned as he followed her, keeping the air around her full of smoke and flame. Arching her back as far as it might go, she continued to curl as he hovered, giving him no respite. At last he tried to cut her off, blasting an enormous explosion of fire and smoke ahead of her path. Instead of rising above or diving below, Bree turned off her wings completely, twisted her body until her wings were pointed the opposite direction she'd been flying, and then punched the throttle. It hurt like hell, much like it had when she broke Argus's record on the obstacle course, but she could endure a little soreness.

The Galen man rotated, bringing his gauntlet around to bear. A much smaller streak of flame roared out toward her. Bree dropped low, then pulled back her shoulders and raced upward, left-hand sword swinging. She cut him at an angle, right hip to left shoulder, and far too deep for any hope of survival. As she soared into the air, she turned, seeking another foe, but then the sound of horns reached her ears. She froze, and it took her a moment to realize what it was: the call of surrender.

Lessening the power of her wings so she only hovered, Bree let her swords drop, and at last she ceased the flow of flame from her gauntlet. The fire faded away as if it had never been. Surveying the battlefield, Bree looked for the blower of the horn, and she found him in a red jacket in flight toward the island of Galen. Relief filled her chest. Galen surrendered. Weshern had won.

"Bree!"

She looked up to see Kael flying down toward her. A smile was on his face, but it looked forced. His eyes were wide. Shocked, she realized. Peeled raw by the sight of battle. In many ways she felt the same, for as the forces of Galen flew away, her comfortable numbness dissipated. The pain in her muscles was no longer an ache but a steadily growing fire throughout her body. She sheathed her swords, undoing the hooks that kept them secured to the cords attached to her wrists, and then opened her arms to accept a very tired embrace.

"I'm glad you're safe," he said.

"So am I."

As she pulled back, she looked over his shoulder at the flood of red-robed men flying in from Center with their gold wings, slowly diving toward the Endless Ocean. The vultures, come to collect treasures from the dead. The ocean would not deny them, for a safety measure built into the harness somehow allowed the light element to keep it afloat. Even if the bodies were not recovered, their wings would be. It made it hard not to know which were more important to the theotechs.

Kael cleared his throat, and when she turned back, she caught him glancing at her swords.

"Bree...," he started to say, but then several horns sounded, calling them to form up. Argus himself flew by, shouting as he did.

"Skyborn! At my side."

Kael gave her a look, a mixture of jealousy and pride.

"You know he means you," he said.

Bree nodded, punched her brother playfully in the chest, and then edged the throttle higher so she could join Argus and his Wolf Squad. Everyone was scattered about, and they flew at a leisurely pace compared to their arrival. Bree settled several yards behind the others with Argus, and she felt strangely worried about how he would react to her previous display. All around her, now in a wide array instead of their tight *V* formations, flew the survivors. Part of her wanted to count, but a larger part feared to know the true number of the dead. *We've won,* she told herself. *Let that be enough for now.*

But what exactly had they won?

Curiosity overcoming her exhaustion and nervousness, she poured a bit more power into her wings so she might fly side by side with the nearest member of Wolf Squad.

"What were the terms?" she said, shouting to be heard over the blowing of the wind.

"The what?" the man asked.

"For our victory. What was this for?"

"To kill them in battle," the Seraph explained as if it should have been obvious. "The theotechs wouldn't accept a surrender until a quarter of their numbers were lost."

Bree frowned. That was it? A battle whose sole purpose was to kill the others, with no greater objective than that? What was the point?

"What if they hadn't flown out to fight us?" she asked.

The elite Seraph shrugged.

"Then we'd have torched Galen's countryside until they did."

Such a realization chilled her to the bone, and she slipped farther back into the crowd. She'd joined the Seraphim expecting battle, expecting bloodshed, but knowing her first battle might have been against civilians from afar? That she might have partaken in a slaughter as they destroyed homes, fields, and cattle? It unsettled her deeply, and she had to conjure Dean's smiling face to banish it with a fresh sense of justified rage.

Though the flight to Galen had felt like it lasted an eternity, flying home seemed to take all the longer. Bree checked her light element once along the way, glad to see that despite how greatly she'd taxed it, she had by her estimate a quarter of its power left. Easily enough to make it back to the academy safely. When they flew over Weshern's edge, the beautiful Crystal River flowing over the side into a magnificent white spray, Bree was nearly overwhelmed with relief. It felt so good to be home, she never wanted to leave again. At the same time, she heard the echo of the elite Seraph's words, this time played out in reverse. If Galen's men had come, and Weshern's Seraphim not come out to meet them, then the beautiful hills below, the fields of grain and winding rivers, would all be pummeled with fire, stone, and ice.

This is what we protect, she thought as they flew over a small town whose name she didn't even know. Its residents waved and cheered at the sight of them. *These are who we serve.*

When they returned to the academy, Argus directed them to the apothecary. Bree landed, and she crossed her arms at the waist as it seemed the entirety of Weshern's forces landed about her in a circle. Too many eyes were upon her, she wished she could slink away, but such a desire was impossible when Argus landed before her, his blue eyes piercing into hers. Before he could address her, Headmaster Simmons stepped through their ranks, the Seraphim respectively parting so he might reach Argus.

"They were ready for us," Jay said.

"It didn't matter," Argus said. "We crushed them."

"Not Galen, *Candren*. They assaulted Sothren the moment our Seraphim left Weshern. From my early reports, our allies suffered a massive defeat."

Argus nodded his head, and it seemed to make his stone face all the harder. Turning away from the headmaster, he approached Bree, and something in his eyes made her wish she could turn invisible.

"How many?" he asked. No dancing around the issue. No discussion, only a number. Bree cleared her throat, and she met his gaze, telling herself not to be prideful, not to boast. Just say the number.

"Seven."

The commander stepped closer, face still unreadable.

"Show me your swords."

There was only one thing he could mean. Bree drew them from their scabbards, and she felt a moment of panic. Could she replicate the feat? She'd bathed them with flame in the midst of combat while fearing for her brother's life. Such panic proved unfounded, though, for as she triggered the flame of her element, she found that having something tangible to focus it on made all the difference. Fire swirled about her twin blades, and tiny globs of it dripped down to the pavement as if it were a liquid. After a moment, Bree ceased it, let it fade away into black smoke.

Argus shook his head in disbelief.

"I want fliers in all directions," he said, addressing the rest of the Seraphim. "Don't let our people dwell on the sour news from Sothren. Instead, tell them of our victory over Galen's forces. Tell them our island will not back down against those who would intimidate us." He turned back to Bree. "And most of all, tell them of the seven kills by the Phoenix of Weshern and her twin blades of fire."

The cheers of her fellow Seraphim washed over her. Bree stood in their midst, unsure what to do, what to say. For the first time since discovering her inability to master her element, she felt like she belonged. Overwhelmed, she dropped to her knees, tears dripping down her cheeks as one name rolled off their tongues, a legendary creature from an age long past, a name now all her own.

Phoenix…

CHAPTER 27

It had been a long day, and Kael was glad to finally see its end.

"God, that took forever," he told Brad as he slumped down onto his bed, an arm across his forehead.

"Can't have been that bad," Brad said, leaning against the interior of the doorway to his bedroom. "Besides, aren't you, like, heroes now?"

Kael snorted. He didn't feel like one. After coming back from the battle, he'd been stuck waiting for his turn for debriefing. He'd spent more than an hour just killing time in the library until Devi called him to come into a private room on the third floor. Inside was a slender table, and seated there were Devi the librarian, Headmaster Simmons, and Argus Summers. As Jay directed the questioning, Devi jotted down nearly every word he said. They asked him for his own recollection of the battle, if he'd scored any kills, or if he remembered anyone else doing so. They also asked him to estimate enemy numbers, the length of the battle, if any particular tactics performed by their enemy seemed unusual, and so on. Kael couldn't imagine how so many mundane details could prove useful, but he answered the questions as best he could.

By the time they finished, Kael had asked only one question in return.

"Is Bree all right?"

"Better than all right," Argus had said, the commander remaining quiet through most of the debriefing and chipping in only to help clarify something Kael couldn't easily convey given the absurd difficulties of tracking chaotic aerial combat. "By the end of today, every man, woman, and child of Weshern will know her name."

In Kael's opinion, that hadn't answered the question at all, but he'd pretended it did and gladly accepted his final dismissal.

"So what was it like?" Brad asked.

"Dull," Kael said, still thinking of the debriefing. He caught his roommate's strange look and realized his error. Shaking his head, he quickly backtracked.

"Sorry," he said. "Misunderstood you for a second."

"No worries," Brad said. His friend came into the bedroom, and he sat down beside him on the bed. He was unnaturally quiet, and Kael couldn't blame him. It'd likely be another year or two before Brad would experience combat for himself, and he was both curious and frightened by the prospect. Kael wished he knew what it was his friend desired from him. Did he want to know how terrifying battle truly was? Or did he want comfort, to be told it wasn't really that bad, all so he might sleep and train and live without the looming fear weighing on his heart?

"I'm not sure I could ever describe it right," Kael said quietly as he sat up. "Thinking back to it is like trying to relive a bad dream. It's just...there's so much happening all around you. People are dying, others are in danger, and you're in danger, too. But you can't think about that, because there's too much else you're responsible for. I just...I just followed Olivia and did all I could to hang on. It's weird, Brad. I've never been more afraid in my life, but at the same time, it didn't seem to matter because I had no time to dwell on it. Despite so much happening at once, I felt like I saw all of it...and yet also felt like there were a hundred things I couldn't follow, and each and every one of those things could get me killed."

He stared down at his hands, feeling ashamed of his words.

"You feel so helpless," he said. "Like your life is completely out of your hands. All you can do is fight. You try everything possible to keep yourself alive, but when the sky's filled with fire and ice, and so many are dying around you despite trying just as hard as you to survive, to live..."

He was crying. He didn't know when he started. He didn't even know why, but he was. Brad put a hand on his shoulder and squeezed.

"Hey, it's all right," he said. "You're here. You made it."

"Yeah," Kael said, and he sniffled. "I did. At least there's that, right?"

He smiled, and Brad returned it.

"Look on the bright side," he said. "First one's supposed to be the worst. It's all downhill from here."

"Damn straight," Kael said. "Just wait until it's *your* turn. I'm going to laugh my ass off when fattie gets his first kill. We'll rub it in Instructor Dohn's face together, how does that sound?"

"Sounds like a plan," Brad said, rising from the bed. "But for now, I think a better plan is to get some sleep. You look exhausted."

Kael wiped at the tears on his face.

"I can't imagine why."

Brad shut the door for him, and Kael leaned back down on his bed. Sleep. It sounded so wonderful. He prayed Bree was at least handling herself better than he was. He'd checked on her before coming to his apartment, and she'd seemed overwhelmed by it all.

"I have a new name," she'd told him, the only thing she offered beyond insistences she was all right. There was no hiding her confusion and shock. If the battle was a dream, then it seemed his sister was still struggling to wake up.

Maybe it's like that for everyone, Kael thought as the last of the daylight vanished behind his curtained window, overwhelmed by the inky darkness that preceded the midnight fire. *Maybe we're all still struggling to wake. Just open our eyes, and have the blood and death be nothing more than a nightmare, a harmless, fading...*

Kael dreamt of the moment just before battle, of flying west as the entire Seraphim forces of Galen stretched out before him. Except this time there were more of them, far too many, thousands of men in red jackets and gold wings. Kael wanted to tell everyone to turn around, to flee. How could they win when facing so many? But despite how loud he shouted, no one heard him. No one cared. The enemy was upon him, but now their wings were no longer golden but instead made of long reams of shadow. Their red jackets burned with fire, and as the multitude of faces sailed past him, the battle raging despite ignoring him completely, he saw fanged mouths and deep red eyes.

And then the shadows began to scatter, for across the horizon rose a blinding white light. Kael squinted, trying to see. A voice called out to him, distant, crystalline. He swore he saw a set of wings, and a face...

Wake up, Kael.

Something hard struck his face, banishing the dream. Kael's eyes snapped open, and he fought off a momentary wave of dizziness so strong he thought he'd vomit. The room was dark, too dark, and before he could ask what was going on a thick piece of cloth rammed into his mouth.

"I said wake up," hissed a familiar voice into his ear.

Hands grabbed him by the wrist, pulling him out of the bed. Kael started to resist, and a punch to the gut rewarded his efforts. He dropped to his knees, retching. His vision finally coming about, he saw that three men surrounded him in his room. The tiniest hint of red light bypassed the thick curtain across the window, and it flickered off the steel of three drawn daggers. Across the hall, Brad's door was shut, and he prayed his friend was unharmed.

"Keep an eye on the door," one of the three whispered to another.

One left for Brad's room; the other two lifted Kael back to his feet. The sharp point of a dagger pressed against his back, and the same rough voice whispered into his ear.

"Walk."

Resisting seemed pointless, so Kael did as he was told. He stepped out into the hall, then spared another glance toward Brad's room as he turned toward the apartment door. From within, he heard Brad's loud, consistent snoring.

At least he's safe, thought Kael.

His three captors pushed him out the door and into the brighter light of the midnight fire. They grabbed his hands and yanked them behind his back, tying them with a stiff piece of rope. His gag they tied as well, knotting two loose ends behind his head. They said nothing as they worked, and trying to keep calm, Kael surveyed the area in search for signs of hope. His apartment faced the stream and the advanced element training field beyond that. Just to his left was the main road that split the academy, and beyond that, the mess hall. The hour was clearly late, and so far he saw no one about.

"Come on," one of his captors said, giving him a push once his hands were finished being tied. Kael stumbled forward, and he glanced over his shoulder at the three once he had a bit of separation. Already tired and confused, his shock only worsened when he realized he knew two of them: Saul and Jason Reigar.

"Saul?" Kael asked, the name coming out muffled. His classmate looked away, refusing to meet his eye. Jason, on the other hand...

"Not a word, you understand me?" he said, putting the knife to his back. "I hear the slightest noise and I'll make you bleed."

Kael bobbed his head in answer. Jason kept the dagger there while putting his other hand on his shoulder, guiding him. Kael had thought they'd head west, toward the empty training fields, but instead they curled around the northern side of the apartment complex and hurried across the road toward the four women's buildings. Before they'd even finished crossing, Kael felt a sinking feeling in his stomach, for he knew where they were going. Bree's room was on the northern side, and as they approached he saw three shadowed shapes hiding beside the door. Two were older students. One he recognized as Jason's friend Alex from when they harassed him at the mess hall. The third shadow was Bree, bound and gagged.

"Anyone hear you?" Jason asked.

"No," one of the other two holding Bree answered.

"Good."

They put Kael and Bree side by side, and he checked her over in fear of wounds. He saw none, and he felt the tiniest bit of relief. To his eyes, she seemed calmer than he did. If anything, she looked furious. Each received a push to move, and while Kael stumbled forward, Bree tumbled to the ground and went limp. One of the older students pulled on her arm for her to stand, but she just lay there like a dead fish. Even when two of them lifted her together, she kept limp, accepting no weight on her legs.

Finally Jason pushed the two aside and knelt beside her.

"They may want you alive, but I'll deliver a corpse before I let myself get caught," he told her. "If you don't want my knife in your belly, stand up, walk, and make no attempts to escape. You got that?"

Bree stared at him for a painfully long time, then nodded. The other two helped her up, and this time when they pushed, she walked alongside Kael toward the east. The five led them all the way to the wall encircling the academy. Up the stairs they went to the top. Kael wondered what they planned to do once there, but an answer was already awaiting him. Coiled rope lay atop the wall, a metal hook on one end. Jason grabbed it, secured it on the interior edge, and then hurried to the other side.

"Tyler, you first."

Tyler, a wiry man with such pale skin he nearly looked orange from the light of the midnight fire, grabbed the rope and began to climb down. After a nod, Alex slithered after. When Jason confirmed him safe, he turned to Bree and cut off the rope around her wrists.

"Go on now," Jason said, careful to keep her surrounded and his dagger pointed at her chest. Bree glared but obeyed, sliding down to where the other two men waited with their own weapons at the ready. Next was Kael's turn. The knife slid through his wrists, cutting the rope. Kael rubbed his already sore skin, pondering an escape. Jason was much bigger than him, and he looked ready for an attempt, almost *eager* for one.

He'd love an excuse to kill me, Kael thought, and it chilled him to the bone.

Kael climbed down the rope, still pondering an escape attempt now that he was momentarily away from Jason. The other two down below were prepared, for Alex held Bree in his beefy arms, a dagger pressed to her throat. It was clear what would happen should he try to run away. Swallowing down his frustration, Kael stepped away from the rope and offered them his hands so they might tie them again, this time in front of him.

Though Kael couldn't see them, he could still hear the two Reigar brothers talking up on the wall, and he strained his ears to listen in.

"Remember, remove the rope and then lie low on your stomach until you see us coming back," Jason told his brother. "If you think you'll be caught, drop the rope and then get as far away as you can. You might be able to explain a midnight stroll, but if the rest of us can't get back inside, we're dead the moment they discover those two missing."

"Stop worrying about me," Saul said. "I got this."

Jason rubbed his younger brother's dirty blond hair and then slid down the rope. When he hit ground, he gave it a single tug, and then Saul started pulling it back up.

"Let's go," Jason said to them, his voice not so quiet as before. "We've a ways to travel before we reach the island's edge."

They curled around to the south, avoiding the roads. Soon they were in the field where the island of Weshern held its executions, and a morbid thought struck Kael. Would he envy the disciple of Johan and his quick death dropping down into the well? Jason had said whoever wanted them had wanted them alive... but that didn't mean very much, did it? Terror struck him at the thought of Jason selling them out to Galen's Seraphim. How great might their torture be? How long would they force the Phoenix that had humiliated them to suffer?

Suddenly the threat of Jason's dagger didn't seem so great. If only he'd tried to escape when they had them split up on the wall!

"We're running behind," Alex said as they reached the end of the field. Beyond that was a stretch of grasslands that sprouted up around a slender river running toward the island's edge.

"You don't know that," Jason said.

"I know time better than you do. We've got an hour or two at most."

Jason muttered something to himself as if he disagreed, but still he pushed them all on harder, forcing Kael and Bree into a light jog. The grass reached up to their knees, and they had to struggle for each step. The effort soon had him sweating, and he gasped in air through his nostrils. When they reached the river, they turned south and followed its bank. Far ahead, Kael saw where the river reached the island's edge and went tumbling over. It'd take twenty minutes to reach it, thirty at most. If they were to escape, it'd have to be soon.

Kael glanced over at Bree, trying to convey his thoughts to

her through sight alone. She saw him, and he flicked his eyes twice toward the river. His idea was to dive in and see if they could reach the other side, using both surprise and the current to gain enough distance so they might flee to safety. Bree saw, and she shook her head.

Why not? he wondered, wishing he could blatantly ask her, but that was a delusional hope. He trudged alongside the water, his legs aching and his lungs on fire. If only he could at least breathe through his mouth. The rag tasted like sweat and blood, and with each passing minute it made him sicker. The remaining four talked little, for Alex's warnings appeared to have made them nervous. Once he and Bree were discovered missing, an investigation would certainly follow. If Jason and his ilk didn't make it back before morning, they might as well immediately turn themselves in for the abduction.

The soft gurgle of the river gradually became a roar as it flowed over the island's side and into open air. Two figures wearing wings and harnesses waited beside it, bathed in red light, and while Kael knew he should be surprised, deep down he wasn't. One was a woman in golden armor, her white tunic seemingly orange due to the midnight fire. With the angelic knight was a theotech of Center.

"Have they been harmed?" the theotech asked. His head was shaved, and his face sported a thin patch of brown facial hair around his lips and chin. Jason's attitude was far more subdued and respectful when he answered.

"Not much," Jason said, shoving Kael closer. "I hope a few bruises don't matter."

The theotech gave cursory looks at the two of them.

"No, bruises don't matter much so long as they're alive and breathing," he said, smiling as if they were guests he'd invited over for tea. "Zelda, my dear, would you prepare them for their travel to Center?"

"Not yet," Jason said, stepping between them. "I want my payment."

A look of utter disgust came over the theotech's face.

"The proper amount will be transferred to your family's coffers, I assure you," he said. "Did you think I would arrive here with a giant bag of coin?"

Jason backed away, and he stammered out a weak apology. Zelda twisted a knob on her right gauntlet, then lifted it up. Electricity sparked from her palm.

"If you remain still, this will hurt less," she said.

As she stepped forward, Kael heard a soft whistling sound, one he was intimately familiar with. Praying he was correct, he dove to his left, straight into Bree. Together they hit dirt, Kael crouching over Bree in a meager act of protection. The others cried out, but before anyone could react, Zelda suddenly staggered backward. A wet cough escaped her lips, followed by blood. A long lance of ice impaled her through the chest, and she dropped to her knees, body turning limp. When she slumped forward, the still-embedded lance caught the ground and propped her up. Her arms flopped at her sides like those of a strange child's doll.

Jason saw, and he turned toward them with his dagger drawn.

"What the f—"

All around them, the night exploded. Fire and lightning blasted into the theotech before he could even raise his gauntlet. Alex started to flee, but another lance of ice hit his left shoulder, ripping his arm off his body. He dropped to the ground, whimpering as he bled out. Kael stared with eyes wide, unable to turn away. A stone came crashing in from the sky, its girth twice the size of Jason's chest. It smashed his lower body, snapping the bones of his legs in a horrifying sound belonging to a nightmare instead of the waking world. Jason collapsed, body convulsing in shock from such pain and trauma. When another stone crushed his skull, Kael felt relieved.

And then just like that, it was over. The theotech and his escort were dead, as were the four who'd dragged Kael and Bree to the edge. Kael pulled the rag out of his mouth, and he sucked in air, hoping to fight off his suddenly light head and weak knees. Five Seraphim of Weshern landed around them, their wings softly humming.

"Are you two all right?" asked a blessedly familiar voice. Kael turned to see Argus among the five helping Bree to her feet. Another Seraph drew a sword and used its edge to cut free their bindings.

"I'll be fine," Kael said, still feeling wobbly on his feet. When Bree's hands were free, she pushed away from Argus and rushed over to him, throwing her arms about him.

"I thought they'd kill me when I first woke," she said as she hugged him.

"A shame you didn't have a broom handle nearby," Kael said, and he grinned despite the grim hour. "Jason would have fled in terror."

Bree wiped away a single tear from her face as she laughed.

"Damn right," she said.

Kael turned to Argus, who was busy inspecting the body of the dead theotech.

"How did you know we were here?" he asked.

Argus turned, then pointed to the sky.

"He told us."

Both followed his gaze to see a sixth Seraph carrying a man in his arms. When they landed, Kael was hardly surprised to see it was Saul. What he was surprised to see, however, was that Saul wasn't tied up or bound in some way.

Saul crossed his arms over his chest upon landing, and he struggled to look them in the eye.

"Jason didn't tell me who we were taking," Saul said. "Only that they were traitors to Weshern. When I saw it was you, I... I knew I couldn't go through with it. Not after the battle we endured."

Kael's jaw dropped as he realized what that meant. Saul had turned on his own brother, sentencing him to die, all to protect him and Bree. To have done that, to be that loyal...

"Saul," Kael said, stepping toward him. The young man had just done something Kael wasn't sure he could ever have the strength to do. Could he condemn Bree to death, no matter what she did? He didn't think so. No, he knew so.

Saul didn't want to hear it. He put his back to them and asked the Seraph to fly him to the academy. Kael watched them go as Bree held his hand in hers. She said nothing, only watched until Saul was a speck on the red sky before turning to address Argus.

"What happens now?" she asked.

"Nothing," Argus said after confirming all were dead. He gave a nod, and the other Seraphim began to fly back.

"What do you mean, nothing?" Kael asked.

"We leave, and come morning, vultures will retrieve their corpses. No charges will be filed, no questions asked by either side. It will be as if this never happened."

"But that's...that's wrong," Kael said, as if that should have meant something. He stormed closer to Argus, wishing his voice could match the strength of Argus's. "A man from Center tried to kidnap us, maybe kill us. How can they go unpunished like this?"

"Because that's how the islands work," Argus said with such finality it made Kael take a step back. "You want us to accuse the Speaker's theotechs? The only way we defend ourselves is with the elements those theotechs trade to us. With Galen breathing down our necks, do you think we'll risk such vital supplies in a futile attempt to punish the failed kidnapping of two students?"

Kael felt his entire body shaking at such a thorough dismissal. He had no argument he could make against it, but it didn't remove the sense of wrongness, the complete unfairness that the theotechs could escape any punishment for their crimes.

"Kael," Bree said, putting a hand on his shoulder.

"I'm fine," Kael said, brushing it off. He glared at Argus as he struggled to control his temper. "So what should we do?"

Argus gestured to the other waiting Seraph.

"We fly you back to your apartment, you crawl into bed, and you go to sleep," he said. "There is a world of mysteries out there, and right now, you should focus on the ones you can control, and that's yourselves. I don't know why a theotech wanted you captured, and I don't want to know. All I care about is that I keep you safe and out of their hands."

"But what if they demand us to be handed over since this attempt failed?" Bree asked.

Argus shook his head, and his look was frightening.

"I said it before, and I'll say it again, Bree. We Seraphim don't hand over our own. If Center demands your lives, they'll get them only with a full-scale invasion of Weshern, and that's something no island, regardless of allegiance, would sit idly by and allow. Whatever they want you for, I highly doubt it is worth the rebellion of all five islands. For now, you're safe, and I'll establish constant patrols around the academy grounds to ensure you remain safe."

He offered her his hands, and beside him, Loramere did the same to Kael.

"You ready?" Loramere asked.

Kael exchanged a look with his sister, and they both nodded.

"We are," Kael said. "Please, take us home."

CHAPTER
28

After the last battle, their equipment had been relocated from the gear sheds to the armory, and inside its sturdy stone walls Kael finished telling Bree his plan as he strapped on his wings.

"Are you sure?" she asked, frowning at him.

Kael bobbed his head.

"It's not without risk, but I think there's a chance we'll learn something we never could from the library's books. If you think it's a bad idea..."

"No, I trust you," she said. "Just be careful, all right?"

Kael winked, then hurried down the road, past the gear sheds, and to the entrance of the academy. Given the incident the night before, Argus ordered Kael and Bree to take the day off, but this sat poorly with both of them. While Bree was fine with practicing on her own, Kael had better ideas. Today was one of his days to accompany an older Seraph to Center to deliver messages, so dressed and wearing his wings, he went to the academy gates. There he found a bored Loramere waiting.

"How's my favorite Seraph-in-training?" Loramere asked.

"Here to go with you to Center," Kael said.

The giant man raised his scarred left eyebrow.

"Uh, no, you're not," he said. "Brad's coming with me today, assuming he can get his ass over here in a timely manner. Argus made it painfully clear you and Bree won't be accompanying anyone to Center for the next decade or so. Or did you think the wisest course of action after avoiding a clandestine attempt to kidnap you would be to fly right into their arms in broad daylight?"

Kael gritted his teeth and accepted the gentle berating. He'd figured something like that would happen, but now he'd have to rely on someone else to get across his message.

"Can you do me a favor then?" he asked.

Loramere shrugged his broad shoulders.

"Name it."

"Inform the theotechs that I wish to speak with Knight Lieutenant Nickolas Flynn."

The older Seraph crossed his arms and frowned down at him.

"And why might that be?" he asked.

"Nickolas has been a friend of the family for years," he said. "Now will you tell them?"

Loramere hardly looked happy about it, but he relented.

"Sure, I will. Don't expect much, though. Center is a big place, and it might be days before Nickolas receives word."

"I understand," Kael said, bowing.

He left and returned his wings to the armory. Now with an entire day to kill, Kael decided he might as well head back to the library. Even if he thought the library a dead end, that didn't mean he was ready to give up on the mountains of books just yet. Devi greeted him at her desk, and Kael smiled politely before climbing to the second floor. After retrieving the same book he'd read for the past several days, he found a comfortable chair, settled down, and began reading about the history of the theotechs.

While there were volumes and volumes of it, the actual meat was frustratingly thin. The theotechs were founded shortly after the Ascension, meant to serve as the Speaker's hands and eyes. His holiness would divine God's desires through speaking with his angels, and the theotechs would then carry out those desires, enforcing them as necessary. Over the past five hundred years, they'd had little reform, and few interesting details were written about them. Kael felt a maddening certainty that whatever errors they'd made had been scrubbed out of history. All he could find were enacted policies, plus various deeds of charity and sacrifice made by more memorable theotechs. What he couldn't find, at least not yet, was a reason why they would have any interest in him and his sister.

Minute after minute he turned the pages, his eyes starting to skim instead of reading. The writing was so dry and dull, and remained so even when discussing minor rebellions that had risen up against the theotechs, or how in 317 A.A. several hundred split away in a desire for more direct control over Center and the five outer islands. Dry and dull, just the bare facts...

Devi shook him awake gently by the shoulder, earning a startled gasp.

"I'm sorry," Devi said, backing away. "But a man is here to see you. A knight from Center, actually."

"Thank you," Kael said, wiping at his eyes and face. His hand came back wet, and in sudden horror he looked down to see he'd drooled on the leather cover of the priceless old book. His body froze, and when he looked up to Devi, he must have had the guiltiest of expressions on his face.

"Don't worry," Devi said, winking as she took the book from him. "Leather cleans just fine, and I won't tell anyone if you don't."

Kael blushed as he hopped out of his chair. Thanking her again, Kael hurried down the stairs, wiping at his eyes and trying to force himself awake. Taking the steps two at a time, he reached the bottom, then paused.

Patience, he told himself. Talking to Nickolas was a risk, and he needed to be measured, not rushing out embarrassed because he'd drooled a little in front of the librarian. Fixing the collar of his jacket, he calmly walked out the door, to where the knight lieutenant waited on the steps. His white tunic was as brilliant and clean as ever, his head still smoothly shaven, his brown eyes calm and dispassionate despite his pleasant smile.

"My little Kael," the man said, embracing him. "You've matured so much since I last saw you."

"A year at the academy will do that," he said as he hugged back.

"I wish you'd contacted me sooner," he said after releasing him. "Though I'm sure you've had more than enough distractions to worry about."

"We've all had our fair share of distractions," he said, leading Nickolas down the steps toward the street. "Last night, for example."

He purposefully kept his wording vague, his tone light. If Nickolas knew nothing, he'd be mildly confused at worst. But if he did...

"Kael," the knight said, halting. "Here is not the place to discuss such things."

I knew it.

"Then where?" he asked.

In answer, he led him around to the back of the library. Nearby was the apothecary, and behind it a garden with rose-bushes carefully planted and surrounded with bricks. Nickolas took him to one of several wooden benches and gestured for him to have a seat.

"I'd rather stand," he said.

"Fair enough." Nickolas stepped back and crossed his arms as he looked around. The wall surrounding the academy marked the end of the garden, and in all other directions there wasn't a man or woman in sight. They seemed alone, but Nickolas still didn't appear happy.

"Last night's incident was … unfortunate," the man said. "A decision by a theotech who acted alone and without approval from Center."

"What did they want us for?" he asked.

"I can't tell you that," Nickolas said, shaking his head. "Even acknowledging last night is incredibly dangerous. All I can assure you is that no harm was ever meant to befall you or your sister."

Kael clenched his jaw and tried to work out his next line of questioning. That Nickolas was being so open about things was a surprise, but that didn't matter if he kept all useful information to himself. Bending down, he yanked one of the roses from a bush so he could twirl it in his fingers while he paced before the knight. The thorns pricked his skin, and he used the pain to focus, to hide how desperate he was for information.

"Why do the theotechs care about us?" he asked. "Why are Bree and I so important to them?"

Nickolas pulled back his shoulders, and his golden armor

rattled from the movement. The way he looked at him, as if he were but a child, made his talk about how mature he seemed just that, talk.

"Center is a whole different world compared to Weshern," he said. "And Heavenstone is another world within that one. Politics and favors run rampant, and in there, the left hand barely knows the right hand exists. A hundred reasons could exist for you to have caught a theotech's eye, and your sister's stunt with her swords in yesterday's battle might well be one of them."

Kael had wondered if Nickolas would bring that up. His sister's fame had spread throughout Weshern like the fire on her blades, but had word of it also traveled to Center? It seemed the answer was yes.

"I know it's not because of that," he said, tossing the rose to the dirt. "At least, not just because of that. Nickolas, can I... can I trust you?"

He felt like such a child asking it, but he had to. Ever since their parents' death, Nickolas had checked in on them, ensuring they were no burden on Aunt Bethy. Revealing their investigation was a risk, but a risk he was willing to take. Nickolas stepped closer, putting gauntleted hands on his shoulders as he leaned close. Kael stared right into his brown eyes, searching for the slightest lie when the knight answered.

"I've already told you things that could get me executed. Of course you can trust me."

At least that Kael knew to be true. If there was anything Center protected most, it was her secrets. He debated just how much to tell. So far, all he'd be revealing were some simple observations, and his curiosity about them. Nothing too terrible if it did get back to whoever was responsible in Center.

"The theotechs interfered with my affinity tests," he said,

plopping down on the bench. It creaked as he leaned against its back. "And they bore witness to both our six-month evaluations. We can't seem to find any reason why they would carry an interest in us except for one thing."

"And what is that?" Nickolas asked carefully.

Kael swallowed down his doubt, and he looked up at the towering knight. Here it was. The first true gamble.

"What do you know about the ghost plague?"

It seemed a bit of color drained from Nickolas's dark skin.

"Kael, I'm only going to say this once: let this go. Some doors should stay shut, some parts of history forever buried. Digging into this will only put you and your sister in danger, do you understand me?"

"We're already in danger," Kael said. "Or did you forget how I was dragged out of my bed last night at knifepoint?"

The man shook his head as he crossed his arms and swayed a bit, as if struggling to control himself.

"I am aware of how it looks to you," he said. "And I know you're young, and used to breaking the rules, but I am asking you to trust me. Stop asking questions. Go back to your lives, and put all this other nonsense behind you. That is what's best for everyone involved, I promise. This course you're on right now? It's going to get you in trouble, Kael, the kind of trouble no one ever wants, and I will certainly take no part in your reckless suicide."

His stern voice had steadily risen in volume, until by the very end even he seemed to realize how close to shouting he was. The quiet of the garden only made it worse, and he glanced around in search of anyone who might have overheard. Kael bit his lip as he did, wishing he could take his advice. It made sense. Things were far beyond his control. If Center wanted him and his sister, for any reason, what could he do to stop it? To change it?

"Perhaps you're right," he said, slumping.

"Of course I'm right," Nickolas said, and he sounded very much relieved. "I want nothing but the best for you and your sister. Since the day you two were born, that's all I've ever wanted."

Kael's entire body stiffened, and he fought to look natural despite the sudden terror that pounded through his veins.

Since the day you two were born...

Kael had assumed the theotechs' interest began during their affinity tests, or perhaps after their parents' deaths. But as he stared up at the smiling knight, he realized how wrong he'd been. Their watchful eye had been upon him and Bree earlier than that. Much, much earlier.

"I should go," he said, sliding off the bench.

"Not yet," Nickolas said. Fear spiked through Kael's chest, but it appeared unfounded. Nickolas glanced around once more before speaking in a low tone.

"I hear a lot of things given my position. Your victory over Galen was significant, but it isn't enough. If anything, it's only made matters worse. Sothren and Candren have already been pulled into your mess. Elern will soon follow, and I fear her strength won't be enough to prevent the coming war. All five islands, warring against one another? This will be the worst conflict we've seen in decades, and it won't remain in the skies. Soldiers from all islands are mustering their numbers. Invasions will soon follow. Please, Kael, be careful. These are dangerous times."

"I have my duties as a member of the Seraphim," Kael said, standing up straight. "I will not dishonor them. Should war come, I will fight."

"I asked for care, not cowardice." Nickolas said. "Leave it to youth to confuse the two as one and the same."

The knight embraced him again, and Kael tried to smile and pretend that all was well. When Nickolas pulled back, he activated his wings, and they came to life with a deep, pleasant hum.

"Speaking of dangerous times," he said. "Have you met with any disciples of Johan attempting to take root here in Weshern?"

Kael shook his head, keeping silent about his meeting with Thane Ackels prior to joining the academy.

"The only disciple of Johan's I've seen was at his own execution," he said.

"Good," Nickolas said, looking relieved. "Try your best to keep it that way. Johan is a dangerous man, and I assure you, Center has her eye fixed upon him. Do not listen to the lies his disciples spread, nor let them gain a foothold in Weshern for even a moment. It will only bring suffering to your people."

"I'll do my best," he said as the knight rose into the air. He waved, smiling calmly, but that smile faded as he stared at Nickolas's shrinking outline.

Johan and his lies, he thought. *Perhaps it is time I hear what these "lies" might be...*

Because one thing was certain: he no longer trusted whatever supposed truth came from the mouths of Center, her knights, and her theotechs.

Bree watched Kael head west toward the academy entrance, still frowning. Making any contact with Center, or one of her angelic knights, felt like too great a risk for her tastes, but given the kidnapping attempt, perhaps it was time to push things harder than some light reading at a library. Checking the sun, she wondered what to do with her own day off. She'd planned to do some training, if only to alleviate her boredom, but her entire body felt sore from the battle. Any sort of flying sounded unpleasant, but she did have her swords. Ever since Argus promoted her to training with the combat squads, she'd neglected her practice with them. Deciding to remedy that, she began to softly jog back toward her apartment and then head south. A bit of stretching and putting herself through some moves might do her good.

Bree retrieved her swords from inside the armory, leaving her wings behind. A quick jog took her to the little clearing just off the road where they practiced swordplay, but only an empty field awaited her. As she stood in the silence she let the losses hit her. Dean, killed during his duel. Sasha, dying right before her. After the battle, Bree had learned of another member of their group lost as part of the completely annihilated Scorpion Squad.

"Of course you're all gone," Bree whispered as she drew her swords. "After losing so many, why wouldn't you be?"

Bree felt tears starting to build, but she shook her head and forced them down with a flash of anger. She was not some young, stupid girl. Her swords had taken the lives of seven men, eight if she counted Eric Drae. Time to be stronger. Time to be a warrior. Hardships were just a way of life.

Twirling her swords in her hands, she began moving from stance to stance, doing all she could to forget how it had been Dean who first taught them to her. The stretching of her muscles felt pleasant, loosening up her body as she turned and twisted in ways she never could while wearing her wings. Her mind settled into a form of trance, the world falling away as her swords looped and cut through the air, so that when a voice called her name she felt her heart jump.

"Yes?" she asked, spinning. Her entire body tensed the moment she saw who was before her, standing at the edge of the road: Argus Summers.

"I see you're not at the obstacle course," Argus said.

Bree tried to shake off the surprise and pull the ire out from her voice. She only partly succeeded.

"I already beat your record," she said. "What more is there to do?"

The commander chuckled.

"Because you're never satisfied, not even with being the best. It's driven you to greatness, and if God is kind, it will allow you to survive far longer than you deserve."

Such a comment struck Bree as strangely cruel, and she lowered her swords to glare his way.

"What does that mean?" she asked.

"You're a fire, Bree," he said, stepping closer. "In all senses of the word. I could not watch you as much as I wished, but I did catch glimpses of you during the battle. You fly with complete, fearless abandon. Reckless doesn't begin to describe what I saw. You're going to shine brighter than anyone else alive, but I fear nothing will sustain it. That same fearlessness that makes you special will be what leads you to your death."

Once again she felt herself brought before the legendary Argus Summers just to be judged and found wanting. Resuming her stance, she began to swing her swords through her training exercises.

"Was that what you came here to tell me?" she asked, not looking at him.

"Not at all."

As her right sword came down in a swing, Argus drew one

of his own and flung it in the way. Bree startled upon their connection, then immediately felt her neck flush red. She sheathed
her swords and turned back to her commander, accepting the
obvious rebuke.

"Forgive me," she said, dipping her head.

"You're forgiven," Argus said, sheathing his own blade. "And
I didn't come here to make you doubt yourself. I came here to
discuss your role in our next battle."

"Am I leaving Olivia's squad?" she asked.

"In a way," he said. The man ran a hand through his short
dark hair, and he glanced west, as if to the very island of Galen
itself. "Our enemies will be ready for you this time. They've
tasted firsthand the danger you present, and they'll try to counter it immediately. This means we must react accordingly."

"And how is that? Do you want me to fly with Wolf Squad?
Come in late to the fight?"

"Far from it," Argus said. "I want you to lead the charge."

If a breeze had been blowing, it probably could have knocked
Bree off her feet.

"Excuse me?" she asked.

"I will accept no argument," he said. "The terror you inspire
is our greatest ally. I want your twin trails of fire leading us into
battle. I want Galen's men to see you coming, and for every
single one of them to remember what you accomplished *in
your very first battle*. That doubt is invaluable. While they can
predict all our formations and initial assaults, you they can't.
Don't you understand, Bree? No one has seen anyone like you.
Try as they like, they can't prepare for you. They can't account
for you. I need you wild, I need you reckless, and I need you
unstoppable. When the Phoenix comes crashing in, I want
them afraid. Can you do that?"

It was a terrible burden she felt him thrusting upon her

shoulders. He wanted her to dominate the battlefield, to frighten her enemies with her very presence as she assaulted their ranks. In short, Argus wanted her to live up to the reputation she'd created from her first battle. Could she handle such a thing? Or would it only backfire as she died during the initial assault, impaled by a shard of ice or crushed by a barrage of boulders?

"I don't know if I can," Bree said, measuring every word. "But I will try."

"Good," Argus said. "I'll also be creating a new squad, aptly named Phoenix. While you won't lead them personally, their sole purpose will be to act as your shadow, protecting you with their elements as best they can."

"Will my brother be among them?"

The commander hesitated.

"If it is important to you, then he will be. I'd prefer more experienced Seraphim, but at least he has spent many hours trying to follow you in flight."

Bree took in a deep breath, then let it out slowly. No turning back now, if she'd had a choice in the first place. Argus had already set the plans into motion. Her acceptance was likely symbolic at best.

"Yes, I want him there," she said. She gestured toward Argus's swords as she took a step back. "So, since I'm being so nice, care to reward me with the privilege of a duel?"

A hint of a smile cracked the commander's cool demeanor.

"After all the praise our island's heaped on you, perhaps a lesson in humility would be worthwhile."

Together they drew their swords.

"Careful," she said. "I've already beaten one of your records and would hate to overtake you in something else."

"The only reason I ceased flying the obstacle course was

because it bored me," said Argus, pointing a blade her way. "But you, little Phoenix, I find fascinating."

To cover her blush, she stepped forward and thrust a sword toward his chest. The commander batted it away, twirled to parry her follow-up attack, and then countered. No smile was on his face, but there was a smile in his icy-blue eyes as their duels stretched on throughout the morning. He won four games to her one, but each game felt closer than the last, and most importantly of all, Bree's earlier loneliness faded away, all but forgotten in the whirl of sweat and steel.

CHAPTER
29

It felt wrong to go behind Bree's back, but Kael refused to put her at risk for his scheme. Not when he could avoid it. One person, though, was integral, and Kael stood before the door to her apartment, knocking, and wishing he didn't feel so ridiculously nervous. The door cracked open, then flung all the way as Clara stepped out and wrapped her arms around him in a surprising but very welcome embrace.

"About time you swung by," she said, squeezing tightly. "I had to hear about Saul's abduction attempt from my father. That was very inconsiderate of you."

Kael shrugged as he grinned down at her.

"Um, sorry, I'll try not to do it again?"

She kissed his lips, which temporarily blanked his mind. At last he kissed back, and he held her far more tenderly as his body relaxed.

"You're right," he said when she pulled back. "Sorry, Clara, my mind's been in a hundred places the past few days. I should have come sooner."

"Damn right."

She pulled him into her apartment. Kael had expected, due to her status as daughter of the Archon, that she'd have far more luxuries than he had. He was wrong. The same blue carpet, the same plain shelves, same basic furniture. As Clara shut the door, Kael forced his mind to remain on the task at hand. His request was dangerous, and not just to himself.

"Clara, I have a favor to ask," he said as he stepped away, arms crossed over his chest. Clara tilted her head slightly, and her smile hardened, becoming practiced, as her sharp mind immediately began debating what he might want of her.

"Which is?" she asked.

Kael took in a deep breath.

"I . . . was wondering if you could tell me who gave you that Johan tract."

He thought she'd be disappointed, upset, or worried. Instead she looked excited.

"And why would you want to know that?"

There was no point in lying. If he did, she'd see through him immediately, and for that alone, likely refuse him. Kael scratched at his neck and peered about the apartment, unable to meet her gaze as he told her everything. He told her about his findings concerning his parents, the ghost plague, the attempted abduction headed by a theotech of Center. He even told her how he'd originally been marked as having light affinity, not ice, before a theotech interfered with the testing.

"That's not surprising to hear in hindsight," Clara said. "Kael, haven't you noticed how seldom you need to replace your light element compared to the rest of us?"

Kael shrugged, feeling embarrassed.

"Not really," he said. "It's not something I ever thought about."

"Well, it's obvious now, trust me. So the theotechs have their eye on you, and might have had their eye on your parents as well. What does this have to do with Johan?"

Kael slumped into Clara's comfortable chair and clasped his hands before him.

"It's a stretch, but everyone from Center has been lying to me from the very start. For once, I want to see if I can get someone to tell me the truth."

Clara's green eyes sparkled. No hesitation. No doubt.

"A family member of one of our servants recently became a disciple of Johan's," she said. "I can find out where he lives and how to meet him, but only on one condition."

"And what's that?"

Her grin spread.

"I'm coming with you."

Kael met her after dark, just as she'd asked. Clara stepped out, hair tied behind her head, uniform crisp and clean.

"Last chance to turn around," she told him.

"This was originally my idea," Kael said. "I should be the one asking you that."

Clara gave him a peck on the cheek.

"Not anymore. Let's go."

"So how are we getting out of the academy grounds?" Kael asked as they walked west.

"Through the front door, obviously."

It hadn't been obvious to Kael, but Clara didn't show the slightest hint of doubt, so he let the matter drop. Together they crossed the path slicing between the training fields, making their way to the guarded gates. Two Seraphs stood on duty, their black jackets shimmering red beneath the midnight fire. Kael recognized neither of them, only that they were clearly much older, likely third to fourth year. As they neared, Clara grabbed his hand and held it, clearly wanting the Seraphs to see.

"The gate's shut for the night," said one. "Go back to bed, or out to a field if you're looking for somewhere quiet."

Clara stood to her full height, her tone taking on an authority Kael had rarely heard her use.

"As third heir to the Archon, I demand you open the gate and tell no one of our passing," she said. "Kael and I would like to have our privacy."

One snickered to the other, but neither put up an argument. The gate slid open, and one made a sweeping gesture before they exited.

"Enjoy the night," he said.

Kael's neck was in full blush as they passed.

"Surely there are other ways we could have snuck out," he said as they walked the road. "Why let ourselves be seen?"

"Because I wanted us to be seen," Clara said. "If we get caught, or interrogated, which would you prefer, that you went to speak with a heretic preaching rebellion against Center, or that you wanted the two of us to have a bit of fun somewhere off academy grounds?"

"That depends. Can I be executed for fooling around with the Archon's daughter?"

Clara shrugged.

"It depends on the mood my father's in when he hears."

Kael dug his elbow into her side.

"You're not helping."

She laughed and squeezed his hand.

"Come on. We don't have that much time, so we'll need to do a bit of running. Besides, the sweat will add to our alibi."

They followed Winged Road, passing by several turns north and south, until arriving at Perryton, the first town on its path. Just before the town's entrance, a single man stood in the center of the road, wearing familiar garb. Kael had seen plenty of it at the Willers' family ball. The man was tall, bald, and bore twin blue lines traveling from ear to ear, the tattoos just barely curling above and below his eyes. He wore thick chain mail, and a blue sash across his waist. A bundle of clothes rested in his arms.

"Thanks, Kai," Clara said as she accepted half of the bundle. The family guard turned to Kael and offered him the other half. Kael took it, saw that it was a pair of brown pants, a loose, long-sleeved shirt, and a pair of boots. A quick glance around showed nothing but tall grass and the road they were on. He looked to Clara to ask where he might change, then realized she was curling around to the other side of her enormous guard. His eyes met the bald man's briefly, and there was no amusement in them, just a chilly stare.

Kael turned around, putting his back to the two, and stripped down to his undergarments. The pants fit well enough, as did the shirt, though the wide collar caused it to hang a bit low on his shoulders. Not a style he'd choose, but that seemed to entirely be the point. Last was a pair of boots, plain and thin, without laces or ties. Done, he hesitated, then called out over his shoulder.

"Ready?"

"Ready."

He turned to see Clara stepping back onto the road around

her guard. She wore a plain brown skirt instead of her uniform's black pants. Her boots had been replaced with open sandals, and her uniform with a loose white shirt similar to his own. Her fingers ran through her blonde hair, pulling out the tight knot she'd tied it into.

Kai snapped his fingers at Kael, then offered his hands. Realizing what he wanted, Kael handed over his old clothes. As he did, the man reached into his own pocket and pulled out two long daggers. Kael took one, sliding it into his pocket, as Clara accepted the other, hiding it in a deep pocket sewn into the side of her dress.

"Wait here until we return," Clara ordered the guard. "If we're not back before sunrise, don't come looking for us. Go to my father instead, and inform him of what we've done so he might organize a search. I release you from your vow of silence for that purpose, and that purpose only."

Kai bowed low in affirmation. Clara took Kael's hand again, and they headed toward town.

"Seems you've thought of everything," Kael said, shifting and kicking his boots into the dirt in a failed attempt to make them fit better.

"If you get caught, you'll be reprimanded, maybe expelled from the academy at worst," Clara said. "If I'm caught, it'll be a scandal, and a great blow to my father's honor. Johan's disciples preach my family is a cowardly lot who bend to Center's every whim. They also say we'll soon be overthrown, so yes, if this disciple we meet recognizes me, I'd like to have every precaution ready." She patted the knife hidden within the folds of her dress. "Even lethal ones."

It was a stark reminder how dangerous Kael's desire actually was, one he shouldn't have needed. He'd been there when

Thane was dropped to his death, head cracking open on the side of a stone well. Touching his own dagger for reassurance, he focused his mind on the task at hand.

"What is his name?" he asked.

"It used to be Ben, but since conversion he's taken on the name of Marrik." Clara chuckled. "His mother wasn't too happy about that. It's how I heard about it in the first place. Marrik's hidin' in a rented home, and it shouldn't be too far from the town entrance. When you see a street marked Lily, we turn north and look for a house numbered seven."

"Does Marrik know we're coming?"

Clara shook her head.

"If he's not there, we try again sometime. No reason risking beyond that. Don't tell him your name, by the way. I doubt he'll ask it, but if he does, just refuse. He'll understand. Our own lives are at risk, and if we keep calm, we should appear to be nothing more than a curious couple."

It made sense to Kael. There was no way for them to know how such a man might react learning of Clara's royalty, or Kael's connection to the now-famous Phoenix of Weshern. Just a simple, poor, curious couple. It wouldn't be hard. For Clara it might be an act, but Kael had spent more than enough days in the fields and hungry nights at Aunt Bethy's.

A line of squat stone homes marked the edge of Perryton. Just beyond was a tall pole dug into the center of the road, and Kael paused before it and frowned. Hanging from thin pieces of rope tied to the top of the pole were two broken halves of a torch, the top blackened and snuffed. The torch was the symbol of Galen, and it was plain to see what the people of Perryton thought of the foreign island.

"They're appearing all over Weshern," Clara said softly, staring at the broken torch.

"Do the people want war that badly?" Kael asked.

"A war they themselves won't fight?" Clara turned away from the effigy. "Yes, I think they do."

They continued on, passing quiet homes, the windows dark, the inhabitants long asleep. Kael felt his nerves growing, and his eyes darted side to side, searching for spies that his mind knew were imaginary but his gut insisted were nearby. The town itself wasn't large, and they quickly spotted the road sign marked Lily and turned north. Kael squinted at the sides of homes, spotting numbers carved into them. They were in the twenties, but counting down, and it took only a few minutes to find the number of their destination.

It looked less like a home and more like a hive, a stone construction of several floors, seemingly haphazardly thrown together, as if each new apartment was an afterthought to the previous. The grand building had multiple numbers carved into it, but the seven was plain enough to see, carved into the stone beside a thick wooden door at street level. Kael softly knocked on the door. The last thing he wanted was to wake other occupants. He waited a few long seconds, listening, but heard nothing. He knocked a second time, just a smidge louder.

Above the door was an open window covered by a thick curtain. The cloth lifted up, blocking the light of the midnight fire so the occupant within was just a blob of darkness and shadow. Just as quickly, it dropped. Kael heard footsteps approach the door, the clatter of a lock, and then it opened.

"Why do you come and wake me in the middle of the night?" a man asked from within, form hidden behind the cracked door.

"We come asking questions," Kael answered. "We seek answers we might not get elsewhere."

The answer was careful enough, and guarded enough, Kael

had no doubt Marrik would immediately understand their true purpose. The door opened farther. Light of the midnight fire trickled in, revealing a man in a dark robe, its hood pulled back.

"Come in," Marrik said. "We will talk further where it is quiet, and will not disturb those around us."

Kael brushed the dagger in his pocket with his fingertips, then led Clara inside. The home was but a single room, with a bed pushed into one corner, a chair in the other, and a stool beside the door that gave access to the window. A stick with a carved hook at the end rested near the door, and Marrik used it to pull the curtain open fully before backing away.

"I am sorry I cannot offer you better accommodations," Marrik said. "If you wish to sit, the floor must suffice."

Marrik settled into the chair, gently rocking in it. Kael folded his legs underneath him and sat, Clara doing likewise. In the dim light, Kael took a better look at the disciple. He wasn't much older than him, face clean-shaven, his skin deeply tanned. His hands rested in his lap, and by their deep callouses Kael knew him to have been a fisherman. His hair was long, and braided in a ponytail that hung far past his shoulders. The red midnight hue gave his pale eyes a fearful glow.

"You said you have questions," Marrik began, sitting up in his chair. "I cannot promise to have all the answers, but I will do my best. I know why you come here, so do not lie nor waste my time. The words of Johan have reached your ears, haven't they?"

Kael and Clara nodded.

"His wisdom spreads. The world is changing, and we will be the catalyst. Now ask, and I shall answer."

The two exchanged glances. Clara held his hand, and he felt her squeeze it tight. She was trusting him. He thought of his research, of the conversation he'd had with Thane months ago, before ever entering into the academy. What did he truly wish to know? What could these disciples of Johan say that might reveal why the theotechs took such interest in him and his sister?

"Who is Johan?" Kael asked, deciding to start with the question most everyone did. It was a question Marrik was clearly familiar with, and he launched into a spiel with practiced ease.

"Johan is the man brave enough to refuse the lies of Center," he said. "He was a theotech before they cast him out, which is why he knows the truth from the lies. Johan dared ask when he was told to accept. He dared doubt when he was told to believe. Very few meet him, for his life is ever in danger, but I am one who has. His wisdom is unmatched. His presence is certainly divine. Perhaps, in a future earned in blood, he will openly walk among us, and you will be blessed to share in his presence like I have."

It all sounded like nonsense no different from how the theotechs spoke of the Speaker for the Angels, Marius Prakt. Kael kept such thoughts far from showing on his face. Instead he did his best approximation of guarded fascination. It wasn't hard. Johan, whoever he was, did intrigue him greatly.

Marrik paused, and Kael sensed him waiting for another question. Still keeping it vague, he approached the next topic most every curious visitor asked about.

"What does Johan want?"

Marrik rubbed his hands together, as if eager for the question.

"He wants the truth to be known," he said. "The Speaker for the Angels is a liar, one who does not hear the voice of the angels, nor share their wisdom with mankind. He is merely a man with power, wielding that power cruelly and expertly to manipulate our five minor islands into servitude. Johan would have this false divine expelled, and the true wisdom revealed to the people. Our islands are kept afloat by the Beam, yet it is Center's theotechs who operate them, not us. Our society thrives on the elements, yet we know nothing of how they are made. This cannot continue, not unless we would submit to Center and admit our independence is nothing but a fraud."

Marrik's presence was powerful and uncomfortable. He spoke with absolute certainty, and a passion that was undeniable. Kael shared a look with Clara, and he could tell she was similarly affected. Part of him wanted to leave immediately, but part of him wanted to hear every single word that came from the man's lips.

"So say you're right," Kael offered. "Say the Speaker is a fraud. What of his theotechs? It is their gifts that keep our islands afloat. It is their work that gives us water to drink. If they seek only power over us, then why serve us in such a way?"

Marrik looked far too pleased with the question. He must have been asked it before, perhaps even asked it himself, and he had an answer immediately ready.

"They serve us only so we might repay them tenfold. We hand over our fortune in food and goods, and in return, obtain just enough elements to keep our fishermen airborne and our military armed. Just enough to protect ourselves from the other islands, which are equally hungry, islands stretched equally thin. It's a cycle they trapped us in centuries ago, and no one yet has had the strength to resist."

Marrik tapped his fingers. Eager. Eyes wide, and hungry.

"Do you know what they truly want from us, my unknown friends? They want to keep our numbers in check. They want us forever angry with the other islands, killing each other, thinning our numbers so we are never as strong as we might otherwise be. And then when we have peace, when it seems we might start posing a threat... why, suddenly there is a shortage in one of the elements. The five islands will offer higher and higher tribute for it out of fear they be the one cut out, and those who cannot afford it, well..."

Marrik shook his head.

"Then it comes to battle, and we spill blood for it instead, exactly as Center desires."

Kael felt his pulse rising, his blood boiling. The battle that had cost Bree and him their parents, it'd been because of a shortage of flame element that year, and Weshern had been forced to take to the skies to battle for their cut. The idea that it'd been completely manufactured, the death for no reason other than calculated manipulation...

"You're saying Center fakes the shortages," Kael said, fighting to keep his voice calm.

"What I'm saying," Marrik said, leaning closer, "is that we don't know. We don't know how it's created. If we don't know that, we don't know what causes years of shortage and years of surplus. But the evidence is before us, my friend. I offer my explanation, the explanation given by Johan to us all. If there is another, let the Speaker himself share it. Bring the secrets into the light. But he won't, you know that. Knowledge is a poison to an iron rule, and Marius will die before he shares the secrets of the theotechs with us."

"So what should we do?" Kael asked. "Threaten war unless our demands be met? Would you have us fly across the skies to battle over Center's streets and fields?"

"No," Marrik said. "We prepare for invasion."

"You can't be serious," Clara said, unable to remain silent

any longer. "You think Center will invade? Why? If all you say is true, and the Speaker's manipulation of us so absolute, why bother?"

"Because without conflict, we threaten their rule," Marrik said, tilting his head her way. "Elern declared herself peacemaker among the five islands, and no matter how many times the Speaker may insist such peace is their goal, it is a lie. In times of peace, we stockpile. Our numbers grow. The stores of elements steadily increase. Should such peace last too long, the minor islands might have enough to withstand being cut off by Center. A true rebellion, a capturing of the theotechs and forced sharing of the knowledge of the elemental prisms, the Fount, and the Beam. Should this happen, Center's power over us is at an end, and no king or theocrat has ever willingly given up power, I assure you. Not without a fight."

Marrik stood from his chair, and he swept his arms wide.

"Mark my words, the time comes," he said. "Johan knows the heart of the Speaker, and it is one of cowardice and greed. We fight among ourselves when we should face the common enemy. Our independence is a sham, and even the Speaker will soon abandon the charade entirely. His knights will fly like legions, his soldiers unending. They will come to conquer, no longer willing to play the game. The risks aren't worth the peace it buys. We must be ready. We must spread the message, for when the time comes, and we rise up against them in the inevitable war, our freedom relies upon our victory. We are the ones brave enough to open our eyes and see. Will you be one of them?"

It was a call to arms, one Kael was unwilling to accept. Too much of what he'd heard was conjecture and assumptions. Despite the claims of Johan having been a theotech, he didn't seem to know any of their actual secrets, or if he did, he wasn't sharing that knowledge with his followers. Worst of all, none of his rhetoric explained the theotechs' interest in him and his sister. They had nothing to do with shortages or elements or the puppet rule Center exercised. They were simple Seraphs, that was all, Seraphs who survived a plague that might never have been.

"Perhaps in time," Kael said, rising to his feet and offering Clara his hand to help her do likewise. "You have told us much, and I would like us to think on it before we return."

"Think, decide, but do not tarry," Marrik said. "I must sow seeds all throughout Weshern, and the dangers of the work are many. The theotechs sense the threat we pose, and they are all too eager to execute those who would deny the divinity of the Speaker."

They left, and Kael was surprised by the immense relief he felt when he shut the door to Marrik's home. The two returned south, toward Winged Road leading toward the academy, and they walked in silence. Marrik's words looped in Kael's mind, mentally chewing on them, deciding what he did and did not believe. To his surprise, he believed more than he doubted.

"Marrik didn't have a shred of doubt," Clara said once they were nearing the edge of town. "No wonder the theotechs are so frightened of Johan and his disciples. A man without doubt in his beliefs is a man who will kill for them."

"Do you think he was right, about any of it?"

Clara shrugged as they passed the hanging pieces of the broken torch.

"I don't know. But at least I know why they hate our family now. We're not leaders to them. We're just the puppets ruling in Center's stead."

She said it with such bitterness Kael winced, and he took her hand in his.

"Thank you for bringing me to him," he said.

Clara winked.

"I got to get away from home and the academy and do something my father would be royally pissed about if he found out. I'm pretty sure I should be thanking you."

Kael laughed.

"Good," he said, for something else had been weighing on his mind, a needed act he'd been putting off as long as he could. "That means you'll help me with something tomorrow, right?"

Kai waited up ahead, alone in the road, bundle of clothes and shoes in hand.

"And what might that be?" Clara asked. "Is it more dangerous than meeting with an outlaw heretic?"

Kael winced.

"Not quite," he said. "And yet perhaps worse…"

CHAPTER 30

K ael hesitated, hand hanging in the air just before the wood.

"Are you sure you want to do this?" Clara asked.

"Want to?" Kael said. "No, but I should."

And so he knocked on the door to Saul Reigar's apartment, then scooted back a step. They heard footsteps within, the sound of things shuffling. When the door finally opened, it yanked inward with violent speed. Waiting on the other side was Saul, black circles under his eyes and blond hair unkempt. He wore his uniform, the shirt pulled free of his pants, which were missing their belt.

"I'm getting ready to grab supper," he said, glaring at Kael. "What do you want?"

Kael almost told him it was too early for that, but he caught himself before uttering such an inane protest. All his prepared statements jumbled in his mind, and the sheer ugliness on Saul's face stole away his ability to conjure up new ones.

The awkward silence stretched on as Saul crossed his arms and leaned against the doorframe. Thankfully, Clara was with him, bailing Kael out when he needed it most.

"Kael wanted to thank you," she said. "Right, Kael?"

"Right," he said, and it felt like a stone fell from his tongue. "To sacrifice what you did, that must have been so hard, and I wanted to…"

"I killed my brother," Saul said, barging past him while tucking in his shirt. "*Hard* doesn't begin to describe it."

Kael frowned, refusing to give up so quickly. After the failed kidnapping attempt, Saul had gone missing from practice for more than a week. That morning he'd finally returned, taking part in the various drills without addressing a soul. Seeing him move through practice like a corpse had filled Kael with guilt, and so he'd come, hoping he and Clara could at least try to make him feel better. Of course, Saul being Saul, he wasn't going to let it be easy.

"You did what you had to do," Kael said, hurrying after him. "It's not your fault your brother was a traitor."

Saul froze, and his body stiffened as if stabbed. Before he even turned around, Kael realized there couldn't have been a worse thing for him to say. Damn it, all he wanted to do was apologize, how did he mess that up so terribly?

"No, it's not my fault," Saul said, glaring fire from his hazel eyes. "My family losing *everything,* that's my fault."

Kael started to protest, but stopped. He was missing something, and he glanced to Clara, saw her own confusion.

"I don't understand," Kael said softly.

Saul grabbed Kael by the front of his shirt, and he yanked him closer. His stare was like iron holding Kael prisoner.

"There was a trial," Saul said. "Archon Willer blamed my parents for the attempt on your lives. Jason swore he acted alone, but it didn't matter. We lost our homes, our lands, our titles...I thought I could live with Jason's death. Your sister killed more in her first battle than Argus did, and to just hand her over...I couldn't allow it. My parents raised me with more loyalty to Weshern than that. My parents, whom Isaac declared traitors and exiled from our island."

"I heard nothing about this," Clara said softly.

"There's a whole world underneath your nose," Saul said, glaring at her. "Of course Isaac didn't let his precious little daughter hear something that might upset her."

Kael struggled to meet Saul's furious gaze.

"I'm sorry," he said. "Saul, I'm so sorry."

"Say sorry all you want, it doesn't fix anything." Saul shoved him away, and Kael stumbled to keep his balance. "I pray to God that Bree does something useful with her life, because I just sacrificed all of mine so she might live."

Kael's throat tightened, and he tried not to let the hurt reach his voice.

"You saved my life as well," he said.

Saul shook his head as he stared at him with such hatred.

"Your sister's the only one worth a damn, Kael. If it'd been just you, I'd have let you die without a second thought."

Kael could endure Saul's anger and frustration. For all his classmate had lost, his anger was justified. But to dismiss him so easily, to say something so hateful and cruel...

"You don't mean that," he said softly.

Saul stepped closer, hands balled into fists.

"Should I repeat myself until you believe me?" he asked. "I'd let...you...die."

His fist rammed into Kael's stomach. When he doubled over, Saul shoved him onto his back. Kael rolled to his feet, hands clenched at his sides. He met Saul's stare, but he did not raise his fists, nor attempt to dodge when another blow struck him in the mouth. His head popped back, his lip immediately swelling as he tasted blood trickle across his tongue. Two more blows to his chest, but he offered no retaliation.

"Fight me, damn it!" Saul screamed. There were tears in his eyes as he struck again and again. "It's your fault I've lost everything, now fight me!"

The blows on his body weakened, and Kael endured them despite the pain.

"Everything," Saul said, voice now a whisper. "You cost me everything."

At last they stopped, and Clara stepped in the way, looking remarkably calm despite what she'd witnessed.

"That's enough," she said.

"It'll never be enough," Saul said, but his words were tinged with defeat.

"It is enough," Clara said. "Or shall I have you join your parents in exile?"

"No," Kael said, wiping blood from his lip as he rose to his feet. "Let him go. This was just a misunderstanding, isn't that right, Saul?"

Before he might answer, the sound of horns blared from the center of the academy grounds. Saul looked completely shaken, and he wiped at the tears sliding down his face.

"The both of you can go to Hell," he said. "Never speak to me again."

The young man hurried past them toward the road, Kael careful to give him a wide berth. Once he was gone Clara turned to him, looking over his wounds.

"You could have fought back," she said as she winced at the sight of his swollen lip.

"Because of me and my sister, he lost his entire family," Kael said. "Saul may never forgive us, but if I struck him at such a broken moment, he'd never have reason to, either." He gently eased her away from him. "I'm fine. My knees feel like they're made of butter, but that's it. Besides, those are the warning horns. I need to prepare."

She stepped on her tiptoes so she could give him a kiss.

"Stay safe," she said.

"Aren't you coming with me?"

Clara shook her head, and she ran a hand through her short blonde hair.

"My father prefers I join him in the holy mansion if there's ever an attack," she said. "When you return, I'll find you, I promise."

She blew him a kiss, then hurried to the road running between the eight apartments and turned north. Kael did the same, only he turned south instead. He tried to walk calmly to the armory, but apparently that wasn't going to be allowed. Seraphim raced across the skies above the academy, and upon seeing him, one dove low.

"Are you combat ready?" the older man asked.

"I am," Kael answered, showing him a newly sewn patch on his right shoulder. "Part of Phoenix."

"Then let's go."

He grabbed Kael's wrists, barely giving him a half second of warning before lifting off. They raced across the grounds to the armory, where Weshern's entire Seraphim forces were gathering. While Kael had thought things chaotic when preparing their previous assault on Galen, this put it to shame. Men and women rushed everywhere, shouting, already forming into squadrons and checking numbers to ensure everyone's presence. Kael had to push through the crowd to get to his wings, and as he strapped them on he was pleased to see his sister join him.

"What the hell happened to you?" she asked as he handed her the pole so she could pull her wings down. "You look like you lost a fight with a boulder."

"Later," he said as he adjusted the wings a little to the left so they weighed evenly on his shoulders. "Do you know what's going on? Are we under attack?"

"Not us," said Bree. "Our allies."

They exited to see a crowd forming around Argus Summers, who must have arrived while they were inside the armory.

"I've already sent a flier to Center," Argus was telling them. "Galen's launched an attack on Elern, but so long as they hold out, we'll arrive in time to turn the battle."

"It's not just Galen," Headmaster Simmons called out as he pushed his way to the commander. He held a crumpled piece of parchment in his left hand, and he offered it to Argus. "Candren's joined in as well, claiming to fight on the side of some minor Elern noble. They're going to replace the ruling family, and if they do..."

"It will be three islands to our two," Argus said. "And Sothren is already weakened."

Rumbles of unease rippled throughout the gathered Seraphim. Elern's neutral status as defender against any invasion was the only thing keeping Weshern safe. If they fell...

"We can't wait until Center gives permission," the headmaster said. "All will be lost by the time they respond. Give the order."

"But it is the Archon's place to..."

"There's no time. You're our commander. Give the order."

Argus looked to the rest of them, and all at once, it seemed the heavy burden on his shoulders faded away.

"Our allies are under attack," he shouted. "Let's go save them."

The Seraphim tore into the air, their chaotic order slowly

shifting into straight lines and even formations. Unlike before, where Kael flew near the very back, this time he joined the front lines, with Phoenix Squad just to Wolf Squad's left. Weshern's rivers and lakes vanished beneath him in a rapid blur, soon replaced by the ocean blue as they made their way to Elern.

"Remember, keeping Breanna safe is our top priority," Phoenix Squad's leader, Olivia, shouted to the rest of them. "Our lives mean nothing compared to hers."

It sounded too much like Saul's bitter proclamation, but Kael tried not to let it bother him. Bree flew just ahead of Olivia, and Kael watched his sister gently weave side to side, dark hair billowing in the wind. He would give his life to protect her. Even before her rise to fame, he'd have done so. What did it matter now that she'd finally mastered her element?

The minutes dragged, long and quiet. Sothren passed by to their left, and Kael hoped to see their own Seraphim flying out to join them. He could even see a few of them circling the air, but they did not stray beyond the island's edge. Waiting for Center's permission was Kael's guess. He shook his head. He remembered his tedious travel there with Loramere, the waiting in lines, and the theotechs' overall disinterest. Getting a response in time to join the fight would be a miracle.

Elern was next, and seeing the island filled Kael's entire chest with anxiety. Having survived one battle should have helped with his nerves, but it only meant he knew just how horrible it might be. Luck had been with him once. Would he manage to endure twice? He clenched and unclenched his shaking right hand, imagining the ice prism contained within its gauntlet. That ice would protect him. That ice would keep him and his sister alive. He had no choice but to believe it.

They flew over Elern's yellow fields, deep chasms, and tall, huddled cities of brown stone. Kael stared at a whole different world he might never walk upon. Did the people down there understand what was at risk? Did they care about the change in ruling families? Selfish as their battle was, he prayed at least Elern's populace benefitted from their defense. No matter what, Galen's aggression had to be stopped. All five islands needed peace.

There they are, thought Kael as they neared the other edge of Elern. In the skies between it and Galen waged the swarming chaos of battle. Elern's Seraphim, marked by their white jackets, flew in small five-person formations. Swarming alongside the red of Galen were Candren's yellow jackets, and Kael prayed he could keep track of them all once the battle began. Having a single enemy to follow was one thing. Two enemies, and an ally? Part of him was terrified he'd take down a friend in his confusion.

Up ahead, Argus split from his squad to fly alongside Bree. He shouted something to her that Kael could not hear, and she nodded. Argus resumed his formation as Bree's wings flared to their maximum velocity.

"Here we go," Kael whispered to himself. "You can do this, Bree. We're here for you."

His sister drew her swords, and as she clanged them together, fire enveloped the blades. She held both at an angle, and they left streaks of flame in a long, burning trail. Olivia shifted Phoenix Squad so they flew directly above and behind Bree, the twin lines of fire passing beneath them. Ahead of all their forces she raced, an unmistakable fiery beacon. Several formations of both Galen and Candren split off from the fight, charging headlong to meet Weshern's arrival. Kael watched them, right hand tensing. This time, he wouldn't be hiding in the back during the initial exchange. This time, his ice would be what kept their nine alive.

"Unleash!" Olivia screamed as the distance between them closed, and the initial volleys soared from either side. Bree weaved left to right, twirling like a dancer on a ballroom floor. From their higher advantage point, Phoenix Squad let loose a barrage of ice and stone, all wide and flat. The elements shot ahead of Bree, intercepting their enemies' counterbarrage. The sound of cracking ice and breaking stone joined the hum of ancient wings. Fire and lightning filled the space between, with such fury Kael could not hope to follow it all. No, he only had one person to follow: his sister.

Bree drifted side to side, avoiding sharp lances of ice that shot past mere feet after. She showed no intention of veering away, no attempt to get around to the back of a squad. Instead she zoomed straight into the heart of their enemies' formations, which meant Kael flew into the thickest, most chaotic part of the battle. He let loose a few round orbs of ice at a Galen group to his right, then turned his aim forward. It seemed their foes wanted Bree dead just as much as she wished to engage them, and they did not attempt to avoid her, only flew straight at her while unleashing an overwhelming display of elements.

"All you have!" Olivia screamed again, and Kael repeated the cry for the others as he braced his right arm with his left hand and let loose. More than twenty enemy Seraphim were closing in. Kael aimed not at them but the air between them, filling it with ice. Fire slammed against his boulders, shards of stone slammed into a thin wall Olivia summoned. Those farther back in the formation struck dead several with lightning, taking advantage of the enemy's refusal to focus on anything but Bree. They wanted the Phoenix dead, and so they'd pay. Breath caught in his throat, Kael watched Bree jump forward with one last sudden burst of speed, and then she crashed into the enemy formations.

Kael had only a second before diving down to follow, but that instant was still breathtaking. Bree spun like a wheel the moment she hit the squad, spears of lightning and fire arcing to either side of her. Her swords lashed out, their trails of fire creating a swirling tunnel. Two men from Galen died, cleaved in half, and then Bree twisted her body so she intercepted a second squad from Candren, cutting right through their *V* formation. The Seraphim broke apart, but not before Bree slashed the rearmost woman with both her blades. The remainder turned around, letting their momentum carry them as they tried to bring their elements to bear on Bree.

Olivia followed those trails of flame, leading her squad onward, and they flew straight toward the now-hovering squad. Kael fired three lances, the first two missing, the third spearing a man through the neck. His body spun in place from the force of impact, his wings keeping him hovering like a macabre ornament of the sky. The others tried to retaliate, but speed was not on their side. Phoenix Squad mopped them up in seconds, then banked hard to follow their protected charge.

Kael felt his muscles screaming as he twisted his body while increasing the throttle. The smoke from Bree's sword trails passed by his face, and he arced his back to try to match her sudden climb. His path sent him flying toward the distant island of Galen, and as it flashed before his eyes, he felt a sudden, immediate instinct something was wrong, but he couldn't place it. Something about the island, or its shimmering Beam beneath...

The naked, Fount-less Beam.

A loud crack met his ears, and he glanced over his shoulder to see a squad of four suddenly on their tail. They were coming in fast, and in perfect position. More sharp stones followed, killing the woman at the back end of his squad. Letting out a curse, Kael rotated about to face their pursuers and lifted his right gauntlet. Bracing it with his left hand, he prayed he caught them off guard as lance after lance of ice shot toward them. One struck a man in the face as he climbed, smashing bone and splattering blood and gore throughout the air. The other three veered aside, whooshing past Kael. Ignoring him, he realized, preferring to chase the far larger number.

Under normal circumstances, Kael would have chased, but no doubt something terrible was happening. Spinning to face Galen, he confirmed the missing Fount, and he stared at the Beam with dawning horror.

Where are the theotechs? he thought, spinning. A boulder flew over Kael's head, missing by inches as he instinctively ducked. To his right, he finally spotted a group of three hovering in their red robes and golden wings. Punching the throttle, Kael abandoned his squad, instead whirling through the combat. Lightning flashed below him as if a thunderstorm raged close to the ocean. Bodies fell, their jackets of all colors. All the while, he prayed his sister would endure.

Before he even reached them, Kael could already see the anger on the theotechs' faces. Seraphim were supposed to ignore their presence during battle, but this was too important, Kael knew it in his gut. Founts never, ever ceased, their creation directly tied to the existence of the Beam that kept all six islands afloat. Slowing his speed so he didn't slam into the three, Kael spun and pointed toward Galen.

"The Fount!" he screamed, drifting past them. "The Fount is gone!"

The theotechs froze, and the nearest turned to follow his finger. Immediately he pulled a horn from a side satchel and put it to his lips, blowing a long, deep note. Kael looked back to the battle, saw the other leaders of the various factions pull out their own horns and sound the note for surrender. Kael felt relief when he spotted Bree's burning swords amid the chaos. If something had happened to her while he rushed off to the theotechs on a hunch...

The thought died as full-blown terror erupted in his heart. Galen's Beam flickered, then dimmed. With wide eyes, he watched the island tilt toward them, just enough to send buildings crumbling, trees snapping, and rivers running askew.

Galen was falling.

CHAPTER
31

The world was a nightmare, and try as Bree might, she could not wake up to escape it. Wings pushed to their maximum, she flew amid a hundred others racing toward the crumbling island of Galen. Allegiances and grudges meant nothing now, the Seraphim from the various islands all sharing the same goal: to save as many lives as possible.

As she closed in on the edge, she more felt than heard the deep rumbling sound emanating from the island's center. Buildings shook, many collapsing in on themselves. Given the tremendous size of the island, there seemed no specific place to go, and Bree felt at a loss. She picked a spot and flew, as did all the others, it seemed. So far it didn't appear Galen had dropped at all, but it had tilted slightly. Men and women fought against the incline as Bree swooped down to the soft earth and grass of the edge. They screamed at her, arms reaching, dozens seeking refuge, but there was only her.

"Give me the children," Bree shouted. "Please, the children, I can carry two, now hurry!"

The group seemed to be a family, and while they were afraid, they were not yet in panic's grip. *Perhaps they are in denial,* thought Bree. She couldn't blame them. The island was shaking, and it'd tilted slightly, but to believe it might fall? To believe an entire world was about to die? Perhaps that was too much, even for her, and she'd personally seen the weakened Beam fading in and out beneath Galen's surface, its Fount ceasing to be.

"Please, take care of them," a mother said, handing over a boy and a girl, each looking to be around six years old. Bree scooped one into each arm, asking them to hold on. Their little hands wrapped around her neck, and Bree shared a look with their mother. The tanned woman's eyes were hollow, her lip quivering from strangled tears.

"I'll come back for you," Bree told her.

Left hand clenched into a fist, she poured power into her wings, gripped the children tighter, and then lifted off the grass and into the chaotic sky.

Thousands of men and women now filled the airways between the two nearest islands, Elern and Candren. Seraphim from all five islands raced in, diving onto Galen and leaving moments later with men and women in their arms. Ferrymen ceased all travels to various islands, everyone with an empty platform turning and heading toward Galen's docks instead. The fishermen were right behind them, slowly plodding closer while carrying enormous nets. Bree glanced over her shoulder at Galen's own fishermen. Half a mile away she saw a dock, and two fishermen were just taking off, each holding the side of a net. Crammed within looked to be more than a dozen children.

Bree turned back, then swore. Too many were in the air, far more than she'd ever seen. It dwarfed the arrival docks at Center, and there were no colored flags to guide people into organized lines. A pair of fishermen were up ahead, each holding a woman by the wrists. Bree banked to the right to avoid slamming into them, and as she did she felt her grip lessen on the girl. She slipped, screamed. Bree felt her heart freeze in her chest, and she lunged to catch her by the wrist before she might fall. The little girl bawled, her dark hair whipping about as she hung there. Bree gritted her teeth hard enough to hurt, but she held on as she pushed her wings faster.

Don't drop her, Bree thought as her hand ached and the muscles of her left arm quivered. *Don't you dare drop her. Just a little longer.*

It felt like an eternity, but at last she arrived at Elern's edge. Bree slowed just enough to drop them onto the grass, two among hundreds as the first wave of refugees arrived. Curling around, Bree put the island of Galen in her sights and then slammed the throttle to its maximum. Her hair danced as she raced toward it, weaving through the traffic as if in the midst of battle. The Beam continued to flicker, and a large chunk of earth broke free from its bottom, falling and falling until it crashed into the ocean. The sound was like a thunderclap, and it chilled Bree to her core.

Fishermen from the other islands had arrived by the time Bree was almost there. They carried two at a time, sometimes three. Men and women hung from their hands, children wrapping their arms around their necks. The nets were proving more reliable, and like a macabre catch of the ocean the fishermen carried them to safety. Fear was spreading like a fire among the populace as more and more people from the interior parts of the island spread outward to the edges. Twice she watched a platform lift off from the ground in the strong arms of the ferrymen, filled to the absolute brim, yet still people leapt at it, trying to catch its sides. Most missed, and they flailed their limbs wildly as they fell to their deaths.

It seemed most were traveling toward the various docks and the towns surrounding them, but Bree had a promise to keep. Hoping she remembered correctly, she flew toward the same stretch of earth that she'd taken the children from. She couldn't concentrate, couldn't think. The rumbling noise was deeper now, but the screams overwhelmed it. So many crying, shouting, begging for safety...

When Bree arrived at the same spot, she felt relief to see the children's mother still there, waiting. She cried out to her, lifting her arms as Bree landed.

"Wrap your arms around my neck," Bree told her.

The woman tried, but by now more families had joined her waiting group, and they pushed and jostled. Bree felt people grabbing onto her wings, others tugging at her clothing. Bree stepped back, trying to maintain control. The side of the island was so close, yet they seemed not to care.

"Get back!" Bree screamed, trying to shove away a dark-haired man with wild eyes and silken clothes. She reached for the mother, but before she could grab her hand, the man drew a knife, stabbed the woman in the breast, and then shoved her over the edge.

"You'll take me!" the man shouted. One hand held the bloodied knife, the other pulled out a handful of golden coins.

Bree flew several feet into the air so she would be free of them, drew a sword, and then sliced open the man's throat. He dropped to his knees, fell to his side, and then rolled off the edge of the island, his corpse chasing the woman he'd killed. His gold fell with him. The rest retreated, horrified, and Bree looked at them with growing terror.

"You," she said, pointing at a young woman who looked Bree's age. "I can fly faster if I carry you."

Bree sheathed her sword and then dropped into the group beside her intended passenger. Knowing she couldn't dare hesitate lest she be mobbed again, Bree grabbed the woman around the waist and immediately flew back into the air. The woman wrapped her arms around Bree's neck as if in a loving embrace, and she put her face against the buckles of the harness, eyes closed as she cried. Bree envied her. If only she could close her eyes...

The air was alive with vibrations. Twin paths, like ant trails, or pulsing veins, stretched out to connect the two nearer islands. Fishermen carrying far too much weight dipped and rose as beside them the ferrymen guided their packed platforms to safety. Seraphim flashed through their numbers, trying to stay at the outskirts, but they were so many. As Bree watched, one net tore open, and an elderly woman slipped through. A nearby Seraph dove after, but Bree could not afford to watch to see if he caught her. Another Seraph flew too fast, failing to notice a fisherman higher above starting to drift. Their bodies collided midair, and as the Seraph spun wildly, he struck the chains of a platform, upending it. Men and women fell screaming. Bree told herself to pretend it wasn't happening. Forget it all. If she dared let it sink in, if she dared think on all the horrible things happening, she'd be paralyzed.

The woman in her arms screamed something, but Bree was too out of it to understand.

"What?" she asked.

"My husband!" the woman shouted, tilting her mouth closer to Bree's ear. "Please, you have to get my husband!"

Bree didn't know what to tell her. Elern was close, and Bree angled for a landing, steadily lessening the power of her wings. As the woman's feet touched down she let go, still screaming as tears stuck her hair to her face.

"His name is Thomas!" she screamed. "Please, you have to—"

Bree flew away, her whole body trembling as she prayed for a way to endure the madness.

She kept to an outer path, hoping to avoid most of the chaos as her wings shone with power. Skipping through the edges, Bree chose one of the cities near Galen's very center. All along the rooftops she saw families gathering, and upon her approach they waved their arms and screamed, crying for her to choose them. No matter whom she chose, Bree could not shake the guilt clawing at her throat. Of the families, she saw a dark-skinned woman with three young children atop a pale stone roof, and Bree landed before her.

"God bless you," the woman said, handing over a boy no older than four. "Please, take them somewhere safe."

Another, a beautiful little girl of six, stepped closer and lifted her arms. Her older sister held her hand, and she looked eight, maybe nine, her long hair braided and tied with a crimson ribbon.

"I can only carry two," Bree said, trying to cut off the woman's thanks. "Please, only two."

Bree took the youngest in her left arm, the older one in her right, and both wrapped their arms about her neck. The mother tried to argue while the remaining girl started to cry.

"I'm coming back," Bree said as she gently lifted into the air. "I'll come back for her, I promise."

"Mommy!" the four-year-old cried, and she pulled an arm back to reach for her mother.

"Hold on to me," Bree told her, and she spun so her back was to the mother, blocking the child's sight of her. "Hold on to my neck. This'll be like a ride. A fun ride, all right?"

The girl sniffled and replaced her grip. Shifting her arms so she held the two better, Bree increased the throttle as high as she dared. She couldn't fly at a proper angle, and the wind blasted against her far more than normal. Doing the best she could, Bree flew back over the edge, more drifting than flying toward Elern.

By now it seemed every set of wings that existed was flying toward Galen. A veritable army of theotechs and their gold wings had arrived from Center, landing together at one of the docks, and they were a welcome sight. Most of the ferrymen had dropped off their first platform full of people and were on their way for a second trip.

Just one more hour, Bree thought. *That's not too much to ask, is it?*

The edges of Elern were starting to overcrowd with people, not only refugees but Elern's native population rushing in to help. Bree searched for an open spot farther inland, then set down the older girl first.

"Take care of your sister," Bree said, handing the four-year-old over into her arms. "You keep her here, all right?"

"I will," the girl said.

Screams sounded from the island edge, loud and unified. Turning, Bree lifted into the air so she might see.

Galen's Beam, already weak, was now gone.

Bree tore into the air, screaming like a shot toward Galen. The Beam flared back to life, barely at half strength, and it seemed the entire island shuddered. Despite the Beam's return, the island was clearly drifting downward. Whatever time they had, it wasn't much. Bree shifted her angle, and she weaved through the fishermen as they desperately pushed their own clunky wings to their limits. Bree's eyes remained focused on the distant city in the heart of the island. She'd made a promise, and she would keep it.

When she was almost there, the Beam collapsed again, and this time it did not return. The island was crumbling. Bree flew forward, telling herself she was unafraid, telling herself she could make it in time. As grass and fields passed before her, she saw those at the docks lifting off the ground as if floating. The wind, which had been soft and ignorable, suddenly raged into a maelstrom as the island increased speed. Bree's downward curve became a dive.

I can make it, Bree thought as she closed in on the city. She saw people on the rooftops, only now they were several feet above them, screaming helplessly. And then she saw the mother, the eldest daughter held closely in her arms. The wind fought against Bree, shoving her away, denying her speed. Bree pushed into it, teeth clenched, painfully aware of the ocean's approach. The two saw her, and they reached out to her. So close now, so close...

Bree's eyes flicked to the side, she saw water, and with a scream she banked upward, knifing into the air until her momentum died. Hovering in place, she spun, and with tears in her eyes she watched Galen's fall.

The island struck the ocean waters. The sound was like the fist of God striking the world, deep, overwhelming. Rumbling followed, a thunder that continued unendingly. All the people who were still there, those who had floated just above the falling ground, were now hit with violent suddenness. There was no pretending to survival, no delusions of enduring. Bree saw the bodies hit, saw them break. Shocked still, she watched as the ground broke into chunks, houses crumbling as if they were a child's playthings. She couldn't think. She couldn't even form cohesive sentences in her mind. The Endless Ocean seethed with fury, rushing in with a terrible roar as it buried the remnants of the once proud civilization. Enormous waves crashed outward, towering so high she saw several Seraphim vanish into their white spray.

Slowly the sounds diminished as the ocean swallowed the island, and it seemed her frozen world returned to life. She heard crying and screaming, but only from above. Above flew an army of sorrow, wailing with terror and anguish. Not below. Nothing from below but the rushing water swallowing fields of grass and destroyed buildings. Bree hovered there, not wanting to move, not wanting to even breathe. Never before had she felt such guilt. It crushed the air from her lungs, and it peeled back her eyelids so that she could only stare and watch, lost, alone, overwhelmed.

"Bree!"

Kael lowered to a hover before her, and his appearance matched how she felt. Blood was splattered across his armor, the left side of his face bruised. Bree opened her mouth, trying to say something, anything.

"I could have saved them," she said, and the words broke something deep inside her. "If I wasn't a coward, I could have . . . I could have . . ."

Kael pulled her into his arms, and she buried her face against his chest and sobbed.

"It'll be all right," he whispered as they hovered there. "It'll be all right."

It was a lie, just a lie, but she needed those words nonetheless.

Bree clutched him as if her life depended upon it. In his embrace, she let the horrors of the day sink in. All their earlier trials and battles seemed so trivial now. Their world, and everything they knew, had irrevocably changed. Tilting her face to one side, she let her tears fall as she watched a legion of grim men and women fly past them to the Endless Ocean below, searching in vain for survivors.

CHAPTER
32

Bree knelt before the wall surrounding the academy. She'd picked roses from the park behind the apothecary and placed seven against the gray stone. Silently she stared at two names, one directly above the other. Liam Skyborn. Cassandra Skyborn. The bright sun, green grass, the gentle breeze; it all seemed in cruel mockery of yesterday's absolute horror. As if it'd never happened. As if, without names written upon stone, the dead had never existed. But something had to be done. Everyone felt it in their bones. Already Bree heard debates between Seraphs on the proper way to show remembrance for the fifty thousand dead.

There is no wall big enough, Bree thought, forever haunted by the image of the bodies slamming down when the island of Galen first struck the ocean. Build one spanning all of Weshern and it still wouldn't have room for the names of the dead.

She heard footsteps in the grass behind her, and she glanced over her shoulder to see Kael approaching. His hands were in his pockets, his eyes downcast.

"Hey," he said once at her side.

"Hey."

A soft gust of wind blew over them, and Bree let it fill the silence for her.

"I still miss them sometimes," Kael said, easily figuring out why she was at that particular stretch of wall. "It's stupid stuff, too. Like, I wish they could have seen me when I first tried on my Seraph uniform. They'd have been so proud, you know? But I'd loved to have seen it on their faces. Or can you imagine what Dad would say after hearing about your swords?"

"He'd probably say they weren't proper weapons for a Seraph."

"And Mom would have immediately elbowed his side and called him a stubborn fool for thinking it," Kael added.

Bree smiled, but it was fleeting. Her head ached, and she'd barely slept more than an hour or two last night.

"What do you think Mom and Dad would have said about Galen's fall?" she asked.

Kael fell silent once more. He had no answer to that, and honestly, neither did Bree. She'd like to think they'd have been compassionate, that they'd have known exactly what to say… but these were the people they'd fought against, the people they'd died fighting. What were the people of Galen to her anymore?

"I couldn't sleep," Bree said when the quiet began to grate, even to her. "I keep seeing the same thing. This poor mother and her daughter. I was flying to get them, right at the very end. But then I turned away. I thought I was out of time. I saved her two other little girls, but they'll grow up without a mother now, all because I was a coward."

Bree rubbed at her eyes.

"It's like a bad joke. I keep seeing her, reaching out for me, crying, and I don't even know her damn name."

Kael sat down cross-legged beside her. He absently picked at some grass, seemingly more comfortable looking at it than at her.

"I'm sorry," he said. "Do you want to talk about it?"

A simple enough question, but the answer wasn't quite so simple. Part of Bree wanted to forget it all had happened. It'd be easier that way. But that way led to constant nightmares and a thin wall of denial that she knew would one day crack. So instead she tried to get her tired mind to form into some approximation of order.

"After Mom and Dad died, I swore I'd make them pay," she began. "I don't know who, just . . . Galen. Her people. Her Seraphim. They took them from us, Kael, took our parents, yet we didn't even have the names of their killers. And when Eric killed Dean, I swore it again. I wouldn't stand by. I'd do something, I'd have my revenge, yet when I slew Eric, I didn't feel happy. I didn't feel satisfied. I had to do more. I had to fight even harder. The people of Galen had all these awful drawings of me, insulting me, and I swore I'd make every single one of them remember my name. I'd make every one of them fear it as I avenged what they'd done."

Bree shuddered. After the fall, Kael and Bree had returned to nearby Elern to regroup with the rest of their squadron. The refugees from Galen had lined the island's edge for miles, an overwhelming, frightened, heartbroken mass.

"Do you remember the looks on their faces?" she whispered. "All those people, shocked and broken. That's who I swore vengeance upon? That's who I spent so much time hating?"

Her tears were growing stronger, and she couldn't wipe them away fast enough.

"I don't hate them anymore," she said. "I don't want them afraid anymore. I don't even want them to remember my name.

I just want to have saved two more of their lives. Just two more, a mother and her terrified little girl..."

Kael's arm wrapped around her, and she leaned limp against him and let it all out. All the lingering pain. All the confusion and doubt. Every aching memory that haunted her failed attempts to sleep, faces of the dead, the crumbling nation, the breaking bodies of her people... she cried in her brother's arms, accepting his silent strength.

"Everyone's scared," Kael said after several long moments. Bree kept her eyes closed and let his voice float over her. "Everyone's confused. The world we knew has changed forever, and we don't even know why, or whom to blame. But no matter what happens, I do know this, Bree. I know you did all you could to save those people."

"You don't know that," she said. "I feel it in my bones. I know I didn't do as much as I could have. Not like you. Not like everyone else."

"You're wrong."

He said it with such sudden anger Bree was shocked, and she peeled away to meet her brother's gaze. There was no hiding the hurt in his eyes.

"Kael," she asked. "What happened to you yesterday?"

He stared at her a long moment, debating.

"I decided I'd try to go to one of the smaller towns," he said, gaze loosening, mind easing into the past. "Somewhere people might overlook, you know? I kept thinking... I kept thinking, if this happened to Weshern, we'd have been forgotten down in Lowville while the bigger towns were evacuated. So I flew... I think I was in shock at the time, and I just flew until I saw someone, a man outside his home on a farm. He had no clue what was going on, only that the land was rumbling beneath his feet. So I told him."

Her brother took in a deep breath, and when he let it out, his upper body shuddered.

"He refused to come with me," he said.

"Did he not believe you?" Bree asked.

"No," Kael said. "It was because I couldn't take them all at once. He had a wife and two sons, and he didn't trust me to come back after I took their sons. *It's your fault this land's dying,* he tells me. *I'd rather we die here at our home than let you tear us apart and raise our kids as Weshern slaves.*"

Bree couldn't imagine how she'd have reacted. At the outer edges, everyone had been so frantic to escape. The idea that someone would refuse was baffling.

"What'd you do?" she asked when he refused to continue.

"I...I told him I was taking his sons anyway," he said. "I told him he was killing them, and I wouldn't allow it. He struck me, I drew my sword..." Kael wiped his own tears away as he fought for strength to speak. "They were so mad, so scared, and I was no better. I brought the youngest son back with me to Elern, a little four-year-old boy. He was the only one. I slew his father, Bree. His own father, just to save him. My only prayer is that he's so young he won't remember when he grows older. After that, I didn't go back. I couldn't. Like a coward, I watched Galen until it fell."

Bree grabbed Kael's hand and held on tight. She couldn't believe how selfish she'd been. He'd not spoken of his own attempts when they met, and she'd not thought to ask. Haunted by her own guilt, of that outstretched hand she refused to grab, she'd not imagined her brother suffering the same. He'd seemed so strong on the outside, so held together, but it only hid his pain and guilt.

Just like his sister, she thought.

Bree wished she had wise words to offer, some sort of

consolation, but she did not. Shifting so she sat before him, she hunched so he'd see her despite his lowered gaze.

"Kael, I want you to make a promise with me," she said. "I want you to promise that you'll let this guilt go, and never blame yourself again. If you do, I'll do the same."

"Like it's that easy," Kael muttered.

"I don't think it's easy. I think this will be one of the hardest things we ever do, but we have to. We have to. The guilt is too much, Kael. Too many people were lost that day, and I don't want my brother to be one of them. Tell me if I'm wrong, but I don't think you want to lose me, either."

Kael sniffled as he looked up.

"Not for anything in the world," he said, and he forced a smile to his face. "And fine. I promise."

Bree fought back another round of tears, these of exhaustion and relief.

"And I promise, too," she said. "Now don't you dare feel guilty about that ever again."

"Or what?"

She laughed, weak, nervous.

"Or I'll find a broom and do to you what I did to Saul."

This time Kael's smile was genuine.

"Then I best not upset the almighty Phoenix of Weshern," he said. "I'd hate to be beaten with a broom handle."

"A burning broom handle," Bree added. "I have an image to maintain."

Kael laughed as he rose to his feet and offered his hand.

"Come on, Phoenix," he said, greatly exaggerating her name. "Let's go find Brad or Clara. I think we need to spend some time with friends. How does that sound?"

"Right now, that sounds like the best thing in the world."

EPILOGUE

On the third day, Center finally issued its response.

"Hurry up," Brad shouted from the door of his room as he slipped an arm through his jacket.

"Trying," Kael said, tucking his shirt into his pants with one hand while grabbing a belt with the other. The call for assembly had come less than five minutes earlier, sending everyone scrambling to dress and prepare. A representative from Center was on his way to Weshern, and all Seraphim were to be ready in greeting. While part of him was nervous, mostly Kael was relieved. It seemed their entire island had spent the past three days holding its collective breath while the theotechs investigated the cause of Galen's collapse. Everyone, even Kael and Bree, had spent their turn at the library being questioned by the men and women in their red robes. At last, it seemed they would have an explanation for the worst disaster ever recorded since the destruction of the old world during the Ascension.

"Maybe it was all Galen's fault," Brad said, stepping into

Kael's room fully dressed and tugging at the collar of his shirt. "They did something so bad God decided to punish them for good."

Kael shifted his belt so its buckle was perfectly straight, then tugged on the edges of his jacket so it wasn't bunched around his neck.

"Do you really believe that?" Kael asked.

Brad hesitated, then shook his head.

"No," he said. "But it doesn't matter what I believe, does it?"

Kael thought of the cold stares of the theotechs as they asked their questions after the island's collapse.

"No, it doesn't," Kael said. "There's only one opinion that matters, and we're about to hear it. Let's go."

Together they dashed out of the apartment to the street. Once there they followed a steady stream of students from all four years hurrying south to the intersection, where a large crowd gathered.

"Suit up!" Instructor Kime shouted from their center. "Everyone to the gear sheds and retrieve your weapons and wings."

The crowd shifted east, and Kael and Brad followed. Though all the preparations were as if for a battle, the entire atmosphere was wrong.

"Feels like we're going to a funeral," Brad muttered, glancing at the dour, nervous faces of their classmates. Kael found it hard to disagree. No excitement or anticipation, just dread.

Once at the gear sheds they waited in line until it was their turn to go inside and grab their set. As Kael strapped on the silver wings, he felt his nervousness start to grow. Why all the pomp and assembly? It was just a messenger from Center. They received similar messengers daily, yet to greet this one they must be suited up and carrying their swords? Something more was going on, and it seemed everyone knew it. This didn't feel like they were preparing to greet an ambassador. This felt like they were preparing for war.

As Kael waited outside the gear sheds, the orders they heard did little to dispel that feeling.

"All combat-ready Seraphim join your squads by the academy entrance," Headmaster Simmons shouted from the center of the street. He then pointed to where several of the instructors hovered off the ground so they might be visible. "First year, gather up with Instructor Kime. Second year, Instructor Dohn. Third year, with me, and fourth year, Instructor Ellis. Line up, follow orders, and keep your mouths shut."

Kael and Brad exchanged a look.

"Good luck," Brad whispered, slapping him on the chest.

"You, too."

Deciding that flying in such a crowd would be reckless, Kael pushed his way through to the west until he was free, and then he powered up his wings just enough to float him along until he joined the eighty Seraphim already waiting at the entrance. Kael thought he was the last to arrive, but that turned out to be his sister, who landed beside him at the gathering place for Phoenix Squad.

"Anyone know what's really going on?" Bree asked the other five.

"No idea," Kael said, and he looked to the others.

"If it were our place to know, we'd already know," Olivia said. She was busy tying her shoulder-length dark hair behind her head with a piece of string, which made the sharpness of her jaw and cheekbones all the more prominent. "Leave speculation and worrying to those with idle time and loose tongues. The truth will make itself known to us soon enough."

Not exactly the answer Kael was looking for, but he dared not argue with his squad's leader. Nodding his head, he bit his tongue and consoled himself with knowing that Olivia was right. He would know soon enough.

Argus Summers flew over to join them, and Kael was quick to dip his head in respect. The commander stood in the center of the large gathering, and he spun until certain that all paid attention.

"I'll be flying to the holy mansion to escort the royal family," he said. "The rest of you, head to the west docks and take up flanking positions on either side of the road. Leave no gaps between you. I want a solid line. The rest of the academy students will line up beside you, but let the instructors and the headmaster worry about them."

The commander paused, and it was that hesitation, that worry in the man's cool blue eyes, that finally made Kael afraid.

"And most of all," he said, "I want you all to remain calm no matter what you might hear. Is that understood?"

Murmurs of acknowledgment filtered in from among the Seraphim.

"Good," Argus said. "The other groups are ready, and they'll be following your lead. Fly on."

The humming of their wings increased in volume as Argus flew into the air. Olivia rose just above their heads, exchanging quick signals with the other squad leaders. Order decided, the squads took off, one after the other, with Phoenix Squad taking up the rear. Though Bree wasn't officially part of the squad, she flew just to Olivia's left, with Kael taking up the right. Above the streets they flew, and Kael gazed below with a strange sense of regret. It wasn't long ago he walked those streets. It wasn't long ago that, come a moment like this, he'd have peered up at the Seraphim flying overhead and wished he was among them. Now he wished he could walk those streets again, oblivious to the dangers, and to the theotechs' ever-watchful eyes.

Their path took them over Lowville, and Kael felt a momentary jolt of excitement when he saw the tiny figure of Aunt Bethy standing on the doorstep to their home, hand to her face to block the sun as she looked up at them. Kael waved to her, and when she waved back, a stupid smile bloomed across his face.

Guess it's not all bad, he thought, imagining his aunt's pride.

Their path angled lower as they approached the docks. All normal traffic had been halted, and blocking off large parts of the street were Weshern's soldiers dressed in full battle attire. The Seraphim landed in the empty streets, taking up stances on opposite sides starting just beyond the wood of the docks. Kael stood beside Bree, and he wished he could joke with her, maybe poke fun at all the seriousness of the day. But Argus had made it clear he wanted them to remain silent, and so he did. The rest of the Seraphim landed, forming a corridor of gleaming silver wings. Several minutes later, Argus arrived, flying low while Isaac and Avila Willer rode on horses behind him, accompanied by Theotech Vyros on foot.

When they reached the docks, the rulers of Weshern dismounted, nearby soldiers rushing over to lead the horses away. The couple were dressed in their finest, he in a blue and black suit, she in a deep blue dress, each adorned with silver gloves, necklaces, and crowns. Compared to when Kael had met them during the solstice celebration, they looked less approachable, more regal. They stood arm in arm before the docks, patiently waiting. Argus stood a step back, wrists crossed behind his back. Like a lurking spider, behind them both waited Vyros.

Time crawled along, and Kael had to shift his weight from leg to leg to prevent them from falling asleep. He kept sneaking glances north, hoping to spot the messenger from Center, but it wasn't the messenger who arrived first. In a sudden rush came the angelic knights. More than a dozen men and women, clad in gold and white tunics, raced in from the clouds in loose formation toward the docks.

"At attention," Olivia ordered, echoing the other squad leaders. Kael stood up straight, and he crossed his arms behind his back, hands holding his wrists. His breath caught in his throat as the knights landed. They stayed together, crowding in along the docks while showing no real hurry. Kael watched them from the corner of his eye, all the more certain something terrible was happening. Rarely was a messenger ever escorted, let alone by an entire squadron of angelic knights. Then he saw four ferrymen carrying a platform, its sides lined with silver, its chains made of bronze, and Kael finally realized what was happening.

This wasn't just a messenger. The Speaker for the Angels was coming to their island to announce his decree.

Don't panic, Kael told himself as the ferrymen lowered the platform to the docks. *He's probably visiting all four islands to tell the people what happened.*

Galen's fall was an unmatched catastrophe, so of course the Speaker would personally deliver whatever information his theotechs had discovered. Clutching his wrists tighter to prevent himself from fidgeting, Kael watched and waited as Marius Prakt stepped out from the platform.

He was a younger man, which surprised Kael for some reason. He'd expected a tired, wrinkled old politician who looked worn down by the weight of his own jewelry. But Marius... Marius looked healthy, vibrant, his skin softly tanned, his short brown hair carefully trimmed. Like the theotechs, he wore red robes, only instead of gold medals and rings, he bore no decoration whatsoever. The most ornate thing on his body was a single black sash tied at his waist. With a bounce in his step, he approached the Willers. Though his face was pleasant, Kael noticed he never smiled, and when he shook hands with the Archon, his eyes seemed to harden, his lips twisting into the faintest resemblance of a frown.

The Speaker said something to Isaac, and though it was far too soft to hear, Kael could easily read the two words on his lips: I'm sorry.

I'm sorry. What does that mean?

Kael had little time to dwell on it, for the Speaker stepped between them, several of his angelic knights accompanying him, one brushing aside Avila as if she were a commoner. Marius greeted Vyros next, vigorously shaking the hand of the theotech and smiling as if he were a trusted companion. Next came a brief exchange of pleasantries with Argus Summers. Then he was moving, with the Willers quickly following, angelic knights flanking them on either side. Manacles swung from the belts of the knights, and the sight unnerved Kael to no end.

If Marius had a destination, he didn't let it be apparent, for he addressed other members of the Seraphim, speaking to each one as if they were old friends. Kael wondered what supernatural power guided the man. Simply being in the Speaker's presence made people look more alive. It was as if Marius were a bolt of lightning wherever he went, always moving, a bundle of energy he gave off to every man and woman he addressed.

And then he stopped right in front of Bree.

"Phoenix of Weshern," he said, reaching out his hand. Bree gave him hers, and he kissed the tops of her fingers. The Speaker smiled, his teeth like pearls, his eyes like sapphires.

"Even my own knights are jealous of your...reputation," he said. "I confess, I am tempted to oversee your next battle so I might witness your skill firsthand."

"Forgive me, Speaker, but I pray there is no next battle for you to witness," Bree said. "Only peace."

Beside her, Olivia tensed as if Bree had openly slapped the man, but Marius smiled all the wider.

"A fine prayer," he said. "A selfless prayer. May God hear and answer you, Miss Skyborn."

Just like that, he was moving on. Kael released a breath he didn't know he was holding. The Speaker continued down past twenty more Seraphim, all eyes following him. Though it seemed he stopped nowhere in particular, Marius pulled himself up to his full height. A change overcame him. He wasn't jovial anymore. He wasn't a bundle of energy. Suddenly he was a towering presence, his voice deep, his arms out wide as he commanded the people's attention, and willingly they gave it.

"Three days ago, our people suffered a terrible tragedy," he shouted, and it seemed his voice might carry for miles. "Three days ago, we witnessed the fall of an island God himself made fly. There is nothing to say that adequately conveys the horror of that moment. There is nothing I may do that will heal the wounds such loss has given us all. But even though we grieve, we must act. The truth must be known, the innocents protected, the guilty...punished."

Kael felt his blood chill. A distant humming reached his ears, and he tore his eyes away from the Speaker to look to the northern skies above the docks. Mouth open, he felt his knees go weak.

"Three days ago, the Seraphim of Weshern acted with reckless irresponsibility," the Speaker continued. "Your forces joined a combat without due process, nor with permission of our theotechs. The angels tell me that these actions were a direct cause of Galen's eventual collapse. The weight of these sins rests on Weshern's shoulders."

No amount of orders could have kept the listening Seraphim

silent, nor the expressions of shock from the gathered soldiers. The noise of the crowd only grew as others saw what Kael saw: hundreds of angelic knights flying from Center, accompanying a seemingly endless number of platforms carried by ferrymen.

"I would reveal more," the Speaker continued, showing no care to the sudden explosion of noise. "But for the safety of mankind itself, I must not. It is possible the collapse may be repeated here, and that is a possibility I must prevent at all costs. Because of this, I issue my decree: until the risk has been averted, Isaac and Avila Willer are to be imprisoned, and the people of Weshern ruled under Center's direct control."

The knights flanking the Archon and his wife removed the manacles swinging from their belts, quickly clamping them down onto the wrists of the shocked couple.

"No!"

Clara rushed out from farther down the line, dashing toward her parents. Kael's heart froze, panic pounding through his veins as the nearby knights drew their blades. Light shimmered across Argus's wings as he moved to intercept, grabbing her in his arms and holding her still.

"You can't do this!" Clara screamed as she struggled to free herself. "This isn't right, we didn't do anything! Let me go, damn it, let me go!"

Kael moved to join her, to do something, but Bree reached out and grabbed his arm.

"Not now," she said, leaning in close and keeping her voice low. "All you'll do is throw your life away."

Marius watched Clara's struggle with a mask of sympathy Kael didn't buy for a second.

"Calm yourself, child," the Speaker said. "Further inves-tigations are necessary, and the lives of your parents may yet be spared. I tell you, I tell all of you, that we do this for your protection. My theotechs will take residence here, as will many of Center's soldiers, but it is only to prevent another catastrophe like that which befell Galen. It is the will of God that none may fall, and though it is a heavy burden, I take it upon myself to ensure your safety."

Argus whispered something into Clara's ear, and she slowly went limp. Still crying, he led her away, through the line of Weshern Seraphim and beyond Kael's sight. Fire burning in his breast, Kael turned to see angelic knights landing upon the docks, one after another in a constant flow. Behind them, the first of many platforms bumped against the docks. From it rushed two dozen soldiers bearing the crest of Center on their shields. They marched with their long spears held high, their heavy boots thudding atop the wood. More and more platforms docked, thousands of soldiers flooding into Weshern, so many it would take hours for them all to land. Accompanying them were the damn theotechs in their red robes. The knights led the way, and Kael stood, locked still, stunned and unsure what to do.

His knights will fly like legion, his soldiers unending. They will come to conquer, no longer willing to play the game.

Marrik had sworn the time approached, and now here it was, before Kael's very eyes. Before they'd dropped Thane Ackels down the well, he'd raved about Center's armies coming on a bloodred sky. Shivers running through him, Kael watched the continual wave of soldiers. The two disciples had been wrong. There was no war. No great battle. Here they stood, peaceful, obedient, the beaten dogs Thane had accused them of being, as the army of Center occupied their home. Teeth clenched, he almost wished they had fought back. Almost. To rebel now would be a death sentence, but if the other islands joined in, if they sensed their own sovereignty challenged under the guise of protection...

As the knights marched on by, Kael spotted one he recognized. He stared at Nickolas Flynn, hoping the man might notice him. As luck would have it, he did, Nickolas turning his head slightly and making eye contact with Kael as he walked past. Kael prayed for something, anything, a sign from the man that things weren't as dire as they seemed.

In answer, Nickolas shook his head slightly and turned away.

Surrounded by golden wings and armor, Marius marched through the streets. Behind them, spines stiff and their hands and feet thankfully unbound, followed the former rulers of Weshern. It didn't seem fair. It didn't seem right. Argus had made the decision to send their Seraphim in early, not the Willers. Why should they be arrested, and not him?

A hand touched his. Kael looked to his left, to where Bree remained in perfect stance except for where she'd slipped her right hand underneath their wings so she might clutch his fingers. It was a breach of protocol, but right then, it didn't seem to matter. Bree was just as frightened as he was, and that realization made Kael pretend to be brave. To be strong.

"We'll fight them," he whispered in her ear. "This isn't over."

"I know," she whispered back. "But who will fight with us?"

There was no denying the obvious truth. Center had come to claim Weshern, and only one man had cried warning from the very beginning. The one man whose disciples had urged the people to resist before the conquering armies came. The name was treason, but Kael spoke it anyway.

"Johan."

The platforms dispersed wave after wave of soldiers, the ferrymen filling the sky, the sound of boots almost deafening. Together, hand in hand, the twins watched the army of Center march into their home, banners held high, theotechs guiding the way.

A NOTE FROM THE AUTHOR

Ever since the third grade I've wanted to tell a story about a civilization in the sky. Something about the imagery has always fascinated me, and it started with the floating land of Zeal from an old Super Nintendo RPG called Chrono Trigger (which, coincidentally, is still my favorite game of all time). Now I doubt Chrono Trigger was the first (and it certainly wasn't the last) to do the floating islands bit. James Cameron's Avatar comes to mind, as does the wonderful game Bioshock Infinite. Heck, I even have a floating city in one of my other series, but it was very much a background thing, and it whet my appetite for a whole world focusing on just that.

Though I'd wanted to do a floating island story for a very long time, I never did. Couldn't decide what story I wanted to tell. People are living on a floating island, awesome...now what? And that was what tripped me up for so long. Now what? So as I started forming this story, I built the world first on a purely mechanical level. What kept the islands afloat? Where do they get fresh water? Food? How does everyone travel? Oh, and of course: how can I make combat awesome and fit my kind of storytelling (i.e., stupid and over-the-top fun)?

One of the things I did *not* want to do was have a segmented caste system, some up high, some down below on the ground. It seems that in every instance of a city on the clouds, the obvious symbolism becomes a bit too enticing. But then the conflict becomes earthbound versus skyborn, and let's face it, the people in the clouds are going to end up the villains in some way, shape, or form. We tend to root for the underdogs, and rarely is the civilization living clean and free high up in the clouds going to be considered the underdog over those living down in the dirt.

So I wanted a civilization in the clouds, and only the clouds. I wanted to fully embrace every aspect of it instead of creating a juxtaposition between earthbound and skyborn. Most of all, I wanted to convey the thrill of flying. If I'm going to have floating islands, why not have people zipping through the air? Aerial combat? I can work with that. But I'm also the guy who likes to fling around giant fireballs, so what can I do to satisfy that itch? I was tempted to just use magic, but this time around, starting off in a brand-new series, brand-new world, I wanted to keep myself a little more under control, keep the setting a bit more structured.

The concept of the prisms came about after a few iterations, but once I settled on the idea, everything grew from there: the wings, the Founts, the Beams, all of it. Once I had the world, well, now it was time to figure out the characters, and the overall story arc. One day, while in the middle of writing a completely different book, and months before I went all-in on this one, I took a day off to write a single chapter that'd popped into my head and refused to leave. It was of two children sitting on the edge of the world, watching the sun set, except instead of seeing stars emerge, they watched the sky be consumed with fire.

That was it. That was when I knew this book had grown from an interesting idea to something I must put to paper. I wrote that single chapter, then set it aside. Weeks later I wrote a second chapter, this time while between projects. The third and fourth chapters I wrote during days of frustration while finishing the sixth and final Shadowdance book. My poor editor would probably strangle me (and likely will once she gets to this note) for how much this book stole my attention from that one. But by the time I finished that fourth chapter, I knew it, felt it in my gut, that this could be something special.

And I believe it is. I hope you do, too, dear reader.

Real quick thanks, so feel free to skip this paragraph. Thanks to my agent, Michael, for helping me fine-tune the book in its early stages. Thanks to my friend Rob, for listening while I bounced off ideas and for keeping me from using the terrible ones. Thanks to my editor, Devi, for coming in with the same energy and excitement on this, book seven, as you did years ago on book one.

Of course, thanks to you as well, dear reader, whether this is the first book of mine you've read or the twentieth. If you enjoyed this book, please tell a friend, blab on your social media of choice, or even better, write a review at wherever you purchased this. Your support is what keeps me going, and I cannot thank you enough. Because of you, I get to live in the clouds telling stories. I couldn't be happier, or more blessed.

David Dalglish
February 29, 2015

extras

orbit

meet the author

DAVID DALGLISH currently lives in rural Missouri with his wife, Samantha, and daughters Morgan and Katherine. He graduated from Missouri Southern State University in 2006 with a degree in mathematics and currently spends his free time wondering how his seven-year-old is so much better than him at *Minecraft*.

introducing

If you enjoyed
SKYBORN,
look out for

FIREBORN

Seraphim: Book Two

by David Dalglish

"Where are we going?" Bree asked as Argus led her down the road, heading farther north. The trade district was far behind them, the tall wooden buildings replaced with the much more familiar squat stone homes akin to those in Lowville. Each kept an eye on the sky at all times, painfully aware of how vulnerable they were to any angelic knights who might fly overhead.

"To a barn just outside town," Argus said. Despite them being alone on the street, he glanced about as if searching for eavesdroppers. "My most trusted Seraphim are gathered there. Flying anywhere is a risk, so most everyone walked there over the past hours. When we do fly out, it'll be together, as a cohesive unit."

Bree nodded, flattered to be considered one of his trusted few. It should seem silly given all she'd done in her past two battles against Galen, but Argus was still the legendary hero of Weshern's Seraphim, while she...well, they might be attempting to craft the Phoenix into a similar hero, but she still wasn't there yet.

"What do we do when we get the elements?" she asked.

"Then we fly the hell out of there," Argus said. "This is a smash and grab, Bree. It should fit your reckless talents well."

"Are backhanded compliments the only compliments you know?"

Argus laughed.

"Perhaps. Once our nation isn't on the verge of complete domination I'll try harder to use tact."

Before she could respond, Argus suddenly grabbed her wrist and yanked, hard. The two tumbled against the stone side of a house, both backs against it, Bree's startled cry muffled against Argus's palm.

"Quiet," he whispered into her ear.

By then there was no need. She heard the thrumming of wings. An angelic knight flew overhead, his form a shadow against the rippling midnight fire. He kept closer to ground than the others she'd seen earlier in the night, traveling in a gentle curve looping about the outskirts of Glensbee. The overhang of the roof was a paltry amount of cover, but it seemed enough as the knight continued on. That, or the two didn't appear worthy of notice.

"It's only going to get worse," Argus said as he let Bree go. "So far we've only hidden what is ours. Once we retaliate, and the Speaker realizes he has a full rebellion on his hands, neither night or day will be safe for us."

"This is our home," Bree said. "We should never feel unsafe here."

Argus gestured to the sky, where the knight had just flown.

"Then you know who to blame," he said.

They continued on, keeping close to the homes they passed in case another knight flew over. Bree saw that up ahead the buildings stopped entirely, meaning they'd soon be traveling on open ground. It was a prospect she was not looking forward to in the slightest. Neither was Argus by the looks of it, for he stopped at the very last home. He did not meet her gaze, only stared at the road splitting the tall grassland.

"I should be honest with you," he said. "There's a reason I want you with us tonight. You're our backup plan, our secret weapon in case things go foul. Do you know what that means?"

Bree wasn't sure what she could be missing, but his apprehension made no sense.

"I'm not sure I do," she said.

Argus turned to face her, his blue eyes shining a deep purple from the midnight fire.

"It means I'm relying on your burning swords to save us. Your burning swords, which no other Seraph on Weshern, if not all the islands, has ever wielded before."

Suddenly it clicked. Bree felt a pit growing in her stomach, and she crossed her arms against a sudden chill worming through her.

"If anyone survives, they'll know I participated," she said.

Argus nodded.

"At night, amid the midnight fire and the chaos of battle, each one of us might go undetected, but not you. The moment you reveal yourself to the theotechs, you'll put your entire family in danger. This isn't something I want you doing lightly, nor feel like you have no choice in the matter. We need you, Bree, I won't deny that, but we need all your heart and soul, without regrets or fear. The moment you fly afraid is the moment I watch you die."

Bree stood up straight, her bruised ego giving her the strength to meet his gaze.

"I will never fly afraid," she said. "And I'll take care to keep my fire unused unless I absolutely must."

"Good." He put a hand on her shoulder. "You don't need to make this decision now. Talk it over with your aunt and your brother. Their lives will be in just as much risk as yours. If all goes well, revealing yourself won't be necessary, not tonight. Surprise will be on our side, I'm confident of that. But the time will come." He squeezed, then released. "Just be sure you're ready to make that sacrifice."

He paused, and she could tell he was waiting for her to make the first move. Swallowing down her nerves, she looked once more to the sky, then back to Argus.

"Time is wasting," she said. "Let's go."

Breaking into a sprint, she raced down the dirt road, the former commander easily keeping up with her. They ran, the tall grass waving on either side of them from the soft breeze. They ran, passing through the red and orange world until Argus finally veered off onto one of several side paths. Up ahead was a barn, and Bree felt relief that they'd reached it without being spotted by a patrolling knight. Despite the clear red sky, she maintained her run until reaching the whitewashed wooden sides and the huge doors cracked open a foot. Bree hesitated, waiting until Argus entered first.

At some point the barn would be stocked floor to high ceiling with hay for the animals in the coming cold season, but for now it was mostly empty, with only a third of the back wall blocked off by tall stacks of hay bundles. The rest of the open space was filled with Seraphs, men and women standing about in uniform, wing harnesses resting on the floor beside them. In the dim crimson light, Bree estimated thirty at most. Their idle conversations dwindled at their commander's entrance, though more than a few eyes stared Bree's way as well. Bree scanned for familiar faces, vaguely recognizing some from her lengthy drills prior to battle against Galen's Seraphim, particularly those few who had been members of Phoenix Squad.

"We're all here," Argus said to them, garnering their attention with a single clearing of his throat. "So suit up. We're taking back what is ours."

Argus turned to her.

"We have a set for you this way," he said.

She followed him to the far side, where atop the hay were twin pairs of unclaimed wings. One had black lines painted on its silver wings and clearly belonged to Argus. The other was slightly smaller, and Bree felt a chill sweep through her as she picked it up. Despite all that had happened, the skies were not yet denied to her. Sliding an arm through the harness, she hoisted it onto her back, put her other arm through, and settled the weight on her shoulders. Immediately she felt more at ease than she had for the past several hours.

This was the life she knew. This was where she belonged. The planning, the strategy, the politics: all that belonged to others far more suited to the challenges they presented. For her, she wanted an enemy in the skies before her, and her swords and fire to bring them down. Everything else was just unwanted complication. Her hands flew over the buckles, tightening them about her waist, thighs, and arms, the preparatory act one she could perform in her sleep.

As she tightened the gauntlet about her right hand, Argus pulled a bag free from a clip on his belt and dipped his fingers inside. He pulled out a single fire prism, which pulsed a soft red. She reached to take it, but when her hand closed about it, Argus did not release immediately. His eyes met hers, and he spoke in a low voice.

"Remember, only if you must, and only if you are truly ready."

"I understand," she said, pulling the prism free, opening the compartment on her gauntlet and sliding it inside. Element secure, she closed the compartment with a satisfying click. As Argus moved about, checking on others, offering them encouragement, one of the Seraphs came over to join Bree beside the hay.

"We won't be flying in formation tonight," Olivia said. Her dark hair was tied tight behind her head in preparation for battle. The light of the midnight fire coming in through the high windows cast a shadow across her sharp features, adding an edge to her beauty. "We don't expect much aerial opposition at first, so when knights do appear, we'll already be scattered, fighting ground troops or loading up the elements. Just stay with me on the way, then break solo when combat begins. With how few of us there are, we should be safe from potential collisions."

"Ground troops?" Bree asked, realizing it was a subject she'd never pondered before. "How do I engage ground troops?"

Olivia gave her a look, then immediately softened.

"Right," she said. "I forget how young you are. If the Speaker had not closed the academy, you'd have begun studying air-to-ground warfare during your second year. Not much we can do now, so I'll tell you the absolute basics. Arrows are a very real danger, so never fly in a straight line. Veer at all times. Beyond that, a braced soldier bearing a shield will not be deterred by your speed, and should you hit at even half throttle, you'll break both your necks. Everything is hit-and-run. Bombard from above with your element, and rush in to use your swords only when you absolutely must." The woman cracked a rare smile. "Which for you I assume will be almost immediately."

Bree felt her cheeks blushing and was glad it'd be all but impossible to notice in the barn. Despite her ability to bathe her swords in flame, she still lacked any control over her fire when used as a projectile. Instructor Kime had compared wielding fire to playing an instrument, and her as being tone-deaf. If that was true, her burning blades were a strange bypassing of her disability.

"Everyone, gather up," Argus called from the center of the barn. The Seraphs shuffled toward him, and Bree stayed at Olivia's side.

"I'm glad you're here," Bree told her.

"Most everyone from Phoenix Squad is," Olivia said. "It seems you're the inspiration Argus insists you are."

More nervous blushing. It was bad enough that someone as skilled and famous as Commander Argus was talking about her, but that he was making claims that she might be an inspiration? For whom? The other Seraphim? The people of Weshern? She didn't know, and she didn't want to know, so she kept her mouth shut and just smiled meekly.

"I'll try to make this quick," Argus began once all were gathered around him. "From what we can tell, the wagons are making their way toward the western docks. By midday tomorrow, they will be off our island, which means we must attack tonight. My hope is that we catch them unprepared. We've been Center's puppets for a long time, and they may not realize the lengths we will go to achieve true independence. Make no mistake; every last one of you here is signing a death warrant by participating in this attack. Should you be identified, you, your family, and all those you love will be in danger. The theotechs of Center have held on to power for centuries, and they will not relinquish it kindly. If we want Weshern pried free from their grasp, we'll need to start cutting fingers."

"My swords are ready to do the cutting," a Seraph near Argus shouted, and the rest laughed. Argus grinned at him, a wolfish gleam in his eye.

"I hope all of you get your chance tonight," he said. "The wagons stopped just outside the town of Melisand. For those of you who don't know where that is, it's fifteen miles west of the academy grounds, following Angelic Road. The theotechs accompanying the wagons appear to have rented rooms in town. A fortunate break for us, for it means many of the angelic knights will be with them to act as bodyguards. As for the rest, we hit hard, and slaughter them while they're unaware. After that, we press our numbers advantage, secure a quick victory, and then move out before reinforcements arrive."

Their commander slowly turned, letting his gaze sweep over them.

"Once the battle ends, flee to Aquila Forest. Deep inside, we're building the infrastructure of Weshern's rebellion. Don't worry if you don't know where inside the forest. Those there know of tonight's attempt, and they'll be watching for returning Seraphim so they may signal you to safety. Just make sure you're not followed. The moment Center realizes where we are, and the Speaker brings his entire forces to bear against us, we're all dead."

Argus pointed to several men and women, listing their names as he did.

"You will be responsible for obtaining the elements and carrying them to safety," he said when finished. "Everyone else, you're to be their guards. Clear out any knights you encounter and any ground troops that might be stationed on defense. Do whatever it takes for us to secure the elements. Is that clear?"

A chorus of nervous cheers were his answer, Bree's included. Fighting Seraphim of Galen, whom Weshern had a long, storied history of conflict with, was one thing. Battling the elite angelic knights of Center? That carried a hint of fear, of the impossible. Bree was about to engage with the best of the best, and potentially without her fire to aid her. It was terrifying, if she gave too much thought to it, which is why she joined the others in cheering instead.

"Very well," Argus said, and he bowed low in respect to them all. "It's time we fly, and we fly unchained."

We fly unchained, cried the rest.

Like a stirred nest of hornets, the Seraphim flew from the barn, keeping low to the ground so as to not alert distant knights of their presence. If they were spotted on the way, and their surprise ruined, then the entire assault would be over before it began. Bree flew a few yards to the left of Olivia, treating her like a squad leader even if she wasn't. The land whirled beneath them, just a blur of grass and hills. Argus led the way, and he kept the group dangerously close to the ground, so that they had to rise and fall with every hill. After a few minutes, Bree realized he was guiding them on an indirect route, avoiding any villages between them and Melisand.

Bree felt her stomach slowly cramping with each passing minute. It was like her first battle all over again, and no matter how much she berated herself, she couldn't remove the growing worry.

This is where you belong, she told herself. *You'll remember that when it starts.*

It'd been the same with the other two engagements. When combat began, a change came over her. The world seemed to slow, and all her tension, all her nerves, eased away. Worrying was impossible with her mind singly focused on the now, reacting on instinct, a primal killing dance in which she excelled. Pulse pounding in her neck, Bree stared ahead, hands bumping against the hilts of her swords, seeking reassurance from their presence.

Hills became fields of farmland. They flew so close above the rows of corn Bree could brush the top of the stalks with her fingertips if she wished. Argus kept the entire pack moving at a blistering pace, her throttle pushed nearly to full. Up ahead, a cluster of small squares marked an approaching town. Bree didn't know Weshern well enough to recognize it on sight, but given how they streaked toward it instead of veering told her they'd arrived at their destination.

Hit hard, and slaughter them while they're unaware, Argus had commanded, and all around Bree the Seraphs activated their gauntlets, eager to do just that. Bree kept her eyes peeled, searching for their target in the glow of the midnight fire. At such speed, they'd have little time before...

And there it was, a circle of three wagons at the outskirts of town. Instead of slowing, Argus's wings shimmered with silver light, bursting him ahead. Bree pushed her throttle to its maximum, and she wished she had greater control of her fire so she could attack at range with her element. At such a speed, she could only watch as they made their first pass over the theo-techs' camp.

Ice and stone led the way, blasting through the wagons and smashing craters into the ground as if the wrath of God had unleashed upon the hapless camp. Bree saw no knights, just a dozen or so men in armor standing in a circle about the wagons. They lifted their enormous shields, the overwhelming volley smashing against them and beating them down. Fire followed, wide swaths encircling the camp and setting every

wagon aflame. There would be no fleeing, not without enduring the inferno. Those with lightning picked their targets more
carefully. Bree saw two soldiers die on their way for their weapons, arcs of lightning tearing through them so that their bodies
collapsed unmoving.

That had to have gotten them all, Bree thought as their Seraphim broke into two groups, one veering left, the other right,
both looping around for another pass. This approach was
slower, with more care to aim, and Bree quickly saw how
wrong she'd been. The rest of the troops had awakened, joining those who'd first been on guard. Not near as many had
fallen against the barrage as she'd expected, and they lifted
dented and scratched shields while bracing with both their legs.
Others beside them lifted bows, and Bree jerked to the right as
she saw one aiming her way. The arrow sailed wide, and then
a ball of flame crashed down between the two, the protector's
armor and shield mattering not. Bree pulled higher, seeing
no reason to risk her life if she wasn't ready to engage in the
melee. She climbed above the others, watching them strafe the
camp, a barrage of ice from Argus smashing the lone remaining wagon into pieces. Bree winced, hoping the elements they
sought could withstand the punishment.

Rotating in air, Bree spotted a hint of gold to the west, the
glint locking her body in place. There, between the camp and
the town…

A barrage of ice and fire unleashed toward them as two
knights suddenly burst into the air, their golden armor gleaming in the night.

Their camp was separate from the others, Bree realized as she
angled toward them, eager to engage. Against ground forces
she was of limited use. But here in the air?

445

In the air, she could dance.

Two Seraphs died, caught unaware by the ambush, one knifed through the stomach by a lance of ice, the other bathed in fire from the waist up. He flew wildly afterward, blind and burned, until crashing into one of Melisand's homes with enough force to crack the stone of its walls. Bree tried to pretend she didn't see and was glad she could not hear the sound of impact over the roar of battle and wind in her ears. The rest of her group turned about to engage, but they'd had their backs to the two knights, preparing for a third assault. Only Bree had seen them coming, so she would reach them first.

Swords drawn, she smiled and pushed the throttle to its maximum.

Thin balls of fire flew like comets toward her, and Bree twisted her body with her waist and shoulders, twirling through without slowing in the slightest. They passed so close she felt their heat on her skin. How well the knight tracked her path cracked her veneer of confidence. Veering hard right, she swerved through the air, avoiding a thick lance of ice that had meant to cut straight through the center of her path. Bree veered immediately back, twirling once as two more comets burned below her, and then she was close enough to strike.

The knight wielding the ice arced away, as if daring her to chase, but instead she closed in on the one still flinging fire. He'd hovered in place, left hand holding his right wrist to brace his aim. Bree saw his palm spreading open with fingers stretched, knew what he intended, and banked at the last second. A wide spray of fire shot toward her, covering a great space of air as it rolled outward, but she just barely skirted its edge. Bree hooked toward him, left hand shooting out to cut. She almost bathed it in flame. Almost.

extras

The sword cut against his chest, but unlike in her other battles, it did not slice through like cloth. Instead she felt a hard jolt, followed by intense pain in her shoulder. She was moving too fast, the sword unable to cut cleanly through to prevent the hard jerk to her momentum. Unable to keep hold, she released her sword. It flew wildly, pulling out a long stretch of the cord that kept it attached to her gauntlet. Screaming against the pain, Bree turned away and climbed, sword trailing after her like a useless appendage. She caught the other knight turning for her, but then the rest of the Weshern Seraphim arrived, preceded by a blistering barrage of ice arrows launched from Argus's gauntlet. The knight dodged the first few, but the awkward movements stole some of his speed. Avoiding a burst of flame pushed him higher, right into a blast of lightning that ripped through his chest.

Bree lessened the throttle as she spun to find the knight she'd cut. It must have gone in deep, for she saw him drifting east, body limp. Bled out, by her guess. Argus launched a single shard of ice, which caved in his skull, then flew over to the body. He grabbed the left gauntlet, shut off the harness, and let the body fall. The Weshern Seraphim looped up and around, converging on the desolation that had been the theotechs' camp. Bree hovered for a moment, gently pulling on the cord attached to her sword to get the gears inside the gauntlet to start reeling it in. Once it was in her grasp, she sheathed it, then lowered to the ground.

"Get the elements loaded up and out of here," Argus shouted. "There's not a chance in Hell the theotechs and knights in town didn't hear that ruckus."

Bree touched down, and she held her aching left arm against her side. Feeling strangely detached, she stared at the charred corpses of Center's soldiers, faces still locked in agony upon death. Most were burned, though a good many had been crushed by ice and stone as well. The ones struck by lightning seemed the most peaceful, their hearts burst inside their chests before they realized they'd been struck. Fire roared in scattered patches all around, the sound of its crackling an accompaniment to the humming of their wings. Bree stared at the corpse of a man lying on his back beside her, a jagged lance of ice protruding from his neck. His bloodstained tabard bore the symbol of Center, a clear circle intersecting five other circles, each bearing the symbol of the respective island's colors. All but Galen, which had been filled in solid black. The sight chilled her, threatening to remove the last of the comfortable numbness that had blanketed her mind since the start of battle.

"Bree?"

She turned to see Argus staring at her.

"I'm fine," she said. "It's... it's nothing."

He didn't look convinced, but he let her be, instead supervising the Seraphs shoving aside pieces of the blasted wagons. Inside were ornate chests, stained wood, and with gold decorations. Carrying those would be impossible, but thankfully they didn't need to. Bree glanced about as they opened up the chests and started pulling out elements wrapped in soft velvet cloth, stuffing them into pouches and bags. She saw only a single dead Seraph of their own, the man lying crashed into the center of the camp, neck twisted at an awkward angle, an arrow sticking out from his forehead.

Feeling like a scavenger, Bree walked to his side, lifted his right arm, and popped open the elemental compartment of his gauntlet. Inside was an ice element, and she pocketed it to hand in later. Eyes sweeping across the devastation their elements had unleashed, she wondered how much they'd expended to recover what the wagons carried.

I hope it's enough to make up for what we've used, she thought. Part of her thought Argus wouldn't care even if it didn't. He wanted to strike a blow against Center. He wanted to let every citizen of Weshern know resistance wasn't a hopeless endeavor.

"Knights coming in," a Seraph shouted, turning Bree's attention their way. Sure enough, the gold shimmer of wings rose above the buildings, three in total.

"Everyone, protect the elements," Argus shouted in response. "Form up, and hit them hard. We need to buy ourselves time!"

Wings thrumming with silver light, Bree led the way, swords drawn as the Weshern Seraphim flew to engage. With three dead and seven staying back to loot the chests, twenty were left to face against the three knights. It should have been over-whelming numbers. It should have been an easy victory.

Then fire and lightning crashed through their formation as three more knights ambushed from high above, lurking so far they were but minuscule dots. Their attacks hit simultaneously with the three at the front, engulfing the battlefield in chaos. Seraphim dropped, bodies burned and scarred, their easy victory now a desperate battle for survival.

introducing

If you enjoyed
SKYBORN,
look out for

THE CITY STAINED RED

Bring Down Heaven: Book 1

by Sam Sykes

STEP UP TO THE GATES

*After years in the wilds, Lenk and his companions have come to
the city that serves as the world's beating heart.*

*The great charnel house where men die
surer than in any wilderness.*

*They've come to claim payment for creatures slain, blood
spilled at the behest of a powerful holy man.*

And Lenk has come to lay down his sword for good.

But this is no place to escape demons.

Prologue

Cier'Djaal
Some crappy little boat
First day of Yonder

You can't lie to a sword.

It's a trait you don't often think of between its more practical applications, but part of the appeal of a blade is that it keeps you honest. No matter how much of a hero you might think you are for picking it up, no matter how many evildoers you claim to have smitten with it, it's hard to pretend that steel you carry is good for much else besides killing.

Conversely, a sword can't lie to you.

If you can't use it, it'll tell you. If you don't want to use it, it'll decide whether you should. And if you look at it, earnestly, and ask if there's no other way besides killing, it'll look right back at you and say, earnestly, that it can't quite think of any.

Every day I wake up, I look in the corner of my squalid little cabin. I stare at my sword. My sword stares back at me. And I tell it the same thing I've told it every day for months.

"Soon, we reach Cier'Djaal. Soon, we reach a place where there are ways to make coin without killing. Soon, I'm getting off this ship and I'm leaving you far behind."

The sword just laughs.

Granted, this probably sounds a trifle insane, but I'm writing in ink so I can't go back and make it less crazy. But if you're reading this, you're probably anticipating the occasional lapse in sanity.

And if you aren't yet, I highly recommend you start. It'll help.

extras

I've killed a lot of things.

I say "things," because "people" isn't a broad enough category and "stuff" would lead you to believe I don't spend a lot of time thinking about it.

The list thus far: men, women, demons, monsters, giant serpents, giant vermin, regular vermin, regular giants, cattle, lizards, fish, lizardmen, fishmen, frogmen, Cragsmen, and a goat.

Regular goat, mind; not a poisonous magic goat or anything. But he was kind of an asshole.

When I started killing, it seemed like I had good reasons. Survival, I guess. Money, too. But the more I did it, the better I got. And the better I got, the less reason I needed until killing was just something I did.

Easy as shaking a man's hand.

And when it's as easy as shaking a man's hand, you stop seeing open hands. All you see, then, is an empty spot where a sword should be. And will be, if you don't grab yours first.

I'm tired of it.

I don't live in lamentation of my past deeds. I did what I had to, even if I could have thought of something better. I don't hear voices and I don't have nightmares.

Not anymore, anyway.

I guess I'm just tired. Tired of seeing swords instead of hands, tired of looking for chairs against the wall whenever I go into a room, tired of knowing lists instead of people, tired of talking to my sword.

And I'm going to stop. And even if I can't, I have to try.

So I'm going to. Try, that is.

Just as soon as I get my money.

I suppose there's irony in trading blood for gold. Or hypocrisy.

I don't care and I sincerely doubt my employer does, either. Or maybe he does—holy men are odd that way—but he'll pay, anyway. Blood is gold and I've spilled a lot of the former for a considerable sum of the latter.

Ordinarily, you wouldn't think a priest of Talanas, the Healer, to appreciate that much blood. But Miron Evenhands, Lord Emissary and Member in Good Standing of the House of the Vanquishing Trinity, is no ordinary priest. As the former title implies, he's a man with access to a lot of wealth. And as the latter title is just cryptic enough to suggest, he's got a fair number of demons, cultists, and occult oddities to be eradicated.

And eradicate I have, with gusto.

And he has yet to pay. "Temporary barriers to the financial flow," he tells me. "Patience, adventurer, patience," he says. And patient I was. Patient enough to follow him across the sea for months until we came here.

Cier'Djaal, the City of Silk. This is the great charnel house where poor men eat dead rich men and become wealthy themselves. This is the city where fortunes are born, alive and screaming. This is the city that controls the silk, the city that controls the coin, the city that controls the world.

This is civilization.

This is what I want now.

My companions, too.

Or so I'd like to think.

It's not as though anyone chooses to be an adventurer, killing people for little coin and even less respect. We all took up the title, and each other's company, with the intent of leaving it behind someday. Cier'Djaal is as good as any a place to do so, I figure.

Though their opinions on our arrival have been... varied.

That Gariath should be against our entrance into any place where he might be required to wear a shirt, let alone a place crawling with humans, is no surprise.

Far more surprising are Denaos's objections—the man who breathes liquor and uses whores for pillows, I would have thought, would feel right at home among the thieves and scum of civilized society.

Asper and Dreadaeleon, happy to be anywhere that has a temple or a wizard tower, were generally in favor of it. Asper for the opportunity to be among civilized holy men, Dreadaeleon for the opportunity to be away from uncivilized laymen, both for the opportunity to be in a place with toilets.

When I told Kataria, she just sort of stared.

Like she always does.

Which made my decision as to what to do next fairly easy. This will be the last of our time spent together. Once I've got my money, once I can leave my sword behind, I intend to leave them with it.

Their opinions on this have been quiet.

Possibly because I haven't told them yet.

Probably because I won't until I'm far enough away that I can't hear my sword laughing at me anymore.

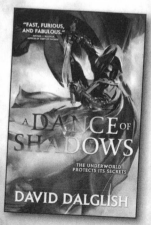